CATHERINE ASARO

THE NIGHT BIRD

LUNA™
www.LUNA-Books.com

LUNA™

First edition July 2008

THE NIGHT BIRD

ISBN-13: 978-0-373-80268-5
ISBN-10:   0-373-80268-4

www.LUNA-Books.com

Printed in U.S.A.

Praise for

CATHERINE ASARO
and the Lost Continent series

"Once again, Asaro skillfully blends romance
with a solid fantasy scenario."
—*Publishers Weekly* on *The Fire Opal*

"This is one heck of a page-turner!... The writing is crisp, the plot
and action are compelling and the sweet ending will completely
satisfy everyone. This is an excellent read!"
—*Romantic Times BOOKreviews* on *The Fire Opal*

"A magical story with complex characters and a love that can heal
wounds, *The Misted Cliffs* by Catherine Asaro is a rare gem from an
author who always delivers."
—*Romance Reviews Today*

"Catherine Asaro has written a beautiful
and vividly descriptive tale that is a cross between a
romantic fantasy and a swords and sorcery tale.... Catherine Asaro
is one of the reigning queens of brilliant romantic fantasy."
—*Paranormal Romance Reviews* on *The Misted Cliffs*

"'Moonglow' by Catherine Asaro is the most amazing and beautiful love story I have read this year...it took my breath away. It's a perfect balance between fantasy and romance, and I am now wondering why I took so long to read Catherine Asaro."
—*Fantasy Romance Writers*

"Asaro has created a magical world in 'Moonglow.' It will leave readers desperate to know more about these enticing characters."
—*Romantic Times BOOKreviews*

"Readers will love this epic romantic fantasy that reads like an adult fairy tale."
—*The Best Reviews* on *The Charmed Sphere*

"'Moonglow' is the first story set in an exciting, magical new world created especially for Luna readers.... The magic of Asaro's world is deep and complex, but very well executed.... The *Charmed Destinies* anthology has a little something for everyone...these stories are excellent examples of the genre written by masters of their craft. If you like a meaty, fantasy-rich story, you can't go wrong with these delectable little treats."
—*Paranormal Romance Reviews*

Acknowledgments

I would like to thank the following readers
for their much-appreciated input. Their comments
have made this a better book. Any mistakes are mine alone.
(Actually, they're due to pernicious imps who sneak on to the
computer when I'm asleep, but I can't keep using that excuse.)

For reading the manuscript and giving me the benefit
of their wisdom and insights: Aly Parsons, Kate Dolan,
Sarah White and Kathy. For their critiques on scenes, Aly's
Writing Group: Aly Parsons with (in the proverbial alphabetical
order) Al Carroll, John Hemry, J. G. Huckenpöler, Simcha Kuritzky,
Jennifer J. Monteith, Bud Sparhawk and Connie Warner.
Special thanks to my much-appreciated editor, Stacy Boyd,
and also to Tracy Farrell, Mary-Theresa Hussey, Kathleen Oudit,
Marianna Ricciuto, Margo Lipschultz, Dee Tenorio and all the
other fine people at Luna who helped make this book possible;
to Binnie Braunstein, for all her work and enthusiasm
on my behalf; to my wonderful agent, Eleanor Wood,
of Spectrum Literary Agency.

A heartfelt thanks to the shining lights in my life:
my husband, John Cannizzo, and my daughter, Cathy,
for their love and support.

To the dancers in the Patuxent Youth Ballet. You're looking great!

THE ROYAL HOUSES OF THE LOST CONTINENT

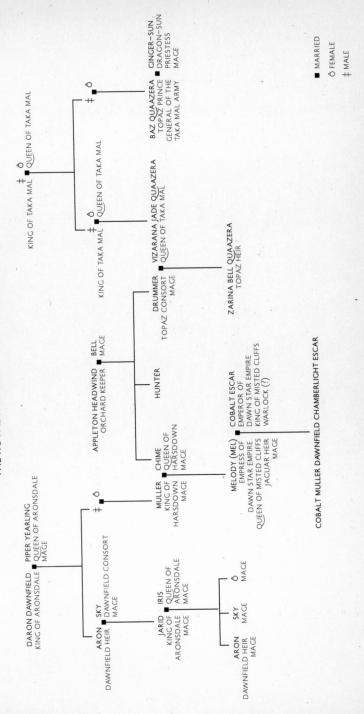

CONTENTS

CHAPTER 1
THE NOMADS

The day Allegra lost her freedom, her world changed forever.

She had been riding all morning, until she stopped at a creek to wash up. In a few hours, she would reach Crofts Vale, home to the Song Weavers Guild. She grimaced at the thought. As much as she loved to sing spells, she felt unprepared for the guild's strict program of study. What if she failed? They might say she had no talent and send her home.

Just do it. She had delayed for three years. That was when the mage mistress from Castle Suncroft had come to southern Aronsdale in search of girls with mage ability. Everyone knew why. Prince Aron, the king's heir, had to marry a mage. Less than one hundred mages lived in all the settled lands, most with minor abilities. Allegra had been excited when she thought they might consider her for Aron's bride, but it turned out she had neither the range nor strength they sought. Well, she shouldn't let it bother her. For all she knew, he was a mean-tempered grouch with bad breath. At least she had done well enough to receive an invitation from the guild. She had felt too young to go then, only sixteen, but now she was ready. She hoped.

She didn't want to arrive at the guild smelling like a horse, though. The creek burbled at her feet, gently frothing over blue-gray rocks, and the sky arched above, squirted with puffs of cloud. She stripped off her clothes, leaving only the pendant around her neck, and eased into the water. Long fronds from a bluespindle tree trailed into the water, forming a screen on the riverbank. She wasn't certain it mattered; people often bathed outside, at least where she lived, and everyone learned to respect privacy. Nor had she seen a person, farm or village during her entire ride this morning. But just in case, she chose an especially secluded spot.

Breathing deeply, Allegra inhaled the loamy smell of mud. She ducked under the sun-warmed water and shot back out, splattering drops that glistened like diamonds. She lathered up with the soapweed plants straggling on the bank and slid her hands over her sore breasts. Those folktales where women jumped onto their steeds and galloped off valiantly into the hills had to be about less endowed women; she always ached after a long ride.

Touching herself that way led to thoughts of Tanner, a boy back home. As children, they had often tussled together, learning throws. Although they had outgrown those games, lately he wanted to wrestle again. She smiled, thinking of his feigned innocence as he challenged her to a match. Up in the loft of his family's barn, they had wrestled in sunbeams slanting through cracks in the wood, laughing and tossing straw. Then he had kissed her. It had been…nice. Odd, though. She felt more sisterly than romantic toward him. Still, she appreciated that he liked her just the way she was, a slightly plump dairymaid with wild yellow curls that never stayed tamed.

The urge to sing stirred in Allegra, and with it, her mage power. But she needed a geometric shape to create a spell. She closed her hand around her pendant, a garnet disk. She had worn it for ten years, since she had learned to make spells from a mage in her village. Today she slid into the "Song of the Lamp Dove," a lilt about the rosy imp who sent innocents chasing after each other.

> Playful little scamp; naughty teasing dove
> Spirit of the lamp; trickster of first love
> You cause such a fuss with your lusty heart
> Tempting young lovers; giving them your spark

The air took on a rosy tinge and light bathed the trees. The clarity of the spell pleased her. It was only color; she could do little more. But she liked it.

Bushes rustled farther up the bank. Startled, she stood up and peered toward the foliage while her spell faded away. A rabbit ran out and dashed down the river, disappearing into another bush.

Time to go, she thought reluctantly. She climbed out and dried off with her tunic. She felt as if her body were humming with a healthy glow. The linen of her shift caressed her skin as she pulled it on, leaving her arms and legs bare. She gathered her other clothes and headed back to Alto, her horse. The mare stood by a cluster of trees, more alert than usual, her ears pricked forward. Allegra's pack sat on a nearby rock. She ambled past a line of trees, swinging her clothes—

Someone behind Allegra jerked her back, the motion so unexpected that her breath came out in a huff. He held her around her waist, pinning her arms to her sides.

"Hey!" Allegra shouted, annoyed. Was some boy she hadn't seen playing a trick on her? She rammed her elbow back and hit a rock-hard torso that didn't feel like a youth's thinner frame. Startled, she twisted, turning his weight against him. She managed to roll him over her hip and flip him onto his back, which surprised her, because she had never been good at throws, which she had only learned for fun.

She had one moment to see a man in black and red clothes; then someone else yanked her backward. Frightened now, she kicked back, hitting his shin. Her blow knocked his leg out from under him, and he lost his grip on her.

Allegra ran for her horse—and a dark blur appeared to her right. *Saints, how many were there?* She swerved to the left, but a fourth man came at her from that side. As she spun away, someone grabbed her from behind and threw her forward. They crashed to the ground, and she flailed, trying to free herself. She ended up twisting so she landed on her back, but it didn't help, for her assailant came down on top of her. He was long and lanky, with wiry muscles under his dark clothes.

"Get off," she yelled, and brought her knee up *hard*. He

groaned as he curled into a fetal position on top of her. She wrenched out from under him and tried to scramble away, but he grabbed her ankle and dragged her back along the ground. Two other people hauled her up, and one of them lashed her wrists together behind her back. Her head spun, and she gulped in air.

The man she had kneed climbed to his feet in front of them, his face dark with anger. He backhanded her across the cheek, and her head snapped to the side. As pain shot through her face, her vision blurred. Her ears rang as if someone had hit a bell.

When he raised his hand again, she cried, "No!"

"Don't do it," one of the other men said. "If you leave marks on her skin, it will lower her price."

Allegra was having trouble breathing. Details jumped out at her in jagged bursts. Her assailants had dark hair and eyes like almost everyone in the settled lands; they wore unfamiliar black clothes with red or green streaks; they had the rangy builds of the nomads in the country of Jazid, which bordered Aronsdale in the southeast. A chill went through her as she looked into their hard faces.

Someone behind Allegra shoved down on her shoulders, and she dropped to her knees. He bound her ankles together, and as pain shot through her legs, her stunned mind finally lurched into action.

Allegra inhaled and shouted, "Someone! Help! Any—"

Her yell cut off as one of the men shoved a cloth into her mouth. When he tied a strip of suede around her head to hold it in, a sense of panic swelled within her.

One of the men walked over to her mare and took the reins. Then he picked up Allegra's pack. He was taller than the others, with black stubble on his chin. *Stubble,* she named him. As he brought the horse to them, he peered inside her pack.

The man who had hit her—Fist, she thought—considered her horse. "We can get a good price for the mare."

Her protest came out as a muffled grunt. They couldn't steal her horse! She had ridden Alto for years, since she was nine.

Fist motioned at her pack. "Is it worth anything?"

Stubble handed the bag to him. "It's mostly just clothes. They're worthless."

Her desperation surged. If they took her pack, she would lose her letters of introduction to the guild and the hexacoins she had saved for this trip.

Fist dumped her tunic and leggings onto the ground and tossed out the letters as if they were trash. When he found her bag of coins, he shook it, making the silver rattle, then unfastened the strings and peered inside.

"Not bad." Looking down at Allegra, he held up the bag and grinned. "A little something for our efforts, eh?" Then he tied her money pouch to his belt.

Allegra swore at him, but the gag turned her oaths into grunts. She strained to pull her wrists free, and the ropes bit her skin.

One of the men leaned down and grasped her necklace. When he yanked, its cord snapped. He tossed the pendant to Fist. "That'll be worth a bit."

No! She struggled futilely. Without the pendant, she couldn't make spells. Although she could do little more than make light, she felt even more vulnerable with that ability stripped away.

Fist studied the garnet. "Nice workmanship." He untied her coin bag and stuffed the pendant inside. Then he picked up her clothes and letters and crammed them back into the pack. "We'll leave this on the other side of the border, as proof we found her in Jazid, in case anyone looks for her."

"She was by herself," another of the men said, incredulous. "Any man stupid enough to let a woman who looks like this bathe alone in a river deserves to lose her."

"Of course he does," Fist said. "But the laws here don't care what we think. It's only legal if we catch her in Jazid." He looked down at Allegra. "Pity you were foolish enough to ride there by yourself. But that isn't our problem, is it?"

Allegra wanted to spit at him. As she fought harder against her bonds, the scrape of metal on leather came from behind her. Then what felt like a dagger pricked her spine. She froze, breathing hard, too scared to move.

"Calm down," Fist said. "Do as we say, and you won't be hurt."

They heaved her to her feet, and the man on her right turned her toward him. His face was wide and weathered by the sun, with lines at the corners of his mouth. His breath smelled of onions and whiskey. Grasping her around the waist, he hefted her up, over his shoulder, so her legs hung down his front and her torso against his back. Her bound wrists fell painfully downward, away from her spine, and she groaned. Someone looped a rope through the bonds and tied it around her waist to hold her arms against her body. The man holding her carried her through the trees, also bringing her horse. It all felt unreal, a nightmare that was happening to someone else.

Within moments, they reached a wagon with rigid sides and a cloth top dyed in green and black triangles. Gold tassels hung from the corners of its roof, swaying in the breeze.

Hanging over the nomad's shoulder, she could barely see as they pulled aside a flap at the back. Inside, the wagon was filled with crates, chests and rolled-up rugs tied with tasseled ropes. When they laid her among the carpets as if she were just another rug, she lost what little calm she had left and struggled frantically with her bonds.

"She's going to cut her skin if she keeps doing that," one of the nomads said.

Stubble took a small bottle and a cloth out of a pocket in his shirt. When he opened the bottle, the pungent odor of suffocating-salts wafted into the air. As he poured liquid onto the cloth, the smell intensified.

"No, don't!" Allegra's cry came out as a grunt.

Stubble leaned over, one hand braced behind her head, and pressed the wet cloth against her nose. She couldn't *breathe*. She gasped, and the repulsive smell of the salts saturated her. Panicked, she fought to pull away, but someone held her in place. The smell intensified until she truly was suffocating. Darkness closed in and she knew no more.

Allegra floated in a haze. Pain burned her wrists and ankles. Eventually one of the nomads untied the strap around her head and pulled out the gag. He offered her wine from a water bag. She drank thirstily, her mouth parched from the cloth. When he laid her down, dizziness took her and she fell back into the haze.

The next time she drifted awake, they were cutting the cords off her wrists and ankles. She groaned as they massaged the circulation into her limbs. The salve they smeared into the burns stung at first, but then soothed the pain. When she instinctively began to fight, though she was only half-conscious, they tied her wrists behind her back and bound her ankles again, this time with soft cloth that didn't bite into her skin. Stubble put another cloth soaked in the salts over her face until she lost consciousness.

Time passed, several days maybe. They tended her, gave her too much watered-down wine and too little water, and twice fed her a thick soup. She was dully aware of her hunger.

Allegra awoke into darkness. Groggy and disoriented, she took a moment to realize she was on her side with someone lying next to her. He had pulled up her tunic and was stroking her breasts. When she gulped in a breath, he put his hand over her mouth and pushed her onto her back, pressing down so she couldn't speak. Her wrists were still bound behind her, and pain shot through them.

He held a dagger by her face. "Quiet," he mouthed.

She froze, able to see the blade even in the dark, it was so close to her face. When the man shifted so he lay on top of her, the pain worsened in her arms and she cried out against his hand.

"Vardok?" a voice asked. Someone dragged the man off her. She could just make out who had helped—Stubble, the one with the salts.

"Leave her alone," Stubble told him. "I meant it when I said I wouldn't let you touch her."

"Why the hell not?" Vardok said. "They'll never know."

"Forget it," Stubble growled, rubbing his eyes.

Vardok scowled at him, but he moved away from Allegra, at least as far as was possible in the cramped wagon.

Stubble leaned over her. "Are you all right?"

She stared up at him, too scared to answer, too dizzy from lack of food, and too drunk from the wine. He pulled her shift down over her body. Then he took that bottle out of his shirt, the bottle she hated.

"No," Allegra said. "Please. Don't."

"Shh," he murmured. "It will help you sleep."

She tried to turn away, but he held her in place while he covered her nose and mouth with the suffocating cloth....

Allegra groaned as she became aware of the bumpy ride. Each bounce added to her nausea. Opening her eyes didn't help; all she saw was a wooden wall a few handspans away. The carpet she lay on felt rough under her legs and smelled of the heavy yarns used in the Jazid rugs traded throughout the settled lands.

After several aeons, or maybe a few moments, she eased onto her back. Her eyes watered as pain stabbed her wrists. Her muscles had stiffened miserably, and the roof swam in her vision.

She rolled onto her other side, facing the interior of the wagon. The bottom half of the walls were wood; the top half had cloth patterned with green and black triangles, like a bizarre chessboard where the "squares" were the wrong shape. Red dragons curled on the triangles, and red tassels hung from bars where the walls met the roof. Goods crammed the wagon: baskets of fruit and dried food, large chests with ornate fittings and bolts of cloth shot through by metallic threads.

The wagon also contained three nomads crammed in among the boxes. Stubble was leaning against a large crate, dozing. Vardok sat by a chest across from her, looking bored. The man who had carried her to the wagon was near the front, sprawled on a pile of carpets, holding a green bottle by the neck. From the strong odor of whiskey, she suspected he had been drinking for a while. When he burped and took a swallow from the bottle, she decided to call him Sot.

"What tribe…?" Allegra's mouth felt cottony, and the rasp of her words trailed off. She wasn't certain how long they had been traveling, but it seemed at least three days.

"What'd you say?" Vardok asked. His Jazidian drawl was hard to understand.

She tried again. "What tribe are you from?"

"You know Jazid tribes?" he asked.

"A little.… Are you the T'Ambera?"

"How did you know that?"

"I heard…they steal women." She had never believed the stories. She kept hoping she would awake and discover this was some sort of delirium.

"What thievery?" Vardok asked idly. "To steal, you must take from someone. We didn't take you from anyone. You were alone. It's our good fortune you were stupid enough to wander into Jazid."

"I was in Aronsdale." She couldn't absorb that they had taken her from her home, her family, everything she knew. In Aronsdale, selling people was illegal. Unthinkable. In all the settled lands, only Jazid allowed it. Aronsdale and Jazid had a treaty for that reason, forbidding exactly what these nomads had done. Such incidents couldn't occur often or she would have heard about it even across the country. She hadn't known Jazid nomads came into Aronsdale.

"You can't do this," she said.

"We seem to be doing it just fine," Vardok told her.

Sot spoke in a slurred voice. "The forbidden is that much more valuable." He motioned at her with his bottle. "With that yellow hair of yours and those pretty violet eyes, we'll get a fortune."

"You can't sell me! I'm a citizen of Aronsdale."

"Not anymore," Vardok said. "We crossed into Jazid two days ago. But don't worry, we won't put you in a public auction. We've private buyers. They asked for an Aronsdale girl. Exotic coloring like yours. Someone pretty. And curvy. Like you." He rose to his feet and stepped toward her. When the wagon lurched, he lost his balance and dropped to his knees next to where she lay.

"Come on," he said, sitting next to her. "You were made for a man, eh? Why else would the Shadow Dragon make you so beautiful?" The smell of peppers on his breath wafted over her.

"Go away," Allegra said. For so long, she had wanted a youth to say he found her beautiful, but none ever had. She hardly saw anyone, given the isolated region where she lived. She hated that Vardok had turned the sweet words into something ugly.

"You don't like us, eh?" he said. "You Aronsdale women think you can do what you want. Now you know you're wrong."

"Vardi, stop it," someone said. "Leave her alone."

Vardok turned with a frown. Following his gaze, Allegra saw Stubble pulling himself up to sit by the crate. His blocky face was creased along one cheek from sleeping against the box, and his eyebrows had drawn into a black ridge over his deeply set eyes.

"Why shouldn't I talk to her?" Vardok asked.

"You're frightening her," Stubble said crossly. "Why do you keep doing that? Can't you tell she's scared?"

"I don't know why you won't let us touch her," Sot muttered. He took another drink from his bottle.

"She doesn't deserve to be mauled," Stubble said. "It's our good fortune we found her, but this can't be easy for her."

Vardok looked baffled. "So what?"

Sot smacked a bolt of cloth next to him. "I don't ask if being sold is easy for this silk." He pointed at Allegra with his bottle. "Why would I ask her?"

"She's a person, idiot," Stubble said. "Not a bolt of cloth."

"How would you like it," Allegra asked Vardok, "if someone dragged you away from your home and put you up for sale?"

Sot gave a rasping guffaw. "Damn sure no one would buy his ugly carcass."

"She's a woman," Vardok told Stubble. "Not a person."

"For saints' sake," Allegra said. "A woman is a person."

Vardok glanced at her. "Not in Jazid."

"Like hell," she said.

"Enough!" Vardok raised his hand, and Allegra flinched.

"I told you to stop it!" Stubble said. "If you keep hitting her, she'll be black-and-blue by the auction, and we won't get horse manure for her. That mark you left on her face will barely be gone by tomorrow."

Allegra hadn't realized she had a bruise, but it didn't surprise her. Tears gathered in her eyes. Would her family think she had died? Surely they would search for her. Although her parents ran a dairy, which filled their days with work, two of her four brothers were old enough to travel. She knew her family; they would look for her even if her brothers spent many seasons traveling. But she couldn't imagine how they would find her in Jazid, the largest country in the settled lands. A long time could pass before they even knew she was gone. It took ten days for a letter to go from Crofts Vale to her home, and her parents didn't know when she would arrive at the guild or write to them.

"We can't show her to either of them if she's not in good shape," Stubble said. "It makes us look sloppy."

"Either of *whom?*" Allegra's voice shook.

No one replied. At least Vardok slid back to his seat.

Allegra closed her eyes, hurting too much to think. Hunger sapped her strength, and the wine blurred her concentration. If she had a shape to hold, and if she could sing, she could create a spell of succor for herself. But the only shapes here were distorted triangles. She was too groggy to remember why they were bad. Reasons swam in her head. Oh. Yes. The more sides to a shape, the more power it gave a spell. Three-dimensional forms were stronger than those with two dimensions. Triangles were the weakest; they could barely create anything, and these were probably too distorted to work at all. She needed her pendant.

"My necklace." She wet her lips. "Do you…have it?"

"We sold it," Vardok said. "With your horse."

"You *sold* them?" Even knowing what they had intended, it was too much. Those were her last ties to home. It crashed down on her then, that they had ended her life as she knew it.

They would sell her to some stranger who could do whatever he wanted to her. She would never again see her home.

"No...*no.*" A sob choked in her throat.

"Oh, be quiet," Vardok said. "It's just a damn horse."

"Let her cry," Stubble said quietly.

She struggled to hold back her tears. "Would you untie me?" she asked Stubble. "It hurts."

"Maybe we should unroll the carpets, too," Sot said with a belch. "Hell, why keep anything tied up?"

I hope you rot into mold, Allegra thought.

Stubble gave them a disgusted look. "Carpets and cloth don't feel. She does." He stood up, swaying as the wagon bumped along, and stepped over to her. He actually smiled. "You should see the look on your face. I'm glad I'm not the one buying you. It might be dangerous."

"Heaven forbid," she muttered.

"She'll shape up," Vardok said. "Especially if the General ends up with her."

Allegra thought she must have misheard. A general? The armies of the Misted Cliffs had conquered Jazid two years ago. The Jazid soldiers who survived had sworn allegiance to the conquering emperor—or been executed. And the people of the Misted Cliffs abhorred slavery. Surely their army here would protect the treaty with Aronsdale.

"What general?" Allegra asked.

Stubble crouched down and rolled her onto her stomach.

"What are you doing?" she asked, alarmed.

"Hold still." He pressed his palm on her spine, keeping her in place. "I can't untie you otherwise."

"Oh." She closed her eyes with relief as he went to work on her wrists. They fell free at her sides, and she groaned when pinpricks scored her muscles.

"Better?" he asked.

Her arms felt as if they were on fire. But it would pass, so she said, "Yes." She looked up at him. "My ankles, too?"

"She'll run off," Sot warned him.

Stubble scooted to Allegra's feet. "She can hardly move."

"You should leave her tied," Vardok said.

Stubble ignored him. Allegra's legs were so numb, she couldn't tell they were free until pinpricks started in them, too. Stubble returned to his seat and took a packet of dried meat out from his pocket. He settled back, eating.

"Can I have some food?" she asked.

"Maybe later," Stubble said.

"But I'm hungry."

His voice tightened. "I said, later."

Apparently his kindness went only so far.

For a while, she just lay, wincing as the numbness left her limbs, but eventually she sat up. Vardok and Sot watched her with curiosity and something much darker. Disquieted, she pulled her shift farther down over her thighs.

"Who is the general you were talking about?" she asked. The more she knew, the better she could plan her escape.

"You'll find out soon enough," Sot said. He tried to drink

out of his bottle, then squinted inside. With an annoyed grunt, he cast aside the empty container.

Allegra wondered if she could use his bottle to make a spell that would ease her discomfort, maybe increase her strength. The circular bottom might work as a shape, maybe even the neck. She needed only to touch it and sing. Of course, they could easily stop her. Although every mage needed a geometric shape, their ways of creating spells varied. She had always appreciated her need to sing for the pleasure it gave her; she had never realized before how easy it would be to stop her from making a spell.

Stubble settled against the crate, one arm on the box. "So many questions," he mused. "Most girls we catch are too scared or crying too much to speak. You Aronsdale girls are tarter, eh?"

"What, you're afraid that will lower my price?" Maybe if she made herself disagreeable enough, they would let her go.

Vardok laughed, but it was an ugly sound. "It will just make breaking you all that much more entertaining for the buyer."

"Women aren't horses," Stubble said.

"Horses cause less trouble," Sot muttered. He was searching in a crate for another bottle, his body swaying as the wagon bounced.

"You know," Allegra said, "it's amazing what you've done in Jazid."

"You think so?" Sot grinned at the others. "See? She's learning already."

Stubble regarded her with a narrowed gaze. "What's amazing?"

"Your population," Allegra said.

"Is it now?" Vardok said.

"Well, actually," Allegra said, "what's amazing is that you have *any* population. Surely your own women grew disgusted with this place long ago and left. It's no wonder you have to kidnap new ones. I can't imagine any woman coming here of her own free will."

Sot's mouth fell open. "I don't *believe* she said that."

Vardok's lips curled in a snarl. To Stubble, he said, "Damn it, Azi, let me hit her."

"Enough!" Stubble said. He glared at Allegra. "You talk too much. You'll get into trouble."

Well, that had certainly hit a nerve. She knew such comments didn't help her, but they were her only shield against her fear that she had lost everything.

🌹 CHAPTER 2
ROSE OF T'AMBERA

Allegra dozed for most of the day, too drunk to stay awake. For dinner, they gave her citrus fruits. Day faded into night, and she slept sitting up against a crate, afraid of what Vardok might do if she lay down.

She woke in the dark with a painful thirst. "Water?" she asked. Her voice croaked.

The wagon continued to jolt along.

"Please," she said, slumped against the chest. Memories of streams, lakes and tumblers of icy relief tormented her.

Something rustled in the front of the wagon. "Eh?"

"I'm thirsty."

"So 'm I," someone muttered. A scratching noise came toward her, and Sot's sleepy voice. "Azi said to give you wine."

Allegra groaned. "No, not that." She could smell him now, onions and sweat and whiskey.

"Here." He raised a bottle to her lips. "'S not wine."

Relieved, she took a swallow—and choked as whiskey burned her throat. Spluttering, she spit some of it out, but the rest went down.

"Don't waste it!" Sot said, pulling away the bottle.

"Wait." She managed to catch the bottle in the dark and fold her hand around its circular base. Power stirred within her. Dents in the glass deformed the shape, but it might still work.

"Would you like me to sing to you?" she asked.

"No! If Azi wakes, he'll get mad at me for touching you." Sot clumsily stroked her hair. "You'll be all right."

She pulled away. "Stop that."

"Come on, pretty, pretty." His lips smeared her cheek. "Kiss me."

Allegra whacked him on the head. "Behave yourself."

"Not so loud," he muttered. Grumbling, he moved away, taking his smell and his bottle with him.

Allegra shuddered and folded her arms on the crate, resting her head on them. This misery had to end. She wasn't safe enough to sleep, had to stay alert…

Allegra awoke into daylight, still slumped against the crate with her head on her arms. Her body ached from sleeping that way, but the pain in her limbs had eased. Either that, or she was too woozy to feel it. Before this mess, she had barely tasted alcohol; now she had been inebriated for nearly four days. She doubted she could run even if she had the chance. Hell, walking would be a challenge.

Sot lay sprawled on his rugs, snoring loudly, his face slack. Vardok had fallen asleep on a pile of rugs across from her, but he had a tensed, alert quality. She realized then he was the one she had called Fist. Stubble was studying a map he had unrolled on his crate.

"Did we ride all night?" Allegra asked. Her voice slurred.

"That's right." Stubble didn't glance up.

"Doesn't the driver have to sleep?" she asked.

"He did. Vardok drove for a while."

"Oh." She had other concerns right now. Before, when she had needed to relieve herself, Stubble had given her a pot and held a rug in front of her. She wanted more privacy, and also a bath. Water. Blissful, clear water.

Allegra spoke awkwardly. "What do you do to, uh, clean up?" She hoped he knew what she meant, because she was too embarrassed to say more.

Stubble didn't answer, and she wasn't sure he heard. Then he climbed to his feet, looming over her. Startled, she pressed back. But he just went to the front of the wagon. Leaning over Sot, he pulled apart two flaps of cloth.

"We need to stop," he told someone outside.

Another man, the driver apparently, answered, words Allegra couldn't hear. Stubble let the flaps fall into place, then came over and crouched in front of her. "We're going to rest the oxen. I'll take you out then. But if you give me trouble, we come back in. Understand?"

As she nodded, the wagon rumbled to a stop. Vardok rolled onto his back and grunted. Sot kept snoring.

"Come on." Stubble stood up.

Allegra tried to rise, but her legs buckled. "Can't," she muttered.

Stubble helped her up. "Just stand until your head clears."

She swayed for balance. When her stomach settled, she looked up at him. His whiskers had thickened into a beard, and he didn't smell so great.

He smiled slightly. "Ready?"

"Hungry," she said.

"Later." He guided her forward, holding her up by the arm.

At the back of the wagon, Stubble drew aside the flaps, and she squinted as morning sunlight poured across them. It was a relief to breathe in the crisp air after the stale wagon.

Then she saw the land.

Saints almighty. Gone were Aronsdale's pretty meadows. To the east, a huge mountain range loomed out of a desert like teeth in the jaws of a gigantic skeleton with its mouth open. Their peaks stabbed the washed-out blue sky, and the rising sun just crested their tips. Closer by, stretches of red and ocher desert alternated with serrated rock formations that stood at the height of a tall man or higher. The land had an eerie quality, as if they had reached a place ruled by the mythical Shadow Dragon, where humans traveled only on sufferance of that Jazidian god.

Stubble indicated the peaks. "Those are the Jagged Teeth."

"Never expected t'see 'em." She tried again. "To see them."

He jumped to the ground. Before she could react, he had lifted her out of the wagon and set her next to him.

"Can walk on my own," she mumbled.

He laughed softly. "Are you sure?"

"Yes." She wanted to sock him for that smirk.

"All right," he said. "But if you run, I'll catch you."

Right. She was tipsy, not stupid. Given how little she knew about survival in the desert, she wouldn't take off even if she were sober. She had no supplies, map or horse. She would bide her time until she had a better opportunity.

"We've been following the Stoneblue River," Stubble said. "You can clean up there."

Water! She set off in the direction he indicated and did her best to walk a straight line. When he rested his hand on her shoulder, offering support, she glared at him and pulled away.

The air smelled strange, so parched and dusty. Its dryness added to her thirst, until she could think of nothing but stoneblue water. She wasn't sure how long it took to reach the river, as her mind kept drifting, but they were soon above it. The water coursed fiercely, as wild as the land, roaring over steep drops, with rapids and small waterfalls. Spray jumped around needled rock formations that jutted out of the froth.

Stubble found a barrier of rocks that created a pool where the river flowed more slowly. He stood on the bank behind Allegra, holding her in place with his hands on her shoulders.

"I don't want you to drown," he said uncertainly.

She shrugged off his hands. "I c'swim fine."

"Sober, maybe."

She ignored him and sat on the bank, her legs dangling in the pool. With a sigh, she eased into the water. She lifted handfuls of the precious liquid and drank and drank and drank, slaking the thirst that had plagued her.

Stubble sat on a boulder a few paces back from the pool. "Don't go anywhere."

Self-conscious with him watching, she crouched behind the riverbank so he could see only her head. Then she pulled off her wet shift and tossed it up on the ground. It wouldn't be dry when she finished her bath, but she had wanted the water so much, she hadn't cared.

"I need to wash my hair," she said. It would give her an excuse to disappear underwater, maybe swim away. More likely she would drown, and she had nowhere to go, but the water had returned a little of her strength, encouraging her to think about escape.

Stubble took something out of his pocket and tossed it to her. Startled, she grabbed it out of the air. It was a rough bar of soap, gritty and orange.

"Stay where I can see you," he warned. "Or I'll come in after you."

"Don't do that," she said hurriedly. He had so far kept the others from mauling her, but no one would stop *him* if he changed his mind about the rules he had set up.

Watching her face, he sighed. "Look, I've a wife at home. Two children. I love them. I don't dishonor my wife by taking other women, and I don't force girls I find in the forest." More quietly, he added, "But I've a living to make, and you're going to bring us a lot of wealth. So if you try to get away, I'll come after you, whatever it takes."

"Well, good for you, not wanting to dishonor your wife," she said sourly as she soaped her arms. "You just sell the girls you find in the forest to someone else to rape. How the hell can you justify that if you think it's wrong?"

"Don't talk to me like that." His fist clenched on the rock. "You're in Jazid now. A horse has more rights than you do here."

"That's appalling."

He started to say more, then stopped and stared at his fist as if he hadn't realized he had clenched it. Taking a breath, he relaxed his fingers.

"Does Vardok have a wife?" Allegra asked. Then she added, "Maybe he likes horses better. I'll bet they don't talk back."

Stubble glowered at her. "He has neither wife nor horse. And before you say no one wants him, he *does* have several children."

"Do they neigh?" Allegra asked sweetly.

"By the Shadow Dragon," Stubble muttered. "Woman, you do have a tongue."

She turned her back to him and lathered her hair. Despite his claim otherwise, he obviously had qualms about his work. Maybe he loved his family, maybe he had a conscience, but that just made it worse, because he went ahead with this anyway, out of his desire for wealth, with no apparent remorse.

Allegra wrestled with her anger. If she was going to get away, she had to keep her wits. Taking off into an unfamiliar desert without preparation was more likely to earn her death than freedom. But eventually an opportunity had to arise. To take it, she needed to be alert and strong, and she would be neither if they kept her drunk and in need of food and water.

She wished she could make a spell to soothe her agitation. She pressed her hand between her breasts where her pendant had hung. She felt more naked without it than without her clothes. Every mage had a maximum shape she could use. The greatest form Allegra had ever managed had six sides, in three dimensions. A cube. The disk on her pendant hadn't been as strong a shape, so it didn't create as powerful a spell, but she liked the sweetness its circular form added. The few times she had tried higher-order forms such as octahedrons, she had managed nothing but a headache.

Floating around, she saw Stubble watching her. She folded her arms over her breasts.

His voice gentled. "What's your name?"

"Allegra."

"I've never heard a name like that before."

"It's the feminine form of the musical term *allegro.*"

"Well, Allegra, listen," he said. "Try to accept what's happened. It will make things easier for you."

"I won't ever accept it. You broke the law, scuzzermug."

"Scuzzermug?" He gave a startled laugh. "What's that?"

"You know those yellow slugs that go under rocks?"

"Ah. I see." He rubbed his hand over his unkempt beard. "I don't suppose it would do any good to suggest you speak with more honeyed words."

She felt about as "honeyed" as a cactus. "Why should I?"

"I would not have you brutalized. And you will suffer if you speak this way to whoever buys you."

"I'm not a possession."

He squinted at her. "Such fire in a woman is strange."

"Why?" she asked, curious. "Don't your women have backbones?"

"I'm sure they all have vertebrae. They also have a better sense of what is in their best interest."

She snorted. "I don't see why they put up with it."

"We've so few women." When she started to retort, he held up his hand. "It's because so many miners come here, not because the women leave. Jazid has a lot of precious ores, gems, that sort of thing. The atajazid offered incentives to attract miners."

"The ata-what?"

"The Atajazid D'az Ozar. The Shadow-Dragon King. He sat on the Onyx Throne before Cobalt the Dark murdered him."

"Oh." Of course. Cobalt Escar, king of the Misted Cliffs, had conquered Jazid, Shazire and Blueshire, and married the woman who was heir to the Harsdown Throne, which meant his son would rule Harsdown as well. Escar was a king no longer; people called him the Midnight Emperor.

"Slavery is illegal in the Misted Cliffs," Allegra said. "I'll tell Cobalt's soldiers what you've done."

He shrugged. "You won't see any of them where you're going."

"I thought one of the buyers was a general."

"That's right." He regarded her intently. "You will go to a man of means and influence. Don't throw that away by running off into the desert. You wouldn't last a day before someone caught you, and chances are your situation with him would be a lot worse."

She noticed more what he didn't say than his actual words. "Why won't you tell me about the auction?" she asked.

He just shook his head, and she wondered if he was protecting himself. Who were these bidders? With a shudder, she turned so she didn't have to face him. She longed for the comfort of a spell. Several holes in the rocks across the pool resembled circles. The pool was only waist deep, but the rippled water helped veil her nakedness. So she swam to the rocks, going underwater to rinse off the soap.

At the other side, she ran her fingers over the stone ridge. Water poured over it and cascaded into the pool, eroding holes in the rock. Most were irregular, but one was almost round. Laying her hand over the hole, she closed her eyes. The uneven shape might allow a small spell.

To do what? She had so few options. Spells went according to color, like a rainbow. Red brought warmth and light, orange eased pain, yellow soothed emotions, green read emotions, blue healed physical injuries and indigo healed emotions. As far as she knew violet spells didn't exist. Just as a mage could use shapes up to a maximum number of sides, she could do any spells up to her maximum color. Allegra thought her limit was probably yellow.

Red and orange mages were most common. Yellow was rarer. The only greens she knew of were the Harsdown queen and the mage mistress of Aronsdale. She wasn't sure about the Aronsdale queen. Blue, maybe? She couldn't imagine an indigo mage; who could survive having that power? Some tales claimed the Aronsdale *kings* were mages because so many of their ancestors had married the strongest mages they could find. Although she knew of only women, she saw no obvious reason why a man couldn't be a mage.

The best Allegra could do was soothe pain and comfort people. She liked to, especially because the spells affected her, too. In theory, she could reverse them and cause pain or grief, but she had no more interest in such spells than doctors had in causing injury or illness. Besides, if she tried such spells on anyone else, she would also experience whatever she inflicted. Now, though, she wished she had learned how.

She laid her head on the stone, her wine-soaked mind filling with sadness. She thought of the songs she had learned for her loved ones, and tears slid down her face. As the oldest of seven children, she had spent a great deal of time helping care for her younger siblings, which included persuading them to sleep. She chose a lullaby from among their favorites:

Sleep little flower, sleep my wild storm
Lie in your bowers, so softly and warm

She went through several verses, crooning to the cherished siblings she might never see again. The spell calmed her, golden in its soothing power. It made her sleepy even as tears ran down her face.

Eventually she let her voice and the spell fade, and she became aware again of the river swirling around her body.

Raising her head, she wiped the tears out of her eyes. Stubble stood by his rock, staring at her, his face flushed. He seemed angry, perhaps because she had taken so long.

He came to the bank and knelt down. "Come here."

Biting her lip, Allegra stayed put. She crossed one arm over her breasts and splayed the other hand over her pelvis, covering herself underwater while she pressed against the rock.

"I'm not going to hurt you," he said, his voice softening. He wasn't angry, she realized, just intense. "That was *beautiful*. You've an incredible voice."

Her voice shook. "Could you move back? So I can dress?"

He stayed there, and she feared he would refuse, that he would pull her out of the water if she came to the bank. Then he exhaled and said, "All right." He stood up and stepped back a few paces.

Allegra swam over, staying low until she reached the bank. She reached for her tunic and pulled it on while she was in the water, soaking the portion from her hips to her thighs. When she climbed out, the cloth clung to her, the top portion damp and the bottom drenched. Water dripped down her legs.

Stubble watched her as if he were hungry. "Ach," he muttered. He spun away and strode to the rock. Then he whirled around. "All right. Let's go back." He was obviously upset, though Allegra wasn't certain if it was at her or at himself.

By the time they reached the wagon, the sun had risen high enough to scorch the day. The fourth nomad was sitting on his driver's bench above the oxen. *Driver,* she thought of him.

The wagon looked like the pictures in geography scrolls, the way it stood in the desert with oxen and its bright colors. Once, those drawings had seemed exotic and enticing to her, but no more. She struggled with the tears welling in her eyes. Damned if she would let them see her cry.

They were soon on their way, bumping among the jagged hills.

Throughout the day, Allegra tried to sleep, to conserve her strength and keep her wits sharp. She managed only an uneasy doze. Vardok exuded hostility, but Sot seemed more interested in his bottle than in her. Stubble read for a while, then sharpened a knife he wore on his belt. Vardok changed clothes, and Allegra averted her eyes, but not before she saw the scars on his back and legs. She wondered if he had fought in the war against the Misted Cliffs.

Later Sot drove for a while. Driver settled in the wagon where Sot had been sprawled and took bread, cheeses and dried meat out of a crate. Allegra's mouth watered; they had given her only a mug of thin stew today. When she turned to Stubble, he shook his head. She clenched her fists so hard, her nails dented in her palm. Hunger gnawed in her stomach.

Eventually Driver went to work on some sort of book-keeping scroll. Allegra wondered if they listed her on those inventories. Angry, she lay down with her back to them and pulled a carpet over her body. The cold night descended like a stone dropping. In the glades of Aronsdale, days were warm and benign, never with the oppressive heat of the desert here, yet the nights were warmer than here. Jazid was a land of extremes and honed edges.

"Ho!"

Allegra lifted her head. The call came from outside. The wagon lumbered to a stop, and the lack of movement felt strange. Vardok had been dozing, but now he stirred, his gaze bleary.

"Finally," Stubble said to no one in particular. He stood up creakily and stepped over to Allegra. "Come on." Grasping her upper arm, he pulled her to her feet. "Let's go."

Apprehension tickled her throat. "Go where?"

"We live here," he said. "My wife will tend to you. Tomorrow we'll have the auction."

Panic swelled in her. "No. I can't."

Vardok scowled at her. "You've been a lot of trouble. Now you're going to get perfumed or coddled or however else women waste their time. So quit complaining."

"Would you call it 'coddling' if four men grabbed you?" Allegra asked. "Trussed you up, hauled you across the desert, then scrubbed you down and put you up for auction?"

Vardok stared at her with incredulity. Then he turned to Driver. "Why don't you hit her?" He waved his hand angrily at Stubble. "He won't let me."

Driver gave him a wry smile. "I'm wary of her punch, Vardi. And her tongue."

"Is that your intellectually subtle solution to everything?" Allegra asked Vardok. "Beat up people?"

"Allegra," Stubble said. "It's time to go." He pulled her to the back of the wagon.

Sunset greeted them outside. The western horizon had turned a red so deep, the sky seemed on fire.

"You wanted me out of there before my refusal to act like a mouse got my face bashed," Allegra said after they jumped to the ground. "Can't rough up the goods, after all." Her words were bravado; she was scared. After the auction, no one would stop the buyer from doing whatever he wanted to her.

"Well, since you asked," Stubble said. "Yes."

"How can you do it?" she asked him. "How can you make your living this way?"

"It's a good living. I'm a wealthy man. How do you think I could buy such a lovely wife?"

"You *bought* your wife? That's horrible."

Stubble seemed bewildered. "How else would I get one?"

"Oh, I don't know," Allegra said. "Maybe court her. Woo her. Treat her well. *Ask* if she'll marry you."

"It doesn't happen that way here."

"Are you selling me as a wife?"

"No. A pleasure girl."

"What's the difference?"

"A woman can be a wife, a concubine or a pleasure girl. A wife has the most status. Then a concubine. A pleasure girl is just for, well—" He cleared his throat. "Pleasure."

"Great," Allegra muttered. She spun away from him and stalked around the wagon.

And stopped.

An astonishing camp lay before her. Brightly colored tents with peaked roofs clustered together. As the sunset darkened, people were lighting lamps that hung from poles, tinted-glass blossoms with flames flickering within. The nomads wore long robes with hoods, men in black and charcoal, women in gold or red silks. No one she could identify as a woman was alone; guards escorted the few who were out this evening.

Stubble came up beside Allegra. "Here." He wrapped one of the charcoal robes around her. "You can't go into camp undressed like that. You wouldn't get more than a few steps."

Right. But it was all right for her to spend four days cooped up in that wagon with their smelly selves. She wanted to pound her fists against him. Instead she drew in a breath, seeking calm. It could have been worse. Regardless of what he may have wanted to do to her, he had held back and kept the others off her. Bitterly she thought that might be why these mysterious buyers had chosen him to set up the auction; they knew the "merchandise" would be in good condition.

Allegra raised the hood of the robe to hide her face. Breezes rippled the cloth around her body, but with night descending so fast, it would probably soon be too dark for anyone to see she wasn't a man.

"You live here?" she asked.

"When I'm not traveling." He rubbed the small of his back. "After the auction, we'll move to our next camp."

"Why move all the time?"

He blinked. "Why would we want to stay in one place?"

"It's home." Allegra thought of her family's dairy. "I lived in the same house all my life."

"Strange," Stubble mused. "I would feel…" He thought for a moment. "Trapped. Confined."

Her voice caught. "Then you know how I feel now."

No answer.

The other nomads unloaded the wagon and saw to the oxen while Stubble took her into the camp. As they walked among the tents, men nodded to him, and he nodded back. She wasn't certain if they recognized him or were giving a ritualistic greeting. They soon reached a yellow tent larger than many of the others, with red tassels swinging in the wind. Two brawny men sat on stools by the entrance, talking, both armed with swords.

As Stubble and Allegra approached, the men rose, their hands on the hilts of their weapons. "What do you want?" one asked.

Stubble pushed back his hood. "Light of the evening."

"Aztire!" The man strode forward and clapped Stubble's arm. "It's good to see you, brother." He grinned at Allegra. "Heh, Vardi."

"It's not Vardok," Stubble said. He motioned to the tent. "Let us go inside."

Stubble's brother eyed Allegra curiously. He wasn't as tall

as Stubble, and his hair was brown rather than black, but they otherwise looked alike.

The other guard at the tent smiled, his teeth a flash of white in his black beard. "It's good to see you, Azi."

"Azi?" Allegra asked Stubble. "Is that your name? Aztire?"

Both guards froze. Then Stubble's brother said, "By the dragon, what do you have in there?"

"Who," Allegra said. "Not what." She lifted her hands to push back her hood.

Stubble caught her arm and swore under his breath. Then he pushed her into the tent. His brother followed. The other man stayed outside, but he stood close to the entrance, undoubtedly listening.

"Don't show yourself in public!" Stubble told Allegra. "It's for your own safety."

"Is it all right in here?" she asked, irked.

"It's fine," he said more calmly.

She pushed back her hood as she looked around. Blue carpets with bird patterns layered the floor. In the corners, braziers shaped like dragons glowed, with smoke curling up from their nostrils. The tang of smoke filled the air, but a hole in the top of the tent let out most of it. Large, tasseled pillows tumbled everywhere, and the gold dragons on them breathed embroidered plumes of fire, probably depictions of the Jazid dragon god.

All these dragons looked strange to Allegra. In Aronsdale, the people worshipped saints. Legends claimed the saints were ancestors who had lived so far in the past, no histories remained of them. Others named them as the first mages, who formed the court of the Dawn Star Goddess, namesake of the House of Dawnfield. Taka Mal had a similar mythology, but rather than a goddess, they revered the Dragon-Sun. They believed their dragon fought Jazid's Shadow Dragon in an endless, daily battle for dominion of the skies.

Saints, hear my prayer, Allegra thought. *Help me.*

Someone was asleep on the far side of the tent, deep in the shadows. From the way Stubble looked there, with such warmth, Allegra suspected she was about to meet his family. Or maybe not. For all she knew, "pleasure girls" weren't allowed such introductions.

"By the dragon, Azi," Stubble's brother said. "Where did you *find* her?"

Startled, Allegra turned back. Stubble's brother was staring as if she were an apparition of smoke that might dissipate any moment.

"He found me in Aronsdale," she said, annoyed he didn't acknowledge her. "Which, by the way, has a treaty with Jazid. Kidnapping Aronsdale women is illegal."

The brother gaped at her.

"She talks a lot," Stubble said.

"She's gorgeous." His brother lifted a length of Allegra's curls. "I've never seen hair this color before. It looks like sunlight." He moistened his lips. "Is she well formed?"

"Stop talking about me as if I'm not here," Allegra said. She barely held back the quaver in her voice. The day was beginning to crash down on her, her disorientation heightened by her lack of sleep and food, and her muzziness from the wine.

"Azi?" A woman's sleepy voice came from across the tent. "Is that you?"

Stubble turned, an expression of welcome flooding his face. "Did I wake you? I'm sorry."

"It's all right." Rustles came from the shadows, and a small woman appeared in a yellow robe that glistened even in the dimness. When she saw Allegra, she shot a startled look at her husband.

Stubble spoke gently. "She's for an auction tomorrow, that's all." He pulled the woman into his arms, and they embraced, Stubble resting his cheek on her head. When they drew apart, he smiled. "The children?"

"Both asleep." She hesitated. "Shall I wake them?"

"No need. I'll see them tomorrow." He inclined his head to Allegra. "The auction is the one I told you about. We've sent word to the buyers."

The woman regarded Allegra with large, dark eyes. She was younger than Stubble, with a heart-shaped face, a small nose and gold hoops in her ears. Her dark hair fell down her back like a black waterfall. "So you found what they were looking for?"

"Finally, yes," Stubble said. "I think they'll be pleased." He sounded nervous.

"I hope so," the woman said. Before, she had seemed to fear Allegra, probably thinking her husband had brought home another woman. Now Allegra had the disquieting impression the woman feared *for* her.

"Can you tend her tomorrow?" Stubble asked. "Pretty her up however you do that."

"Of course," his wife said. She wouldn't look at Allegra.

"You really come from Aronsdale?" Stubble's brother asked.

"Yes." Allegra met his gaze. "Your brother broke the law."

He glanced at Stubble. "She's lively."

Stubble regarded him dourly. "That's a polite way to put it."

The woman took Allegra's arm and drew her away. "Don't mind them," she said. "They act rough, but they're a good lot."

Allegra wondered how she could call men who sold people a "good lot." Then again, Stubble had bought her.

The woman gave her a tentative smile. "I am Rose."

"I'm Allegra." She glanced at the small heaps under a rug several paces away from them. "Your children?"

"Two daughters. We are blessed." She tugged Allegra down on a pile of carpets near the children. Stubble and his brother stayed across the tent, conferring about who knew what.

"How would you feel," Allegra asked Rose, "if a 'good lot' of men hauled off your daughter and you never heard from her again?"

Rose shot her a terrified look. "Don't say that!"

"Then you know how my mother will feel when she finds out I've vanished."

The woman sat cross-legged and folded her hands in her lap. "You weren't well guarded?"

"I was my own guard."

"Well, then." Rose spoke as if that answered everything and reflected poorly on Allegra and anyone else involved in her life.

Allegra tried again. "In Aronsdale, what your husband and the other men did would be considered repugnant."

"That doesn't matter here." She spoke with a painful gentleness. "Were I your mother, I would mourn. But that changes nothing. It is the way of life. Men die and women suffer."

"Do you really see life that way?"

"Of course." Rose patted the carpet where Allegra was sitting. "You may sleep here tonight. Tomorrow we will prepare you to meet the buyers."

"I don't want to." Allegra meant the words to be firm, but instead she sounded afraid.

"Shh," Rose murmured. "It won't last long. They will look at you, talk to you, touch you some and then it will be over and you will go with a powerful man. You will have nice things and a rich life."

"I don't need nice things, and I already had a life as rich as I wanted." Allegra didn't miss what else Rose had said. *A powerful man.* "Do you know the bidders?"

Rose paused, and Allegra thought she would be as taciturn as her husband. But then she said, "They are fugitives."

"Tell me."

"They are under a death sentence from Cobalt the Dark. If they are found, they will be executed."

Great. Just great. "I thought one of them was a general."

Rose nodded uneasily. "General Dusk Yargazon. He wants a pleasure girl to replace one he lost, a girl with fire hair."

"Another woman from Aronsdale?"

"She came from Taka Mal," Rose said. "But they say her grandfather was an Aronsdale man. He married her grandmother and went to Taka Mal with her." She sounded perplexed. "I've no idea why."

"That's how it's done where I live," Allegra said. "The man moves to his wife's home. And it makes sense if the grandfather came from southern Aronsdale. It's the only place in all the settled lands where yellow or red hair is common."

Rose touched a tendril curling over Allegra's shoulder. "Gold. Like the sun. It is an astonishing color."

Allegra had a question about the General. She dreaded the answer, but she had to know. "What happened to the woman?"

"The official story is that the Taka Mal military rescued her." In a low voice, Rose said, "Really she escaped his interrogators. No one knows how. But he can never get her back."

"Because it's illegal to own people in Taka Mal?"

"No. She is the wife of Queen Vizarana's cousin in Taka Mal!" Rose seemed pleased to have someone to gossip with. If women were as scarce here as Stubble had implied, she might have few female friends. "She had married Baz Quaazera," Rose continued. "But no one knew. Several nomads captured her and sold her to the General." Her face paled. "That night the General racked her, to see what she knew about the Taka Mal army. He left her to be cleaned up, so he could have her later. And she escaped!"

"He did *what* to her?" Allegra was certain she had misheard.

"He put her on the rack and interrogated her."

Good gods. What if this general decided Allegra knew secrets of the Aronsdale military? She was having trouble breathing. She inhaled deeply and let it out slowly. "His name is Yargazon?"

"Dusk Yargazon. People call him the General. He commands the outlaw Jazid army that supposedly doesn't exist." She spoke with intensity. "They have the boy king in their protection. One day they will rise against Cobalt the Dark and throw his forces from our country! Emperor Cobalt has put a great price on the General's head. Even the Dark Emperor fears him."

"You know," Allegra said wanly. "This isn't helping. Maybe you should tell me about the other bidder."

"Well, I'm not sure…" Rose wouldn't look at her.

"He's that bad?"

"You could do no better." She wasn't smiling.

Allegra felt as if butterflies danced in her throat. "Then why do you look as if I'm going to the gallows?"

Rose finally looked at her. "His name is Markus Onyx. He is the eldest son of the atajazid who died in the war."

That caught Allegra off guard. "A *nine-year-old?*" She gave an uneven laugh, giddy with relief. "This is the dire fate you don't want to tell me?" It seemed silly for the boy-king's advisors to encourage him to pick out a pleasure girl, but what the hell.

"I'm not talking about His Majesty," Rose said. "The atajazid is not the oldest son."

"He's not?" Her mood plunged. "Then why is he the king?"

"He is the only legitimate son. Prince Markus is his older half brother, and the imperial regent for the Onyx Throne. He is thirty and some years. I don't know exactly."

"Oh." Allegra's shoulders slumped. So this Markus was illegitimate but not without power. "Who was his mother?"

"A concubine of the deposed atajazid." Rose nodded as if verifying the half brother's fitness as regent. "Prince Markus is called the fiercest of all men."

Allegra didn't want to hear about fierce. "Why is Markus a prince, if his mother wasn't the queen?"

"His father legitimized him. Apparently the new atajazid has made Markus his heir until the boy is old enough to sire his own." Rose leaned closer. "Markus has no mercy. He kills as easily as you or I can cry. He will defeat Cobalt the Dark and place the despot's head on a pole in front of the Onyx Palace. His warriors will destroy the armies of the Dark Emperor and lay waste to the Misted Cliffs."

"Doesn't sound like he'll have time for a pleasure girl," Allegra muttered. "What with all that killing."

Rose gave her a dry look. "Men always have time."

"I don't understand why the regent is betting in an auction against his own general. Won't that cause rancor between them?"

Rose shook her head. "It is an ancient custom, that two men of power each have the opportunity for a woman of extraordinary beauty. Because there are so few such women. The prince regent has invited Yargazon to show his esteem for the General. Whoever wins, the other will respect and honor his claim."

Right. Extraordinary beauty. She had two heads, too. "Do they?" she asked. "Honor the other's claim, I mean."

"It is expected," Rose said. "I don't really know. This sort of auction is rare. But nothing could interfere with them working together to destroy the armies of the Misted Cliffs in vengeance for what Cobalt has wrought in Jazid."

Allegra squinted at her. "What exactly has the Misted Cliffs wrought here that is so terrible?"

"They are monsters," Rose confided.

"What do they do?"

"Make changes."

"Like what?"

Rose looked scandalized. "They say that women should have the same rights as men."

Allegra groaned. "And this is terrible *how?*"

"Shh." Rose glanced across the tent, where Stubble and his brother were drinking and laughing. "Don't let them hear."

"I already told them that about women."

"You didn't!"

"I did indeed."

"Did they beat you?"

"No." Allegra grimaced. "Vardok wanted to, though."

"You must never say such to Prince Markus or the General. They will put you on a rack or some such." She regarded Allegra with sympathy. "I am glad I am not you."

"Well, that's reassuring."

"Ah, I'm sorry." Rose took her hand. "Let's talk about other matters and have a good time tonight. You'll feel better. Tomorrow we will make you the most beautiful of women."

"How about we make me the most ugly of women?" Allegra said. "Maybe they'll lose interest and leave."

"Come, don't be silly." Rose regarded her expectantly. "You must tell me about Aronsdale. Is it as exotic as they say?"

"Well, I don't know what they say. But I would love to tell you about it. Did you know women own all the property there?"

"Oh, you are funny." Rose smiled. "But no joking. I would really like to know."

"I'm serious. My parents run a dairy, but my mother owns it."

Rose seemed bewildered. "Your mother cannot own a dairy. She cannot own land. Or livestock. Or anything."

"Of course she can."

"But how?"

"Her mother owned it before her. And her grandmother before that. For many generations."

"If you say so."

"It's true."

"Well, you are gone now. So who will own it?"

That felt like a kick in the stomach. Allegra had always assumed she would marry, probably after she finished her studies at the guild, and she had hoped she and her husband could help in the dairy. Or she might teach, as she had done for the last two years, helping an older instructor in the village of Spindle Vine. As a mage, she would be asked to help ease the lives of the people in her village, singing warmth, light and health. Of course, she might have fallen in love with a man who didn't want to milk cows. Nor was she sure why the guild had invited her to study there. It seemed far-fetched to think the invitation was connected to Prince Aron, but she had seen the looks her parents passed when they didn't know she was watching. They wondered. She lacked the mage strength the royal family sought, but if no one else had it, either, they might consider her.

Allegra had thought of asking Tanner if he would marry her. He had come around a lot before she left for Crofts Vale, and he had hinted he would wait for her. She didn't love him as a woman should love a husband, but she could do worse than to marry her best friend. The passion might come, someday.

Surely that couldn't all be gone. Someone ought to tell his purportedly perfidious Majesty, Cobalt the Dark, that nomads in his conquered territory were selling Aronsdale women as pleasure toys to insurgent warlords. Maybe he would throw this general and prince regent in chains.

"Don't look so grim," Rose said. Her wistful gaze went to Stubble and his brother. "Azi can stay over there tonight. I'll stay with you, to talk if you want, or just to be here. Things will seem brighter in the morning."

"I hope so," Allegra said.

She feared it would only get worse.

❧ CHAPTER 3
THE GLITTERING PAVILION

In the morning, Rose took Allegra to bathe in a small lake fed by the only river in the otherwise barren desert. Vardok, Driver and Sot helped guard the area, but only Stubble sat where he could see them. Allegra supposed she should think of him as Azi, but the name Stubble was too fixed in her thoughts. He settled against a rock with his hands behind his head and his legs stretched out. Watching two women bathe each other was so obviously a treat for him, Allegra wanted to slap the smug look off his face. Instead she drank her fill of water, which he had denied her since her last bath. It cleared her head.

She wished she could make a spell for strength. Triangles showed everywhere on wagons, but they were distorted. She saw nothing resembling a polyhedron. She even dove down in the lake and dug along the bottom. She found a metal ball, but she couldn't use it, for a sphere was the most powerful shape, a polyhedron with an infinite number of sides. Rumor claimed that Cobalt's wife, the empress, could wield such power. Well, maybe. Allegra certainly couldn't. She would burn out her gifts if she tried to use the ball. Just concentrating on it hurt her head. Bilious colors swirled in her vision until she dropped the ball into the river.

After they returned to Stubble's tent, the nomads gave Rose the clothes they wanted Allegra to wear. Allegra couldn't believe it. The "skirt" covered almost nothing. The front panel was a beaten gold triangle the width of her palm and length of her forearm, its scalloped edges curved too much to form a useful shape for spells. The back was the same. The panels hung from a chain that rested low on her hips. Slender gold chains of diamonds, rubies and topazes formed a skimpy fringe from the hip chain down to about midthigh, swaying and clinking when she walked. Rose told her the skirt was made from real gems and gold, in honor of the bidders.

The halter was just as bad. Gold chains secured little gold cups over her nipples and held up her breasts so they appeared to have the most remarkable engineering, as if they could stand up on their own despite their size and weight. It was mortifying.

Rose didn't like the outfit, either. "Might as well send you in there with nothing on at all," she muttered as she helped Allegra dress. Her sympathy helped a little, but Allegra still felt as if she were going to a funeral. Her own. She had passed on, replaced by this barbaric pleasure girl in chains, jewels and little else.

Rose coiled Allegra's hair on top of her head and threaded gems into the locks, with curls framing her face and wisping down her neck. "It's lovely," she told Allegra. "So few women have curly hair here. And you sparkle. Gold, topaz, ruby and the purest of all colors, diamond. For your purity." She lowered her voice. "I have to tell them."

Allegra scowled at her. The blasted nomads had insisted Rose check her virginity. She wished now she had taken Tanner up on his offer that day in the barn and given away her purportedly precious commodity.

"How about you tell them I'm not a virgin?" Allegra said. "Maybe they'll cancel the auction."

"They won't," Rose said. "Besides, you should be glad. This means the buyer may treat you more gently your first time." She hesitated, then said, "It depends on his…preferences."

Allegra winced. "Don't tell me what that means." She looked across the tent to where Stubble sat with Vardok, Driver and his brother. They were joking among themselves, but their impatience practically snapped in the air.

"Do you think the buyers are here yet?" Allegra asked.

"Probably." Rose sat on her haunches and gave Allegra an apologetic look. "I've redone your hair five times. I don't think I can come up with any more excuses to hold them off."

Allegra managed a smile. "Thank you for trying."

"I wish…" Rose took a breath. "I have been happy here with Azi and the children. I've not wanted for anything. But sometimes—" She sighed. "You talk about your home with such love. It's hard for me to imagine, but it has clearly been good to you. I'm sorry they took you away from that."

Allegra couldn't answer without tears threatening her eyes. Footsteps sounded nearby, and she looked to see Stubble standing a few paces away, holding a charcoal-gray robe.

"Are you ready?" he asked.

Rose went to him. "She's ready," she said softly.

Stubble put his hand under Rose's chin and kissed her. "You look beautiful today."

Rose's blush added a lovely tinge to her creamy skin. It was a moment before Stubble pulled his gaze away from his wife and turned to Allegra. He offered his hand, but she stood on her own. She didn't want to appear even more dependent on them, but it was also for Rose. It didn't take a genius to see she feared her husband would bring home a concubine. Although Allegra doubted he would, it obviously wasn't unheard of for men in this culture. Rose might believe him to be good, but as far as Allegra was concerned, his gentleness didn't change the fundamental brutality of his chosen profession.

"Is she ready?" Vardok demanded from the other side of the tent. "I don't see what takes them so long. Just put on the damn skirt and go—" He stopped as Stubble moved aside so he could see Allegra.

"Gods above," Driver muttered.

Vardok let out a noisy breath. "Now that *is* worth waiting for. Oh, yes! We're going to be rich." He grinned at Stubble. "Rolling in treasures."

"Why don't you just keep this damn outfit?" Allegra muttered.

Vardok laughed, the only time he had ever shown pleasure in her company. "Oh, girl, what we're going to get for you will be worth far more than that little skirt."

Stubble's brother wasn't smiling. He just stood, staring at Allegra. He spoke hoarsely. "I'd buy her, Azi. As my wife."

Well, that was about as romantic as having her teeth pulled. But it might be a stroke of luck. He was the brother of the most tolerable nomad Allegra had so far met, he wasn't a war criminal with a price on his head and he wasn't known for the tortures he inflicted or the numerous people he killed. He would also probably be easier to escape from than a general or regent who almost certainly would have bodyguards.

"Yes," she told him quickly. "I'll go with you."

He started over to her, but Stubble grabbed his arm. "Don't be absurd," Stubble said. "The buyers are already here. You couldn't come close to affording her, anyway."

His brother shot him an angry look. Then he exhaled and nodded. "Sorry."

Oh, well. Allegra knew it had been a long shot.

Driver and Vardok joined them, and they surrounded Allegra until she felt trapped.

"Here." Vardok offered her a blue-crystal glass with what looked like water.

Puzzled, she took the glass. She had slaked her thirst at the lake this morning, but it might be best to drink again, when she had a chance. She swallowed half the liquid—and gagged. "Ai! It's so bitter. What's in it?"

"Finish it," Vardok said harshly.

She wrinkled her nose. "I'm not thirsty."

Driver took the glass and raised it to her lips. "Just one more swallow. You can do it."

"No." Allegra jerked back her head.

They held her in place then, while Stubble's brother forced open her jaw. Driver poured the liquid into her mouth, and Vardok manipulated her throat so she swallowed convulsively. It happened so fast, she barely realized what they were doing before they finished. As she coughed, Driver and Vardok let go of her, but Stubble's brother slid his hand down to her behind. When Stubble frowned at him, he let her go.

"Why did you do that?" Allegra asked, bewildered.

"You'll like it fine," Vardok said. His eyes glinted.

She liked it less by the moment. "What was it?"

"Probably nothing you've heard of," Driver said. "An extract from a plant that grows only in this region of Jazid. Miradella."

The blood drained from her face. *No.* She knew of the extract from teaching her students about other countries. "Miradella is a lethal poison!" She couldn't believe they would kill her after all this trouble. "Are you *crazy?* Why are you doing this?" Did Vardok hate her so much?

"Shh," Stubble murmured. "It wasn't a fatal dose. You'll have a fever, but it should start to cool by tonight."

Driver stroked her hair as if he were calming a skittish horse. "You'll be fine. Just less resistant."

Soaking her with alcohol and starving her wasn't enough? They needed poison, too? What if they made a mistake and she flaming *died?* The hell with them. She rubbed her hands over her face, her arms trembling. "This can't be happening."

Stubble offered her the charcoal robe. "You needn't walk through camp like that. We're going to another tent."

She grabbed the robe and covered herself up. At least no one would stare at her while she died. She looked around desperately for Rose. She couldn't face this alone, surrounded by kidnappers. The nomad woman was standing a few paces back, her face strained. Allegra stared at her, imploring.

Rose turned to Stubble and started to speak, but he shook his head. "I don't want them to see you," he said. "If they decide they would like two girls instead of one, I can't refuse them."

The blood drained from Rose's face. Her gaze darted to the carpets where their five-year-old daughter was playing with the toddler.

"They're too young to catch anyone's interest," Stubble said. "But I want you all to stay in the tent today. My brothers will remain here as extra guards. Just in case."

Rose let out a relieved breath. "Thank you."

"How can you bear to live this way?" Allegra asked.

Rose glanced at her, then looked away, her face red.

Stubble pulled up the hood of Allegra's robe. "For the sake of your health, don't talk during the auction. Please."

"If you were worried about my health," she said, "you should have damn well left me in Aronsdale." Before he could say or do anything else, she stuck her finger in her mouth, so far down her throat that she started to choke.

"Hey!" Driver yanked down her arm. "What are you doing?"

"She's trying to throw up the miradella," Vardok said. He smirked at her. "Perhaps you'll be quieter from now on, eh?"

"Go rot in sheep dung," she ground out.

"You just talk that way to whoever ends up with you," he said, smug. "Go ahead. Be my guest."

She thought of running, but she knew they would catch her and drag her to the tent. She hoped Emperor Cobalt captured them all, including the buyers, and they putrefied in his dungeons.

They took her out of the tent then. With her hood up, she almost blended with them, except for her bare feet. She clenched her fist in the cloth of the robe, painfully aware of how little she wore under its thin protection. A few women were out in bright silks, with hoods hiding their faces, each escorted by nomads in dark robes. It was obvious the women were status symbols for the men, but that just increased the need to guard them. It sounded like a nightmare, that two men of high stature could come here and take away people's wives, if they so chose.

A pavilion stood in the center of the camp. Unlike the other brightly hued tents, this one was silver, with a white fringe on its peaked roof and white poles at its corners. Sculptures of silver-glass birds swung from its eaves, gleaming in the morning light. Rose had awakened Allegra before dawn, but the sun had since risen over the serrated peaks of the Jagged Teeth Mountains.

The interior was brighter than Allegra had expected. White hangings lightened the walls and sheer white drapes separated its interior into two rooms. The silvery-white carpet was so thick, it covered her toes. The sensuous brush of the pile on her skin only agitated her more.

Two nomads were waiting for them, men in dark trousers and gold and green shirts, their leather belts studded with fiery stones. They also had swords hanging in sheaths on their belts. While Stubble spoke with them, Allegra shivered. Vardok, Driver and Sot loomed over her, and she could almost feel their tension coiling in the air. The maddening aroma of curry and rice wafted through the tent, and her mouth watered. Her hunger had become a physical pain.

Stubble came back to them. "Jasper is letting them know we're here." As he spoke, one of the men with a sword parted the gauzy drapes and stepped through to the other room.

"Why are those men armed?" Allegra asked.

"The swords are ceremonial," Stubble said. "To honor our guests."

"Oh." She was glad she hadn't tried to run. Ceremonial swords undoubtedly worked on escaping prisoners just as well as ordinary weapons.

Vardok took hold of her robe and pulled it down. He caught her unawares as it fell around her waist, but she instinctively folded her arms to keep it from slipping any farther. Driver pulled apart her arms and let the robe fall the rest of the way, pooling at her feet. Then they all stood and looked at her, the four nomads and the guard with the sword.

"By the dragon," Driver muttered. "Lucky bidders."

Allegra's face flamed.

"Come." Stubble took her arm and led her forward. Her skirt clinked, and her head felt heavy with her bejeweled hair piled up.

Panic flared within Allegra and she balked. "I can't go in there. I can't do this."

"Allegra, this isn't difficult," Stubble said, his voice strained and impatient. "They just want to look at you."

"Don't force us to drag you in," Driver said.

She would die before she let herself be dragged in front of the two most notorious men in Jazid. When Stubble pulled her, she walked forward with her jaw clenched. The man with the sword pulled aside the drape, and they all escorted her into the other room.

It *glittered*. The wall hangings were metallic gold and white. Blue-glass lamps fashioned into dragons shone with gold plate. Gold and ivory chests gleamed in corners, and metallic dragon patterns curled across the white carpet. Two men sat at a low table across the room, reclining on white cushions. The table was set with china and gold, and they drank from crystal goblets. Allegra felt excruciatingly vulnerable in the unrelenting brightness. She wanted to curl up and hide, or flee this place of cruel, hard beauty.

Stubble guided her forward, his hand on the small of her back. The stares of the buyers could have burned her skin.

They both had black hair and eyes, but their resemblance to the nomads ended there. These men were to the T'Ambera as jaguars were to stray cats.

It was obvious which was the General. His black uniform glinted with silver on the cuffs, and its severe cut accented his broad shoulders. The heavily corded tendons in his neck slanted into his shoulder muscles and under his collar. Jazid's unforgiving sun had weathered his face and prominent nose, turning his skin leathery. He had a cold, steely demeanor. Wrinkles bracketed his mouth and creased the corners of his eyes, but she had no doubt he could easily best warriors half his age.

She looked at the other man.

Markus Onyx. Even reclined on a cushion, he looked violent. Nothing gentle showed in the planes of his face, only a sense of brutality deepened by his intense stare. His sculpted features might have been handsome if he had looked human, but no hint of compassion showed on his face. He wore dark trousers with an elegant cut and a leather belt studded with rubies and onyx. More onyx edged the cuffs of the dark red shirt that pulled over his powerful shoulders. His gaze raked Allegra with an appraising possessiveness.

Stubble and one of the armed men brought Allegra over to the buyers. Someone behind her pushed on her shoulders, and she dropped to both knees on a cushion in front of the glittering table. The nomads knelt on one knee to the prince regent, each with one arm resting across his thigh and his eyes downcast. The General sat relaxed in his chair, watching them with a predator's gaze. Markus, however, watched Allegra. She knew because, unlike everyone else, she hadn't averted her eyes. She stared at him as if she were a skylark doe mesmerized by torchlight, and his dark stare seemed to bore through her.

Markus waved his hand. How the nomads knew with their eyes downcast, Allegra had no idea, but they immediately rose to their feet. She started to, as well, but someone caught her shoulder, holding her down. She wanted to cross her arms over her breasts, but it would only draw more attention, and she would feel even more exposed when they forced down her arms. She struggled to breathe as her panic grew.

Inhale slowly, she told herself. *Out. Slowly.*

Yargazon narrowed his gaze as if she were a poor substitute for whatever he expected. "Her hair is the wrong color."

Stubble spoke with deference. "My apologies, sir. We couldn't find one with the fire-hair."

Fire-hair? He must mean red, like the girl Rose mentioned. Stubble didn't sound perturbed, which made her wonder if he thought Yargazon was just trying to bargain.

The prince waved his hand at the nomads. "You may all wait outside."

Allegra would have never thought she wanted nomads to stay with her, but being alone with these two was even worse. Or not completely alone; eight men in black uniforms stood around the room, at attention, swords on their belts. She shot a frantic look at Stubble. He hesitated as if he hadn't expected the buyers to tell them to leave, either.

But he shook his head almost imperceptibly at her. No surprise there. As far as they were concerned, Markus was their sovereign rather than Emperor Cobalt. They wouldn't refuse him.

After Stubble and the other nomads left, Yargazon spoke. "You. Girl." His deep voice rumbled. "Look at me."

Perspiration was gathering on Allegra's temples. She turned to the General, then flinched at his hard stare.

"What's your name?" he asked.

"Allegra." She wondered if Markus had told the nomads to leave so they wouldn't figure out what he and Yargazon liked about her. Another bargaining tactic.

"Allegra?" Yargazon said. "That makes no sense."

"It's a musical reference," Markus said lazily, sprawled on his cushion. He sounded relaxed, but his posture spoke more of aggressive tension than anything else. "They do that in Aronsdale. Name people after useless concepts."

Allegra stiffened. "I don't consider music useless."

Markus raised an eyebrow as if surprised she knew how to speak. "I imagine you wouldn't." His voice was like a well-oiled weapon. He motioned at the meal before them, steaming silver platters of curry and rice in a saffron sauce. A bowl of oranges stood next to the decanter of blood-red wine, and an enticing aroma wafted up from a loaf of spiced bread.

"Serve us," Markus said.

Allegra gritted her teeth. She hadn't had anything resembling a good meal in days. Now he wanted her to wait on them while she practically swooned with hunger? The hell with them.

"Serve yourself," she told Markus.

He glanced at Yargazon. "Did she just say what I thought?"

"I believe she said, 'Serve yourself,'" the General answered.

"So she did." Markus considered Allegra. "I wonder what our good general thinks we should do about that."

"I racked the last one," Yargazon said. "Perhaps that would help here."

Allegra jerked around to him. "That's sick!"

Markus spoke in a deceptively quiet voice. "What do you say, Allegra, hmm? Shall I let my general stretch you out?"

Sweat gathered on Allegra's palms, and it was all she could do to keep from wiping them on her legs. "No."

He indicated the dinner. "Then perhaps you will serve us."

She knew she should just do it and get it over with. But their casual attitude was too much. Her fist clenched on her thigh, and before she had time to think, she said, "Yes, you can torture people without any consequences. That doesn't make you better than anyone else. Putting a woman on a rack isn't powerful. It's weak and it's brutal."

A muscle twitched in Markus's cheek. But he only glanced at Yargazon and spoke with a deceptively mild tone. "She talks a lot."

"Indeed." Yargazon beckoned to her. "Come here."

She was having trouble breathing. Their mild tones didn't fool her. They were angry; she saw it in the glint of their eyes. She stayed put, kneeling before the table with one of them on each side.

Yargazon leaned forward. The table was so small, he easily closed his hand around her upper arm. "I said, come here."

Then he yanked.

She cried out as she flew forward and slammed into the corner of the table. The edge gouged her belly, then raked her leg as Yargazon dragged her forward. She sprawled across his lap on her stomach, her hair flying loose from its coil. The General jerked her upright and backhanded her across the face. With a gasp, she flew backward and landed on her side on the pillow where she had been kneeling. She lay gulping in breaths, too stunned to move.

Yargazon spoke in an icy voice. "I believe you were going to serve His Highness."

Allegra lifted her head to look at Markus. She couldn't read anything in his dark eyes, no hint of remorse for what Yargazon had just done in his name. She had read of such tyrants, who would just sit back while their people committed atrocities for them, as if that absolved them of responsibility for the damage.

"Get up," Markus told her. "And don't talk."

Allegra pushed up on her palms. Blood ran down her stomach, and a red splotch stained the pillow. The chains of her skirt were disarrayed over her thighs, leaving her almost naked.

Then she saw what Markus was holding. A quirt. He tapped it idly against his fingers as if he had forgotten it.

Where he had taken the whip from, she had no idea, but that he brought it to the auction told her far more than she wanted to know about him.

Allegra was gritting her teeth so hard, her jaw hurt. She pushed herself up on her knees and sat catching her breath. She didn't know what they wanted, food or drink, but Markus's goblet was empty. So she picked up the crystal decanter of red wine. Her hand shook as she filled Markus's glass, and dark red drops splattered on the pristine white tablecloth. Picking up the goblet, she looked into Markus's covetous stare.

Then she threw the wine in his face.

The prince whipped his arm up in front of his head. He swore and grabbed Allegra, moving so fast, she had no time to shrink back. Catching her wrists, he knocked the empty glass out of her hand and pulled her forward on her knees, then yanked her against him with her arms caught in front of her body. His large hands gripped like a vise, bruising her skin.

"Are you out of your *mind?*" he said. "Do you have a death wish?" He grabbed a cloth napkin and wiped the wine off his face. "Because the sentence for what you just did is execution."

"Fine." Allegra spat the word at him. "Kill me. For surely death would be a better fate than living with either of you."

The General rose to his feet, his face darkening. Markus dropped his quirt and stood, as well, hauling her up with him.

"We should tie her across the table." Yargazon bent down

and grabbed the quirt. Even as he straightened up, he snapped the lash. It caught Allegra across the back of her thighs and she screamed with the slash of pain. She twisted in Markus's hold, staring desperately toward the far end of the room, frantic for Stubble to free her from this nightmare.

"Dusk, wait," Markus said. "Neither of us has bought her yet." Dryly he added, "And you'll get me with that thing."

Yargazon lowered the whip. "My apologies, Sire."

Stubble stepped into the room, his face taut with alarm. "Your Highness?" he asked. "Is there a problem?"

Markus threw Allegra down on the cushion stained with her blood. She fell on her side, catching herself with her hands, then looked up at Stubble, her hair falling in her face.

"We're done here," Markus said curtly. "Take her."

Stubble strode to the table with an impassive expression, but he took Allegra's arm gently. Drawing her to her feet, he nudged her toward the exit. He spoke in a low voice. "Hurry."

Allegra stumbled with him. Her vision blurred, either from the blows or because the poison was taking effect. It wasn't tears. She refused to let the bastards make her cry.

As soon as Stubble ushered her out of the terrible glittering room, her knees gave way and she collapsed. As he caught her, he spoke quickly to Vardok. "Go tell Rose we're coming back and she'll need to tend Allegra. Hurry."

Vardok swore under his breath. "She threw wine in his *face.*" He watched Allegra as if he could sear her to ashes. "If you've ruined this for us, girl, I hope your execution is long, drawn out and painful beyond imagining."

"Vardi," Stubble said. "Just go."

Vardok clenched his fist and hit at the air. Then he swept from the tent, his robe billowing out behind him.

"Can you walk?" Stubble asked Allegra.

She took a step. When her legs buckled, she groaned.

"By the dragon," Stubble muttered. He picked her up, one arm behind her back and the other under her knees. Driver covered her with the charcoal robe, except for her face. Then Stubble carried her out of the tent. Allegra didn't know why he bothered. It seemed pointless to tend her wounds when the prince regent planned to kill her for insulting the wretched House of Onyx.

CHAPTER 4
THE DRIFT BASIN

Rose was ready for them. She had a bowl of water, pots of salve and bandages. Vardok, Driver and Stubble's brother stayed back while Stubble laid Allegra on a carpet.

"This is a bad sign," Rose murmured, leaning over to swab the gouge on Allegra's stomach.

Stubble knelt on Allegra's other side. "Why couldn't you just do what they wanted? Do you *want* them to execute you?"

Allegra sat up, wincing. "They deserved a lot worse."

"You're bleeding," Rose said. "And you're fevered. You must lie down." She touched the welt on Allegra's thigh that curled around from the back. "They whipped you, too?"

"General Yargazon started," Allegra said.

Rose shot a frightened glance at her husband. "What do you think will happen?"

"I've no idea. I have to find out." With a grunt, he rose to his feet. To Allegra, he said, "Stay here. And by the dragon, girl—no more trouble."

Allegra just shook her head. Something had snapped within

her when she saw the prince and his general sitting there with that sense of entitlement, arrogant and cruel, believing they had a right to inflict whatever they chose on anyone they wished. But saints, despite what she had said, she didn't really want to *die*. Would they execute her for the insult she had given?

She feared it was true.

Allegra sweated in a delirium for hours. Her fever soared, and she tossed on the carpets, throwing off any coverlet Rose put over her. She managed to swallow some soup, but nothing else. Stubble hadn't returned. Vardok and Driver were gone, as well, but Stubble's brother stayed on guard with two other men. Rose sat by her, laying damp cloths on her forehead.

Late in the afternoon, Allegra's fever began to ease. When she realized the worst had passed, that she would survive the poison, a sob wrenched out of her.

A rustle came from across the tent. As Allegra rolled onto her side, Stubble ducked inside the tent. Her pulse surged, and she dragged herself into a sitting position. The jeweled chains fell away from her skin with clinks, leaving creases along her thighs.

"Azi!" Rose hurried over to him. "What happened?"

Stubble grasped her around the waist and lifted her up. "You're beautiful, my love!"

"Goodness," Rose said, blushing. "Put me down." When he set her on her feet, she searched his face with a worried gaze. "Are they going to execute her?"

"I sure as hell doubt it." He grinned at Rose. "I could use a bit of wine, eh?"

"Azi! Don't tease," Rose said. "Tell us what happened."

"Why do you 'sure as hell doubt' they'll kill me?" Allegra said, twisting one of the chains on her skirt around her fingers.

Stubble laughed, shaking his head in amazement. "Who would have thought a talent at hurling wine would push up a girl's price? The bidding went all afternoon. Given how much he paid for you, I doubt he'll let anyone put you to death."

"They went through with the *auction?*" Allegra's pulse was hammering. "Even after what happened?"

"I've never seen anything like it!" Stubble beamed at his wife. "We're rich! We'll give some to the tribe, of course. Even with the wealth split so many ways, I'll never need toil again if I don't want. Gems, gold, silver, silks, urns, pearls, crystal, china and more hexacoins than I've ever seen in my life. The chests filled the room!"

Allegra sagged back. The universe surely had some cosmic imbalance, that the nomads should be so immensely rewarded for what they had done to her. The coverlet that had fallen around her waist scratched painfully on her legs, as if she were oversensitized to every texture. Her fevered mind was too hazed for her to think past the fact that she would soon go with one of those monsters.

"Don't you want to know who bought you?" Stubble asked.

"I don't care," she said dully.

"But you should know!" Rose said.

Allegra rubbed her eyes with the heels of her hands. She

thought about what he had said. *I doubt he'll let them put you to death.* "It's the General?"

"No, not Yargazon." Then Stubble said, "The prince regent."

Rose gave Allegra a yellow silk robe to pull over the skirt and halter, covering her body. Allegra wished it could become a spell of invisibility, hiding her from the brutal man who had paid a fortune to steal her life and freedom.

Her sellers were outside, Stubble, Vardok, Driver, Sot. She heard them talking as they waited for the prince's retinue. Stubble's brother had taken his nieces to their cousin's tent, to keep them out of anyone's notice. Allegra stood inside with Rose, a tear on her face.

"Don't cry," Rose said. "Maybe he won't be so bad."

"Do you really believe that?"

Rose shifted her weight. "Tales of royal houses are always exaggerated."

"Tales of what?" Allegra asked bitterly. "Torture?"

"He is a fugitive king," Rose said. "He escaped the conqueror who sought to kill him, and now he plots Cobalt's overthrow. His survival is a great inspiration to our people. It is natural stories would circulate of his power, his courage, his strength."

"That wasn't what I asked," Allegra said.

"I'm sorry," Rose said softly.

That was answer enough. Allegra couldn't bear to hear more. Her injuries ached, and the miradella fever sapped her spirit.

Rose laid her hand on Allegra's arm. "It will be all right."

Allegra's voice caught. "I thank you for your kindness."

A commotion rumbled outside, horses stomping and men's voices. The ground vibrated with the pounding of hooves.

"Farewell," Rose said. "Be well."

Allegra squeezed her hand. "You, too."

Someone swept aside the tent flap, and Allegra stepped back with a start. Stubble stood there with a man in a black uniform. Allegra wasn't certain of the hierarchies here. The man would be Yargazon's officer, since he was military, but that meant he served Markus. She wondered uneasily how Markus and his general settled this business of bidding for the same woman. Each had to keep the other happy, Yargazon because he commanded Markus's army, and Markus because he commanded Yargazon. She just hoped whatever agreement they reached didn't involve them hurting her.

As Stubble and the officer entered, Allegra backed away. Stubble caught her arm before she could retreat more than a step.

"It will be all right," he murmured as if to a thorough-bred horse that spooked easily.

"Bring her outside," the officer said. "His Highness wants to leave immediately."

"No," Allegra said. Matters were whirling out of control. She couldn't stop this and she couldn't escape, but she couldn't face the future they thrust onto her. Stubble pulled her forward. Then they were outside, and the evening sun slanted across the desert, gilding the tents, turning yellow into gold, red into ruby, green into emerald. Such a harsh people, yet they created such beauty.

A group of mounted officers waited, horses stepping restlessly, bridles clinking, saddles gleaming. She didn't see Yargazon, but Markus was on the far side, conferring with another mounted man, a colonel it looked like, if she read the silver ribbing on his shoulders correctly. The prince rode a massive horse, which of course was the color of onyx. Black. How depressingly apt.

The officer with Stubble said, "I can take her from here." He nodded with respect to the nomad. "His Highness is pleased."

"It is our honor to serve the prince regent," Stubble said. "May he always be favored by the Shadow Dragon."

Allegra gritted her teeth. Favored indeed. This dragon of theirs ought to reduce them to ashes.

The officer lifted his hand as if he were inviting Allegra to dinner. He never touched her, but with all the warriors here, she felt as coerced as if he had dragged her in chains. In her yellow silk robe, she was the only one not wearing a dark color, and it drew attention like a visual shout.

Markus glanced down as they reached him. "Is she ready?"

The officer bowed. "Yes, Your Highness."

"Does she have any things?"

"I don't know, Sire."

"You could ask me," Allegra said tartly. "I'm standing right here."

Markus regarded her impassively. "Do you?"

"Nothing. The nomads stole it all." She squinted up at him, dizzy from the fever. "I thought you were going to execute me."

Incredibly Markus smiled. "I hardly think so, after what I just paid." He glanced at the officer. "Lieutenant Borjan."

Whatever Markus wanted, the man understood. He put his hands around Allegra's waist and lifted her. At the same time, Markus reached down and grasped her just above Borjan's grip, his thumbs pressing into her breasts. He hoisted her in front of him on the horse, sideways, so her legs hung down one side. Unlike his men, he had a riding blanket instead of a saddle. Taking her leg, he eased it over the horse so she straddled the animal. Her robe hiked up, baring her legs, and the evening breeze whispered across her skin. She still had that unsettling feeling of being oversensitized, and it magnified her awareness of every touch and texture.

Allegra looked down—and inhaled sharply. She was up higher than on any horse she had ridden before. It gave her vertigo to see the ground so far below. Markus trailed his finger along her thigh, then put his arms around her waist and settled her against his chest. She hated the way she had to close her eyes and sag against him, wretched with fever. She felt as if she were burning alive. She needed to lie down.

Markus shouted, "Hai!" and snapped his quirt, the same whip the General had used on Allegra earlier today. With a snort, the horse pranced forward. The men still on foot swung up onto their mounts, and the company surged into motion. One of the men raised a pennant, red and black triangles with a gold dragon roaring flames. The cloth rippled in the light of the setting sun until the dragon seemed as if it were in flight.

As the company passed through the camp, the nomads stood outside their tents, men, women, even children. The adults went down on one knee as the prince rode by, the women with their bright silk hoods hiding their faces. Apparently children were exempt from the kneeling business, for they all waved and threw desert-orchids into Markus's path.

The horsemen soon reached the outskirts of the camp. More of the prince's men joined them there, swelling the company to several hundred. Markus leaned forward, one arm around Allegra's waist and the other gripping the reins. He prodded his horse, and it surged into a gallop. Within moments, the company was racing across the desert, deeper into the badlands of Jazid.

Evening folded over the riders as they rode through the stark foothills of the Jagged Teeth. It didn't surprise Allegra that no one lived here, given the inhospitable land. The desert buckled in ridges of black stone, congealed during ages long past from the breath of volcanoes, those dragons who roared below the earth and flooded the land with living, molten rock.

The men were all soldiers. Cavalrymen. They rode hard, leaving the nomad camp far behind. It surprised Allegra to see so many. In choosing to ride with Markus, they also became fugitives.

Eventually they slowed down, and Markus let his horse walk. He was in the center of his company, with men all around, though a pocket of space surrounded him. The alert attitude of the four riders nearest the prince and their constant presence made Allegra suspect they were his bodyguards.

"You're so hot," Markus said, shifting her in his arms. "Like a Kazlatarian furnace."

"It's a fever." Just saying those few words took too much energy.

"A fever, eh?" He tugged the sash on her robe. "Who is your fever for, sun girl?"

Sun girl? Probably he meant her hair. "It's the poison."

He opened her robe as if she were a present he was unwrapping. "What poison?"

She tried to close the robe, but he nudged her hand away, and she was too drained to resist. He kissed her ear, but she had too little energy even to move her head. At least the cool evening air breathed mercifully on her skin.

Her hazed mind only slowly comprehended what he had asked. Then she said, "The nomads poisoned me before the auction."

He stopped kissing her. "What?"

"They poisoned me."

"Why the blazes would they do that?"

"To make me fight less, I think."

Anger snapped in his voice. "And if you die, after I've paid more for you than any other woman they've probably ever sold?"

She just wanted to lie down somewhere. "They said they didn't give me enough…to kill."

"What did they give you?"

"A miradella extract."

"Oh." The anger went out of his voice. "That's different."

"It is?" She couldn't for the life of her see why.

He splayed his hand across her stomach, and his calluses grazed her skin. "How long ago did they give it to you?"

"This morning, before the auction."

"So your fever has peaked already?"

"I think so."

He laughed softly. "Good."

Good? What was wrong with him, that he found it amusing? "I don't feel 'good.' I feel half-dead."

He touched the scab on her abdomen. "Does this hurt?"

"No." It did, but she had no intention of telling him.

His touch became a caress as he slid his hand to her breast and traced a circle around her nipple, which was barely hidden by the skimpy halter. With his head bent over hers, he spoke against her ear. "Does that feel half-dead?"

"Don't." Her face burned as she pushed him away. Her nipples hurt, and they had swollen in the cold air. Everywhere he touched her, she felt raw. Her oversensitized skin tingled and ached, and she wanted nothing more than to lie down someplace cool and quiet, in the dark, *alone,* until the fever passed.

He stroked her hair off her left shoulder, baring her neck, and bit her gently, pressing his teeth down as he sucked at her skin. Then he lifted his head just slightly. "I'm no expert on miradella. But I think the fever will go soon. The other effects will wear off in a few days."

"Other effects?"

He laughed against her hair. "You are so sweetly naive."

Probably, but she was finally getting the idea. With her face burning, she said, "What, it's an aphrodisiac?"

"Some people say so." He ran the tip of his tongue around her ear. "Others claim it just makes a woman more receptive. I don't know. I wouldn't use it on anyone, given the danger. It's hard to find the plant, anyway, and harder to make the extract. But the T'Ambera are experts. It's their living, after all." He sounded amused. "A little extra for me thrown in, eh?"

Allegra wanted to punch him. His "little extra" came at the expense of her health, even at the risk of her life. She didn't care how callously "expert" the T'Ambera were at selling illegal pleasure toys to unscrupulous warlords; they could have killed her if they had misjudged her response.

"It doesn't work on me," she said.

He trailed his fingers over her thigh as he bit at her neck and ear. Sensations flared within her. The air's chill sharpened, and the perfume of a night-blooming flower overpowered her sense of smell. Everywhere Markus touched her, she burned. She wanted it to *stop*. But every time she pulled away from him, he shifted her back, and she didn't have the energy to keep fighting. She finally just turned her head, her cheek against his chest, and stared across the darkening rocks, unresponsive as he caressed her body.

After a while, another rider came up next to them on the other side from where she was looking. Markus pulled her robe closed and sat with his arms around her waist, the reins loose in his hand. Turning her head, Allegra saw General Yargazon riding alongside them. Even silvered by the moonlight, his features had a relentless, hardened quality.

"We should set up camp," Markus told him.

Yargazon surveyed the darkening land. "It's not far enough here from the T'Ambera."

If the General held rancor toward Markus over the auction, he showed no sign. It didn't actually surprise Allegra; she doubted it was normal for a prince to let his general bid against him, and Yargazon surely realized it. Given what Rose had told her, it suggested that either Markus wanted Yargazon to know the prince held him in esteem or else Yargazon had some power over him. She wondered, too, why Markus was willing to relinquish such a large amount of wealth when he was a fugitive without the full resources of his title.

"We're coming up on the Drift Basin," Markus was saying.

"Yes, that should work," Yargazon said. "It's easy to defend."

Markus scanned the riders ahead of them. "Have you seen any sign of Escar's men?"

"Nothing we could identify," Yargazon said.

Allegra knew the name Escar, but in her daze, it took her a moment to remember. Of course. Emperor Cobalt's surname wasn't really *The Dark;* it was Escar. It meant jaguar in the ancient language High Alatian. Cobalt Escar. Maybe he would devour this renegade Jazidian prince like a jaguar on the prowl.

"Let the men know we'll be stopping soon," Markus said.

"Very well." Yargazon saluted Markus by extending his fist so the heel faced the sky. His gaze scraped over Allegra as if she were the dregs of some mistake. Then he rode off.

Allegra considered what she had heard and then spoke slowly, thinking her way through the details. "You're fugitives, so you're always moving. Hiding this company can't be easy. But Cobalt can't monitor the whole country. It's too big, and he has the other lands he conquered. That's why you can do this."

Markus ran his hand down her leg. "Military matters aren't for females."

"Oh, stop." In her five days in Jazid, she had thoroughly wearied of their hammerheaded ideas about women.

Markus twirled one of his fingers in her hair. "Shall you put on armor and ride into battle, my lovely singer?"

"What makes you think I'm a singer?" Did he know about her spells? It seemed unlikely, and she preferred it that way. The more resources she had in reserve, the better.

"Aztire T'Ambera says you have a beautiful voice."

She was pretty certain he meant Stubble. "He exaggerated."

"You will sing for me tonight," he decided.

"I need a disk." She knew it sounded ridiculous, but what the hell. She might as well try.

"A what?"

"Disk. A round shape. I had one as a pendant, but the

nomads stole it when they took me from Aronsdale." Even knowing it would make no difference, she added, "Which is illegal, as you know, since you were one of the signers on the treaty that set up those laws." She wasn't certain of that, but it seemed a good guess.

"I know what 'disk' means," he said. "And if you didn't want to come to Jazid, you shouldn't have wandered over the border." His voice lightened. "Though were I the Jazid-Aronsdale border, I would surely shift myself to be closer to you."

Allegra blinked. It sounded like he was teasing her. But that would mean he had a sense of humor, which hardly fit his image as a brutal, murderous despot.

"I wasn't even near Jazid," she said.

"Aztire said you were wandering in the desert, lost and confused. He and his men rescued you."

"Oh, for saints' sake. That's ridiculous."

"Fortunately for you, I happened by." He didn't sound the least bit remorseful.

"You didn't happen by. They invited you."

Markus sighed. "You know, Allegra, I do truly believe you have no idea of your trespass."

She crossed her arms. "The only trespass was when Aztire and his men went into *my* country and grabbed me."

He pulled her arms apart. "I'm referring to now."

"What, talking is a trespass?"

"Even my highest-ranked men rarely contradict me." He opened her robe and stroked his hands from her hips up to her breasts. "And you are definitely *not* a man. Yet here you are, challenging me."

"I'm terrible. Appalling." She shoved away his hands and closed her robe. "Obviously you should send me back to Aronsdale and find a pleasure girl with better manners."

He laughed softly. "She would be far less interesting."

Good gods. He *was* teasing her. Allegra shook her head. "I don't understand you."

"Ah, well. We have something in common after all."

"Why are you acting nice? A few hours ago you were going to whip me and then have me executed."

"I never said I would execute you. Only that it was the sentence for your actions." He touched his tongue to her ear and ran it over the ridges. In a low voice, he added, "But I have no objection to the whipping. You humiliated me in front of the commanding general of my army."

Anger sparked within her. "You and your general had me dragged in there almost naked, made me kneel while the two of you ate, knocked me around, he lashed me with your damn quirt and you say *I* humiliated *you?* That's so turned around backward, it's like riding an ass with your back to its head."

He made an incredulous noise. "I truly cannot believe you said that to me."

"I can't believe half of what you say." Maybe if she annoyed him enough, he would send her home.

"I tire of this conversation," he growled. "You will be silent now."

Allegra let it go. She had used up her energy.

Night cloaked the land, and the riders were picking their way below a huge moon that glowed orange above the mountains. A rock spire loomed out of the darkness, its needled peak silhouetted against the stars. In Aronsdale, mist often dimmed the night's splendor, but in this parched air, the sky sparkled as if the legendary Shadow Dragon had painted diamond dust across its arch.

Eventually they entered a basin ringed with peaks like a giant, ancient fortress. The company was surprisingly quiet. The lack of tenders bemused Allegra. In Aronsdale, civilian men and women traveled with the army to look after the soldiers, but these riders seemed to tend to themselves. Although only a few lit torches, the men knew when Markus rode by. They stood to salute him, turning their fists to the sky.

Markus stopped at a large tent surrounded by soldiers. As he dismounted, he motioned to Lieutenant Borjan, who had stayed close during the ride. "Help her down."

Borjan swung off his horse and gave the reins to a youth waiting there. Then the lieutenant came over to Allegra. Self-conscious, she pulled her leg over the horse and slid into his hold. The rocky land hunched around them, all charcoal shadows, with darker patches where none of the silver moonlight reached. Markus had moved a distance away and was conferring with several men. Although he seemed to have forgotten her, she doubted she would be so lucky.

Soldiers moved everywhere, quiet and cautious. It didn't surprise her that only a few had uniforms. They were renegades, an army in exile within their own country. Allegra thought if she could find a shirt and trousers, she could pass as a youth in the dark. Maybe she could slip out after Markus went to sleep. She would have to secure supplies, a map and a horse, and sneak past whatever sentries he had posted, but if she managed, she could be well on her way home before dawn. She tried not to think about what would happen before Markus went to sleep.

Shivering in the cold air, she drew her robe tighter. The silk shimmered in the starlight, but pretty cloth did her no good. It was too thin.

"Here," Borjan said. "You can use this." He pulled off his jacket and settled it around her shoulders. It enveloped her, coming down to her hips.

"Thank you," she said. Unsure how to deal with Markus's people, she added, "I appreciate your kindness."

"Such courtesy," a dry voice said. "You should try that with me."

She spun around. Markus had come up to them, his presence a subtle invasion because he stood closer to her than a stranger normally would. She stepped away and collided with Borjan. The lieutenant nudged her back to Markus.

The prince looked over Allegra's head at Borjan. "Major Taliz caught a man stealing weapons from the armory."

"I could have provided him a replacement weapon, Sire, if he needed one," Borjan said. "He had only to ask."

"I know." Markus rubbed the back of his neck. "Apparently he wanted an extra dagger to send home to his son."

"Just one dagger?"

"Just one. But I can't have the men stealing weapons. If a theft goes unpunished, others will break discipline on a larger scale." He dropped his arm. "An example must be made."

"I understand, Sire," Borjan said. "I'll take care of it."

While they talked, Allegra stepped discreetly away, until Markus's presence felt less invasive. He seemed to occupy more area than the extent of his body, as if his personality filled space in some intangible manner.

Two men were coming toward the prince regent, bringing a third. When their prisoner stumbled and almost lost his balance, Allegra realized his hands were tied behind his back. His guards shoved him to the ground in front of Markus. He landed on his knees and stayed there, his eyes downcast.

Markus spoke coldly. "So you are the thief who put his own wishes above his oath to his country."

"Sire, please, I meant no ill." The man looked up at him. "I swear. It was for my boy. I haven't seen him in two years."

"So you risk the army?" Markus asked. "Our weapons aren't toys for children. And if you die here, who will send gold home to support your family?"

Allegra froze. What did he mean, "die here"? Surely he wouldn't execute a man just for stealing a knife. Saints, he had stolen her from Aronsdale, and he knew it even if he refused to admit it. Did he consider a knife more important than a woman? Then again, maybe she didn't want the answer to that question.

The man's shoulders hunched. "Your Highness, please. I'll pay back double out of my wages for what I tried to take."

Markus glanced at Borjan. "Give him thirty. And have him chained for three days."

Allegra went cold in a way that had nothing to do with the night air. Surely he didn't mean they would lash the man thirty times and drag him in chains for three days. Depending on what they used, thirty lashes could strip the flesh from his body, even kill him. For *one knife?* Her protest came out before her better sense stopped it. "You can't whip him! It's wrong."

Everyone went silent. When Markus turned to her, she wanted to shrink into a point and disappear. His voice was like ice. "Are you offering to take the lashes for him?"

She suddenly couldn't breathe. "What?"

He glanced at the lieutenant. "Give her the thirty lashes."

"No!" The man on his knees shot an alarmed look at Markus. "Sire, I will take the punishment."

"So which of you shall I have whipped?" Markus asked, looking from Allegra to the thief. "Perhaps both?"

Allegra had had enough. "Go ahead," she shot back at him. "Whip me for objecting to your tyrannical despotism. Show what a powerful force you are, terrorizing a girl half your age and strength. There's real bravery."

"Enough," Markus said. He ripped the jacket off her shoulders and tossed it to the lieutenant. As Borjan caught it, Markus said, "Thirty," and jerked his chin toward the thief.

When Markus turned to Allegra, she backed away. He caught her arm and forced her to the tent, then shoved her through the entrance, using her body to push aside the flaps. Barbaric splendor filled the interior, huge cushions strewn everywhere, thick rugs and ornate chests inlaid with jewels and precious stones. Dragon braziers burned in the corners, and even their dim orange glow seemed bright after the pale moonlight outside.

As the flap fell into place, Markus spoke in a resonant voice that carried. "You will never speak to me that way again."

Allegra wished she had kept her mouth shut. *No, damn it.* He deserved what she had said.

"You'll learn respect." He grabbed something off a chest by the wall and drew back his arm. She froze, staring at the large whip. He snapped it *hard,* and its crack split the air.

CHAPTER 5

THE COMPASS

Allegra gasped and jumped away. It took her a moment to comprehend that he had missed her.

"That was one of thirty," Markus said. "Here's two." He cracked the whip.

"No!" Allegra cried. Then she realized he had missed a *second* time. She stepped back from him, confused.

"Three," he said harshly as he snapped the whip.

And missed.

Bewildered, she stopped backing up. As glad as she was that he had missed three times in a row, it made no sense. He mouthed a word she couldn't read in the dim light. When he did it again, she realized he had said, *scream*. He cracked the whip so close to her that she had no trouble at all letting out a loud cry.

Markus tossed the whip onto a pile of rugs. He unbuckled his leather belt and pulled it off his trousers. When he snapped the belt against his hand, the smack of leather hitting skin sounded loudly in the air. "Five," he said.

What the blazes? She was trapped with a crazy man. He swung the belt, and the blow came so close, air whooshed past her. As she jumped away, the leather hit a chest supporting two small gold vases, and they clattered on the ground.

"Six," Markus said. Under his breath, he muttered, "Scream, damn it," and cracked the chest just a hand span away from her.

"Don't!" Allegra cried, genuinely alarmed.

So they went, Markus following as she backed around the tent. With great—and loud—force, he hit trunks, chests or his palm and methodically counted off the blows, up to twenty-eight. His hand had to be burning, given how hard he was hitting it. Just as she allowed herself to believe the incredible fact that he had chosen to hurt himself rather than her, he lunged forward and grabbed her. She gasped as he threw her onto a pile of carpets. She landed on her hip and caught herself on her hands, her hair flying around her shoulders.

Markus dropped next to her and flipped her onto her stomach. He held her down with his big hand splayed against her back while he yanked her robe up to her waist. When she struggled, he pressed harder against her, half sitting, half lying on the carpet. He pinned her torso with one arm and both of her legs with one of his legs. As he swept aside the jeweled chains of her skirt, his calluses scraped her behind. With a grunt, he lashed her across the buttocks. Allegra cried out, her eyes tearing up with pain.

"Twenty-nine," he said. In a low voice, he added, "That is for throwing wine in my face." He belted her again, making her scream. "That was for defying me in front of my men."

She stared at him over her shoulder, tears streaming down her face. "No more." Even without the miradella increasing her sensitivity, it would have hurt; now it was agony.

"Be grateful it was only two." He dropped the belt behind her on the carpets. Then he tugged the robe off her shoulders, baring most of her body.

"No!" Allegra turned over and scooted back on the carpet, wincing and holding the robe closed in front of her breasts.

"Take it off." He almost seemed to vibrate with tension.

She shook her head, her heart beating too fast. He caught her thigh and slid over to her. When she brought up her arms to protect herself, he tugged them down. Then he pulled the robe off the rest of the way and tossed it behind her.

"Don't hurt me," she said, terrified. "Please."

Markus stared at her, breathing hard. Instead of grabbing her, he grabbed several of the big, wine-red cushions scattered on the carpet and piled them up next to Allegra. He sprawled in the cushions, half reclining, and dragged her next to him. She resisted, pushing against his torso as he pinned her against his side. He just nudged her hand away and shifted her so she lay in the hollow where his arm met his shoulder. Then he wrapped his arms around her, sagged into the cushions—

And closed his eyes.

Allegra lay still, breathing hard. Gradually her pulse slowed. When he continued to lie there with his arms around her, a splinter of hope worked into her thoughts. Could a chance possibly exist that he would let her alone tonight?

After a moment, she said, "Is Lieutenant Borjan really going to give that man thirty lashes?"

"Of course." He opened his eyes and stared at the ceiling. "I wouldn't have ordered it otherwise."

"You didn't give thirty to me. You pretended. Except for the last two."

He rolled his head toward her. "I didn't pay that huge amount so I could tear up that spectacular body of yours. I want to enjoy it, not ruin it."

Spectacular? Was the man blind? She was a fat dairymaid. Then again, the nomads had starved her for five days.

"Why would you pay so much for me?" she asked. "And then whip a man for stealing a knife?"

"What I paid for you came out of my royal coffers," he said. "Specially marked coins, jewels identified with my family, that sort of thing. I had to get rid of all that—it was too easily identified with me. Every time I used some of it, I gave away my location. So I exchanged a substantial portion in one place for something of equal or greater value. You're an investment."

Her pulse stuttered. In the bizarre logic of Jazid, it made sense, but unlike gold or gems, her "value" wouldn't increase with age. "Does that mean you're going to sell me to someone else when you need more wealth?"

"It's possible." He nuzzled her hair. "Though I have to admit, I can't imagine now why I would do such a stupid thing. I want you right here. With me."

If she hadn't known better, she would have thought he sounded affectionate. Lack of food must have addled her mind. Although Markus had shared his trail rations and water, it had only taken the edge off her hunger.

"Did you and General Yargazon finish breaking your fast this morning?" she asked. They had ended her part of the auction so abruptly, maybe he hadn't eaten enough, either, and would consider having food brought for them here.

"Dusk was too angry," he said, leaning his head against hers. "He wanted you right then."

"Why?" Allegra regretted the question as soon as it came out. She didn't want to know, not for a man who had spoken so casually about torturing her. "Never mind. Don't answer."

Markus spoke drowsily. "I'm not Dusk Yargazon."

"Is that good?"

"Some men find the pain of an unwilling woman erotic. I'm not one of them." He reached across his body and stroked her breast. "Pleasure is much better." He fumbled with the gold cup over her nipple. "Must be a way to take these off," he mumbled.

Apparently he wanted *her* for dinner. She pushed at him, but he found whatever fastener he was searching for anyway and flicked the cup off her breast. The entire contraption fell away, leaving her bare except for the skirt. As she grabbed futilely for the halter, he pulled her against his body. The chafing of her nipples on his shirt sent a jolt through her body. She felt vulnerable and raw, and she wanted it to stop, all of it, Markus's attentions and these hypersensitized reactions. She tried to twist away, but he held her tightly, her front pressed against his side.

"Don't fight me, night bird," he murmured, fondling her breasts.

"No. Leave me alone. Please."

Markus grunted, but he actually stopped mauling her and sank back into the cushions. "It's been so long anyway," he grumbled. "I suppose I can wait until you're ready."

I won't ever be ready. But incredibly, it didn't seem as if he intended to force her.

"By the way," he said, closing his eyes.

"Yes?"

"Don't try sneaking off. I have bodyguards outside. I've told them you might try to leave."

"Oh." *Damn.*

"'Tyrannical despotism,'" he muttered. "Where did you learn such words?"

"From reading, I guess. Or reading to my students."

"Reading!" He turned onto his side, rolling Allegra onto her back, and pushed up on his elbow so he could look at her. "How can you read?"

She frowned at him. "I open the book and look at the words."

"Well, yes." He actually laughed. "So do I. But I'm a man. You're a woman. And women can't read."

"Oh, stop." She turned over, putting her back to him.

"Allegra." He rolled her back toward him. "I'm not trying to insult you. Jazid women are illiterate. It's illegal to teach them reading, writing or anything else."

"That's the stupidest thing I've heard yet."

Scowling, he said, "I would appreciate it if you refrained from denigrating my intelligence."

"I didn't mean you. I meant denying girls their education."

"It's always been that way." Shifting his weight, he pinned her legs with one of his while he trailed his fingers over her stomach. "A woman has one purpose in life. To please a man. If you let women read and write and do numbers, it distracts them from their purpose."

Allegra snorted. "I can't believe you actually said that horse manure with a straight face."

"Maybe if you spent less time reading," he said crossly, "and more time learning the ways of your sex, your personality would be more pleasant."

"I like my personality fine. It's yours I'm finding insufferable."

"Do you have any idea what could happen to you for speaking that way to the prince regent of Jazid?"

"So where is he?"

He spoke wryly. "Well, I can't say for certain, but I believe he is lying next to you, attempting quite unsuccessfully to obtain pleasure from his pleasure girl."

Allegra reddened. "I meant, if you're the regent, where is the king? The atajazid?"

"Someplace hidden." He slid his hand over her leg and under her skirt, between her thighs. "And no, I won't tell you where."

Sensation burst within Allegra, starting where he touched her and spreading through her body. Embarrassed by her reaction, she pushed away his hand. No one had ever touched her this way, not even Tanner when they tussled in the barn. "Please, don't," she said. "I can't do this. The only way you'll get what you want is through force. Is that what you intend?"

"I won't hurt you, Allegra." He slid down her body and shifted so he was on top of her, his hips between her knees. His voice gentled. "Try to relax. The miradella will help." Then he lowered his head and suckled her breast, his unshaven chin rough on her skin.

Allegra groaned as sensations shot through her body. Had he been someone she loved and trusted, it might have felt good. Now it frightened her. When she tried to wriggle away, he caught her wrists and pinned them on either side of her body.

Just get it over with, she thought. She stared at the cloth of the tent and tried to imagine herself somewhere else.

Markus lifted his head. "You're as stiff as a plank."

"Please d-don't—" Her voice caught with a sob.

"Ah, hell. Don't cry." He slid up along her body until he was looking into her face. "Love shouldn't upset you."

She rubbed her face with her palm, smearing the tears across her cheeks. "It's not love. It's coercion."

"You should try harder to please me," he grumbled.

"Why? Why don't *you* try to please me?"

"I swear, you are the strangest woman I have ever met." He rolled off her and lay on his side with his head propped up on his hand. His gaze traveled along her body. "Strange, but erotic. When you walked into the tent yesterday, I couldn't believe it. I've never seen a woman like you. Gold hair and violet eyes? I hadn't really believed such existed." He put his hand around her waist. "You're so small here. And this womanly shape. An hourglass. You could drive me mad."

Allegra was certain now about his lack of sanity. Sure, she had a small waist, in comparison, because what went above and below it were so much more ample.

"I'm fat," she said.

"What idiot told you that?"

"I can look in a mirror."

"You're just right." He brushed his lips over hers. "Most Aronsdale women are too skinny."

She was at a loss for a response. From him, the compliment didn't have the ugly edge it had when Vardok had said something similar.

Markus smiled. "What, no cutting insult to humble me?"

"Humble," she said, "is not a word I would use for you."

"What words would you use?"

"Arrogant." She paused, uncertain. "Are you cruel? I thought so, but now I don't know."

"I am what I am." He laid his palm over her breast and rubbed her in circles. "I don't know if it is cruel or not."

"Thirty lashes and three days dragged in chains?" She knocked his hand away. "That was cruel."

His voice hardened. "It's the principle. If the men start thinking of our armaments as supplies for their personal use, it will be a disaster."

"He hasn't seen his child in years! You could have ordered him to pay it back in double or do hard labor. Instead you'll have him damn near killed and then humiliated in front of your company. And you think he'll serve you with loyalty after that?"

"He will fear to do anything else."

"That's no way to command an army."

His voice cooled. "And you are an expert in military discipline?"

"It's common sense."

"You've a good deal of arrogance yourself, to so blithely dismiss my leadership."

"You really want people to follow you out of fear? Wouldn't you rather they followed you out of respect?"

"They won't respect me if I appear weak." He seemed more puzzled than angry. "I would have lost their respect if I let you humiliate me without an appropriate response."

She didn't doubt that was why he had spoken loudly while he was cracking the belt. "Then why did you mostly pretend with me?"

"I told you why."

She didn't believe him. "I don't understand how you can be brutal one moment and compassionate the next."

He studied her face as if she were a puzzle he needed to solve. "Those are your judgments. Not mine."

"If you go through with those thirty lashes, it will tear the flesh off his back."

"He's already been lashed by now." Markus scowled at her. "And stop trying to distract me."

"From what? Committing rape?"

"Saints, woman!"

"What, am I supposed to pretend I like it? I'll never do that, no matter how many ways you threaten or drug me."

Markus glowered at her. "I don't need women to 'pretend' with me. Any other would be honored by my attentions."

She felt as if she had a lion by the tail, and that if she relaxed for a moment, he would devour her. "I'm not other women."

"That's certainly true." He rolled onto his back, his torso half-raised in the cushions, his long legs stretched out on the carpet. "I'm tired, and I can't sleep. Sing to me."

"All right." Maybe she could make a spell. For what, though? Creating light would serve no purpose, and she had no particular wish to offer comfort. She didn't know any other spells. Surely, though, even someone as minimally talented as herself could manage something useful. He obviously had trouble sleeping, and her last spell had made Stubble sleepy. It had also aroused him, and she didn't need

Markus any more worked up, but if she could put him to sleep, he would leave her alone.

"I really do need a disk to hold," she added.

"That makes no sense," he grumbled.

"It helps me focus." Which was true.

He waved at a chest behind his head. "You may look there."

Allegra pushed up on her hands, and this time he let her go. She went to the chest quickly, so she could get what she needed before he changed his mind and decided he wanted her instead of her singing. She wondered if he was always like this, so mercurial and restless.

Ornate dragon patterns in emerald, gold and onyx inlaid the chest. Inside, she found a man's toiletries: rough soaps, washcloths, a wooden brush with stiff bristles, a shaving blade with a pitted hilt, a strap to sharpen it and picks for cleaning the teeth. It told her how "dangerous" he perceived her to be, that he let her rummage through personal items that included a knife. Even more mortifying was the accuracy in his estimation of her. She had little experience with blades; if she threatened him with the knife, he could easily take it from her.

A compass in a circular case lay in one corner. Picking it up, she closed her eyes and reached with her mage sense. More than a disk but less than a flat cylinder, it stirred her power. Yes, she could use this.

"Bring the brush, too," Markus said drowsily.

Allegra picked up the brush. When she stood, her head swam. The constant strain of the past few days had taken its toll. She couldn't even call it a nightmare, because she awoke from dreams and this had no end.

When her head cleared, she returned to the pillows. Markus was lying on his back, breathing deeply, and relief washed over her. But then he opened his eyes. "What do you have?"

She showed him the compass. "Is that all right?"

"If you want." His lashes lowered over his eyes again. "Put my head in your lap while you sing and brush my hair."

Brush his hair? She would never have expected that from Jazid's notorious outlaw prince.

The pillows were worn and large, with embroidered dragons similar to the Jazid flag. Self-conscious, she slid under him until she was sitting cross-legged with his head in her lap. With a sigh, he turned his head and pressed his lips against her inner thigh. His constant intimacy flustered her, and she was so tired, she feared she would fall over backward with nothing to lean against.

Allegra set the compass on the cushion by her hip so its cool metal pressed her skin. She lifted a length of his hair and ran the brush through it. Or tried. The heavy locks were so knotted, she could only untangle a few strands.

"Your hair is a saints' forsaken mess," she said.

"Hair is hair," he mumbled.

"Don't you ever brush it?"

Markus yawned, showing a row of healthy white teeth. "Not really."

"It's all ragged." In the back, it curled down his neck to his shoulders, but on the sides it only went over his ears. She hadn't even realized he had bangs until she worked out their knots. The tangles had kept them off his face, but after she brushed them, they fell into his eyes.

"Whoever cut it did an appallingly bad job," she said.

"I cut it," he said sourly.

Even when she didn't intend to insult him, she did. "Well," she amended, "it's clean." After a moment, she said, "I'm surprised the prince regent of Jazid has to cut his own hair."

"I'm hiding from an invading force that conquered my country," he growled. "We don't have the personnel to spare for amenities."

"Oh." She could see his point.

Allegra contemplated the man lying with his head in her lap. Brushing his hair comforted her for some odd reason. It took her a while to figure out why. Most people in the settled lands had straight hair; curls were only common in eastern Aronsdale. Markus's mop of curls reminded her of the boys back home.

She gazed at his body stretched out before her. He had a magnificent form. Under different circumstances, she might have desired him. In fact, if she had met him in Aronsdale, she would have considered him far out of her league and been intimidated by his sexuality and fierce beauty. He seemed larger, darker and so much more intense than any man back home.

Yet he lay quietly while she brushed his hair, the tension easing in his shoulders. The unlikely combination of his banked ferocity and his wish for her to play with his hair was appealing, even erotic. When she turned his head so she could reach the other side, he put his arms up around her hips and stroked her bottom, then let his arms relax back onto the cushions.

After Allegra worked the knots out of his hair, it took less concentration for her to brush it. At that point, she focused on the compass, which still pressed firmly into her leg.

And she sang.

The compass wasn't exactly a cylinder, but the shape was regular enough to bring her spell alive. The lullaby poured out of her, smooth and hypnotic:

Sleep my child, sleep my love
Through the night, my sweetest dove

None of that applied to Markus, except perhaps night as a metaphor, but it would do. She wound the song around him in a golden spell, the color that soothed physical or emotional pain.

Markus fought.

He never moved, never opened his eyes, and she didn't think he even realized he was fighting. But his body wouldn't let him sleep. She tried adding a touch of emerald to the colors, and to her surprise it worked. A mood spell formed, letting her sense emotions. He had no idea he was resisting a spell. She felt his fatigue, his tired muscles, his hardened thoughts of Emperor Cobalt, the man who had stolen his country, his people and his birthright. And she felt his need to sleep. He *wanted* to sleep. But tension coiled within him, and worries plagued his thoughts.

A haze of eroticism overlaid it all. He wanted her with a lust of bewildering intensity. He barely controlled his urge to take her as hard and as rough as he needed to satisfy that hunger. Yet despite how much his culture approved his using his pleasure girl however he pleased, he held back, for it mattered to him how she felt.

Her spell even absorbed bits of his memories as they affected his mood. They painted a grim picture of a land whose angry, violent men felt they had nothing to lose. Cobalt had taken everything, including their pride. In this country with far fewer women than men, the soldiers from the Misted Cliffs too easily seduced Jazidian women with promises of a better life. The fury of the men here simmered, ready to erupt.

She sang softly, verse after verse, fighting Markus's anger and insomnia, until finally he surrendered to a deep slumber.

Allegra opened her eyes. Gradually she realized the spell had put her to sleep, too. She was slumped over Markus, and her legs had gone stiff with the weight of his head.

The cold prodded her into action. The braziers had burned so low, they shed almost no light or heat, and she wore nothing except a few chains around her hips. When she slid out from under Markus, her muscles protested, and she winced. Even if he hadn't posted guards, she doubted she could have gone anywhere. She teetered on the verge of collapse.

Rising stiffly, she rubbed the ache in the small of her back. She retrieved her robe, but the silk offered little warmth against the night. Barely able to stay on her feet, she pulled at carpets until she found one supple enough to use as a blanket. Then she retreated across the tent, as far from Markus as she could go, and lay down, wrapping herself in the carpet, with the compass cradled against her stomach. The weave of the rug chafed her sensitized skin, but its warmth was lovely.

The moment she closed her eyes, the oblivion of sleep dropped over her and she knew no more.

❧ CHAPTER 6
THE BARN

Tanner and Allegra wrestled, rolling in the hay that filled the loft. Sunlight sifted between planks of the barn, and dust motes danced in the shafts. He pinned her on her back, holding her down with his weight, while she struggled under him, pressing her body against his. The first time they had wrestled, he had kissed her with tenderness, but this time he took her lips as if he would take command of the world. He grabbed her hands and held them by her shoulders, holding her in place with the weight of his body and the demands of his kiss. She had never known this side of Tanner, fierce and hungry.

Arousal spiraled through her. Her shy explorations, alone in her bed at night, had never roused this intense response. Her skin felt fevered, hyperresponsive to his touch. She had known Tanner all her life and felt safer with him than with anyone else, but today he had changed. His dark edge excited her.

He released one of her hands and fondled her breast. She didn't remember undressing, but she lay beneath him with nothing on except a chain around her hips. No man had ever touched her this way before. She felt exposed and helpless, unable to stop him—and incredibly aroused. He slid down her body, his clothes rough on her skin, and settled his hips between her knees in a way that felt familiar, though she had never lain with him like this. He took her nipple into his mouth and suckled, pulling hard, his teeth against her skin. She sighed as sensations tingled through her, and she ran her free hand through his hair. The curls felt thick and soft, longer than she remembered, more ragged.

He came back up and kissed her while he stroked her sides, his palms sliding from her breasts to her hips. He was moving his pelvis against hers in a steady rhythm, and she felt his erection through his trousers. His chest was strong, more muscled than she remembered. She fumbled at his shirt, trying to pull it off so she could feel his body against hers. But instead of buttons, her fingers caught on complicated fastenings, loops and ties. Then he grasped her wrists in one hand and pulled her arms over her head. Holding her wrists down in the hay, he captured her.

Let me go, she said, straining to embrace him.

He slid his hand between their pelvises, and she murmured a protest, wanting to feel his hardness against her. She couldn't free her hands to pull him closer, couldn't do anything but strain against him. Never would she have expected Tanner to affect her this way. He smelled different, an intoxicating musky scent. His palms were rough with calluses, but more like those of a swordsman than a farm boy. He stroked her between her thighs where she had never felt a man's touch, and she groaned as shudders of pleasure shot through her.

Tanner unfastened his trousers, pulling at the ties, his knuckles rubbing her sensually. Then his fist pressed between her thighs. No, not his *fist*. He was trying to enter her, and she tensed, suddenly afraid.

It's all right, he said. *I'll go slow. Relax, sweet night bird. You're ready for me.*

Warmth swirled within her. Her body strained toward him, and he finally freed her wrists. She embraced him, pressing against his muscled torso while he slowly pushed into her.

Ah, gods, he said. *I can't hold*— With a groan, he thrust hard and buried himself inside her. She cried out, barely able to take him, and he stopped, lying on top of her, his heart beating hard, so hard. But she didn't want him to stop. Her dreamlike urgency overwhelmed the pain, and she rocked against him. He began to thrust then, with a strong, steady rhythm, stretching her, filling her. It was so different from how she had imagined, delicious and frightening at the same time. Sensations flooded her like the crest of a wave, and she never wanted it to stop. She was so close, so close to the top.

"Beautiful Allegra," he murmured.

His unshaven chin scratched her cheek with a day's growth— and it was far too heavy for Tanner. She struggled awake. She *wasn't* dreaming, she did actually hold that incredibly beautiful body in her arms, and he was moving steadily, his rhythm quickening, his breath urgent. It *wasn't* safe, secure Tanner. He had never had this sultry, powerful hunger.

"Markus?" she whispered.

He lifted his head in the darkness and gazed at her, his eyes glazed. The entire time, he kept moving, stronger, faster. Bending his head, he kissed her with a passion almost out of control. Then he groaned, giving a huge thrust, and held himself deep inside her, his body rigid, his muscles like steel cables. His hips jerked and he arched back his head, the tendons in his neck standing out.

With a gasp, Markus collapsed on top of her, breathing heavily. She lay under him, stunned. She had let him take her, *urged* him, but he wasn't the boy she had loved all her life. On some level she must have known, but when she comprehended what had happened, tears welled in her eyes.

Markus sighed, then rolled off her, onto his back. Pulling her into his arms, he laid her head on his shoulder. "So lovely," he murmured.

Allegra lay still, too stunned to respond.

After a while, he brushed her inner thigh tenderly. "You're bleeding."

"I never— Not before this…"

"I know." He kissed the top of her head. "Even if they hadn't told me, I would have known. You're so innocent."

She couldn't answer. He thought she had welcomed him into her arms.

"Allegra?" he asked. "Are you all right?"

"Yes," she lied. She felt as if she were an instrument played just long enough to warm up, then left without a performance of the concerto. But she couldn't go any further.

Markus turned on his side and gently slid his palm between her thighs. "Did I leave you hungry, night bird? I can help." He rubbed circles with his palm, and pleasure surged through her, but now it felt overwhelming, too much. She pushed him away.

"Are you sore?" he asked.

"I— No. A little." She didn't know what to say.

"Later, then," he murmured, smiling. He sat up, rubbing his eyes. "I wish we could lie here all day. But it will be dawn in about an hour, and I want to be on the move before the sun rises."

Too much had happened. Allegra had reached saturation. She just stared at the ceiling, her hand resting over the triangle between her thighs as if to protect herself from her own desire.

Markus looked back at her. "You're quiet this morning."

"You surprised me," she said. "I was dreaming."

His lips curved upward. "Of me?"

She thought of lying, but she couldn't dishonor Tanner that way. Miserably she said, "Of my boyfriend in Aronsdale."

A long silence followed her words. Then he spoke in a curt voice. "*Gods.* I have never met a woman so capable of humiliating a man with so few words."

"I'm sorry." Her voice caught. "I thought I was going to marry him. Then you took away my life."

He spoke tightly. "So you sought refuge from me in dreams about him?"

"No. I mean, I've *never* had a dream like that."

Markus leaned closer, his eyes intense. "That's because you don't want this boy the way you want me."

"No. That's not true."

"Then why haven't you dreamed of him before? Why do you crave him only when I touch you?" Anger edged his voice, but she needed no mood spell to know it masked hurt.

Allegra had no glib answers, so she spoke the truth. "He has been like a brother to me. A friend. I've never thought of him as a lover. I thought perhaps if we married, that would change."

"Those were moans of passion, Allegra. You were loving me, not some callow Aronsdale boy."

"It wasn't love," she said, bewildered.

"You can't deny what you felt."

"You think making love is the same as loving someone?"

"Of course it is." He leaned over her, his voice sharp with his hurt. "You can't deny it. It was me you wanted."

She wondered if he even saw her as capable of more than a sexual response. "You've taken away my life, my family, everyone I love. You think you're entitled. You tell me I must be whatever you want. And it's true, you've caught me. I can't resist drugs and bonds and starvation forever." With pain, she said, "But even if you have my passion, you can't force me to love you."

Silence followed her outburst, and she regretted revealing so much of herself. The words had torn out of her before she'd had time to think.

Then Markus spoke heavily. "Come. We must go." He

took a cloth off the carpet, one he must have brought over, since it hadn't been there when she had lain down earlier. He cleaned himself off, then climbed to his feet and fastened his pants. "I want to change. And we must prepare to ride."

She stared at him. He was fully clothed, even in his boots, exactly as he had fallen asleep last night. She wore nothing but a slender chain around her hips. In her dream, he had held her down when she tried to remove his shirt. She sat up, hurting in a way that had nothing to do with physical pain. Tears blurred her eyes as she felt around the carpet for her robe.

He knelt and pressed the robe into her hands. "Don't cry."

"Why do you care?" She wiped at the tears. "You got what you wanted."

"I thought you wanted it, too." He brushed her hair back from her face. "What did you mean by starvation?"

"I've hardly eaten in days."

"We ate on the ride yesterday."

"Trail rations. I had nothing but water in the morning. The T'Ambera hardly fed me more than once a day, usually only soup."

"Dragon's breath," he muttered. "I didn't know. Whenever you're hungry, just tell me. I'll get you food."

Allegra wasn't certain she believed him, but she so much needed it to be true, for him to be the decent man he sometimes seemed. She said only, "Yes, please. I'd like to break my fast."

He studied her face. "Will you be able to ride with me today? We don't have a litter to carry you."

"Why would I need a litter?"

He touched her inner thigh. "I wondered if you were sore."

"Oh." Her face heated. "I'll be all right." She actually had no idea, but given how ready her dream and the miradella had made her for him, she thought she would be all right.

"I'll see what I can do," he said.

He turned away, and she hoped he would leave. She needed time away from the force of his presence. She also wanted to wash up and put on real clothes if she could find any that would fit. Maybe she could use one of his shirts.

He didn't go outside, though. Instead he rummaged in a trunk across the tent. He came back with a blanket, some filmy scarves and a bundle of fur. Crouching down, he showed her the blanket. It had fleece on its inner side.

She brushed her palm across the fleece. "It's so soft."

"I can put it over the saddle blanket."

His unexpected consideration touched her. "Thank you."

He showed her the scarves. "You can wear these."

Wear what? Perplexed, she took the clothes. The fur turned out to be a pair of knee boots, soft rather than heavy, with crisscrossing thongs to keep them up. They were designed to be sexy rather than useful, and she doubted they would hold up well if she walked in them. At least the fur was light enough that the boots shouldn't be too hot during the heat of the day. The scarves were a skimpy skirt and halter sewn from red silk and inlaid with jewels, garments she had no more desire to put on than she had wanted to wear the jeweled chain-skirt.

She regarded him dubiously. "Do you always carry clothing like this?"

He laughed softly. "No. I bought it from the T'Ambera along with you."

"Trousers and a shirt would be more practical. They'll protect my skin from the sun."

He stared as if she had suggested she grow a third arm. "Good gods. Do you want to look like a man?"

"I don't mind. I'd rather be comfortable."

"It pleases me for you to wear what I give you."

She scowled at him. "It doesn't please me."

She thought he would get angry, but instead he smiled. "You can wear the robe to protect your skin."

"Fine," she muttered. "Make me look like an idiot."

"Allegra, you'll look beautiful." He indicated an ewer across the room. "You can wash up there. I'll go to the hot springs. If you're ready when I return, we'll have time for breakfast."

She just nodded, too hungry to argue.

After Markus left, though, Allegra just sat. The bruise on her face throbbed, the gouge on her stomach stung and her buttocks ached from Markus's belt. She hated to think what condition she would be in if he had struck her thirty times instead of two. How could he hurt her and then expect her to want him in bed? And it had been obvious his officers expected him to treat her much more harshly. If all men here felt that way, it was no wonder they had a shortage of women.

She thought of the soldier who had stolen the knife.

Markus had said *lashes,* which implied a whip rather than a belt. Even if the man lived through his sentence, she doubted he would survive being chained and forced to run behind someone's horse for three days. Yet none of Markus's men seemed surprised by the punishment. Such a cruel place. Its people were like the land, hardened by the stark desert they refused to let defeat them.

Finally she went over to the ewer. It held beautiful, clear water. After she drank her fill, she used washcloths and soap from Markus's chest to clean up. Then she dressed. The translucent red garments slid silkily over her skin. The skirt fit low on her hips and came to midthigh. The halter just barely covered her nipples and pushed her breasts together in a most embarrassing manner. Rubies, diamonds and topazes sparkled on the skirt belt and in the chains that formed the halter. She felt like an ornament.

The entrance flap crinkled as Markus entered. He froze when he saw her. Then he strode over and, with no preamble, took her into his arms and kissed her deeply, with his tongue, while he ran his hands up her sides. Water dripped off his hair onto her cheek.

Flustered, she pushed against his upper arms. He wore a sleeveless leather thing that resembled a jerkin, and it left his arms bare. His huge biceps felt like rocks under her hands. A wide armband circled his left arm as if he were some barbarian warlord. Which, she supposed, was apt.

She drew back her head. "I thought we had to leave."

"Hmm." He put his hand behind her head to hold her in

place and went back to kissing her. He slid his other hand up and caressed her breast through the silk.

"Let me go." She tried to twist away. When he held her in place and kept stroking her, she hit his shoulders with her fists. "Don't be such a bastard, Markus."

He released her as if she had a plague, and for a moment she felt only relief. Until she saw his fury. Then she realized what she had said. *Bastard.* He was, literally; it was why he was the prince regent rather than the atajazid.

She looked up into his smoldering, furious gaze. "I'm sorry. I didn't mean that the way it sounded."

"My birth may have not been royal," he said tightly, "but my father gave me full rights to his name."

"I know. The word is used differently where I came from. It means a boor." Her voice cooled. "A man who forces his attentions on a woman."

He grasped her chin. "Adapt, Allegra. You have no choice."

"Why?" she asked, bewildered. "Surely many Jazidian women would jump at the chance to be with you. Why do you want one who fights you?"

"I wish I knew," he muttered. He took her arm and pulled her across the tent.

They came out into a crystalline morning. The sun had yet to rise, though the sky above the mountains on the horizon was lightening. A large man with a sword on his back waited nearby, and Markus drew him aside. Allegra couldn't hear their discussion well, but she gathered something had happened last night, and this man, apparently one of Markus's bodyguards, feared the prince's reaction. Markus, however, seemed more intrigued than upset.

"I'll check it," Markus said. "You did well to let me know."

"It is my honor to serve, Your Highness." The guard sounded nervous.

Markus stood for a moment, lost in thought. Then he came back to Allegra. "The sergeant just told me something odd."

"I didn't hear much," Allegra said. "Your guards left their posts last night?"

He traced his finger along her lower lip. "Such a lovely mouth to sing such sweet songs."

Where had that come from? Her spell couldn't have put his guards to sleep. They had been outside the tent, farther away than any spell she had ever done could reach. But what if it *had* affected them, and Markus suspected? Sweat gathered on her palms, and she wiped them on her thighs. Her spells were her secret defense. If he realized what she could do, he might learn to counter them.

"No comment?" he asked.

"I don't know what you expect me to say."

A smile softened his face. "I slept better last night than I have in years. I didn't wake until this morning."

"Is that a problem?"

"Not for me. But two of my bodyguards also went to sleep—on duty." He leaned closer and spoke by her ear. "Do you know what else, Allegra? Those two guards may have been close enough to hear you sing."

Well, hell. To distract him from his dangerous train of thought, she glared. "Are you saying my song is so boring, it puts people to sleep?"

"Oh, it wasn't boring at all." He set his hands on her shoulders. "By the dragon, woman, what a weapon! How many people can you knock out? Three? Six? A hundred? Could you do it to men during battle?"

A weapon? "That's absurd." She didn't have to fake her astonishment. "I can't do that."

"How many can you put to sleep at once?"

"None!"

"Tell me the truth," he murmured, "or I'll have to keep you in chains all the time so you can't escape if you make me sleep."

She scowled at him. "If I could knock out people, I would have done it to the nomads and gone home."

"You wanted the compass last night." He scratched his chin. "Something about it being a disk. What does that do?"

"Nothing. I just sing better if I have something to hold."

"You said it helps you focus." His smile flashed, all those healthy white teeth. "The spell? Hah! That's it, isn't it? The disk focuses your spell."

Allegra wished he weren't so blasted intelligent. "Don't be silly. Spells are nothing more than children's fables."

His smile faded. "No one who fought at the Battle of the Rocklands would agree with you."

"The what?"

"The battle where the armies of the Misted Cliffs, Jazid and Taka Mal fought two years ago."

Although she didn't recognize the name, she knew about the battle that decided the fate of Jazid. "My people call it the Dragon-Sun War."

"I was nearly killed."

"In the fighting?"

"No." He grimaced. "From lightning."

"I heard something about a thunderstorm."

"No! That's just it. Cobalt's wife stood above the battle like some avenging goddess. She brought down lightning. Sheets of it! Out of a blue sky. I was struck by a bolt."

"You were hit by *lightning?* And you survived?"

His smile quirked. "I've a hard head."

She could believe that. But the rest made no sense. "You're saying Cobalt's wife started the storm?"

He regarded her uneasily. "People claim she's the reincarnation of the Dawn Star Goddess."

Even in her isolated rural life, Allegra had heard that name given to Cobalt's wife, the daughter of the king and queen of Harsdown. The Dawnfield name derived from ancient myths of a warrior goddess who had become the stars. Mel had done something far less ethereal than rise into the heavens, though. She had married Cobalt Escar to stop him from invading Harsdown.

"You're talking about Mel Dawnfield," she said.

"Yes. The empress." Markus paused. "Her father is the cousin of your king in Aronsdale, isn't he?"

"That's right."

He considered Allegra, his face thoughtful. "Her parents

came from southwest Aronsdale. Like you. They have yellow hair and so does she. Like you."

Allegra didn't doubt Mel Dawnfield could do spells. Most Dawnfield women had the ability. But lightning? "No mage could do what you describe. It must have been a freak storm."

He raised his eyebrows. "Mage?"

Damn! She would give herself away without realizing it. "A person who casts spells. I don't know much about them."

"Yes, you do." He tapped his finger on her cheek. "You're one of these mages, hmm?"

She glowered at him. "If *I* hit you with lightning, you wouldn't survive."

His grin flashed. Taking her arm, he drew her toward where a groom was readying several horses. "We can discuss your mage abilities while we ride."

"Wait!" She had to run to keep up with his long strides. "You left my robe in the tent."

Markus called to another guard as he strode past. "Bring me the silk robe from my tent." To Allegra, he added, "I'll let you put it on when the sun rises. I wouldn't want to burn that creamy skin of yours."

"Markus, slow down!"

He blinked, then slowed down. "I forget that you're small."

"No, you're large." As they neared the soldiers around the horses, she flushed under their stares. "I really, really don't want to ride in this outfit." Maybe he would get jealous and cover her up. "Your men will see. A lot of me."

"They will all envy me." He didn't sound the least fazed. "For having the prettiest girl in Jazid on my horse."

"They'll know you didn't really whip me. You can see through the damn skirt!"

"Only if you look close." He scowled. "And I would execute any man who looked that closely at you."

"Why not get a thicker skirt?"

"Because I like the way you look in that one. And if I like it, woman, you *will* wear it."

"You're a pig," she muttered.

His laugh rumbled. "Ah, but a pig who has *finally* had enough sleep. So I am a happy pig."

"Oh, stop."

"Stop what?"

"Having a sense of humor." It made it harder to hate him.

They soon reached the horse he intended to ride today, a huge animal with a gray coat. A soldier made a cup with his hands to help Allegra mount. When she was astride the animal, she realized they had indeed put the fleece over the riding blanket, a much appreciated softness against her skin. Markus swung up behind her and slid his arms around her waist. When he snapped the reins, the horse headed out and they joined a group of other riders already on the move.

Then Allegra saw him: the dagger thief. He stood behind a horse with his hands shackled in front of his body and his head down. A chain from his manacles stretched to the saddle of the horse in front of him. Allegra flinched when she saw the flayed skin and red welts on his shoulders where his shirt hung open. As she watched, Lieutenant Borjan mounted the horse.

Allegra turned back to Markus and motioned toward the shackled man. "He won't survive your punishment."

Markus let out a breath, but she couldn't tell if he was angry or not. After a moment, he veered off and rode over to Borjan. The lieutenant saluted him with his fist turned upward. To Allegra, the salute looked as if the men were offering their prowess as warriors to the sky, the realm of their Shadow Dragon.

Markus tilted his head toward the thief. "Can he ride?" he asked the lieutenant.

"I don't know, Sire," Borjan said. "Possibly."

Possibly? Allegra felt ill. If doubt existed as to whether the man could even ride, he certainly couldn't run behind Borjan's horse for three days.

"Give him a horse, then," Markus said. "Take off the shackles and let him ride."

A flash of relief lit Borjan's eyes. "Right away, Sire."

As the lieutenant vaulted to the ground and strode to the shackled man, Markus went on, riding his horse forward.

Allegra let out the breath she hadn't realized she was holding. Again Markus surprised her. She hadn't expected him even to listen to her, let alone act on her words.

"Thank you," she said quietly.

"For what?"

"Sparing his life."

"Why are you thanking me? Do you know this man?"

"No. But he didn't deserve to die for stealing a knife."

"He might not have died. Jazid men are strong."

"Even so."

Markus just grunted. Then he said, "Do you want to eat?"

"Very much."

He took food out of his riding pack, oranges and peaches. When they finished the fruit, he gave her creamy cheese, a delicacy given how easily it could go bad under these travel conditions. They washed it down with clear, fresh water. His consideration confused her, for she didn't want to like him, and he was making it far harder to hold back that response than she would ever have thought possible.

They continued to ride as they ate. The company was soon moving through foothills, penetrating deeper into the desolate badlands.

# CHAPTER 7
STONEBLUE SKY

As the sun rose, the prince regent's company cut across the northern foothills of the Jagged Teeth and came out into open land, headed toward the distant peaks of another sharpened range. They had seen no other people since leaving the T'Ambera, and nothing lay ahead but splintered mountains.

Markus's bodyguard soon rode up alongside them. When the prince slowed down, the man gave him a bundle of blue silk.

Markus squinted at the silk. "What is this?"

"You asked for a robe, Sire," the guard said. "I found this in one of the chests."

"I meant the yellow one."

"My apology." The man hesitated. "The yellow was crumpled. I thought you might like a fresh one for her."

"Ah." Markus grinned at him. "Yes, that's good."

The guard spoke in a carefully neutral voice. "I also rolled up the rug and stored it."

Allegra wondered which rug he meant, given that the

tent had so many of them. Then her face burned as she realized what they were talking about—the rug with the proof of her virginity.

"Thank you, Izad," Markus said. "You've done well."

"It is my honor, Sire."

Markus thrust the robe into her hands, then kicked the horse and took off again, racing across the desert. She had a feeling he went fast because he liked it rather than because it served any need. His horse stretched out his powerful legs, and if her added weight tired him, he gave no sign. Markus held her around the waist, and the wind whipped back her hair in the exhilarating ride.

Eventually he slowed to let the horse rest. When they resumed a saner pace, she pulled on the robe and was surprised to inhale its scented fragrance. "Did you buy this from the T'Ambera, too?"

"I think so," he said. "I didn't look much at the clothes. I concentrated mostly on the weapons."

She blinked. "The T'Ambera sell weapons?"

"To me, yes."

"Charming people," she said. "Slave traders and arms dealers."

"They brought me you." He nuzzled her hair. "That alone was worth the trip."

"Markus, where are we going?"

No answer.

She indicated the distant range. "To those mountains?"

"Perhaps."

"Why won't you tell me?"

"I don't consult a pleasure girl about my military plans."

"Well, you should."

He gave a startled laugh. "Whatever for?"

She didn't really have an answer, so she gave one she knew would outrage him. "I can tell you if they are good plans."

"Is that so?"

"Indeed."

"I will say this, Allegra. You are never boring."

"I would like to be boring. So much that you tire of me and let me go home."

His words burst out. "I would never throw away a woman because she wasn't new and perfect, especially not after I got her pregnant three times."

Where had *that* come from? She spoke carefully. "You must have a lot of children."

"Actually, no. Just one." After a moment, he added, "His mother doesn't acknowledge I am the father. But everyone knows he is mine. He looks just like me when I was fourteen. And he has three joints in his big toe. Who else has that? Only me, my father and my grandfather."

"How can your concubine refuse to say you are the father?"

"She wasn't a concubine." He shifted behind her, gripping the reins so hard, his knuckles whitened. "I don't have any women. I haven't for years. Except you, now."

Only her? "Then how—" She stopped, uncertain she wanted to hear the rest.

"She lived in a town I visited with my father and Dusk

Yargazon." He spoke in clipped sentences, unlike his usual drawl. "Dusk saw her. He liked her. So he took her. He shared her with me. That's it."

Allegra had a feeling that wasn't "it" at all. "Does she say Yargazon is the father?"

"No. She says the boy's father is her husband."

"Her husband!"

His voice had gone flat. "I didn't know she was married."

"You didn't *ask?*"

"No. I thought Dusk did. I didn't know him as well then."

"Gods, Markus, what did you do to her?"

"I made love to her." He sounded defensive. "It isn't a crime."

Like hell. "What about Yargazon?"

His voice turned leaden. "I didn't know."

"Know what?"

"His tastes are…harsher than mine."

"He hurt her, didn't he?" Her voice cracked. "The two of you grabbed some girl, raped her, hurt her in saints only know how many ways and left her like a broken doll."

"Stop it!" His fist jerked on the reins, and the horse neighed in protest.

"You feel guilty," she said. "All these years, you've hated what you did." Despite what his people allowed, what his title and status gave him, despite everything, he had a conscience.

"We broke no laws." He sounded almost as upset as she felt.

"Of course not. Your family *makes* the laws." Allegra took

a breath to steady herself. "That means you also have the power to fix wrongs. The moral responsibility is yours, too."

"By the Dragon, you talk a lot!"

"No, I don't. I just say things you don't want to hear."

"I didn't *know*." He spoke with unexpected pain. "Usually Dusk shared his girls with my father. I knew they did, but I never thought about it. I hadn't realized my father— I mean, he never treated my mother that way."

That you knew. "Your mother was his pleasure girl?"

"Concubine. He was good to her."

She didn't believe it. "Always?"

It was a moment before he answered. "Until he tired of her. I was about five. She was pregnant with my second sister."

Allegra hesitated, unsure if she should ask more. This man had a lot more to him than it had appeared when she met him. She spoke with care. "Do you have a lot of siblings?"

"Not as many as…before the war." He paused for a moment. Then he said, "I don't know what my father was like with the mothers of my other siblings. But maybe it was fortunate he tired of my mother. He hardened as he grew up."

"Grew up?" It seemed a strange way for a son to characterize his father.

His arms moved as he shrugged behind her. "He was only twelve when I was born."

Her mouth fell open. *"What?"*

"He wanted a concubine." Markus sounded uncomfortable. "So grandfather gave him one. She was sixteen."

Allegra could think of many responses to that. Choosing tact, she said, "You had an unusual childhood."

"But a good one." After a pause, he added, "I think."

"You think?" It didn't sound good to her.

"I lived in a palace with a mother who doted on me, a father who gave me all the riches I could want and servants to cater to my every need. I wasn't the heir to the throne, so I didn't have to learn all those lessons my grandfather drummed into my father, and my father later expected from my half brother. I could do whatever the flaming hell I wanted. Yes, I would say it was a good life."

Then why are you angry? It sounded to her as if he had missed a great deal, like parents with the maturity to raise a child and love him without spoiling him.

"What happened to your son?" she asked.

His voice warmed. "He's done well, actually. I used to visit the family several times a year." He didn't hide his longing. "I liked those visits. And I sent gold coins regularly. I also offered him a commission in the army, when he was old enough." Dryly he added, "That was before Cobalt put a death sentence on my head. Now, what army can he join? I can't commission him in the official one, with Cobalt in charge, and mine is outlawed." His mood lightened again. "He's very good at engineering, you know. He designed an irrigation system for his village, and it works beautifully. He's a strong, kind boy."

She smiled, touched by his affection. "He sounds like someone to be proud of."

"So he is." After a pause, Markus spoke wryly. "I think this talks-too-much affliction you have is contagious."

"You have interesting things to say." It was true. He had lived a strange life, privileged certainly, though not one she would have wanted. She had a feeling he knew he had missed as much as he had enjoyed, but she doubted he could actually say what his sumptuous life had lacked.

"Come, let's ride," he said. "Shadow has had enough rest."

"Shadow?"

"My horse. Named for the dragon, of course." With that, he surged into another mad race across the desert.

In the late afternoon, they stopped to rest at the southern border of Taka Mal and Jazid. To Allegra, the badlands of Taka Mal looked just as stark as those of Jazid.

"How do you know where the border is?" she asked. They were sitting on the top of a small mesa that thrust up from the desert like the isolated, broken molar of some giant.

"By the cairns," Markus said, pointing. "Look over there."

Allegra squinted. A solitary pile of red boulders stood like a sentry in the desert, gnarled and weathered.

"Is someone buried there?" she asked.

"A border guard," he said. "If they don't have family to accept their remains when they die, the army buries them on the border, to honor their service to the atajazid."

It sounded so lonely. "Does it bother them?"

"Not at all. It's considered an honor. Often they have a place picked out ahead of time for their burial." He bit into a slab of meat he had taken from his riding bag. "The army doesn't have enough sentinels to guard the border anymore, though."

It didn't surprise her. Jazid had lost many men in the war, and Cobalt had executed those soldiers who refused him their fealty—except these outlaws who had escaped the long reach of his power.

"It must be strange, living as an exile in your own country," Allegra said. She bit one of the grapes he had given her.

He scowled at the border. "It's even more aggravating that Taka Mal is free when we aren't, given the way they betrayed us."

Allegra knew little about Jazid's northern neighbor beyond the geography she taught her students, but she had thought Taka Mal and Jazid shared similar cultures. A queen ruled in Taka Mal, though, which she could never imagine happening here.

"I'd heard that Taka Mal and Jazid were allies," she said.

"No longer."

"How did they betray your country?"

"How *didn't* they?" He tore a bite of meat off with his teeth and chewed and swallowed angrily. "They allied with *your* country. Their infernal queen married a man from Aronsdale, some weak, pretty boy with yellow hair."

Allegra had heard about the marriage; such delicious gossip reached even her home, for the man came from south-western Aronsdale. The stories always described him as handsome and charming, a minstrel and lithe acrobat with a dazzling smile.

"I can see how an alliance between Taka Mal and Aronsdale might surprise Jazid," she said. "But why call it a betrayal?"

"The queen had agreed to marry my father, to cement the alliance between our two countries. Together, we would stand against Cobalt the Dark."

That didn't sound right. "If she wed your father, wouldn't Jazid laws have constrained her?"

"My father would have expected her to behave as befits a Jazid queen, if that is what you mean."

Allegra scowled at him. "In other words, he gets her throne."

"I don't know what they would have done," he admitted. "Both of them were strong personalities. But it's irrelevant. Instead of keeping her word, she took that boy as her consort." He clenched his fist on his knee. "Cobalt the Dark cut off my father's head, and now the queen of Taka Mal sleeps with Cobalt's kin."

"I'm sorry about your father," she said quietly.

He stared out at the desert. "I saw it."

She stared at him, stunned. "You saw—" She couldn't finish, couldn't say, *You saw a man behead your own father?*

"Cobalt violated the Alatian Code of War." Markus's gaze had become distant, as if he viewed images far different from the empty desert below. "He called my father to meet him during the battle. A truce applies when leaders talk this way. But Cobalt attacked him. They were on a mesa above the battlefield. I was in the combat, leading a company. I saw Cobalt and my father fighting." In a dull voice, he said, "While I was riding to help my father, Cobalt killed him."

The blood drained from her face. "You saw it all?"

"Yes." His eyes focused on some distant point. "I had almost reached them. But I never made it. The lightning hit first."

"I'm sorry," she murmured. No wonder the emperor was called Cobalt the Dark. He sounded horrific.

Markus drew in a breath and turned to her. "My father was not an easy man, and he grew harder each year. But he loved me, and I loved him. I *will* avenge his death. I'll never rest until I hold the severed head of the Dark Emperor in my hands."

"I'm not surprised you hate him." The more she understood about Markus, the less he seemed like a tyrant and the more like a strong, desperate leader doing his best to survive an intolerable situation.

"But, Markus," she said. "No mage could bring lightning down out of a clear sky. It isn't possible."

"I saw her do it." His gaze darkened. "You can, too."

"I can't!"

"I know you're lying."

Every time she started to see him in a different light, he turned around and showed his other side, the atavistic warlord. She had to convince him before he decided to do something drastic, like tie her up until she sang the spells he wanted. She took a breath. "Yes, I admit, I can do spells. But only to soothe people, create light or warmth, help you sleep. I'm telling you the truth when I say that's my limit. I didn't know I had put your guards to sleep. I wasn't sure I could even put *you* to sleep."

He smiled. "I know you didn't realize about the guards. You would have snuck out of the tent otherwise."

Damn. It hadn't even occurred to her to check on them. She had been too exhausted to do anything last night, though. If she had tried to escape, she would have collapsed in his camp, which would have brought her a lot more grief when someone found her.

"Why did you need the compass?" Markus asked.

"It's the curved surface," she hedged. "It focuses the spell."

"Curves." He laughed and brushed his hand over her breast. "That's how you put a spell on me."

She wondered if he would ever stop pawing her. It flustered her, especially when he made her want to laugh at his jokes. If anyone had told her a few days ago that the prince regent of Jazid could be sensually charming when he wanted, she would have thought they were crazy.

"*Geometric* curves," she said. "Like a circle."

"How many people can you put to sleep?"

"Maybe five? I've never done it before." She got up and went to the edge of the mesa. His company was spread out below, in the shade of the rock formation. Far to the east, small figures rode across the red desert, scouts he had sent ahead to check the land.

Markus came up behind her and put his arms around her waist. "Even five is an incredible weapon. A lovely girl, singing like a night bird. No one would ever suspect."

"I won't be your weapon. I could never hurt people with spells." She shivered despite the heat. "It's another reason the empress couldn't have attacked with lightning. What we do to others, we do to ourselves."

"You didn't fall asleep last night." He kissed her temple. "You moved across the tent. You had to be awake to do that."

"I did sleep for a while," she admitted. "But spells usually don't affect me quite as much as the people I direct them at."

"Hmm." He slid the robe off her shoulders and it fell down around her elbows. Nuzzling her neck, he fiddled with the gold clasp that fastened the halter between her breasts.

"Markus!" She swatted his hand. "If anyone looks up here, they'll see you mauling me."

"They'll wish it was them instead of me." He opened the clasp.

"Behave yourself." She grabbed the clasp, holding the halter closed so her breasts wouldn't fall out.

Markus suddenly hefted her up into his hold, with one arm under her legs and another behind her back. He carried her away from the edge and then set her down on her feet. "Better?"

It was better, but she was still annoyed with him. When he pulled her into his arms and tweaked open her halter, baring her breasts, she tried to twist away. He held her close, trapping her arms between them. She wished he didn't smell so good, with soap and leather and some indefinable smell that was just him.

"You quit that," she told him, trying to free herself. She wasn't sure what she wanted him to stop—touching her or being desirable.

"I can't quit that," he said, laughing. "You *are* a spell-caster, I know, because you've done something to me. I'm useless! I can't stop thinking about my luscious pleasure girl." He bit gently at her neck as he slid his hand from her breasts to her back, then over her bottom and between her legs from behind. "You must take pity on me and release me from this torment."

"You don't sound tormented to me." He was doing maddening things to her. She was still aroused from this morning, and his touch sent shivers through her that she really, really didn't want to feel for this unrepentant scalawag.

Markus blew into her ear. "You're ready for me, Allegra. You can't hide it." He stroked and teased her in the most distracting way. "Such sweet honey."

This morning she had come so close to her peak. And then stopped. Without completion. Now he held her against that beautifully muscled physique of his, and her traitorous body reacted.

When she stopped fighting, Markus relaxed. She immediately twisted around in his arms, putting her back to his front, and jabbed back with her elbow, hitting him in the stomach. When he grunted, his hold loosened and she wrenched free. Turning to face him, she stepped away from both him and the edge of the mesa.

He glared at her, holding his side where her elbow had hit. "What the blazes was that for?"

She fumbled with the clasp on her halter, trying to cover her breasts. "Stop pawing me."

"Oh, no, night bird. You can't tease me this way." He grasped her arm and pulled her forward. Then he kissed her hard, with his tongue, his hands cupping her bottom as he lifted her pelvis up against his. Startled, she squirmed, trying to get down.

Markus abruptly set her on her feet again. Then he put his thumb against her shoulder and gave a push. She backed up a step, away from the edge of the mesa. He thumbed her shoulder again, and she backed up more. He did it a third, then a fourth time. Confused, she kept backing away—right into a cluster of rock spears. It was why he had chosen this lookout; the spears formed a wall that offered shade from the sun. Or so he claimed. Now she wondered if he had other reasons. He trapped her against the wall and kissed her while he worked off her robe and dropped it on the ground.

"Mmmph," she protested.

"That was articulate," he murmured against her lips. Then he went back to kissing her. He tugged down the chains that held her halter over her shoulders, fending off her attempts to hinder him. The halter slid off and hit the ground with a clink.

Allegra pulled her head away. "If you don't stop, I'll put you to sleep for a century."

His wicked smile flashed. "Only if you can use your own delectable curves." He slid her up the wall, lifting her until his pelvis pressed against hers, his erection rubbing the silk of her skirt where he had teased so mercilessly.

Allegra struggled, her hands sliding against his biceps, her body moving against his. Her attempts to free herself backfired; the more she fought, the more it aroused him. It affected her almost as much to feel his strong body and the

144

flex of his muscles while she inhaled his smell, sweaty and soapy at the same time.

"Prince Markus?" a man called from somewhere distant.

"Not now," Markus muttered, tugging on her skirt.

"You'd better answer him," Allegra said.

He bit her earlobe while he rubbed his erection against her stomach. "He'll go away if I don't."

She tried to wriggle down from where he was holding her, but he just slid her up higher on the wall, enough so he could suckle her breast. She groaned as her nipples hardened. Damn man. Somehow he knew just how to arouse her.

Embarrassed as much by her own reaction as by what he was doing, she thwacked him on the head. "Quit groping me, Your Hedonistic Highness."

"My what?" Laughing, he let her slide to her feet. "Come on, Allegra," he coaxed. "Stop fighting me. Admit it. You like the way I touch you."

"Sire?" the man called. He sounded closer, maybe even near the top of the path that led up the mesa.

"Ah, hells," Markus said. He scooped her clothes off the ground and thrust them into her hands. "Cover yourself up."

By the time the man came around the wall of rock, she had the halter back in place and had almost finished pulling on her robe. Markus stood in front of her, blocking her from view, but she saw who had arrived. Lieutenant Borjan.

"Sire, General Yargazon sent me—" Borjan stopped when he saw Allegra quickly tying the robe. "Ah. Oh." He scratched his ear. "My apologies. I didn't mean to disturb you."

"What does Yargazon want?" Markus asked.

"A scout just came in. He thought you would want a report."

"Oh. Yes, I do." Markus pushed his hand through his hair, disarraying the locks Allegra had so carefully brushed last night. "Tell him I'll be right down."

"Right away." The lieutenant made a fast exit.

"I have to attend to this," Markus grumbled. "We'll finish later." Under his breath, he added, "If I don't go crazy by then."

She couldn't help but smile. "You mean you haven't already?" she asked innocently.

"I swear, you will drive me to it." He gathered up his pack and motioned her toward the path. "Come."

"I can wait for you up here," she offered.

"And run away as soon as I'm gone, no doubt." He stretched out his arm, pointing at the path. "Come. *Now,* woman."

"Markus, can't you at least be courteous about it?"

"What?"

"'Come,'" she said in a deep voice, mimicking him. "'Now, woman.' You order me around like I'm your dog."

"You're not my dog," he said crossly. "You're my slave."

Allegra folded her arms, glared at him and stayed put.

Markus lifted his hand as if inviting her to dinner. "Allegra, will you please accompany me down to my tent?"

Saints above. He *could* actually be courteous. She lowered her arms. "Yes, certainly."

The path wound down the outside of the mesa. It dropped

off to their left, but it was wide enough that she didn't fear she would fall. She kept her hand on the cliff to her right for support. Although sand dribbled off under her palm, the stone was solid.

Markus followed her. "How deeply can you make a person sleep?" he asked.

"I don't know."

"Could you do it so they didn't wake up?"

Allegra froze. Then she swung around to him. "Are you asking me if I can *kill?*"

He stood above her on the path. "Well, no. But it's a good question. Can you?"

"No! Even if I could, I never would. How could you ask such a thing?"

He came closer to her. "I'm the outlawed sovereign of a conquered country. I have to think in those terms to survive."

She spoke more quietly. "I don't know what the empress did, but it's not something I could replicate even if I were willing. I have nothing resembling that kind of power."

He cupped his hand under her chin. "I don't know what you can do. But I'll find out."

"If I hurt others, Markus, I hurt myself."

His voice softened. "I would never wish that."

She took a breath, trying to calm her agitation. Then she turned and resumed the descent. He was a leader of contrasts, compassionate one moment, harsh the next, and she was discovering a compelling man beneath the emotional armor of his exterior. She didn't want to be attracted to him.

Too much danger existed on that path. He couldn't force her to use her spells for violence, but now that he knew about them, he would be even more vigilant about keeping watch over her. With every step she took farther into this parched desert, her hope for freedom faded, becoming as pale as the stoneblue sky.

CHAPTER 8
THE ANVIL

Markus's company camped among the eerie stone formations that marked the first ranks of the new mountain range they had been approaching all day. Jutting columns of rock alternated with stretches of sand, all red and ocher in the daylight, with flecks of other colors: metallic blues, violet and the false gold of feldspar. Stubby plants clung to the rocks, dark green and tenacious. Dust drifted in the air, stirred by the passage of so many horses and men. Night dropped its star-dusted cloak with the speed of a hawk descending for its prey.

After supper, Markus met with his top officers: General Yargazon, General Ardoz and Colonel Bladebreak. They sat in his tent at a low table, drinking wine as they talked. Candles on the table shed gold light across their faces. Allegra lay on a blanket across the tent among a tumble of pillows. Markus had insisted she take off her robe, leaving her in only the red skirt and halter. He claimed it was because the braziers warmed up the tent, but she knew perfectly well he wanted the others to see her. It was some annoying status thing among the men. They all looked at her when they came in with a disquieting hunger, especially Yargazon. She tried to ignore them, but it was difficult when they stared.

Although she pretended to sleep, she kept her eyes open enough to see them. And she listened. Military advisors in Aronsdale would never have discussed their plans in front of someone who hadn't sworn loyalty to their cause, asleep or not. These officers didn't even seem to see beyond the sexy clothes and curves of her body. It was an advantage to their attitude she hadn't realized before; they lowered their guard around her in ways they would never do with a man. They plotted strategy as if she wasn't in the room.

Yargazon was speaking. "I had thought last year, after the queen's people discovered the assassination plot, that they killed the assassins. But it appears one may be alive."

Markus lowered his wineglass. "Where is he?"

"My agent has infiltrated the palace," Yargazon said. "He thinks our man is in a cell, but he doesn't know the location."

General Ardoz, a large man with a shock of black hair sprinkled with gray, reclined on a cushion. "If they've had him for a year, he's probably broken by now. The queen may know our plans to put the atajazid on the Topaz Throne."

Allegra stiffened. The *Topaz* Throne? That was Taka Mal, not Jazid. It sounded as if they had tried to murder the queen of Taka Mal and install the boy atajazid in her place. The plan must have failed.

"They already know," Markus growled. "That damn priestess told them." He scowled at his officers. "I fail to understand how one girl could escape an armed war camp and reach the queen in less than a day."

"She obviously had help," Yargazon said.

"It doesn't add up." That came from Colonel Bladebreak, a heavyset man with bristly gray hair and a stomach tending to fat. "No matter how many times I analyze it, the facts don't fit. Even with an unusually fast horse and help from the Taka Mal army, she needed over a day to get so far. She managed in less than twelve hours."

"When we get her back," Yargazon said coldly, "I'll question her myself."

"Get her back how?" Bladebreak demanded. "She's the consort of the queen's damnable cousin."

"I don't care if she's the consort of their Dragon-Sun," the General said. "She was in Jazid when I bought her. Legally she's my property."

"Well, she's in Taka Mal now," Markus said. "If we took her, it would be tantamount to an act of war. Her husband is second in line to the throne."

"An act of war?" Bladebreak raised an eyebrow. "I'd say we did that last year, when we sent agents to murder the royal family."

"They have no proof those men were ours," Markus said. "The word of one girl, even a priestess, is hearsay."

"It's been a year," Ardoz said. "Surely they would have acted by now if they had evidence we backed a plot against the queen."

Markus glanced at Yargazon. "Could our agent have held out this long against interrogators?"

"Had they been trained by myself or your father, no." Yargazon moved his hand in dismissal. "This queen is weak. Afraid of extreme measures. So against her people, yes, it's possible."

"I'd like to interrogate the queen," Bladebreak said sourly. "I'm surprised that cousin of hers hasn't deposed her. What madness possessed her father to leave her the throne?"

"Don't underestimate her," Markus said. "If she couldn't hold her own and then some, she wouldn't have survived for ten years as queen. And she's well liked among her people."

Yargazon snorted. "What idiot wants a woman on the throne?"

"They think she's the ultimate priestess of the Dragon-Sun," Ardoz said. "They tell themselves the Dragon-Sun is the true ruler of Taka Mal, and it makes a female sovereign more palatable."

Markus smiled wryly at Ardoz, showing more warmth with him than with the others. "If you can figure that out, you'd think her own people would see it, as well."

The laugh lines around Ardoz's eyes crinkled. "I'm sure they do, Mark. It's a justification they let themselves use."

Allegra blinked. Mark? She hadn't known Markus had a nickname. No one else seemed to use it.

"Well, assassination didn't work," Bladebreak said. "And the attempt alone wasn't enough to cause the chaos we needed."

Allegra could see why they needed the confusion that would

follow the sudden deaths of the royal family. With only a few hundred men, Markus otherwise had little hope of countering the Taka Mal army, which surely had several thousand.

"The longer we wait in hiding," Yargazon said, "the more it drains our resources."

"I concur," Bladebreak said. "The strain is showing. That fellow who stole the knife isn't the only one worried about his family. We can't keep on like this, with no relief for the men."

"The army needs a focus," Ardoz said. "The men have nothing to do but worry while our supplies diminish."

Markus regarded them intently. "The solution is obvious."

"I agree." Yargazon nodded with satisfaction. "A wise idea."

"Perhaps," Bladebreak said dryly, "you might share this idea with the rest of us?"

"Invade now," Markus said. "We've more men and weapons than last year. We're better prepared."

Allegra was surprised to see the other men nodding. Did they really believe a few hundred men could conquer Taka Mal? Surely not. She recalled Markus's comments about weapons and the T'Ambera. Maybe they had found something that would give them an edge.

"This could be a good time for other reasons, too," Yargazon said. "According to my reports, Emperor Cobalt's forces are stretched thin and their morale is terrible, especially since he sent one thousand men into Taka Mal and left only a thousand here. Trying both to protect Taka Mal and hold Jazid demands more resources than he can spare."

Markus nodded to Yargazon. "That assassination plan of

yours was brilliant, Dusk. Even though it 'failed,' we came out ahead because Cobalt had to reduce his forces in Jazid as a result."

Bladebreak and Ardoz nodded their agreement. Allegra felt queasy, hearing their plans for killing and how they honored someone for his brilliance at bringing about death.

"Cobalt's men also aren't used to desert fighting," General Ardoz said. "They don't know how."

"We've had reports of strife," Yargazon said. "The men ask why they must hold this land so far from their own." His smile could have been a knife. "The Misted Cliffs is foggy and cold. They hate the desert. Jazid demoralizes them."

"Well, then," Markus said. "We are decided. I'll present our recommendations to the atajazid."

That intrigued Allegra. It sounded as if they planned to meet up with their hidden king. Asking his permission was probably a formality; she couldn't imagine these sun-hardened warriors putting off their battles at the order of a nine-year-old child.

"There is one other matter," Yargazon said. "My agents have picked up some odd rumors. Something about an engineering guild associated with the Topaz Palace."

"Have they developed a new weapon?" Markus asked.

"I don't think so," the General said. "It's something called kindle-powder." Wryly he added, "Actually the rumors are about the failure of this kindle-powder. It doesn't work."

"What is it?" General Ardoz asked.

Yargazon shrugged. "We've no details. It may just be a myth."

Markus glanced at Yargazon. "Keep checking it."

"We've another point to consider," Ardoz said. "The royal family. Do we still want them killed, except the queen's consort?"

"He's an excellent hostage, as Cobalt's kin." Markus rubbed his chin. "I've been thinking on this. I'm not so sure killing any of them is a good idea. After we have the throne, we'll want Queen Vizarana's army to fight with us against Cobalt. They are far more likely to do so if we let their queen and her baby live. And she could give us valuable information."

Yargazon frowned. "Any time some king—or regent— lets his enemy live, a survivor comes back for revenge. Look at Cobalt. His family ruled Harsdown for centuries. Then his father invaded Aronsdale. When Aronsdale defeated Harsdown, they should have executed its king and his heir. Did they? No. They imprisoned the king in a supposedly impregnable fortress. And Cobalt, his heir, who was just a little boy? He grew up into a monster, raised an army to free his father and then turned those godforsaken forces against the rest of us." He shook his head. "We can't let either the queen or her heirs live."

"Well, we will see what happens." Markus raised his goblet. "To Taka Mal."

The others lifted their cups. "To Taka Mal."

After they drank and refilled their goblets, Markus reclined on his cushions. Bladebreak smiled at him. "You seem in a good mood."

"Hmm," Markus said.

Yargazon spoke sourly. "Has she had any wine lately?"

Markus grinned at him. "I don't give her any."

"Perhaps you should," Yargazon said. "You could keep your belt ready for another thirty."

"Aye, that I could," Markus said, laughing.

Allegra wanted to slap them. Belt indeed. During their ride today, she had walked part of the time because she was stiff after riding so much. But she knew what Markus let everyone think, that she couldn't ride because of the thrashing he had supposedly given her. If he brought that up now, she was going to throw more than wine in his face when she had the chance.

"She sings, too," Markus said. "She has a gorgeous voice."

"Really?" Ardoz said. "You're fortunate."

Markus stretched indolently. "Maybe you would all enjoy a song, eh?"

As the others murmured their agreement, Allegra went cold. Surely he wouldn't ask her to go over there. They were all turning toward her, so she closed her eyes all the way. Fabric rustled as someone stood, followed by the tread of boots crossing the tent.

The footsteps stopped. "Allegra?"

She sighed and stirred, opening her eyes. Markus was crouched in front of her, blocking her view of his officers.

He kissed her languidly. "Wake up." He put his hand on her waist, and his thumb stroked the underside of her breast.

Allegra decided she had better "wake up" before he started pawing her in front of his military advisors. "Are they gone?" she asked. Wishful thinking, but it was worth a try. Maybe he would send them away.

"Still here," he murmured. "We want you to sing for us. Come to the table."

"Markus, I don't want to." She meant to sound firm, but the words came out frightened.

"Come. Sing." He silently mouthed, *Put them to sleep.*

What the blazes? She sat up in the pillows. As she rubbed her stiff shoulder, she gave him a questioning look.

In a voice so low, she barely heard, he said, "Come, my night bird. If they are sleeping, they can't harm you."

For saints' sake. He wanted her to do a spell. Whatever for? She almost said no, but then she changed her mind. If she put his officers, his guards—and him—to sleep, she could sneak out of the tent, assuming she didn't knock herself out, as well.

Markus stood up and offered his hand. As she took it, she felt the sword calluses on his palm exactly like in her dream. A shiver went through her, and this time it didn't come from fear.

He drew her to the table, and the men watched her with appraising stares that among her people would have been considered extraordinarily rude. She wanted to cover herself with her hands, but Markus had her arm in his large grip.

"Here." He set her at the table between his and Yargazon's places, by a pole that supported the tent. The men sat drinking their wine, seeming relaxed in their cushions, but with an ingrained tension that she doubted they ever lost.

Markus went to a chest across the tent and removed something that glittered. Straightening, he detached a small piece from it, then turned and showed it to her. Squinting, Allegra realized he had a key. He closed the chest and set the key on its top. Then he came back, holding the larger object. No, two objects, bracelets it looked like. As he drew nearer, she blanched. Those weren't bracelets, they were gold shackles joined by a gold chain. Rubies, diamonds, topazes and onyx glinted in the metal.

As Markus knelt next to Allegra, she drew back. "What are you doing?" she asked, frightened.

"Just making sure you don't fly off," he murmured. He lifted her hand. She strained to pull it away, but he clicked a manacle around her wrist. The metal felt cold on her skin. He wrapped the chain around the pole and closed the other manacle around the chain.

I can't do this. She was surrounded by warlords in a culture that obviously valued their ferocity, height and physical power far more than any kindness. She feared if they sensed her apprehension, she would seem like prey to them.

Exactly *why* Markus wanted her to knock out his advisors was another question altogether. Convoluted tangles of power swirled here. If she put them to sleep, including Markus, she would be trapped without the key to the manacles. But maybe she could figure out a way to free herself. However slim her odds for escape, they weren't zero.

Markus had picked up the compass, and now he handed it to her. He took his goblet off the table then and settled next to her in the pillows.

"Sing, beautiful songbird," he said, raising his goblet. Had they been alone, his sensual expression might have aroused her. But the calculating stares of his military advisors were frightening. She didn't know what they intended.

Allegra stared at the compass in her lap so she wouldn't have to see their harsh faces. She chose the lilt that had put Markus to sleep last night. As she sang, she focused on the compass and poured out a comfort spell...soft, sweet, soothing. Although she wanted her voice to carry to the guards outside, she had to be careful. If she sang too loudly, Markus would know why and the others might wonder. She couldn't risk their suspicion.

Allegra soared into the high notes, caressing them with her voice, and wove a green spell. It came more easily this time, swirling their moods around her. *Sleepy.* They all were, even Markus. Good.

She caught wisps of thoughts, nothing concrete, emotions more than words. They liked her singing, Ardoz and Markus especially. In fact, Markus loved it. Yargazon was impatient to reach some place, she wasn't certain where, and his mood dominated. He wanted to fight. Go to war. So did the others. A restless anger drove them, prodded by their smoldering resentment of Cobalt, the hated emperor who had stolen their country and their lives.

Sensuality overlaid their moods, woven into the aggression, especially with Yargazon and Bladebreak. The pairing of violence and arousal disturbed Allegra. They associated warfare with sexual desire and believed taking a woman increased their power as warriors. It terrified her, especially given her vulnerability.

Markus's responses were much healthier, rich and sensual, robust. To her surprise, he felt a great deal of tenderness toward her, which he strove to hide, thinking it would be perceived as weakness. He had been deeply lonely, but she was changing all that for him. In different circumstances, knowing he desired her so much would have pleased her.

She recoiled from Yargazon. He wanted her as much as Markus, and having her shackled next to him heightened that desire. But his lust smothered. He wanted to hurt her, to hear her cry. He didn't see her as human. In his eyes, she was incapable of true emotion, a temptress who deliberately weakened men. He found her exotically beautiful and voluptuous, unbearably so, and that translated into a need to punish her. Overriding it all was his fury at her defiance. He admired Markus, considered him a good leader and regent, a man worthy of respect. He felt *fatherly* toward the prince. He knew the honor Markus had given him with the auction, and he wanted Allegra to suffer for the insult she had done Markus, for her resistance, just for being herself. He would conquer her as he conquered on the battlefield, laying waste to both.

Bile rose in Allegra's throat. How could he hate her so much? She withdrew her concentration, shutting him out of her spell. As his mood receded, the others became clearer.

Ardoz surprised her. Although he considered her pretty, his response had more kindness to it than desire. The blood-lust for war burned within him even more than in Yargazon, but it had no sexual component. To him, Allegra represented softness, the reward after the battle, the place where a battered warrior laid his head. When she realized where else he wanted to lie, she blushed. What would Markus do if he realized his military advisor found *him* more attractive than his pleasure girl? She caught images from Ardoz, fantasies—memories?—where he held a younger Markus. It bewildered her, and she almost stumbled in the song.

Colonel Bladebreak was a different story. His interest in her had a hard edge, aggression intermingled with lust. With dismay, she realized he assumed Markus brought her to the table because he meant to share her with them. Bladebreak expected her to fight when he took her, and the bastard looked forward to it. His response so distressed her, she lost her place in the song.

Distraction rippled from the men as she stuttered. She jumped back into the lilt, determined to knock them out before anyone hurt her. Even without a spell, she knew Markus would never consent to let them touch her. So why flaunt her? For status, obviously. It established his rank in some subtle male hierarchy. But he walked too close to the edge. Jazid men might dress their women in almost nothing for their pleasure, but in public the women wore robes. The bright colors identified their sex, with the associated status it gave their men, but covering them up decreased the chance of an assault or kidnapping. Markus wanted it *both* ways, to show her off and to keep her only for himself. He had the power and bodyguards to protect her, but he was taking a risk. He had better know what he was doing, because she would pay the price if he lost control of the situation.

Reaching beyond the tent with her spell, she touched the minds of soldiers, distant and vague. She focused on them even as she redoubled her efforts with the officers here. Markus fought, but his resistance softened as his starved need for sleep caught up with him. His mood grew more diffuse, saturated with drowsy contentment.

A loud snore broke into her song. Startled, she looked up. Ardoz and Bladebreak were sprawled in their pillows, fast asleep. Yargazon had collapsed on his side and dropped his wine goblet. A red stain was spreading on the blue and violet carpet. Markus lay on his back, his chest rising and falling with the even rhythm of sleep. His eyes twitched under his lids as if he were dreaming.

"General Yargazon?" she asked. "Would you like more wine?" If he were the least bit awake, *that* ought to provoke him.

No response.

"Colonel Bladebreak?" she asked. "General Ardoz?"

Bladebreak snored, and Ardoz didn't budge.

Saints above. It had *worked*. It was fortunate, because she couldn't have maintained the spell much longer without falling asleep herself. The effort had strained the limits of what she knew how to do with her gifts. Before her kidnapping, she hadn't even thought she could do green spells. She felt drained, ravenous and sleepy.

Allegra twisted the shackle on her wrist and tugged the

chain around the pole. The metal felt too hard to be pure gold. She couldn't bend the manacle, nor could she do anything with the pole; to support such a large tent, it needed to be sturdy, and they had driven it deep into the ground.

Markus sighed and rubbed his eyes. Sitting up slowly, he smiled at her. "Hmm…pretty songbird."

"Oh." She blinked at him sheepishly, her hands gripped on the chain she had been trying to wrest free.

"You can't unlock that," he said.

Allegra flushed and released the chain. "You woke up."

"I've spent the last ten years fighting to sleep. Who'd have thought I would have to fight to stay awake?" He regarded the others with a grin. "Looks like they lost the battle."

"They were easier than you," she admitted.

"That's amazing! You can even knock out experienced officers who should know better."

"Don't you trust them?"

He leaned toward her. "I don't trust anyone. Especially you. But they're excellent officers."

She kept her opinion on that to herself. "So why did you want them to sleep?"

"To see what you could do." He considered her. "What about the guards? You tried with them, too, I'll bet."

"I don't know," she hedged.

"Hah." He climbed to his feet. "I'll go check."

"Markus, wait!"

He turned back. "Eh?"

She tugged at the shackles. "Don't leave me like this!"

His eyes took on a bedroom look that had nothing to do with sleep. Although he didn't have Yargazon's or Blade-break's hard edge, she needed no spell to realize that seeing her chained excited him.

"I'll come back," he murmured.

"Your men might wake up," she said, trying not to panic. "They would find me alone here, without you."

His smile faded. "No, that wouldn't be good." He strode across the tent and took the key off the chest. He came back and released her, then tossed the shackles on the table. "Come on." He grabbed her hand. "Let's go visit my guards."

She stumbled along with him as he strode across the tent. "Slow down."

He moderated his pace. "I keep forgetting your legs aren't as long as mine." He sounded immensely pleased with himself.

Outside, the moon glowed with a red tinge from dust in the air. The man who guarded the entrance was lying on the ground. Snoring.

"Hah!" Markus toed his bodyguard's arm, which was flung across the ground. "Izad. Wake up!"

The man grunted.

Markus pushed Izad's shoulder with his boot, rolling him onto his back. "What kind of protection is this, eh? An assassin could have slipped into my tent and knifed me between the ribs."

"What—?" The guard peered blearily up at Markus. Then comprehension dawned on his face. "Your Highness!" He scrambled to his feet, clumsy with sleep. "Sir! I—I— Gods almighty." Even in the dim light, it was easy to see his face had gone deathly pale.

"Why were you sleeping, Izad?" Markus asked mildly.

"Sire! It won't happen again!"

"Yes, I know. But why did you go to sleep?"

"I don't— It's never happened before." Izad seemed as bewildered by Markus's calm response as by finding himself snoring on duty. "I don't know."

Markus nodded. "Carry on." He took Allegra's arm and headed around the tent.

Allegra glanced over her shoulder at Izad. He was staring after them with his mouth open.

"That was astonishing," Markus said. "He had no idea why he fell asleep."

"He was terrified of what you would do to him."

He snorted. "If he really had fallen asleep on duty, he would have been endangering the person of the prince regent. That's an executable offense."

"Is that why you threatened me with execution over the wine?" she asked tartly. "Because I endangered your exalted person with my fierce, bellicose behavior?"

His laugh rumbled. "Ah, well. If all dangers were so lovely, I'd die a happy man." When Allegra glowered at him, he grinned.

"You're not going to tell Izad what happened, are you?" she said.

"I doubt it. The fewer people who know what you can do, the better weapon you make."

"I'm not a weapon," she said, exasperated. "And for saints' sake, Markus, your military advisors are going to wonder why they passed out in your tent."

"Why? It wouldn't be the first time we drank too much and fell asleep." He laughed with satisfaction. "This is incredible. Think what I could do."

"*You* don't make the spells."

"You're dangerous, you know, knocking out my bodyguards." He thought for a moment. "I need to figure out how I'll stop you from doing spells when I don't want them to happen."

Great. Just great. Saints only knew what he would think of.

They found two more of his guards asleep. Only the one on the far side of the tent was awake. Markus admonished the others enough so his reaction was less out of kilter with their expectations. As punishment, he ordered them to muck out the horse stalls. The confused guards asked which stalls he meant, given that the company had none, but Markus was already moving on, and he just waved. Allegra wondered what they would think when they realized they had all fallen asleep at the same time.

Markus returned to the entrance and peered inside. With a soft laugh, he said, "Look," and lifted the flap. Yargazon, Ardoz and Bladebreak were still fast asleep, sprawled on their cushions. With a grin, he dropped the flap.

"Izad." Markus beckoned to the guard. "Get the others. We're going for a walk."

As Izad went for the other bodyguards, Allegra shivered,

her arms folded. The night's cold seeped into her bones. "I'm cold. I should get a—"

"No." He caught her as she started into the tent. "You'll wake our sleeping beauties."

"Saints, Markus." She couldn't stop her shivering. "Can't you be considerate?"

"What, it's inconsiderate to let them sleep?"

She was too cold, hungry and tired to deal with him. "If you can't see the problem, I give up."

His expression tightened. "I must be too stupid, eh? After all, I am—what was it? A tyrannical despot who inflicts brutal punishments and terrorizes girls half my weight and age, a man sorely limited in intelligence, unbearably rude, illegitimate and with bad hygiene. Oh, I almost forgot. A pig, too. The dragon only knows how you can stand to inhabit the same world as me."

Allegra blinked. "You have a good memory." She hadn't thought he listened that closely to what she said, but apparently he remembered the parts he didn't like.

He beckoned to someone behind her. Turning, she saw his four guards waiting far enough back so they weren't intruding.

Izad came over to Markus and saluted. "Yes, Sire?"

"Assign four men to guard this tent. Then meet me at the Anvil." He glanced at Allegra, then back at the guard. "And bring me one of those ocelot blankets."

"Right away, Sire."

Markus nodded to him, then grasped Allegra's arm and headed off, striding through the camp. The other three guards came with them, one on either side and one behind, all easily matching the prince regent's stride. Allegra had to run to keep up. The soft soles of her fur boots offered little protection against the rocks stabbing her feet. She tried to slow down, but Markus kept up his pace and wouldn't let go of her arm. By the time they left the camp, a stitch burned in her side. She stumbled on the stony ground and pitched forward.

Markus barely caught her before she fell. "Careful there!"

She braced her hands on his arm while she gulped in air. The company had camped in a basin deep in the foothills of the Fractured Mountains. Here on the rim of the basin, columns jutted up, and shadows lurked among them, dark spaces like holes that could swallow a person into some inky hell.

Markus shifted his weight from foot to foot. "Are you ready?"

"No," she said, knowing it wouldn't matter. Her attempts to be so disagreeable that he would want nothing more to do with her had so far failed miserably.

"Come." He took her arm and started off at the same pace.

"No!" She braced her feet, really digging in this time, and refused to go. "I can't go that fast!"

He stood next to her. "That was fast?"

"Yes." She tried to pry his fingers off her arm. "You're hurting me." She was going to have another bruise tomorrow.

He seemed ready to snap with tension, but he did release her. Maybe it wasn't tension as much as his inability to stay *still*. He was always restless, always moving, never able to concentrate for long. That combined with his sharp intelligence reminded her of a boy she had once taught. The fellow could never sit; he had to be up and about. He hated being indoors, particularly in confined places. He had a sweet nature, charming and funny, and she had soon realized he genuinely had a hard time controlling his hyperactive need to move. Although he had outgrown it a bit as he matured, he would always be that way to some extent. Markus seemed a lot like him.

"Why do you stare at me so oddly?" he asked. "You look as if I've sprouted dragon wings."

She rubbed the small of her back, which ached from all their horseback riding. "Don't you ever slow down?"

"What for?"

"You're exhausting."

"I'm not tired."

"I wasn't referring to you."

"Oh."

"Oh? That's it?"

"What did you expect me to say?"

She glowered at him. "How about, 'I'm sorry for dragging you all over creation, and I'll attempt to be more aware of your needs in the future.'"

"Men don't talk that way to women." He crossed his arms. "It is your pleasure in life to serve my needs, whatever they may be, however it pleases me. That's why you exist."

"Well, goodness me," she said. "I can't imagine why women don't want to immigrate to this lovely country."

He lowered his arms. "Allegra, I don't want to argue." He held out his hand. "Come with me. I want to show you something. A special place I've always loved."

Again he caught her off guard. When he cleared his throat awkwardly, she flushed and took his hand. He started off again, this time at a more moderate pace. It felt odd holding his hand, more like something she would have done with an Aronsdale boy. She had no doubt that if Yargazon showed up, Markus would drop her hand as if it were an ingot in a furnace. Even so, it was nice.

"Where are we going?" she asked.

"It's called the Anvil." He indicated a place up ahead where darkness blocked the stars. "There."

"What about the men sleeping in your tent?" she asked.

His laugh was low and satisfied. "They'll be fine. And if I'm gone when they awake, they can't ask me questions."

She doubted they would find it so amusing, but she was glad to be away from them. Although in military terms, Ardoz was probably the most violent, he didn't frighten her like the others. She had absolutely no idea what to make of his interest in Markus, though. She had never known a man could feel that way about another man.

They were approaching another rock formation, this one taller than the others, at least the height of ten people. It jutted up from the desert like, well, a huge anvil, impressively massive, blocking the rich canopy of stars.

Markus turned to the three guards. "Two of you wait here. When Izad returns, send him up."

The men bowed. "As you wish, Sire."

The hike up the Anvil was steep, and the path wound into the formation rather than around it, which relieved Allegra. She didn't want to be on an edge, in the dark, so far above the ground. The walls on either side rose up until they met overhead and formed a tunnel. The path was too narrow for more than one person. Markus went first, she followed and his third guard came after her, his tread heavy in the inky darkness. Rocks poked her feet through her flimsy boots. With no light, she had to feel her way along with her hands on the walls.

They came out onto the flat top of the Anvil under the icy stars. Far below, the desert stretched in plains of sand and distorted shadows, all etched in silver by the moonlight. To the east, the Fractured Mountains rose in broken spires against the sky.

"Saints above," she breathed. "It's incredible."

"Worth the walk?" Markus asked.

"It—it's—" A gust of wind hit her, and she gasped from the chill, wrapping her arms around herself. She had never thought before that people's teeth really could chatter, but hers were doing it.

"Eh. Come here." Markus drew her against his side, folding her in his arms. Even through his shirt, his body felt like a furnace. She pressed closer to his warmth, her arms between their bodies, her cheek against his chest.

"That's why you won't give me clothes," she said. "So I have to do this."

"I like to look at you." He stroked her back. "To touch you. Everywhere. You're so soft."

"You shouldn't freeze me just because you like my body." She could hardly get out the words, she was shaking so hard.

"By the dragon," he growled. "You're as bad as my mother."

"You froze your *mother?*"

"No! She was always telling me such things, about being considerate. My father told me not to listen, that she was just a woman and I could do as I pleased."

"Oh, well, there's an example of fine parenting."

"My father was a great man." He rubbed his hands up and down her bare back. "You really are shaking."

"I'm cold!"

"I can help." Markus glanced over her head at his body-guard. "Wait here. This is the only access to the top."

"I'll send Izad up with the blanket when he arrives, Sire," the guard said.

"Excellent."

Markus led Allegra to an edge of the Anvil where a small half dome of rock faced the desert. As they stepped within its shelter, the wind eased. He drew her to the back wall and sat down, settling her between his legs with her back to his front. He bent his legs on either side of her and enfolded her in his arms, surrounding her with the warmth of his body.

"Better?" he asked.

"Much." She turned sideways so she could burrow deeper in his arms. "You're like a campfire."

He kissed the top of her head. "It's another of my plots, to make you behave as if you want to be with me."

That gave her pause. Beneath his joking, it sounded as if he cared how she felt about him. Maybe that wasn't so surprising. Most people wanted their lovers to like them. Given his lack of remorse for what he had done to her, though, she hadn't expected it to matter to him. Probably she was reading too much into his tone because she hoped it would make her situation more bearable. And yet...the tenderness toward her that she had felt in his mood tonight had been real. He could be far more appealing than he had any right to be, given his life, and if she were being honest, she had to admit his mischief made her smile.

In his arms, she continued to warm up. After a while, when her shaking stopped, she said, "You should have listened more to your mother and less to your father."

She expected another of his proclamations about the supposed nature of men and women. Instead he said, "When I behaved as he saw fitting for his son, he spent more time with me."

She knew nothing of his father except stories she had heard in Aronsdale, which all painted him as a brutal man. "Did you like to be with him?"

"Of course."

"You said before that he was harsh."

"You have to be, to rule this country." He slid one of his hands inside her halter and fondled her nipple. "But even the harshest kings need succor."

"You can't buy succor," she said. "No matter how much you pay the T'Ambera."

"Yes, I can." He unfastened the halter's clip between her breasts. "I own you. That's just how I want it."

"I cannot even begin to tell you," she said, "how unromantic that sounds."

Markus pulled off the halter and dropped it in a glittery pile on the ground. As he petted her breasts, he murmured against her ear. "You're not telling the truth. Your nipples are so hard, they're saying, 'Markus, kiss me, please, *now.*'"

Oh, honestly. "It sounds to me like they're saying, 'Cover us up. We're cold!'"

He laughed softly. "You don't fool me. You're mad with desire for my incredible body."

Allegra snorted. "Matched only by your incredible modesty." He was teasing, though. She had felt the truth earlier tonight in her spell; he had no idea how beautiful he looked. How would he know? He spent all his time around soldiers, and they were hardly about to tell their commander he was sexy. Not even Ardoz.

"Markus?"

"Hmm?" His calluses rasped on her skin as he caressed her.

"Isn't Ardoz young to be a general? He's not even as old as Colonel Bladebreak."

"True. But Ardoz is a notorious warrior. And strategist. That's why I promoted him."

So Markus had given Ardoz his rank. "Is that the only reason?"

"What other reason would there be?"

"Friendship."

She thought he would ask what the hell that meant, or tell her military ranks had nothing to do with favoritism. Instead he spoke quietly. "Sometimes friendship turns onto unexpected paths. You may soon turn back and leave that path, which isn't for you, but that doesn't mean you regret it." He pressed his lips against her temple. "My path is with you, night bird."

Saints above. He *knew* how Ardoz felt. She felt certain of it. She doubted he would tell her more, but she would always wonder now if what she had seen in Ardoz's mind had been memories.

"What about my path?" she asked.

"You were lucky. It led you to me."

"Oh, for saints' sake."

He kept caressing her. "You like being here, this way, with me. I can tell."

"Only because I'd freeze otherwise." In truth, she did like the way he stroked her. But this morning, even with the miradella, she had needed to see him with another man's face before she could enjoy his touch.

Markus tugged at her skirt. "The T'Ambera claimed this comes off the chain—ah, there." He pulled away the silk, leaving her naked except for a jeweled chain around her hips. His hand roamed between her thighs, leaving no hidden places. "You're not fighting me tonight."

"It's too cold." After what had happened this morning,

she felt tuned like a string on a harp, ready for him to play. As the miradella wore off, it actually became more effective because the sensations were no longer so intense that she felt overwhelmed. She didn't want to encourage him, but she was too aroused to ask him to stop, either, so she just sat and let him do as he pleased.

He sighed. "Someday, Allegra, you will say to me, 'Markus, come here, I want you.' And I'll fall over in shock."

She couldn't help but smile. "That would be a sight."

"Why don't you try saying it and see what happens?"

She didn't answer, but she curled closer against his chest.

"Hmm." He kept stroking her, but he took it slower, his attentions less demanding than this morning.

After a few minutes, a man said, "Prince Markus?"

"Gods," Markus swore. "Don't they ever go away?"

"That sounds like Izad," Allegra said. "You asked him to come up."

"Oh. Yes. I did." Markus raised his voice. "Here."

"Wait!" Allegra splayed her hands against her breasts and pelvis. "Not yet."

"I won't let him see you." He shifted her weight and stood up with an ease she envied. She gasped when icy air blasted across her bare skin and she curled into as tight a ball as possible.

Markus stopped and said, "Oh." He unfastened his jerkin and pulled it off, leaving only a dark red undershirt. His arm muscles bulged. With his broad chest, narrow hips and long legs, he was a sight well worth the look. Kneeling down, he put the jerkin around her shoulders. "There. I'll be right back." Then he quickly left the hollow.

Relieved, Allegra pulled the jerkin closed with her arms inside and inhaled its leather smell. Cold air leaked in through the armholes, but the garment came down past her hips. The intricate fastenings baffled her, all beautifully woven loops with ties to thread through them. She left them undone and overlapped the jerkin across her front for an extra layer of warmth. She tried to put her skirt back on, too, but she couldn't figure out how it attached.

When she finished bundling up as best as she could, she explored the hollow. Near the edge, the wind picked up. The Anvil dropped down from her feet, and the moonlit desert lay far below, rolling to the horizon. The scene reminded her of Markus, starkly beautiful, often too hot, sometimes icy, and at its best, just warm enough. She returned to the back wall, which hadn't lost the day's warmth, and huddled against it, trying to soak in leftover heat.

Markus appeared around the edge of the hollow, silhouetted against the stars. "You look scared, all curled up like that."

"I am scared," she admitted. "Of you." She tilted her head in the direction his bodyguard had gone. "Of him."

"But why?" Kneeling down, he laid a blanket over her body. With its pattern of light and dark splotches, it did look like an ocelot pelt. A rich scent of animal hide surrounded her.

"My bodyguards protect me," Markus said. "So they protect what belongs to me. He would never hurt you."

Her face burned. "I was naked."

"You're wearing a lot. My jerkin."

She didn't argue. She was too cold. Maybe in Jazid, people considered this a lot of clothes for a woman.

Markus rolled several rocks toward the edge, then swept away the pebbles in front of them. "There. That should be better."

The blanket was beginning to warm her up. "For what?"

"Us." He tugged the blanket away and spread it on the ground. She shivered as he laid her out on the pelt. She curled up on her side for warmth, but he rolled her onto her back and unfolded her arms. When he opened the jerkin, the cold seared her skin.

"Don't be scared," he said, his voice softening. He stretched out on top of her, offering the warmth of his body. "I won't let you freeze." He kissed her, teasing her mouth open so he could go more deeply with his tongue. It wasn't the first time he had done it, but it confused her. She hadn't known men and women kissed that way, and it sent heat through her body.

He murmured against her lips and he rolled the chain around her hips. "This is sexy."

Allegra didn't feel sexy, just uncomfortable. "Your clothes are scratching me." Too late, she realized he might mistake her words for an invitation to undress.

His tongue flicked over her lips. "You'll get used to it."

Used to it? That made no sense. "Don't you undress when you're with a woman?"

He brushed his lips over her forehead. "Never."

"But why?"

Instead of answering, he slid down her body, licking her neck, breasts and belly. Then he went all the way down and kissed her between the legs.

"What are you doing?" Mortified, Allegra tried to roll away.

He gently held her in place, his large hands gripped on her hips. "Relax, night bird. I want you to enjoy it."

"No!" This morning she had been half-asleep, affected by her dream and warm in his tent. None of that was true now, and without his body covering hers, the cold came back with a vengeance. "I—I don't want to do this."

He came back up her body until he was covering her and looked down at her. "What's wrong, kitten? Don't cry."

"I'm n-not." She wiped away the tear on her cheek.

"Allegra." He sounded bewildered. "What do I have to do to make you believe I won't hurt you?"

"Let me go."

"I can't do that." Awkwardly he said, "I am becoming—fond of you."

"You hardly know me."

For a long moment he looked at her. Then he said, "Suppose I were to agree you will no longer be my pleasure girl. Would you consent to love me then? No fighting or crying?"

She was so startled, she almost said, *You would really let me go?* Then she felt like a fool. Of course he wouldn't. "Don't play with me. If we have to do this, just get it over with."

"'Get it over with?' That's terrible."

She had no argument there.

"I want you to enjoy yourself." He brushed his lips over

hers. "Tell me. Would you consent if it meant you would no longer have to be my pleasure girl?"

"Does that mean you would let me go?"

He exhaled. "If you mean would I help you to leave me, then no. I wouldn't. But I would give you legal documents that made it clear you were no longer a pleasure girl."

She clenched the blanket under them. "Why do you say 'pleasure girl'? Do you think calling me that instead of 'slave' makes it all right? Because it doesn't."

"I'm not lying. I mean what I say. Pleasure girl, slave, whatever you want to call it."

"I'm not even sure what you're saying. You're offering to free me, is that it? But you won't help me leave this camp."

"Yes."

So she would still be trapped with him. They were deep in an arid, barren desert where she wouldn't last a day without supplies. Only the legalities of her situation would change. But…if she found a way to escape, he would have no claim on her. In fact, it would dilute his control so much, she didn't believe he would do it. She wanted to hit him for offering her hope when they both knew he would never willingly allow her to leave.

"I don't believe you would let me go," she said.

He moved his hands up her sides and grazed his roughened thumbs over her breasts. "I want to have you of your own free will. It's worth a lot to me, even as much as I paid for you. If freeing you is what it takes to win your consent, I'll do it."

"You're just saying that."

"I keep my word." His voice cooled. "If you think other-wise, you know nothing about me."

Well, she didn't. If she had learned anything, though, it was this: he had far more depth than she had believed in that excruciating moment when she had first seen him. The brutal killer she expected had never appeared; instead she faced a complex man who had a great deal of good in him, even greatness. She felt out of her league with Markus, faced with a powerful leader in a culture so at odds with her own, she could barely deal with it, let alone judge the nuances of his attitudes.

She spoke carefully. "If you have documents that say you own me, will you have new ones drawn up saying you've freed me?"

He didn't hesitate. "Yes."

"When?"

"As soon as we go back to camp," Markus said. "When we reach the base, I'll ask the atajazid to approve them."

"What if he says no?"

Markus scowled at her. "He's nine years old. He's not going to tell me what I can do in my personal life."

"Are you sure?"

"No," he admitted. "But it would be as out of character for him as it would have been for me to tell my father such things when I was nine."

She wasn't so certain Markus wouldn't have tried. Whether his father would have listened was another story, but the point was moot. As a child he couldn't have controlled his father's actions. The same wasn't true with the child king. The atajazid had the power to refuse him. Maybe Markus wanted that to happen.

What else could go wrong? "Would you 'forget' to tell anyone I was no longer your slave?"

"I'll tell whoever you ask me to. My guards. My officers. Even Yargazon, if you want."

That felt like a punch in the stomach. "Would that mean Yargazon could take me as his slave girl?"

"No!" Anger snapped in his voice. "I would never let that sadist touch you. Neither him nor any other man here. Ever."

His vehemence surprised her. He and Yargazon obviously worked well together. His father and the General had shared women, which implied his father had accepted Yargazon's cruelty, even participated. And Markus had loved his father. She hadn't expected him to condemn Yargazon's private life. She also had the impression that after that one time, when Markus fathered his son, he had never again joined the General in taking a woman. In fact, she thought Markus was a far kinder man inside than he let show. What that said about this "bargain," she didn't know. He had made it nearly impossible for her to leave. With what he knew about Jazidian women, he might assume she would stay with him rather than venture into the desert alone. If he believed that, though, he knew nothing about her.

If she agreed to lie with him in return for his rewriting the documents, it was still coercion. But she could think of worse prices to pay for her freedom than to let this sensual man do what he wanted—*if* he was telling the truth.

"If you're making this up," Allegra said, "I'll fight you every day for the rest of my life."

"I'm not lying." He kissed the tip of her nose. "Say yes."

"If you undress."

He lifted his head. "What?"

"Take off your clothes."

"No! Why would I do that?"

"Are you afraid?" she asked, genuinely curious.

"Of course not."

"Is it about control? You feel vulnerable when you take them off." She certainly understood that reaction.

"I'm never vulnerable." He paused for several moments. "It's too cold."

She knew it was a false excuse. "But it's all right for me to freeze? I'm supposed to believe that someone who can't see the hypocrisy in that will keep his word to me?"

"Hell and damnation," Markus growled. "If I take off my blasted clothes, will you consent?"

"Yes. I will."

"All right." He sounded surprised. "But give me a kiss first." He laughed softly. "To build my courage up."

Allegra smiled. "All right." The thought of him needing courage to take off his clothes had its own charm.

He nibbled at her lips. His body pressed on her, and rocks poked her back. After a moment, though, his hands went still.

He raised his head, and his eyes caught glints from the star-light. He exhaled, stirring the disarrayed curls on his forehead.

"I can't do this," he said.

Her heartbeat lurched. Did he mean undressing—or freeing her? "Can't do what?"

"Lie with you under these conditions."

"You promised!"

Markus sat back with his knees on either side of her hips. "It's wrong for me to do it this way."

When she started to shiver, he slid to the wall and held out his hand. Shaking, she went to him. He put her between his legs and wrapped her in both his jerkin and the blanket. Curving into his body, she folded her arms inside the warmth of his embrace.

"Does this mean you won't let me go?" she asked.

"I never said I would let you go."

"Right," she said bitterly. At least he hadn't forced her to go through with the charade. It was especially hard because he *had* chosen to do the right thing and tell her the truth. She didn't want to see good in him, not when he had stolen her life.

"I meant what I said about the bargain," he told her. "I still do."

Allegra froze. She must have heard wrong. "You would let me leave even now? And tell your guards not to stop me?"

"You shouldn't walk around alone," he said gruffly. "It isn't safe in an army, especially when you're one of the only women." Then he added, "But I'll tell my guards about your change in status."

That didn't sound quite right. "You mean that you no longer own me. But I have your protection."

Markus held her head against his chest and stroked her hair. "You'll always have my protection."

Her pulse stuttered. "What aren't you telling me?"

He answered in an oddly quiet tone. "As soon as I prepare the documents, you'll no longer be my slave."

Then he said, "You will be my wife."

CHAPTER 9
A KING'S REFUGE

Of all the responses she had expected—tricks, lies, force—that had never been one of them. "Don't taunt me!"

"I'm not." He was tracing his finger over the ridges of her ear, touching her as he always did, as if he couldn't stop, couldn't get enough.

"It's crazy," she said. "I won't."

"You know, Allegra," he said wryly. "Most women, upon being told they are to become a queen, don't say, 'It's crazy. I won't.'"

"Don't be cruel."

"Making you queen is cruel?"

"You can't make me a queen. You aren't a king."

"Consort to the Prince Regent, then. It's essentially the same thing." His voice lightened. "Unless you plan on marrying the atajazid. Then you could be queen."

"This isn't funny."

"Taking you as my wife isn't supposed to be funny."

"And you just had this idea?"

"Actually I decided this morning after we made love." After a moment, he said, "No, I think I decided when you threw wine in my face."

Allegra blinked. "That makes no sense."

"I know." Markus sounded as confused as she felt. "Nothing about my reactions to you makes sense." He rested his cheek on top of her head. "I need to marry someone. I am thirty-six years old and have no heirs. You're a good choice."

"I can't imagine *one* reason why I would be a good choice."

"You're perfect," he said. "A man in my position needs a woman who will give him strong, tall, intelligent sons. That's how we pick our wives. It's why all the men of the House of Onyx are strong, tall and intelligent."

"Well, goodness," she said. "That was a moving declaration of love." Then she added, "Besides, I'm neither strong nor tall."

He rubbed his cheek on her hair. "I like your size. You fit just right with me. And strength can be of character rather than physique. A man should marry a woman who makes him more than he is. As much as I hate it, you do that, even when I wish you would be quiet."

She felt as if she were sinking into a quagmire. "I'm not a brood mare. And I'm not a mirror for your reflection."

"You see, no one else would dare tell me that. I wouldn't tolerate it from anyone else." He blew out a gust of air. "With you, I don't know what happens. Something is wrong with me. I would think you used a spell, but you obviously hate me, so why enchant me? None of this is sensible. Yet I can't think of anything else. Only a few days with you, and I'm turned upside down."

"You want to marry someone who hates you?"

"Apparently so."

How *did* she feel about him? He angered her—and made her laugh. Just when she was convinced he was hopeless, he would surprise her with his sensitivity. She could see the true leader in him, not the hard exterior he presented to his men, the severity his culture demanded, but a greater man within. And yes, she desired him. He was the most sensuous man she had ever met. Unfortunately he was also the most over-bearing and arrogant.

"I'm afraid of you," she said. "And I hate the way you control everything I do. But I—I don't hate you."

"It's a beginning," he murmured. "Maybe in time you'll come to care."

In time. He had never intended to offer her a choice. She felt as if walls were closing in. "You let me think I could leave."

"If you could convince someone to help you." He held her close, one hand on her stomach under the blanket and the other around her shoulders. "I doubt any sane man in Jazid would help my consort leave. He'd know I would execute him."

"Markus, no! You mustn't."

"I would kill any man who took you away from me." He lifted her chin so she was looking into his face. The moon had set, leaving only a cold brilliance of stars to silver his features. "When we see the atajazid, I'll ask for his blessing. Then I'll march our men into Taka Mal and put the atajazid on the Topaz Throne. When we've added their army to our own, we'll drive Cobalt's forces out of Jazid and retake the Onyx Throne. For *my* king. My brother. The boy I swore to protect. We will do this, Allegra, and you will sit by my side."

"No! I don't want any part of it."

"Yet you have one." His voice quieted. "When I'm with you, it changes me, and I don't like it, but for some reason I don't want it to stop."

"Why? Why me?"

"I don't *know.*" He touched his fingers to hers under the blanket. "You challenge me. You defy me. You demand I be more than I am. And yes, damn it, I want you so much, I can't think when you're near me."

She felt as if she were drowning. "I can't handle this."

"You'll have a good life, anything I can provide."

"I want to provide for myself. Not be your bird in a cage."

"But you're a beautiful night bird." He brushed back a curl that had straggled into her face. Then he leaned against the wall, holding her in the warmth generated by his body. "Sleep if you can. Tomorrow I'll have the documents prepared."

"You want to sleep here?"

He chuckled. "My tent is full of smelly, snoring men."

Allegra smiled wanly. She couldn't sleep in this place of stone, especially not after what he had just told her. Yet despite everything, almost the moment she leaned into him and closed her eyes, a blanket of exhaustion settled over her....

★ ★ ★

Cold prickled Allegra's face, bringing her awake. The blanket had slipped off, and the night's chill bit into her. She and Markus had slumped to the ground, she with her back against his front, he with his arms around her. A stone ridge jutted into her thigh, and she tasted dust. She lifted her head, remembering what Markus had told her. Consort. It seemed little different from pleasure girl, except their children would be legitimate. She had a feeling that mattered a great deal to him.

Markus was asleep, perhaps an aftereffect of her spell or maybe simply because exhaustion had overcome his insomnia. In slumber, his face relaxed, gentling his features, bringing out the beauty that his normal visage disguised. Such a handsome man. Confusing, though. She didn't understand why he wanted her. Insulting him seemed to have had the opposite effect from what she had intended.

She lifted her hand to touch his face, then stopped. Yesterday he had given her pleasure. She may not have fully realized it was him until they were nearly finished, but at some level she had known it wasn't Tanner in her dream. She had yet to sort out how she felt about it. That didn't matter, though, for he was fast asleep and she wasn't, which meant she could leave. She stood up and headed for the entrance to the hollow. She needed to find a shape and sing his guards to sleep.

"Allegra?" Markus pushed up on his elbows. "Bah," he grumbled. "I have dust in my nose."

She stopped halfway to the edge of the hollow.

"I've a guard at the top of the path," he said, watching her. "And I checked myself. No curves, circles or spheres are anywhere on top of the Anvil. Nothing except you, me and rocks."

She went back and knelt next to him. "You have dust in your nose because we slept in the middle of the wildlands."

He pushed at his bangs, tangling them on his forehead. A whiff of his soap drifted to her. At least he kept clean. Given the way some of his soldiers smelled, she appreciated such favors. She would have liked to dump the rest of them in a big tub.

"Why are you smiling?" Markus asked. "It's luminous, like seeing the sun at night."

Allegra touched her lips, surprised to find them curved. "I was thinking your men needed baths."

He laughed quietly. "Probably." Stretching his arms, he cracked his joints. "It'll be dawn in less than an hour. We should get back."

Allegra didn't move. For once, he wasn't pressuring her. Without that influence, she might find out if what had happened yesterday was a fluke. *Did* she want him? Maybe it was only the miradella affecting her, but she wanted to know. Before she had time to change her mind, she leaned forward and kissed him.

Markus went very still. For a moment, he didn't react. Then he put his arms around her and pulled her forward until she was straddling his lap, her knees on either side of his body. When she felt his erection through his trousers, a mixture of arousal and panic flickered through her.

Just see what happens. It wouldn't change her wish to go home, but her life with him would be so much more bearable if she didn't feel forced every time he came to her as her husband.

Markus opened the jerkin and slid one hand around her waist, but he kept her in his lap with the blanket around her body. She held him close, her arms around his torso, and breathed in his scent, soap and musk. He smelled good, even his sweat. She was too nervous to know what to do, but her lack of experience didn't seem to bother him. He grasped her hips and rubbed her against his erection while he dusted kisses down her neck. When he reached down to unfasten his trousers, though, she caught his hand.

She tugged up the hem of his undershirt. "Take this off."

He regarded her with a drowsy, sensual gaze. Bedroom eyes. "You really want me to undress?"

When Allegra gave a shy nod, he pulled the undershirt over his head. His muscles flexed in the process, and watching them, she felt warmer than she had all night. He lifted her off his lap, setting her at his side, and pulled off his boots and trousers. He started to pull her back into his lap, but she put her hand against his shoulder.

"Lie down," she murmured. "On your back."

"Why?" He kept trying to lift her to straddle him. His eyes were only half-open, and his breath was coming faster.

"I want to look at you," she said.

"You do?"

"Yes."

"Oh." He seemed startled, then intrigued. "All right."

He spread out the ocelot blanket and lay down on his back. Starlight sheened his body. Allegra sat next to him, supporting her weight on one arm, and took in the sight as if he were a draught of wine: his wide shoulders, muscular chest and flat stomach. His erection in its nest of black curls. She had never realized an aroused man looked that way, and it excited her.

"You're beautiful," she said.

Markus groaned as if she were tormenting him. He rolled on his side and pulled her down onto her back. As he stretched out on top of her, he pushed apart her thighs. Even with the miradella affecting her, she wanted to pull away. She had never felt attractive, yet he treated her as if she were irresistible temptation. He got up on his knees, drawing her with him, until he was sitting on his haunches with her thighs on either side of his hips, her back arched over his arm and her head hanging back, leaving her nipples pointing upward like an invitation. He suckled her breasts, and ripples of sensation went through her.

"Markus, please." She didn't know whether she was asking him to slow down or go faster.

"That's it, kitten," he whispered. "Stay with me." He brought her up and embraced her, then he lifted her hips and brought them down, entering her. She held on, hugging him while they rocked together, slowly at first, then faster. She kept building, wanting him more, until she couldn't take it any longer.

When Allegra cried out, Markus groaned into her hair

and laid her down, on her back, lowering his body on top of her, still moving, steady and fast. He gave a final, huge thrust and pinned her to the ground while his hips jerked. Then, with an exhale, he collapsed on top of her.

Allegra closed her eyes as the tremors in their bodies subsided. For a while she didn't think. She felt languorous. Content. Eventually he slid over to her side and laid his head next to hers. "Beautiful night bird," he murmured. "So lovely."

She rolled her head against his. "I can't be both a bird and a kitten. Cats hunt birds."

"Then I'm a satiated lion." He pulled the blanket over them, throwing his leg across hers so they could both fit under the half of it they weren't lying on.

As Allegra drifted, Markus lay still, breathing deeply. He gave a snore, then jerked his head and mumbled, "Mustn't sleep." After a while, he sighed. "We have to go."

Markus slowly sat up, letting the blanket fall over Allegra. She watched him dress, wondering if he had any idea what aesthetic things his muscles did when they flexed. When he reached for the jerkin, though, she tugged it away.

"It's so cold," she said, sitting up so she could pull the jerkin around her. "And I can't get that skirt on."

"You can keep the jerkin. I have a lot of them." He smiled at her. "I've never removed my clothes that way with a woman. It was odd. But pleasant. I love the way your skin feels on mine."

"You *never* undress when you make love?"

"No man does."

"Of course they do!"

"Not in Jazid."

"Why ever not?"

He started to answer, then stopped. "You'll get mad at me. And right now I feel quite fine. I don't want to argue."

So it was one of those things. "Is this something you came up with, or something that's true for all men here?"

"All men." His smile turned languid. "Though I doubt I'm the first to discover how pleasant breaking that custom can be."

Well, the customs of a country weren't his fault. "I won't get mad at you."

"Humans wear clothes," he said. "Animals don't."

"What?"

"You said you wouldn't get mad."

"You take mine off when you make love to me." In fact, he was *always* taking them off.

"Men are human."

"And women are animals?" It was astonishing that he could actually look her straight in the eye and spout such horse manure.

"Legally a woman is above a goat but below a horse."

"I can't believe you said that."

"Ah, night bird, let's not argue." He drew her into his arms, sitting side by side with her.

She pushed back from him, her palms against his shoulders. "You just called me an animal."

"It is Jazid law," he said firmly.

She glared at him. "Yes, well, then men must be below pigs."

His grin flashed. "Oink."

"Oh, stop."

"Allegra, of course I think you're human." He tried to pull her back. "But the laws have been with us for centuries."

Although she kept her hands on his shoulders, this time she didn't push back. "It's about control. If you're dressed and I'm not, it makes me vulnerable."

"I suppose. If we were attacked, I would be better prepared to defend us."

"Attacked?" She gaped at him. "You think you're likely to be attacked when you're with a woman?"

"Of course. A man is vulnerable then." He shrugged. "I never thought much about it. I just like being dressed when you're not."

"But why?"

"Maybe for the reasons you said. Your vulnerability is erotic."

"For you, maybe. Not me." She lifted her hands, then dropped them in frustration. "It's this country. It's too harsh, too cold. It hurts all of you, even if you can't see that."

"Contrary to what you think, I'm not a blind idiot."

"Markus, I don't think you're an idiot." If he wasn't so smart, it would be easier to escape.

"Gods," he said. "One and a half compliments in one night. I'll fall over in shock."

"One and a half?"

He murmured in her ear. "First you say I have a beautiful body. Now you tell me I'm not stupid. The second counts as half."

She smiled. "I'd better be careful. You'll get cocky." As if he wasn't already the cockiest man she had ever met.

He stared pensively past her at the night beyond the hollow. The hint of dawn showed in the lightening of the eastern horizon. "The thing is, I see the problems we have in Jazid, but not a solution. Except to conquer Taka Mal."

"How does it solve Jazid's problems to attack Taka Mal?" she asked. "I don't understand why men always think they have to kill each other."

His voice softened. "You're so naive."

She frowned at him. "Calling people like me naive is the excuse kings always give for not finding peaceful alternatives."

"Tell me, how many people do you think live in Jazid?"

She blinked at his change of topic. It didn't sound like he was evading her comments, though just coming at them obliquely. She considered his question. Although Jazid was huge, it consisted mostly of inhospitable peaks or the killing desert. Beyond these mountains, a barren wasteland went on and on, a place where no one lived or traveled, until many leagues in the east it met the sea. From the geography she taught her students, she knew most of the population lived in the western edge of Jazid, either as nomads or scattered among villages. They had no centralized capital like Crofts Vale in Aronsdale or the legendary city of Quaaz in Taka Mal.

"The population is about a million, isn't it?" she asked.

Markus gave a bitter laugh. "You aren't even close."

"I thought I had heard that number."

"We let people believe it," he said. "But it's closer to one hundred thousand."

She stared at him. "For the *entire* country?"

"It's a hard land. No one wants to come here. Especially not women, and without women you can't have children." He let out a breath. "Our infant mortality rate is the highest of any country because we have the fewest healers and midwives. We have no guilds to train doctors, as you do in Aronsdale, so we have no doctors. Girl babies die more than boys because boys get better care. Most people never question that bias, and I think many don't see it. Girls who survive into adulthood are sold. More die in childbirth than in any other country because of our execrable medical system. And some situations—" He stopped.

"Yes?" she asked.

He spoke tiredly. "If a man loses a woman due to mistreatment, the law considers it the same as if his livestock dies."

"That's horrible."

"I'm not defending it." He shook his head. "But you have to understand, many of my people feel the way you live in Aronsdale is perverse, like giving inheritance rights to animals."

Saints almighty. "Is that what you think?"

He touched her cheek. "No. You're very human to me."

Berating him for centuries of traditions wouldn't solve anything. He was a product of all that he described, yet he seemed able to step outside of it and look at the effects.

"I'm surprised your women don't run away," she said.

"Some do," he admitted. "A few go to Aronsdale, but most choose Taka Mal because the cultures are similar. The numbers that leave aren't huge, but it's enough to increase our imbalance. We've had very few wars in modern times.

Except for the losses in the Battle of the Rocklands two years ago, none of our men die in combat."

"That's an awful way to balance a population."

"Yes. It is." He rubbed his eyes. "Now consider this. Our brutal, inhospitable land has incredibly rich deposits of jewels and minerals. We supply almost all the gems and precious ores in the settled lands. But without anyone to mine them, what good does it do us? Hell, my father used to give away huge tracts of land to anyone who would immigrate. In return, they gave him twenty percent of their profits. Even with that, it is the most lucrative trade in any land. Do you have any idea of the wealth owned by some Jazid miners? We have a constant influx of men. Some return to their own countries when they've made their fortune, but many stay."

"So the imbalance grows."

He nodded. "If it happened only in one or two generations, it wouldn't be a disaster. But this has gone on for *centuries.*" He leaned his head against hers. "Seventy thousand men live here. Most are old enough to want a woman. Those with power and wealth have first choice, and many take the younger women, which leaves a population of angry, restless young men. This, in a country with thirty thousand women, less than ten thousand of marriageable age. You do the math."

"It's impossible," she said. "Jazid can't survive."

"So you see. Taka Mal also has an imbalance, but their population is forty-five percent female. And they've over two million people." He lifted his head and looked over the desert, toward the border. "The solution is obvious. We conquer Taka Mal."

"Markus, listen. You can't destroy all those people's lives, killing their men and taking their women." She wanted to shake his shoulders. "The 'obvious' solution is to change what causes the problems. Treat women like human beings. Give them a reason to stay. Make Jazid a place where men are willing to bring their families. Instead of spreading the problems to other countries, why the bloody hell don't you try to solve them?"

He met her gaze, his own dark and angry. "Why should we be the ones to change? Taka Mal betrayed us, and my father *died*. They live as if they are right and we are wrong, and who the 'bloody hell' are you to say that's true? To us, your people are immoral."

"That's crazy."

"Why is what I believe crazy and what you believe right?" He exhaled and went on in a quieter voice. "I see why you hate this way of life, even if sometimes I seem as dense as that proverbial pig. But even if I wanted to change Jazid— and I'm not convinced I should—I can't just decree it to happen. Taka Mal has taken centuries to reach the point where they are now, and her people have resisted every step of the way. Their queen seeks even more changes, but she walks an edge and she could fall so easily. She *knows* that. She takes great care in changes she brings about, maybe even more than a man because she faces such hostility for holding a throne in a country where traditionally women have had much less power than men."

Allegra knew she was out of her depth. In her short life, she hadn't thought much about politics even in her own country. "You need a wife with the experience to sit by your side and help you. Not a girl some nomads found in the woods."

"You're exactly what I need." He gave a wry smile. "You'll berate me every time I make a decision you think is stupid. I may even have to admit you're right."

"I don't want that role."

"I know. But you have it."

"No!" When it came to nations and dynasties and wars, what could she say? The last crisis she had dealt with had been an argument between two dairymaids that her mother asked her to help settle so the girls would go back to work. "I'm no queen, Markus."

He watched her pensively. "Do you know why I want to marry you when I've never wished to take a wife before? It isn't only that I've never desired a woman as I do you. It's not even your mage abilities, though that turned out to be one hell of an extra. Other women I took to my bed thought about—well, I don't know. It was hard to talk to them. They spent a lot of time making themselves beautiful and trying to please me, but they had so little to say. What they desired most seemed to be riches, pretty baubles and an ease of life. What do you say? That I need a woman by my side who can help me with the problems Jazid faces. That, Allegra, is why you should be my wife."

She didn't know how to answer. She had thought he *wanted* a woman who spent all her time trying to please him. This wasn't the unfeeling overlord she had seen in the auction tent. Behind that facade lived a man of intelligence and courage. And he had chosen *her* as his queen.

She spoke quietly. "You should tell the atajazid how you feel about the problems Jazid faces. You're his guardian, yes?"

"So will you be, after we're married."

That threw her. "I'm not qualified."

"You mentioned something last night about reading to your students. Do you teach children his age?"

"Well, yes. But that's not the same."

"It doesn't need to be." He stretched out his arms. "If we are going to see him today, we should get going."

"Today?"

"Yes." Then he said, "Today you'll meet the most fortunate—and unfortunate—child in the settled lands."

Allegra didn't realize they had reached their destination until Markus indicated a large ridge that cut across their path. It buckled up into the bright daylight like a fat wrinkle in the land. Beyond it, the Fractured Mountains rose as if the Shadow Dragon had thrown them down from the sky, cracking them against the desert in gigantic broken spires.

"The atajazid's camp is on the other side," Markus told her.

Camp. Allegra suspected the boy had many soldiers with him, perhaps as many as rode with Markus, possibly even more.

Sitting astride Shadow with Allegra in front of him, Markus rode up the slope. The air smelled different than in Aronsdale, more arid, wilder. The wind increased near the top of the ridge and tossed her hair against Markus, a bright contrast to the sun-darkened skin of his arms. His company rode around them, and the thunder of hooves on the stony ground vibrated through her. It seemed to come from everywhere, growing louder each moment. After the silence of the last three days, the noise was unsettling. She would have thought a freak thunderstorm had hit the land, but the washed-out sky remained relentlessly clear.

They reached the top of the ridge.

Markus reined in Shadow and surveyed the land below. His company halted, as well, fanning out around and behind him. Allegra stared out—and felt the blood drain from her face.

They had come upon an ocean of soldiers. Men filled the land, from the bottom of this ridge to the distant base of the Fractured Mountains. Humanity swirled around great, jagged columns of stone in rivers of people.

"Saints almighty," Allegra said.

"That's my little army," Markus said.

She gave a ragged laugh. *"Little?"*

A fierce satisfaction saturated his voice. "About three thousand men. Another five hundred tenders." He raised his hand, and when he gave a shout, his company surged down the ridge. Two color bearers rode up to flank him, each carrying a flag with the gold dragon of Jazid on a field of red and black triangles. They rode gorgeous, long-legged Jazidian Blacks, the most coveted horses in the settled lands. Allegra had never known anyone who could afford such a spectacular animal. But then, these were the people who bred and raised them.

Markus untied Allegra's robe and pulled it off her shoulders.

"Don't!" She grabbed at the robe. "Everyone will see."

"That's the point." He tugged off the robe and tossed it to Izad, who was riding on their left, behind the flag bearer.

Allegra's face burned. She had on nothing except fur boots, a translucent violet skirt that barely reached her thighs, and a skimpy halter encrusted with jewels. Gold bands circled her upper arms, and a gold collar curved around her neck. Markus wore a black jerkin and trousers, boots, a belt encrusted with gold and a huge sword on his back. A massive armband circled his left bicep. It all felt surreal to Allegra, as if some capricious trickster had thrust her into this world of violent, barbaric splendor.

He displayed her like a trophy. No, not "like." She *was* his trophy. *Bah.* She had hoped she might use the armbands or collar for spells, but with his savvy intellect, he had guessed that if he bent the shapes until he distorted the curve, it rendered them useless. Even without the distortion, the armbands wouldn't have worked because they didn't form a complete circle, and she couldn't fix the collar because she couldn't take it off. He might have decided to call her a queen instead of a slave, but she saw no difference in how he treated her.

However, he apparently *hadn't* guessed she could use shapes besides curves. She kept a lookout for boxes or similar forms she could touch. She had tried with the faceted gems on her clothes, but either they weren't ideal enough shapes or she didn't have the skill for such unusual forms.

They passed sentries, men in leather and metal armor. High on the rock pillars, more sentries stood with bows and arrows. It didn't surprise her that the soldiers wore only short leather kilts with jerkins, thin robes over their clothes, and hoods or scarves for their heads. In this heat, they had to protect their skin, but anything more could cause heatstroke. In the basin, the army overflowed the land, men, horses, carts and tents everywhere. The soldiers saluted Markus as he rode past.

"So many people," Allegra said.

"Before the war, my father had five thousand," he said. "Taka Mal lost many men, too. They have about two and a half thousand left, and also a thousand men that Emperor Cobalt moved from Jazid to Quaaz in Taka Mal." He ruffled her hair. "You'll like the Topaz Palace in Quaaz. It's beautiful, especially the mosaics."

She didn't want to hear that, for she would see that palace only if his army took the Topaz Throne for their boy-king.

Yargazon rode up alongside them. "It's good to be back," he said to Markus. He glanced at Allegra with eyes as hard as onyx, then looked away as if dismissing a detail of no consequence.

Allegra wished he would leave. Ever since she had touched his mood and felt that terrifying mix of hatred and lust, she had wanted to stay as far from him as possible.

"We need to bring in the outlying companies," Markus said. "We should be ready to ride soon."

"Two years was a long time," Yargazon said. "It will be a relief to take action."

"A long time to wait for vengeance."

"Your father was a man above all others," Yargazon said. "His name will be remembered."

Markus's voice warmed. "My brother's, too."

Although Allegra couldn't see Markus's face, she could almost hear his smile. She had thought he might resent the boy who had inherited the throne that should have been Markus's by the timing of his birth. It sounded, though, as if he genuinely liked his brother.

"Indeed," Yargazon said. "Did you know he bested Major Gaizz at sword practice last month? He's going to be as good as your father. Maybe better." The General shook his head. "Cobalt was lucky to defeat Ozar. Your father was an unparalleled swordsman."

"It wasn't luck," Markus said. "I saw their fight. Saints, Dusk, I've *never* seen a man move as fast as Cobalt. It was unreal. He put out eleven of my father's men first. Granted, he was on horseback and they were on foot. But it was unnatural. He seemed to know where they would strike before they moved."

Yargazon rubbed his chin. "You aren't the only one who has said the way he fights seems unnatural."

"People claim his wife is a sorceress." Markus set his hand on Allegra's shoulder. "I suppose he could be a warlock."

Yargazon laughed curtly. "I'm sure the kings of Aronsdale would like to hear you say that, with all their nonsense about their wives being mages."

"Maybe it isn't nonsense," Markus said.

Allegra felt as if a band were constricting around her chest. She wished he would stop talking about it with Yargazon.

"Then why haven't they overrun the settled lands with these mage queens of theirs?" Yargazon shook his head. "You've seen how weak Aronsdale men are. They let their women drain their vitality." He glanced at Allegra, and his mouth tightened. "A man must take a strong hand with such a woman."

Markus wound his hand in Allegra's hair and jerked back her head so she was looking up at him. "What do you think of that, night bird?"

She tried to pull away her head, but he kept his hold, forcing her head back. "Don't," she said.

"Don't what?" Markus said, his gaze dark, his smile cold.

"Don't pull my hair. It hurts."

"Then be respectful," he murmured.

She wanted to slap him. "Don't, please," she said through gritted teeth.

Markus chuckled and let go of her hair. "Dusk, I do believe she doesn't like me."

Yargazon smiled, an expression far uglier than most scowls. "Good. You must be stern with her."

Allegra wanted to spit in Yargazon's face. She even started to gather the saliva. Then she thought, *Choose your battles wisely.* If she spit at him, he would expect Markus to punish her, and Markus obviously didn't want to lose face. The result wasn't worth the energy the fight would take from her. So she swallowed the saliva. But Markus's behavior hurt, especially after how tender he had been with her this morning. In those moments, she had seen him in a different light, a man she could honor, perhaps even feel affection for. She had been a fool.

Get over it, she thought, angry at herself. She wanted him to be different because if she didn't escape this mess, she could be with him for the rest of her life. He had told his top officers he intended to marry her, but she had yet to see any documents changing her status. Of course none of them expressed open disapproval. She could tell, though, that Yargazon thought she didn't deserve the title.

Allegra couldn't imagine Markus as the husband she had dreamed of—a friend, partner and confidant. A lover, yes; even now, thinking of his hands on her body aroused her. But it wasn't enough. He wanted a prize. A trophy. She wanted a life.

Markus indicated a cluster of men riding in their direction. "Dusk, look. It's Ozi's honor guard." His arm brushed Allegra's cheek, and the faint smell of his sweat wafted over her.

Ozi? It sounded like an odd name for someone who merited an honor guard. "Who is Ozi?" she asked.

Markus spoke near her ear, his breath stirring her hair. "You may never use that name. Unless he gives you permission."

She crossed her arms. "Well, since I have no other name, I can't call him anything else, can I?" He was probably talking about his brother, but she wasn't going to acknowledge anything after the way Markus had treated her.

"God of the Dragon," Yargazon said. "Markus, just *hit* her."

Markus lifted his head. "Well, it's true, you know. She doesn't know who we're talking about."

"It's irrelevant," Yargazon said. "You need to teach her respect. Better yet, teach her not to speak at all."

"And you need to learn to speak *to* me," Allegra told him, "instead of talking about me as if I'm not here."

Yargazon's face hardened as he jerked up his arm. He caught his reflex before he landed the blow, but his icy gaze terrified her. If Markus hadn't been here, she had no doubt the General would beat her senseless.

"Allegra." Markus spoke in a low voice. "Not now." He motioned toward the approaching retinue. "They are part of the bodyguard for His Magnificence, Ozarson Falcon Onyx, Atajazid D'Az of the House of Onyx, the Shadow-Dragon King." In a lighter tone, he added, "My little brother."

"Oh." She had no argument with their atajazid; he had done nothing to her. She felt sorry for him. Given the boy's pivotal role in the politics of the settled lands, many powerful leaders wanted to find him, most so they could kill him. He was a threat to everyone: Cobalt the Dark, Queen Vizarana of Taka Mal, King Jarid of Aronsdale, and saints only knew who else.

"Come," Markus said. "Let us go meet the true king of Jazid."

CHAPTER 10

JASMINE

The pavilion was no less beautiful for being a temporary structure in the camp of an outlawed military force. It resembled a pagoda with walls of a thin, translucent wood that took on a golden glow in the late afternoon sunlight. Although Markus had told her every structure in the camp could be taken down and stowed away, this one had a more permanent appearance. Dust drifted in the sunrays, and the Fractured Mountains towered behind the pavilion.

Markus rode with Yargazon, Ardoz and Bladebreak, surrounded by the atajazid's retinue, eight warriors in helmets with black plumes that rippled in the wind. Their Jazidian Blacks were bridled in red and black, with saddles edged in gold. Two guards flanked the entrance of the pavilion and both saluted as Markus dismounted. They stared at Allegra, and her face heated, surely turning the color of a rose.

Markus reached up for her. "Slide down."

Self-conscious with everyone watching, she slid into his arms, holding her skirt down with one hand. He set her in front of him and smoothed the skirt, his hand lingering on her bottom.

"Don't do that," she said in a low voice.

He didn't answer, but he did stop. Stable boys swirled around the horses, taking reins and the animals away. Yargazon, Ardoz and Bladebreak joined Markus, and they all walked to the pavilion. Allegra stood by herself, unsure what to do. Follow him? If he couldn't treat her with courtesy, the hell with him.

Someone touched her shoulder. With a start, she looked up at Lieutenant Borjan.

He lifted his hand to the pavilion. "I'll take you."

"Does His Majesty live here?" Allegra asked as they headed toward the structure.

"Not the atajazid," Borjan said. "Colonel Bladebreak. His wife will prepare you for your audience with the king."

Bladebreak was *married?* The bastard. He had felt no qualms at the prospect of raping Allegra, even looked forward to it, yet here he had a wife waiting for him? She hoped he rotted in the pit of some vile slime.

As far as Bladebreak, Ardoz and Yargazon knew, they had drunk too much wine that night and fallen asleep. It scared her the way Bladebreak and the General watched her today, as if speculating whether Markus would invite them to hear her sing again. She suspected Markus noticed, as well. She had a feeling he wanted the marriage to take place immediately because a man's wife was off-limits. Of course, he could have quit showing her off, but saints forbid he should give up his precious status.

The pavilion had no door, just a curtain of jewels that swayed in the wind. Inside, the air was still. White ceramic bowls of oil with flames in them rested on ornate lamp-stands and added radiance to the glow of the sun coming through the walls. Wicker chairs with blue and white cushions stood around a table tiled in blue and green. Drapes and carpets in marine colors gave the room the feel of an underwater grotto.

"It's lovely," Allegra said, surprised to find such beauty in so desolate a place.

Borjan smiled. "All His Majesty's top men have such quarters. You will, too."

She nodded absently, her attention caught by a girl across the pavilion. Glossy black hair poured over her red silk robe, and she wore a necklace embedded with rubies. The chains of a halter similar to Allegra's showed on one shoulder where her robe had slipped. She knelt in front of Bladebreak, her eyes downcast. He stood in his dusty clothes, a day's growth of beard on his chin, and watched her with satisfaction. His wife? Allegra gritted her teeth. It grated that he expected this girl to kneel to him after he had hoped to assault another woman just the night before.

The rest of Markus's party stayed on the other side of the room, as if an invisible barrier separated them from Blade-break and his wife. Four of the atajazid's honor guard had remained outside; the other four were here with Markus. Probably they were his honor guard, as well, given that he was the fugitive sovereign until his brother came of age.

Yargazon and Ardoz stood talking with Markus. They were three of a kind, all with the height and powerful musculature valued in Jazidian men. The sun had darkened their faces, and the dark stubble of their beards showed less than a day after they had shaved. Yargazon was twenty years older than Markus, and Ardoz at least ten, but they all had the hale physique of youth. To Allegra, the greatest difference between Yargazon and Markus showed in the harsh lines around Yargazon's mouth and the laugh lines that crinkled Markus's eyes. Markus had frightened her the first time she saw him, but that had come in part from her expectations, and she had misinterpreted his guarded demeanor as a lack of compassion. She doubted his face would ever show the cruelty stamped on Yargazon's features.

Bladebreak spoke to his wife in a low voice, and she rose to her feet, her eyes downcast. Allegra wondered why she wouldn't look at him. She hoped it wasn't another wretched Jazidian custom. If Markus expected similar from her, he would be waiting a long time.

The girl turned toward Allegra, and Bladebreak lifted his arm. Allegra wasn't certain if he was beckoning her or giving Borjan a sign. She glanced up at the lieutenant.

"They want you to go over," he said. "I must stay here. No man may enter that side of the pavilion except her husband."

"Oh." Allegra had no desire to go anywhere near Bladebreak. She glanced at Markus, but he was deep in conversation.

Ill at ease, Allegra went to the colonel. His wife watched

with dark, enigmatic eyes that revealed nothing of what she felt. She was smaller and younger than Allegra, with delicate features and eyes too large for her face.

When Allegra reached them, they all stood waiting, like some bizarre tableau. The woman's eyes widened, and Allegra had the distinct impression she had horrified this fragile, lovely person. Puzzled, she glanced at Bladebreak—and almost stepped back from the fury in his gaze. Well, now what?

Belatedly it occurred to her that they expected her to kneel. Too bad. She stayed put. Standing.

Bladebreak looked beyond her to Markus. The prince continued talking to his generals, for all appearances oblivious to everyone else. Allegra suspected he knew exactly what was happening and pretended otherwise because he didn't want to be involved in Allegra's confrontation with the colonel.

Bladebreak spoke coldly to Allegra. "Jasmine will tend to you in preparation for your audience with the atajazid."

Allegra smiled at his wife. "Jasmine?" she asked.

The girl nodded, her gaze averted as if she couldn't bear to look at someone who had so terribly insulted her husband.

"I'm Allegra," she added, more to irritate Bladebreak than because she thought Jasmine cared.

Bladebreak left them and went to Markus. As the men spoke, Allegra grimaced. Yargazon and Bladebreak were trying to convince Markus of something, no doubt concerning what he should do to her.

As Allegra turned to Jasmine, the girl finally looked at her.

"You must do what they want, or they will hurt you," Jasmine said. She seemed subdued, pulled within herself, so different from Rose T'Ambera.

"Does he hurt you?" Allegra asked.

"He is a fine man," Jasmine said. "A good, strong husband."

Allegra had her own thoughts on that, but she doubted his wife wanted to hear them. "Why do you kneel to him?"

"What else would I do?"

Allegra had numerous suggestions, none of them pleasant for Bladebreak, but she held back. If she said the wrong thing, and the colonel found out, he might vent his anger on his wife because he couldn't touch Markus's consort. What could she tell Jasmine, anyway? Revolt? Right. With women so outnumbered, isolated, uneducated and beaten down, it was a wonder any of them even spoke. The cruel life bred by this cruel land was killing its people, both the men and the women.

"Nothing, I guess," Allegra said. To her relief, everyone else was leaving the pavilion.

"Come." Jasmine smiled shyly. "I will bathe and perfume you. You may wear my bridal dress."

"Goodness," Allegra said. "You don't have to do all that." Bladebreak must have already told her about the wedding.

Jasmine hesitated. "I don't mean to presume. It's just…I never have anyone to talk to."

"You're not presuming," Allegra told her, mortified she had troubled the girl. "It's kind of you to offer your dress, and I would love to visit with you."

Jasmine's face relaxed. "It would be fun. Ivan lets me visit my friends if he is here, if he approves of them and it doesn't interfere with his duties. But that isn't often."

"Ivan?"

"My husband."

Ivan Bladebreak. Even his name was harsh. "Maybe you and I can visit."

"I would be honored, Your Highness."

Allegra reddened. "I'm no 'Highness.'"

"You will be, in less than an hour." Pleasure glowed in her gaze. "You must be excited! To marry Markus Onyx. Women throughout Jazid will envy you."

Allegra was tempted to say, *They can have him.* She didn't, though. She told herself it was because it would upset Jasmine, but in truth, the thought of Markus with another woman bothered her far more than she wanted to admit.

"Jasmine." Allegra chose her words carefully. "When people marry here, do they sign a contract scroll?"

"Of course." Jasmine beckoned her to a stool inlaid with blue and green mosaics. It stood next to a table with a blue porcelain ewer in a white bowl. "The atajazid must witness and accept Prince Markus's contract."

Allegra sat down. "Who decides what goes into the contract?"

Jasmine wet a cloth with water from the ewer. "His Highness and the atajazid will write yours." She set to washing Allegra's face. "You are so lovely. I know of no other woman with your coloring. It's pretty."

"Thank you." At least Jasmine didn't share Yargazon's distaste for people from Aronsdale. "Is it part of the contract that a husband won't have women other than his wife?"

She stopped cleaning Allegra's face. "You mean that the woman will have no other man, yes?"

"No. I mean it for the man."

"I don't think so. But men are expected to be faithful."

"Even prince regents?"

Jasmine wouldn't look at her. "Onyx men are special."

Given what Allegra had heard about Markus's father, she had no desire to know what "special" meant. She tried telling herself she didn't care what Markus did, but it was a lie. She didn't want to think about what her reaction meant, that the idea of Markus with another woman hurt so much.

A memory came to her of his voice: *I would never throw away a woman because she wasn't new and perfect, especially not after I got her pregnant three times.* He had been a little boy when his father lost interest in his mother. It must have hurt a great deal, that he would swear such when his culture probably allowed, even encouraged, him to do exactly as his father had done. It added another layer of complexity to this man she was beginning to realize had far more to him than most anyone else she knew.

Jasmine helped her bathe and pinned up her hair with curls cascading down her neck. Then she brought out the wedding dress. Allegra had hoped it would be just that: a dress. But it covered little more of her than the other outfits. It had the usual hip belt, this one solid gold with diamonds, emeralds and sapphires. Slender chains hung from it to the floor.

When she moved, they swayed, revealing skin, then hiding it. The halter was metal. *All* of it. More gems inlaid it, and a fringe of chains hung from its lower edge against her abdomen. A man had to have dreamed up the blasted outfit; what woman would design metal underwear for herself? The halter constrained her breathing and pushed her breasts together into cleavage. The skirt tangled around her legs. Bah.

"Why are you frowning?" Jasmine dusted powder over the fading bruise on Allegra's face and the traces of the gouge on her stomach, hiding both. "You look beautiful."

"Do women here dress like this all the time?"

Jasmine laughed, a lovely chiming sound. "Not at all. Only when they wish to please the men."

"That figures," Allegra muttered.

"Oh, they are all just like little boys, even the ones with gray hair and wrinkles. We must humor them."

Allegra scowled. "Why, pray tell, must we humor them?"

"It's that pride of theirs," Jasmine said, amused. "They grouse and growl and are quite pleased with themselves."

"I've noticed."

"There." Jasmine stepped back and surveyed her work. "Prince Markus will be speechless when he sees you."

Allegra couldn't imagine Markus ever being speechless. It relieved her, though, that the preparations hadn't taken long. "That wasn't so bad."

"It is fun, yes? I never have a chance to do this anymore, since the colonel brought me here. I never see anyone."

Allegra had never been much for primping, but Jasmine

seemed to enjoy it. With Bladebreak out of the room, she had relaxed, becoming a girl sharing confidences with a friend instead of the constrained wife of one of the army's most powerful officers.

"Are there many women in the camp?" Allegra asked.

"Some wives or concubines," Jasmine said. "A few pleasure girls. Not many, though. After the problems, Prince Markus told the women they had to go home or stay out of sight."

That didn't sound good. "What happened?"

"It was mostly with the tenders." She shifted her weight. "If a woman worked where men could see her, it started fights among the men. Or else they took her away, to share among themselves. Prince Markus was afraid someone would get killed. So he sent the women home." She hesitated. "He sent a few of the men home, too."

"For attacking the women?"

"No." Her face reddened. "Because they were too pretty. It put them in danger."

"Oh." A few days ago, Allegra wouldn't have known what she meant. Now she had a better idea. With so few women, maybe the men sometimes turned to each other. But *Markus?* She had felt the intensity of his desire for her. Yet his loneliness had also been strong. If anything had happened with Ardoz, it had been years ago. She wondered how it would have affected the young prince regent, whose people seemed to see him as the epitome of the intensely masculine Jazidian warrior. His ability to step so far outside that role, even in secret, might help explain why he could also see past the ingrained customs of his culture to understand someone as different as Allegra.

Jasmine brushed the curls on Allegra's neck. "I've never seen such hair. It's sunlight."

"Most people where I live have hair this color."

"You must be so far from home."

Allegra's voice caught. "Too far."

"Aye." Jasmine sighed. "It's hard. But this evening will be exciting, yes? You must be nervous about meeting the atajazid."

"A little," Allegra admitted.

"If you're ready, I'll call the men."

"I guess so." Allegra doubted she would ever be ready. She couldn't believe she was about to be married. She didn't know *how* she felt, except confused.

Jasmine went to the entrance and spoke to a guard outside. His response rumbled, and his silhouette moved away from the pavilion. The day had darkened into sunset, turning the walls crimson. Night-blooming lilies scented the air, which felt cool on Allegra's skin, neither the searing heat of day nor the chill of night.

When she joined Jasmine by the entrance, the girl said, "This is the first wedding I've been to." Another blush tinged her cheeks. "Except my own."

Allegra smiled. "When were you married?"

"Last year. Ivan came through our camp with a company of soldiers to buy supplies and weapons. He saw me drawing water from the spring and spoke to my parents. They wrote the contract that afternoon. My wedding was that night."

It seemed an odd way to form unions, to see someone and marry her that same night. She could imagine what her parents would have said if the nomads had offered them wealth for Allegra. Her mother would have blistered their ears. By Aronsdale law, the nomads had committed crimes by abducting Allegra and robbing her; by Jazid custom, they had robbed Allegra's parents. Either way, she hated that they benefited. She wished she could strike a blow, not just at the nomads who had destroyed her life, but at all those who profited from the misfortune of their victims.

"Were you glad to go with him?" Allegra asked.

"Of course." Jasmine's voice lost its vibrancy. "He is a great man."

If he's so great, Allegra thought, *why do you shrink when he enters the room?* Their marriage wasn't her business, but she liked Jasmine, and neither of them had friends here. Hell, she hadn't seen a woman since she met Rose T'Ambera.

"Do you miss your family?" Allegra asked.

"Always. I may never see them again." Her voice caught. "Ivan says we can't leave here, except to hide somewhere else."

Allegra put her hand on the girl's shoulder. "You'll see them. I'm sure." Softly she added, "Both of us will see home again. Somehow, someway."

A voice outside grumbled, "So where are they?" Several tall silhouettes appeared against the darkening wall of the pavilion.

Allegra frowned at the jeweled curtain separating her from the owner of that voice. "My aggravating groom seems to have arrived."

Jasmine's look turned aghast. "You mustn't speak that way! He might hear."

"It's good for him," Allegra said.

Markus pulled aside the curtain and looked in, his face perplexed. "Are you two coming?"

Jasmine averted her eyes and sank gracefully to her knees. "I am sorry for our delay, Your Highness."

"For saints' sake," Allegra said.

Markus spoke to Jasmine in a gentle voice. "Rise, please. Your husband is waiting outside."

"Yes, Sire." The girl stood and slipped out of the pavilion.

Markus raised an eyebrow at Allegra.

"I'm not going to kneel," she said.

Markus stepped inside and spoke quietly. "When we meet my brother, don't shame me. If you were given an audience with the king of Aronsdale, you would kneel, wouldn't you?"

Allegra had nothing against the atajazid, and it was true, she would kneel to her own king. "I'll respect your protocols for an audience with the atajazid, if that's what you're asking."

"Good." He took her arm, his gaze intent. "Understand me. If you disrespect my brother, there *will* be consequences. I'd rather that not happen."

His words heightened her sense of being trapped. She had no wish to humiliate him in front of his little brother, though. "I'll be careful. Just let me know what I need to do."

Relief showed on his face. "Come, then. Let us meet the Shadow-Dragon King."

CHAPTER 11

OZARSON

The royal pavilion wasn't larger than Bladebreak's, but what it lacked in space it made up for in opulence. Diamonds sparkled in its jeweled curtain, unusually large gems of a remarkable clarity that could have bought an entire farm in Aronsdale. They splintered the rays of the setting sun into rainbows. The roof rose in terraces, light and airy.

The honor guards held the curtain open for Markus and Allegra, also for Yargazon, Bladebreak and Jasmine. Inside, red and gold rugs covered the wooden floor, designed with dragons that roared gold-threaded fire. She saw no chairs; like his brother, the atajazid seemed to prefer low tables surrounded by cushions. Two curved swords were crossed on one wall, their hilts carved from ebony and adorned with gold. Red-glass lamps shaped like dragons sat on black lacquered stands. Dragon braziers glowed in the corners, and incense burned in red-glass stands, giving the air a bittersweet odor that made Allegra wrinkle her nose. It wasn't unpleasant, just different.

Four of the guards entered with them. Even with ten

people in the room, it didn't feel crowded. However, Allegra saw nothing resembling an atajazid, a boy or a shadow dragon anywhere.

The chains of a jeweled curtain in the back wall clinked as a fifth guard entered. Another man followed, and they took posts bracketing the entrance. Allegra stood by Markus, with Bladebreak to her right, and then Jasmine. Yargazon stood on Markus's left. As they waited, the back curtain swayed and then parted.

A boy walked into the room.

Allegra's breath caught. His black curls tousled over his collar just like Markus's hair. He had Markus's large, dark eyes. His red shirt was very much like the one Markus had worn the first time she had seen him, and he wore black trousers with a belt studded by gold. He was tall for his age and slender, though judging from his size, Allegra suspected he would someday fill out with the muscular build so valued in Jazid men.

The brothers didn't look exactly alike, however. Although Ozarson had a child's softer features, it was obvious that when he grew up, he would have a blockier chin, larger nose and heavier brows than Markus. She didn't doubt his appearance would be compelling, but with less of Markus's sheer masculine beauty. It didn't surprise Allegra, if men of the royal family chose wives for strength and intelligence and concubines for beauty. The boy's regal posture had a charming modesty, as if he hadn't quite learned the nuances of presenting himself. When he saw Markus, his smile flashed like the sun breaking through clouds.

One of the guards spoke. "His Magnificence, Atajazid D'az Ozarson of the House of Onyx."

Markus had his hand on Allegra's shoulder, exerting a subtle pressure. As she sank to her knees, he went down on one knee with his arm folded across his thigh. In her side vision, she glimpsed Yargazon and Bladebreak doing the same, their heads bent in deference to their king. It bemused her to watch these powerful, arrogant men kneel to a child.

Footsteps whispered on the carpet, and Allegra looked up to see the atajazid walking toward them, flanked by two men in uniforms. When she met the boy's gaze, he faltered and looked confused. At first she thought it was because he didn't know her. Then one of his guards frowned, and she realized everyone else had their eyes averted. Remembering her promise to Markus, she lowered her gaze.

The boy came to stand before Markus. "You may rise." He had a rich voice, but he sounded so very young. His bodyguards stood a step back, towering over his slender form.

Markus lifted his head and discreetly took Allegra's hand, drawing her to her feet with him. He grinned at his brother. "My greetings, Your Majesty."

"And mine to you." Ozarson was trying to be formal, but a child's eagerness underlaid his words. He glanced at Allegra, and a blush reddened his face.

Following the boy's gaze, Markus said, "I've come to ask your permission to marry."

So this was it. Allegra wondered what he would do if his brother said no.

Ozarson's smile burst out like a candle lighting. "A wife? She's so pretty, Markus! You must marry her right away."

From the boy, the words were sweet rather than coercive, and Allegra's heart softened. She had expected to dislike the boy, but instead found herself charmed. She wondered, though, if he would soon gain the harsh edge of the men here.

"Marrying her right away was my thought," Markus said.

"We can have scrolls drawn up immediately," Ozarson told him, his eyes lit with delight. Then he turned to Yargazon and spoke more formally. "Good evening, General."

Yargazon bowed. "You honor us with your presence, Your Majesty." He sounded like he genuinely meant it.

"I've heard your recruiting efforts on this last trip were successful." Ozarson seemed stilted with the General, as if he were trying to sound older. "The men told me you nearly doubled the size of the company. Very good."

"Thank you, Sire." Yargazon's face showed a paternal fondness Allegra hadn't thought him capable of feeling.

Ozarson nodded to Bladebreak. "You look well, Colonel." He stole a glance at Jasmine, then blushed and looked away.

"Thank you, Your Majesty." Bladebreak was as formal as Yargazon. It was surreal to see them act this way with a child.

"Well." Ozarson pushed an unruly curl out of his eyes. He sounded relieved to have the protocols done with. "Let's eat!"

"As you wish, Your Majesty," Markus said.

Allegra glanced around for signs of the boy's mother or other children, but she saw nothing. The pavilion could have belonged to any officer of the army.

"Oh, wait," Ozarson said. "Markus, I have to sign something, don't I? Before you can marry her."

"That's how it works," Markus said. His voice had a gentler quality than his usual cocky self-satisfaction.

The boy indicated the back entrance. "Shall we do it now? I have parchments and quills, I think."

"That would be good, yes," Markus said.

Ozarson turned to one of his guards. "Please make sure my guests receive every anemity—" He paused, looking uncertain, then said, "Every amenity while I tend to the documents for my brother."

The guard bowed to him. "As you wish, Sire."

"Thank you." Ozarson swung back around to Markus, his face bright with excitement. "Let's get started!"

Allegra had a sense Markus wanted to reach out to his brother. He took her hand instead, though, and followed the atajazid to the back entrance, leaving the guards in the outer room.

The chamber beyond the curtain was far different from the other room. Pillows lay heaped up in a play fort, and blocks had tumbled into a haphazard pile, sparkling. With a start, Allegra realized gems encrusted the toys. Quills lay scattered across one table, and a sheet of parchment amid the clutter bore the carefully drawn letters of a penmanship exercise. The slate next to it was covered with algebra exercises she wouldn't have expected from a child Ozarson's age.

As soon as they were out of the other room, the boy threw himself at Markus, and the prince regent caught him in a hug, laughing, his face more at ease than Allegra had ever seen. Then he set the boy back a step and beamed at him.

"By the dragon," Markus said. "I do believe you've grown just in the month I've been gone."

Ozarson pulled himself up to his full height. "I did." He held up his hand with his thumb and finger a short distance apart. "This much, Major Gaizz says."

Markus tousled his hair. "At this rate, you will be taller than me. Just like Father."

Some of the light dimmed in the boy's face. "I should like to honor his memory that way."

Markus's voice quieted. "It would be good."

"Oh, look, I almost forgot." Ozarson waved at the toys in the corner. "I took out everything with curves and circles, just like your messenger said. But why, Markus?"

The regent shifted his feet. "We can talk about that later."

"Don't wait on my behalf," Allegra murmured. "Do tell this delightful young man." Naughty Markus, hiding his discovery about her abilities from his brother.

Markus glared at her, and she smiled sweetly. He had no idea. A wealth of pyramids, cubes, tetrahedrons and other shapes were strewn everywhere. Some were too powerful for her to use, but cubes she could manage. Nor had Ozarson eliminated every circle. A cart filled with blocks had round wheels. They had ridges and dents, but they might be round enough for a spell. She looked away from the cart, not wanting Markus to notice her interest.

Allegra spoke to Ozarson. "It is a great honor to meet you,

Your Majesty." She had to admit a certain satisfaction in being the only person outside Jazid to see this boy everyone wanted to find.

Blushing furiously, the boy said, "We are m—meeting, um, pleased to you."

She held back her smile. "Thank you, Sire."

Markus surveyed the cluttered room. "Do you have somewhere we can sit in all this?"

Ozarson went to the table with his schoolwork. He brushed most of it to the floor, then stopped, squinted at the mess and retrieved a blank parchment, which he spread on the table. He almost knocked the ink bottle over, too, but he caught it before ink splattered his gorgeous, rumpled carpets.

Markus settled at the table, piling cushions behind him for support. Allegra sank onto the pillows next to where Ozarson had scattered his lessons. Her bridal finery clinked and rattled, and she had to sit carefully to keep from pulling the chains of her skirt. A parchment rustled as she leaned back on a large cushion. Curious, she picked it up. Neat script covered the sheet.

Allegra showed it to Ozarson. "Is this your schoolwork?"

He froze in the process of sitting and shot a panicked look at his brother.

"She does that a lot," Markus told him.

"Does what?" she asked. It seemed a reasonable question.

"Perhaps," Markus added to Ozarson, "you might give her permission. To speak."

"Oh." Ozarson sat down and regarded Allegra, obviously

trying to appear dignified. It was sweet and awkward and funny, and she thought it a shame that Jazid might someday wring the charm out of this boy—if someone didn't assassinate him first.

"It would please me," Ozarson told her earnestly, "to give you permission to speak."

"Thank you, Your Majesty," Allegra said. "May I read your school papers?"

The boy shot another bewildered look at Markus. Allegra wondered if he ever spoke with women. She had seen no indication of his mother or a nanny, and the only person he had mentioned was a Major Gaizz, which hardly sounded female.

"She can read," Markus said.

Ozarson's mouth fell open. "Truly?"

"Truly." With satisfaction, Markus reclined in his cushions.

It seemed incongruous to Allegra that in a place where women were deliberately kept illiterate, their prince regent considered his bride's education a point of pride. Granted, it benefited him and any children they had together, but that was true for most anyone. Markus was one of the few who acknowledged it. That his family sought intellectual as well as physical strength for their progeny spoke to their foresight. Unfortunately it also manifested in her groom's maddening ability to anticipate her actions.

Ozarson spoke shyly to Allegra. "You may look at my lessons if you like. Major Gaizz teaches me."

"Thank you," Allegra said.

As the brothers talked about Markus's trip, she went

through the boy's schoolwork. Not only was he doing algebra, but he also appeared to understand it well. And more. At the bottom of a sheet of classic Jazid poetry, he had solved problems with right triangles inscribed in circles. In the margins of a long treatise about ancient military strategies, he had penned sophisticated games of number theory. "Smart" hardly began to describe it; if Ozarson had done all this, he was brilliant.

When Marcus began to discuss the marriage contract, Allegra quit reading and listened. The logic behind the requirement that he obtain Ozarson's permission soon became clear. Markus was next in line for the throne. Until Ozarson grew up, married and had a son, Markus was his heir, which meant any son Allegra bore him would be second in line. It was a strange and unexpected thought, that her child could inherit the Onyx Throne.

Markus's relationship with Ozarson had a different dynamic than she had expected. From their references to the past, she soon realized Markus hadn't just assumed guardianship of the boy after the death of their sire; he had always acted as a father to Ozarson.

Although their father had died two years ago, his presence filled the room. It was soon obvious, from Ozarson's comments, that he longed for the affection and attention of his sire, the man he considered greatest of all men. She wasn't so sure about Markus. The boy who would have done anything to please his demanding father had grown into a more cynical adult. She had no doubt Markus had loved

Ozar, but she had the impression he no longer saw his father with the shine of childhood worship.

Their comments about the late king's friendships startled her. He had counted Stonebreaker Chamberlight as a blood brother—King Chamberlight, who had ruled the Misted Cliffs. Emperor Cobalt's grandfather. Stonebreaker had raised Cobalt. She didn't understand how Cobalt had ended up killing a man his grandfather had considered a sworn brother.

She hoped Markus and Ozarson would say more about their father, but they concentrated primarily on phrasing for the contract. Markus did most of the work, explaining it to his brother. The sections about succession and inheritance fascinated Allegra, but when they reached the portion about the expected behavior of the consort, her ire rose.

"Shouldn't it say 'She must obey'?" Ozarson asked. "'She must ever obedient be' sounds strange."

"I know." Markus penned the second phrase on the parchment scroll in a bold script. "That's the historical wording, though."

"And what is the historical wording for the husband?" Allegra asked. "'Must obey'? Or 'Ever obey'?"

They both looked up with a start, and Ozarson flushed. He didn't seem to know whether to be aghast or enthralled by her.

"It doesn't say either," Markus growled.

She bestowed him with her most dulcet smile. "To remedy that, I suggest 'Always and ever obey his wife, the Princess Consort.'"

Ozarson gave a startled laugh. "Markus would never put that in his marriage contract, Lady Allegra."

"Markus takes many risks," Allegra said.

"Does he now, my soft little bird?" Markus reclined in his cushions. "Perhaps it would suit his fancy to fly his warbler to the top whenever she interrupts. She would be too distracted to sing then."

Fly her to the top? What the blazes did that mean? Knowing him, he was talking about sex. She gave him an unimpressed look. "Maybe his fancy isn't so formidable as he thinks."

"Formidable fancy?" Ozarson asked, confused. "What does that mean?"

His brother picked up the quill. "Nothing important. Let's finish."

"Markus." Allegra spoke quietly. "There is something I would like to put in."

He glanced up sharply, the quill poised. A drop of ink fell from its tip and splattered on the table. "You have no say." His voice had chilled. "None."

"It's important to me," she said.

"No." He turned to the parchment and began to write.

"Wait," Ozarson said. "I'd like to hear what she has to say."

Markus's jaw clenched. He set down the quill and sat back with his arms crossed as he regarded Allegra implacably. "What?"

"I would like you to write this," she said. "That you swear you will never turn me out for another nor ask me to share you. That you will never put another woman before me." An edge came into her voice. "That you will never break your child's heart by forcing him to see you treat his mother as if she means nothing."

Markus stared at her, a flush spreading across his face.

"I'm not sure that goes in a contract," Ozarson said uneasily.

Markus spoke in a low voice. "He didn't walk away from her. Or from me."

"No?" Allegra was suddenly angry for both him and Ozarson. "He only made you feel as if you were never good enough, that you had to vie for his attention every day of your childhood."

"Enough!" He grasped the quill and began writing, his script jagged on the page. An inkblot spread as the quill scratched.

"Markus?" Ozarson asked. "What does she mean?"

"Nothing." Markus wrote a few more lines, then let out an angry breath and set down the quill. For a moment he just looked at Ozarson. He brushed a curl off the boy's forehead. Gently he said, "Nothing, Ozi."

The boy watched him, his dark eyes bewildered.

Markus turned to Allegra. "I will put in this—I swear, as your husband, to honor the vows of our union. Also, I will never take our children or forbid you to see them."

Saints above. She hadn't expected him to agree to anything. That he felt the need to assure her access to her own children scared her. It would kill her if they had children and he tried to take them away. Honor the vows of their union sounded promising, but she didn't know what it meant in Jazid.

She said, "I don't under—"

"No." He held up his hand. "Don't push me. Or I'll write nothing."

Allegra let it go. He had given more than she had expected. Ozarson was listening to them with his forehead furrowed, but he made no protest when Markus penned the words on the parchment.

They finished the contract with less banter than before. One disturbing section outlined Markus's right to kill any man who took liberties that could impregnate Allegra. She went cold when she realized he could execute her, too, if he chose, even if she had been forced. At least the historical wording included an admonishment for the husband to look to the circumstances. It outlined less severe sentences he could impose against a man who took other freedoms with her. It surprised her how few such actions were punishable. Markus was expected to protect her if he didn't want anyone to touch her. Then she realized the subtext; if she wanted safety, she had to abide by whatever constraints he imposed on her life, because the law gave her almost no protection.

Several clauses exhorted him to see to his wife's learning. It was, apparently, the one exception to the laws forbidding the education of women. The reason was typically Jazidian; the mother of a royal heir should have the ability to teach her son, so he could become a better leader. Allegra wondered if some savvy queen from long ago had used that reasoning to convince her husband he should allow her education.

When Markus and Ozarson finished the document, they both signed it. After the ink dried, Markus rolled it into a scroll and tied it with a red-tasseled cord. Then he gave it to Ozarson. "You'll need to have three copies made, one for me, one for the archives and one for the court clerk."

"I will." Ozarson gave him a brilliant smile. "Now we can eat and celebrate."

The prince regent tousled his hair. "Indeed we can."

Ozarson and Markus rose with an ease Allegra envied. In her metal clothes, she found standing even harder than sitting down. She discreetly slipped her fingers under the bottom of the halter and pulled it out so she could breathe as she got up. She was beginning to flag. She and Markus had slept only a few hours last night, and the fatigue was catching up to her.

As they crossed the chamber, she glanced at Markus. "Do we have a ceremony?"

"If we were at the Onyx Palace, among the Dragon Court, then yes, there would be a long, ornate and excruciating ceremony with guests from all over the country." He still sounded angry at her. "This is a military camp for an outlawed army. We don't have time for frivolities. The documents are signed, so we're married."

"Oh. All right." She wasn't certain whether to be relieved or disappointed.

Glancing at her face, Markus relented. "We will dine with my brother, Yargazon, Bladebreak and Jasmine."

The last people Allegra wanted at her wedding dinner were the general and colonel. No, that wasn't true. The last person she wanted at this marriage was herself.

Are you sure? She couldn't sort out her feelings for Markus. She had no doubt about wanting to be free, though. Homesickness flooded her. She had always expected her marriage to be a joyous event with family and friends. But her chances of ever seeing her home again faded more each day.

❧ CHAPTER 12
WEDDING DINNER

When Markus brought Allegra and Ozarson back into the main room, night had settled across the desert. Many candelabras were lit now, filling the pavilion with a warm glow. Less than an hour had passed since they had left the room, but someone had already prepared and laid out the dinner. Yargazon, Bladebreak and Jasmine reclined in cushions around a low table. One guard stood near them, and the others were posted around the walls.

Yargazon and Bladebreak were drinking and talking lazily. Jasmine sat with Bladebreak's head in her lap, stroking his hair. Her robe shimmered in the light, and the red silk had fallen open to show her long legs and a gleaming red halter and skirt similar to what Allegra had worn yesterday. With his head resting on her thighs, Bladebreak looked content. Yargazon also seemed at ease, but Allegra didn't believe it. She had never seen him without that coiled sense of lethal power, like a cobra ready to strike.

When Ozarson entered, Yargazon and Bladebreak started

to stand, and Jasmine to kneel. The boy stopped them by waving his hand.

"You don't need to do that," Ozarson said, smiling.

They settled back, though Bladebreak didn't lie down again. Ozarson gave the marriage scroll to one of his officers with the directions Markus had explained. As the man left, Ozarson settled next to Yargazon. Markus nudged Allegra to sit by Jasmine, then put himself between her and Ozarson. Allegra wished she had a chair. If she leaned back, the cushions would give until she was lying down, and she would fall asleep at her own wedding dinner.

As Allegra rearranged her skirt so it covered more of her legs, Jasmine smiled shyly. "Congratulations on your wedding." She tilted her head toward Markus. "He is a fine man."

"Thank you." He could be a fine man, if he wanted—except for the "small" matter of keeping her against her will.

She salivated at the sight of so much sumptuous food. Curry steamed in ceramic bowls, and dishes with graceful spouts held sauces that wafted enticing aromas. Raw vegetables lay heaped on a square plate—carrots, broccoli, cauliflower, radishes, squashes, string beans—and a dish of sauce sat next to it. Breads warm from cooking added their delicious smells to the dinner.

Something about the settings looked odd, but Allegra was too hungry to concentrate. Ozarson wasted no time ladling curry onto his plate. The man standing by the table looked startled, and she suspected he was supposed to serve the atajazid. When he offered the boy some wine, Ozarson grinned and nodded. He stopped nodding when Markus scowled at him. With a sigh, the boy shook his head at the man with the wine.

As soon as Ozarson started to eat, everyone served themselves. With relief, Allegra filled her dish and spooned up a bite of the sauce-soaked rice. It tasted heavenly.

It finally hit her why the table settings looked strange. No curved shapes. In fact, she saw no useful shapes at all. Although some plates were squared off, they had scalloped sides for artistic effect, which looked beautiful but made them useless for spells. The wineglasses twisted in graceful spirals that destroyed their symmetry. Even the spoons were squared off and angled.

Eventually Ozarson slowed his attack on his food and sighed. Then he beckoned to his guard. As the boy spoke to the man in a low voice, Markus tensed. The prince regent said something, and Ozarson just smiled and shook his head. The guard bowed to them, then went to a chest across the room.

"I wonder what that's about," Allegra said to Jasmine.

"Don't stare," she murmured. "Avert your eyes."

She almost said, *Why the blazes would I do that?* She didn't have the energy to keep protesting, though. Resisting them wore her down. Instead she listened to their war council.

"We can have the army ready in three weeks," Yargazon was saying. "We'll march on Quaaz. In this region, we can move with secrecy, but that won't last once we're in the open. And when we start taking towns in Taka Mal, they will send messengers to their capital."

"Can't we stop the messengers?" Ozarson asked.

"Some," Markus answered. "But eventually someone will get through. They can also send carrier birds."

"The last time you almost reached Quaaz," Ozarson said.

Allegra listened intently, remembering the meeting from last night. They had intended to assassinate the royal family of Taka Mal and attack in the ensuing chaos. After someone warned the queen, her army had met Yargazon's forces, and they hadn't fought. Allegra wanted to ask how they had explained their presence in Taka Mal, but she held back. They probably wouldn't tell her, and if they realized how closely she was listening, they might become more guarded. She wanted to hear as much as possible.

"We were camped closer to Quaaz last time," Yargazon said.

"How long is it from here?" Ozarson asked.

Candlelight glinted on the General's crystal goblet as he lowered the glass. "I could ride there in about four days, if I stopped only to rest the horse. If I slept in the saddle, maybe in three. But for an army? We'll be taking towns and setting up outposts. Six, seven, maybe eight days, depending on how much opposition we encounter."

"It's still so fast," Ozarson said. "It could be over in less than two months."

Markus exhaled. "Yes. That's right."

"It's been two years, Your Majesty," Yargazon said. "We've prepared, built up the army, trained the men. It's time. If we continue hiding, it could weaken morale. Nor can we evade Cobalt's forces forever. The longer we wait, the more chance we will have to fight him here first."

"We've more chance of success in Taka Mal," Markus told his brother. "They've a smaller army than Cobalt. If we move fast, we can have it under our control before we face his men."

"He has soldiers in Taka Mal, too," Ozarson said.

"Some, yes," Yargazon said. "But they're spread thin. And we can reach Quaaz faster than the forces Cobalt has in Jazid. We're closer. By the time they arrive, we'll have taken the capital. If they try to take it back from us, the queen's army will likely fight *with* us, to defend Quaaz. Better we have it than him."

"He can't pull many forces out of Jazid, either," Blade-break said. "Or our people will rise against those left behind."

"Then we must move soon," Ozarson said. He tried to appear confident, but Allegra could see the prospect frightened him. Many boys she knew would have been excited at the idea of a battle. Such stories thrilled her students. But as *stories*. None of this was abstract for Ozarson. He would learn the truth of war firsthand, and if it didn't go as they hoped, he could die.

Markus was watching the boy intently. "You aren't going into battle, Ozi."

"I won't sit in a tent while you all fight!" Ozarson said.

"Your Majesty is very brave," Yargazon said. "But we can't risk your life. It's for you that we do this, so you may reclaim your throne."

Markus laid his hand on Ozarson's shoulder. "You're too young for battle. You *must* survive. Otherwise all this was for nothing."

"It's never for nothing," Ozarson said, with pain and pride. "It's for Father. And Mother."

A fierce intensity came into Markus's eyes. "Yes."

Allegra felt a sinking in her stomach. Had the boy lost his mother, too? If he had other siblings, she had seen no sign of them. In fact, she had seen no children here at all. If that was true, it meant Ozarson had no friends his age, no family but Markus and no home but this army that stood ready to wreak havoc in his name so that someday he could reclaim the Onyx Throne and rule a dying country. He should have been running in fields and playing games with his friends, not planning a war. Instead both he and Markus could be dead in a few weeks.

The officer Ozarson had spoken to earlier had returned and was standing a few steps back, holding a box about a hand span wide. Markus touched Ozarson's hand, and when the boy glanced at him, Markus tilted his head toward the officer.

Ozarson turned to the man with a relieved smile. "Thank you, Major Gaizz."

Gaizz. This was the tutor Ozarson had mentioned earlier. It made sense he would be an officer; the boy had to learn far more about the military than a child his age should have needed.

Gaizz knelt by the table and gave him the box. "I checked the contents. They're sound and undamaged."

Ozarson beamed at him. "Wonderful!"

As Gaizz moved back, Ozarson looked around at the others at the table. "No more war talk. This is a celebration for Markus and his bride." As he turned to Allegra, his face lit with pleasure. "I have a present for you."

Allegra smiled. "You're very kind."

He gave the box to Markus. "Here. For her."

The prince regent watched him intently. "Are you sure, Ozi? You don't have to do this."

"I'm sure. She's your bride. She deserves the best."

Markus smiled, that same flash of white teeth that was so appealing on Ozarson. On Markus, it took Allegra's breath.

"You're generous, my brother," Markus said.

"Not until you give it to her!" Ozarson told him, laughing.

Markus offered the box to Allegra. "His Majesty, the Atajazid D'Az, wishes you to have this in honor of our wedding."

Her pulse leaped as she took the box. It was a perfect three-dimensional shape. Power thrummed within her. The box was large, which would add strength to a spell, but it had only six sides, keeping it within her ability. If she could put everyone to sleep, she might find the supplies here she needed to escape. To reach the horses, she would have to affect people outside, but a box this size could give the power she needed.

Slow down, she thought. *Don't get ahead of yourself.* She traced her hand over the top of the box. Onyx and ivory tiles inlaid the wood, fitting together to form a roaring dragon. Its ruby eyes glowed, and topaz flames curled from its fanged mouth. The care it must have taken to place all those tiny pieces spoke eloquently of the artist's talent.

"It's lovely," she said, looking up at Ozarson.

"Open it." His eyes shone, but it looked like tears rather than happiness gave them that luster.

She raised the top. A tiara lay inside on a bed of red velvet, a delicate gold circlet inlaid with onyx, rubies, topazes and emeralds. Astonished at the fine workmanship, she lifted the scrolled headpiece. It sparkled in the candlelight. "I've never seen anything like this," she said. "It's incredible."

"It was my mother's," Ozarson said.

Her heart lurched. No wonder the boy had tears in his eyes. How could she accept such a keepsake? She looked at Markus, trying to understand, and saw the fear in his eyes. She knew then, without doubt, that if she rejected this gift his brother offered, Markus would never forgive her.

She spoke gently to Ozarson. "You are generous, Your Majesty. I thank you for this unparalleled gift."

He smiled with a blush. "Try it on."

Allegra settled the tiara in her mass of curls. "How's that?"

"Beautiful," Markus murmured.

Ozarson nodded and wiped his eyes with his palm.

Yargazon spoke. "That piece has been given by Shadow-Dragon kings to their wives for centuries. It's an heirloom of great meaning to the royal family and the country." He regarded her implacably. "It should have gone to the atajazid's wife, when he reached his age of majority and took his own queen." If his stare had been a dagger, he would surely have run her through.

Bladebreak was harder to read. Although he didn't look

as if he approved, she didn't sense the same hatred as from Yargazon. Here with Jasmine, he seemed more at ease. Jasmine smiled at her with what looked like hope, though why, Allegra didn't know. Maybe because Jasmine so clearly wanted a friend, and with Ozarson showing his approval, Bladebreak might let her visit with Allegra.

"I'll probably never get married," Ozarson said. "Someone should wear it."

Allegra expected Markus or someone else to chuckle and say he would feel otherwise when he was older. Instead silence fell over the table. She saw the anguish in Markus's gaze and felt the tension as if it were tangible. Then it hit her. Ozarson didn't believe he would live long enough to take a wife.

"You will have the loveliest bride in all Jazid," Allegra told him. "She'll bear you sons just as smart and handsome as you, and the most beautiful daughters in all the land."

Ozarson's face turned red. "I will not!" Now he sounded nine again. With dignity, he added, "Girls giggle too much."

"I suppose they do," Allegra allowed, trying not to smile.

Markus spoke kindly to her. "Sometimes they sing beautifully, night bird."

Allegra knew he meant her words to Ozarson. She felt a lurch at the thought of leaving him. She might not have another chance like this for some time, and she couldn't turn away from it, but it was going to hurt in ways she hadn't expected.

"She does sing well," Bladebreak said. "You should hear her, Your Majesty. It's a pleasure."

"You sing?" Ozarson asked Allegra. "Oh, do sing for us!"

"She can't," Markus said curtly.

"Why not?" Ozarson asked. "I'd like to hear her."

Markus glanced at the tiara Allegra was wearing, then said, "It would interrupt dinner."

Allegra wondered if he thought she could use the tiara for a spell. Although circular, it had too many deviations from an ideal shape. He didn't even glance at the box in her lap. Well, he had only seen her use curved forms, and he knew she had been around squared-off objects. They hadn't been ideal shapes, so she couldn't use them, but he didn't know that. No one else at the table showed any suspicion that her songs could be anything more than a musical diversion. It didn't surprise her; even in Aronsdale, song mages were rare. She had heard of only about thirty other mages, and of those, only three or four needed songs for their magic to work.

"Just one song," Ozarson persisted.

"Some other time," Markus said.

"My people have a custom," Allegra said. "At weddings." She was making up the "custom" as she went along, looking for some way she could convince Markus to let her sing. He would never agree as long as she was touching the tiara. So she said, "The bride asks her new husband to hold her flowers."

Markus squinted at her. "What?"

"What flowers?" Ozarson asked.

"She wears flowers in her hair," Allegra improvised. "A circlet. To show her love to her husband, she offers the flowers to him." She looked straight at Markus. "He gives them back later, to share his love."

"That's a lovely custom," Jasmine said.

Bladebreak snorted. "It sounds like something women would think up. What if the flowers wilt?"

"Well, that can happen," Allegra admitted.

"You don't have flowers," Ozarson said. "I don't think we could find any here. It's mostly just sand and cacti."

"I'm probably allergic to Aronsdale flowers, anyway," Markus grumbled.

Allegra held back her laugh. Honestly. The things he came up with. Sometimes she couldn't tell if he was serious or teasing.

"You aren't allergic to this." She lifted the tiara off her head and offered it to him. "If you would do me the honor of holding this for me, my husband, until later. Please accept it as an expression of my affection."

"Oh!" Ozarson grinned at her. "That's clever."

Markus accepted the tiara. "I'll return it tonight." His smile quirked. "Perhaps when we decide to sleep."

Bladebreak guffawed at him, his face flushed from wine. "I'll wager you'll never return it, then." Jasmine reddened and Ozarson looked confused.

Yargazon took a long swallow of his wine. "How civil of our young bride, to pretend she loves her groom. Amazing what a little persuasion can achieve. Thirty persuasions, so to speak."

"Dusk," Markus warned.

Allegra narrowed her eyes at the General. If he thought

anyone could break her spirit by hitting her with a belt, he was mistaken. He met her gaze, and she saw the hatred in his icy stare. It chilled her to know she could have ended up with *him,* but it hadn't happened, and he had no say in her life. Watching him, though, she feared he wouldn't be satisfied until he saw her suffer for what he considered her offenses.

"I still want to hear her sing," Ozarson said, oblivious to the undercurrents of tension in the room.

"Ah, well." Markus glanced around the table, scrutinizing the objects. He reached over and took Allegra's spoon, which had a curved section.

"Why did you do that?" Ozarson said.

He tapped the spoon against his tumbler, causing the crystal to chime. "Singers need to hear a note before they start."

"Oh, good!" Ozarson beamed. "Then you'll let her perform?"

"All right." Markus glanced at Allegra, his gaze narrowing. She understood his unspoken warning; if he felt the hint of a spell, he would stop her.

Allegra spoke to Ozarson. "I would be honored to sing for you, Your Majesty."

Bladebreak settled in the pillows and pulled Jasmine against his side. Yargazon looked bored and rubbed his ear, as if it hurt. Allegra wondered if he meant it as an insult against her singing. She tried not to let it bother her. Markus reclined in the cushions next to her and trailed his finger along her leg, pushing aside the chains of her skirt. He looked as if he simply wanted to touch his bride, but she had no doubt what else he was telling her; lying that way, he could stop her if she tried to cast a spell. It took several minutes for her spells to work, and the last time he had been awake again within moments.

The box lay in Allegra's lap. She feared that if Markus kept stroking her, he would decide it was in the way. So she moved it to her other side and took his hand, for all appearances showing affection to her new husband. It surprised her how natural that felt. Holding his hand also kept it from wandering too far up her leg and embarrassing her. She discreetly left her other hand resting on the box. As long as she was touching the shape, she could build her spell. She didn't know what she could manage with Markus so alert; she would have to see how the spell felt.

She chose a ballad that pleased many audiences, though its archaic language was rarely heard anymore. The melody started high, and she hadn't warmed up her voice, but she drew in a breath and reached for the note. It poured out clearly, a lyrical match to the chime of crystal:

In the ancient hills of Aron
Find the hidden red lark
Send it to the dying barrens
Before the sky turns dark

Send it from these meadows green
With their purple edgerows
To that land in starkest need
For when the lark sings, life grows

Power built within her. These past two days, she had stretched her abilities beyond what she had ever tried before, but instead of draining her, the effort seemed to strengthen her abilities, as if she were exercising muscles she had never challenged. The box provided more clarity than the compass, for the shape was cleaner. Still, she couldn't do a spell if Markus stopped her the moment he felt drowsy.

Unless he has no time. Mages usually released their spells gently. A mage would no more use a spell as a weapon than doctors or midwives would use their knowledge in violence. A healer *could* do harm and a mage could use her spells for ill, but in both cases they swore to help rather than hurt. However, she *could* use speed. Maybe she could put Markus to sleep before he stopped her. Normally she wouldn't have thought she had the strength, but these past few days had revealed resources she didn't know she possessed.

Unfortunately the spell might put her to sleep, too. She tried not to imagine what Markus would do if she was here to face his anger when they both awoke. Seeing his advisors and guards knocked out had amused him, but if she did anything to Ozarson, she had no doubt he would be furious.

The spell swirled within her, burnished by the soaring notes of the song. She could barely contain its fullness. She hit the highest note, the E above high C—and released the spell with a great swoop of power.

It swept through Allegra, across the diners, across Major Gaizz and the guards, out of the pavilion and beyond. It filled her, and she fought the enveloping peace even as she fell into it like a baby into a down comforter. Markus's eyes widened, and his fingers stiffened on her leg. Then the tension flowed out of his body and his head fell onto her thigh as his eyes closed.

Everyone at the table slumped into the cushions. Ozarson sprawled on his back, and Yargazon's glass fell out of his hand, soaking the pillow with wine. Jasmine and Bladebreak settled down side by side. The colonel snorted, his breath ruffling his wife's hair. Some of the bodyguards managed to sit before they fell, but the others crumpled straight to the ground. They were trained to defend Ozarson and Markus against attack or kidnap. No one had ever taught them to fight the most harmless of spells. Slumber.

Allegra sat, dazed, struggling to stay awake. With care, she lifted Markus's head off her leg and set it on the pillow. Looking at him relaxed in sleep, she felt a sharp pang of regret. She couldn't deny a part of her wanted to be his queen. But she couldn't live that life; it would force her to give up too much of herself.

As she stood, spots danced in her vision. When her head cleared, she went to Ozarson. He was sleeping soundly, his face angelic. She touched his cheek, wishing she could offer him more than the life and possible death of an exiled warlord. For all his power, he had so little.

She rose to her feet, deep in thought. Ozarson probably had maps here, maybe other records that would help her—

Someone clenched Allegra's ankle and jerked. It happened so fast, she had no time to gasp as she toppled into the pillows. She kicked out, frantic, as someone dragged her away from Ozarson. Twisting onto her back, she looked up—

At Yargazon.

The General was awake and furious. He knelt over her with one hand beside her neck and grasped the collar around her throat.

"No!" She choked as he pulled on the metal. Twisting hard, she wrenched out of his hold. He grabbed for her, but his motions were slowed. Groggy. She rolled out from under him and scrambled to her feet even as he struggled to recover. But when she whirled to run, the chains of her skirt tangled in her legs and she tripped.

Yargazon caught her arm as he lunged to his feet. He slapped her hard across the face, and she reeled with the blow. When he threw her down on the carpets, she barely caught herself on her hands. She flipped onto her back as he reached for her. Grabbing his hands, she thrust her feet up into his stomach and heaved backward, using his bulk against him, rolling him over her head. He thudded down with a grunt behind her head.

Allegra jumped up, and this time she pulled the chains away from her legs. Had she thrown one of her friends, it would have taken him time to recover, but Yargazon rolled easily to his feet, no longer groggy. As he came at her, she backed toward the pavilion entrance. She couldn't run outside and risk that someone was awake. He didn't bother to call for help; she doubted he even considered it. She knew why, and it wasn't only because he would consider the idea of needing help against her ludicrous. He wanted her to suffer for her defiance, and he intended to be the one who made her pay.

In the same instant he lunged for her, Allegra dropped to her knee and grabbed one of the braziers. She hurled its smoldering coals into his face.

"Ah!" Yargazon swiped his hand across his eyes, knocking away embers, his face contorted. As Allegra jumped up, he said, "You fool! Are you trying to start a fire?" He threw the burning coals into the curry, dousing their heat and splashing sauce all over the table. No one stirred; they all remained fast asleep.

Allegra backed away as he came at her. When he grabbed her, she tried to roll him over her body, but he anticipated the throw and turned it against her, swinging her around. He hit her openhanded across her face, then with his fist on her back.

"Oh, gods," Allegra groaned, stumbling.

Yargazon knocked her over, and she fell on her stomach. She tried to crawl away, but he dragged her across the carpet, the gems and metal on her clothes grinding her skin. He flipped her over, then lay on top of her, breathing faster—and the bastard was *aroused,* pushing his erection against her. He thrust his hand between their bodies and pulled on the ties of his trousers.

"You slime-scum asshole," Allegra said—and kneed him *hard* in the crotch.

With a shout, Yargazon curled forward, his face contorted.

She heaved him off her body, desperate to free herself, and pushed to her knees. Even rigid with pain he managed to shove her off balance, and she fell onto a chest with a candelabra. Grabbing the metal holder with its burning candles, she swung it at his head. As he jerked up his arm to deflect the blow, he called her a filthy name she had never thought anyone would say to her. Then they were on their feet, both swaying. As Yargazon grabbed her arms, she swung away from him, unbalancing them. He fell sideways—

And hit his head on the edge of the chest.

When Yargazon slumped forward, at first Allegra couldn't comprehend what had happened. She stood, heaving in breaths, staring at him, her hair tangled around her body.

"Ah, gods," she whispered, when she realized he wasn't going to move. Allegra knew what such a blow to the head could do. She hadn't meant to kill anyone! Dropping next to him, she leaned over his body—and realized he was breathing. But when she pushed his head forward, blood ran over her hands from a gouge in the back of his head.

Yargazon groaned, and stirred, his eyes starting to open.

"No!" Allegra heaved him onto his stomach. With a silent apology to Jasmine, she ripped a chain off her wedding dress and bound his wrists behind his back. She tied his ankles with a second chain. She ran to the table for the sash on Jasmine's robe, and also snatched a cloth napkin. Returning to Yargazon, she stuffed the cloth in his mouth and tied the sash around his head, gagging him. Her pulse was racing. He probably wouldn't have killed her, but she doubted she would have felt much like living by the time he finished. It would have been his word against hers for what he had done. She could prove no more than a beating, and Markus might not censure him for it, given that she had also acted against Ozarson.

Allegra drew in a breath, shaking. It looked as if a whirlwind had struck the room, tables knocked over, rugs thrown around and the dinner ruined, with curry sauce splattered everywhere. The candles were no longer burning in the candelabra that lay broken on the rug, but the stench of the scorched carpet saturated the air.

Then Allegra noticed the white blob in Yargazon's ear. She dug at it, and a wax plug fell into her hand. He hadn't rubbed his ears earlier; he had stopped them up so he wouldn't hear her sing. Maybe Bladebreak and Ardoz believed they had fallen asleep from wine in Markus's tent that night, but not the General.

As Allegra took the plugs out of his ears, her arm trembled. "Come on," she muttered. "Don't fall apart." She climbed to her feet and swayed, so dizzy. Her pulse was slowing, and she began to think more clearly. As much as she wanted to *run,* to leave this place as fast as possible, she needed a plan or she wouldn't survive in the desert. She also had to ensure everyone stayed asleep long enough for her to escape.

She ran into Ozarson's cluttered room, sweeping aside the jeweled curtain. She searched quickly through his cart of toys. Many of the blocks were perfect cubes, more clarified sources of power than a rectangular box, but they were smaller, which meant what she gained in the purity of the spell she would lose in power.

Then she hit gold: a block with eight sides, two four-sided pyramids glued together, base-to-base. An octahedron. When she picked it up, she uncovered an even more powerful form, two six-sided pyramids set base-to-base. Twelve sides. A dodecahedron. They were both small, fitting into the palm of her hand, but their lesser size didn't matter, for a little eight-sided shape was far more powerful than a big one with six sides.

Allegra had never tried a shape with twelve sides. She had thought it beyond her ability, but she wondered after these past few days. She understood better now why the mage mistress had wanted her to study at the guild. But whatever they might have hoped to learn about her suitability for Prince Aron had become moot, for even if she succeeded in her escape she was the consort of the man who commanded their enemies.

"Concentrate," she told herself. She needed supplies and information about the land. A quick search of Ozarson's room turned up several maps, but nothing to carry water or food. She dumped the blocks out of the cart and wheeled it into the other room. The whole time, she held the octahedral block. And she sang. Her spell wavered with the surging power of the unfamiliar shape, but it deepened the sleep spell so it would last longer and take Yargazon. She also strove to reach the guards outside the pavilion.

Allegra placed the tiara back in its box and set it by

Ozarson. "It was a beautiful gift," she said. "It would be wrong for me to take it." She paused, her gaze caught by Markus. Her sense of loss was already building, and she pushed it away, afraid of where it would lead her.

Drawing in a breath to steady herself, she went to the smallest of the sleeping guards. She unclasped her bridal dress with relief and let it drop, rattling and clinking, into a heap. "Thank you for your kindness," she murmured to Jasmine.

Allegra changed clothes with the guard, drew his belt tight to keep up the pants, and rolled the legs into cuffs. She pulled a drape off the wall and ripped off a strip, then tied it around her chest, squashing her breasts, so she appeared flat under his shirt. Then she searched the other guards. One had a bag of gold and silver hexacoins stamped with the profile of a regal man, probably Ozarson's father. Another had a pouch used to carry messages, which she emptied and stuffed with vegetables and bread from the table. Dried food would last longer and take less room, but this would do for now. She could find water wherever they had the horses.

She paused and took a breath as reality descended on her. How would she outrun Markus and his men when they had so many more resources? Regardless of what she did, this army would march on Taka Mal. If they took the Topaz Throne, they would take on Cobalt's army. If they persevered against him, then what? Aronsdale lay on their border, rich and fertile.

She had to warn someone, either King Jarid in Aronsdale or the queen of Taka Mal. But why would they believe her?

Allegra was nobody. Nor did she have proof, except the marriage scrolls, and Ozarson's man had taken those. Jarid might think she made up the story to avoid marrying Prince Aron. She wouldn't be the first reluctant mage bride. Even if he did believe her, they had no leverage against Markus. He had lost everything; he had nothing else they could take.

Except…

Allegra stood, breathing hard, and knew the solution lay in front of her, her proof, a hostage, the way to stop the fighting. Ozarson was possibly the most valuable human being alive, and if he stayed here, a good chance existed this luminous boy would be dead before his tenth birthday.

If she took Ozarson, Markus would never forgive her. At that thought, her anger stirred. No matter how much they beat, whipped and starved her, they couldn't break her. They had stolen her life, violated a treaty and drugged her. And what sentence did they suffer as a result? The nomads were rewarded by extraordinary wealth. Markus kept her for his own pleasure. Bladebreak and Yargazon would have raped her, and Yargazon wanted to torture her as well. She had never done anything to any of them, yet they used her with no remorse, and when she resisted, they hurt her. Damn it, *they had no right.*

Allegra gritted her teeth. She knew what they valued, what mattered to everyone in this godforsaken country more than anything.

She knelt next to Ozarson. "I'm sorry," she said softly.

The boy was heavier than she expected, but she managed

to lift him into the cart. His legs hung out the back and his head rested against the pole with the handle she used to push it. He murmured in his sleep, asking for his mother. It made her want to weep. She put the bags of food and coins on his lap and set the dodecahedron by his side, but she kept the octahedron clenched in her hand.

Then she wheeled the cart out of the pavilion.

CHAPTER 13
THE KING'S COURSEWAY

Allegra sang.

She crooned sleep to the guards who snored outside the pavilion. She rolled the cart in the direction the stable boys had taken the horses and sang for anyone who might cross her path.

The horses were in a pen rather than a stable, under a rock overhang. She wheeled the king of Jazid into the enclosure and stopped singing, letting out a breath as she saw the stable boys fast asleep on the ground. Unfortunately the horses were also asleep. She couldn't rouse Shadow at all. She bit her lip, wondering what she had done. She had never managed a spell like this before, and she had no precedent to judge the results.

Allegra leaned her head against Shadow's neck and sang so only he could hear, murmuring the lilt she used to wake her youngest brother, who was only four:

Rise little sprout
Someday a mighty tree
Come softly child
Come softly with me

Shadow whinnied in protest, as if the idea of waking offended him. She kept singing, easing him awake, until finally the great horse nuzzled her shoulder. She gave him part of an apple she had taken from the dinner.

Allegra found riding supplies in a hut by the pen. She took a blanket, stuffed a second bag with trail food, filled sacs at the water trough and added feed bags for Shadow. She changed her uniform with a stable boy's nondescript clothes, and pinned up her hair under the cap to hide the yellow color, which would otherwise stand out in Jazid and Taka Mal like a sunrise at midnight.

Shadow stepped restlessly as she prepared him for the ride, but he didn't protest. It surprised her. Granted, he had carried her for several days, but she had expected him to resist any rider except Markus. Perhaps the spell had affected him somehow. Or maybe he liked her. Who knew? She was just glad he consented to her presence.

Ozarson remained fast asleep, his legs hanging out one end of the cart and his head balanced against the pole. She had no idea how she would lift him onto the horse.

"I know you want to stand," she told Shadow. "You even sleep standing up, eh? But I need you to kneel, beautiful horse."

Shadow shook his head and stamped. He knew they were ready, and he wanted to go.

"Come on," she coaxed, tugging on his bridle. "Here you go."

After some persuasion, and the rest of the apple, he knelt for her. She heaved Ozarson onto his back and shifted the sleeping atajazid so he straddled the horse. Sliding on behind him, she put her arms around the boy to hold him secure. Then she lifted the reins and said, "Ho! Now you can go, my restless Shadow."

The horse surged to his feet. He knew how to leave the pen; he even nosed aside the gate. Allegra left it open. If the horses did wake up sooner than the men and wander into camp, well, it would take that much longer to organize search parties when all the people awoke.

She crooned the lullaby as she rode past sentries asleep on the ground. It astounded her that so simple a spell could neutralize an armed camp. Or maybe it wasn't so simple; it drained her so much, she had trouble staying upright. She switched to the waking song for Shadow and herself, but when Ozarson stirred, she went back to the lullaby, to keep him asleep.

They passed the outskirts of the camp and rode into the desert. Worried about sentries, she continued to sing softly, with green in her spell so she could touch the moods of soldiers on patrol. With that warning, she was able to avoid them. She didn't let the spell fade until she was far out into the barrens, well beyond the foothills where the army had hidden their camp. Her voice was hoarse, and she prayed for its recovery, for without it, she could do no spells. Even with her voice, she wouldn't be able to do much for several days. She had stretched too far. With rest and proper care, her magic would probably return, but she had used everything she had tonight for her escape.

Ozarson had become a heavy weight in her arms, and she groaned as fatigue pressed on her. But she couldn't risk dozing while she rode because the boy might slip out of her arms.

The call of a night-wing eagle came from above her. Raising her exhausted gaze, Allegra saw the bird gliding on currents of wind. *Fly far and long,* she thought to the magnificent creature. *And I will fly with you, for if I am truly a night bird, then I shall be as free as you.* Markus had given her the name, and the part of her that had begun to care for him wanted to keep it. If her escape succeeded, it would be all she had left of him. But if she were to be a night bird, it would be on her terms—as wild and as strong as that glorious eagle in the sky.

Allegra rode on, her weary mind in a haze, rousing only enough to guide the horse by the stars. With the border of Taka Mal so close, Shadow would cross it sometime in the night, but she had no idea when. The maps indicated they were south of a tributary to the Saint Verdant River in Taka Mal. A few days' ride along the smaller river should take them to the great Saint Verdant, with its thriving communities. She hoped the waterway would help disguise their trail, and that they would be harder to locate in more heavily populated regions than out here in the desert.

Quaaz, the capital of Taka Mal, was a logical destination. She could reach it in four days. But then what? She knew neither the people nor the customs, nor what to expect for a woman and a boy traveling alone. Markus and his advisors would probably assume she went there, since it was the closest major city where she could find help. If she went to Aronsdale instead, it would take longer, but they were less likely to search in that direction.

She reviewed the geography in her mind. The nomads had ridden eastward for about four days from where they had caught her. Markus had ridden east for three more days. That put her roughly seven days out of Aronsdale. If she rode straight to the border, she could probably reach Castle Suncroft in six or seven days.

If Markus didn't catch her.

She brushed her hand over his cheek. "Please be different. Be a man I could love."

Markus touched her lips. "I can only be what I am…"

Allegra jerked awake as someone jolted her. Confused, she tried to orient herself. She was on a horse—

It all rushed back. *She had escaped.*

Shadow had slowed to a walk across the desert. Another sigh brought her fully awake, and she remembered what else she had done. The king of Jazid sat slumped in her arms.

"Are you waking up?" she asked. He needed water and food, which he couldn't take in his sleep, and her arms ached terribly from holding him upright.

The boy shifted, but showed no sign of rousing.

"Wake up," she sang softly, holding the octahedron. "Wake little sprout, someday a mighty tree, come softly my child, softly with me." She didn't know if she had enough strength left to affect him. No matter what, this would be her last spell for a while.

Ozarson sighed and opened his eyes. "Allegra?"

"Good morning, Your Majesty."

He lifted his head. "Where are we?"

"In Taka Mal. We've been riding all night." The sun had just risen above the distant mountains. "Would you like some water?"

"Yes, that would be good," he mumbled groggily.

She pulled out a sac and gave it to him. "Try not to go through it too fast. I'm not sure when we'll reach the river."

He took a few sips. "How did we get out here?"

"I put everyone at dinner to sleep with a spell."

"A spell!" He laughed sleepily. "Do you know magic tricks?"

"This isn't a trick," she said. "I knocked out your body-guards, put you in a cart and stole Shadow. Then I rode away."

He gave her the water bag. "You kidnapped me?" He sounded more perplexed than alarmed.

"Well, yes, I did." She stowed the bag with their supplies.

He was silent for a while. Then he said, "When they catch us, Allegra, I won't let them execute you."

She grimaced. "I'm hoping they won't catch us."

The boy rubbed his neck. "I'm stiff."

"You've been sleeping while we rode." His lack of concern surprised her. She would have expected more indignation from a king, even one who was only nine.

"I had a lovely dream," he said. "It was the place you sang

about, the hills of Aron and the purple edgerows. Everything was beautiful there, and no one wanted to kill me."

It broke her heart to hear him talk so matter-of-factly about something that would chill most adults. She felt guilty for taking him as a hostage. A part of her just wanted to get him away from the warlords perpetrating violence in his name and destroying his childhood. They treated him with deference, and she didn't doubt it was genuine, but she also had no doubt they were in control of his life. It wasn't her business, and it could be what Ozarson wanted, but she couldn't help the maternal feelings he evoked in her. Perhaps that made her a fool; she knew only that she didn't want him hurt.

"Maybe we can find you a place like that," she said.

"Are we going to Aronsdale?"

"I was thinking of it."

"Markus and General Yargazon will catch us."

"They might." Uneasily she said, "If I didn't kill Yargazon."

"What a thing to say." He seemed more amused than outraged.

"I'm not joking," she said. "We had a fight. I pushed him, and he fell onto one of your chests. His head hit the corner."

"By the dragon," he said, sounding like a youthful version of Markus. "Was he breathing?"

She nodded, then realized he couldn't see, sitting in front of her. "Yes. He started to wake up."

"He's all right then. He's tougher than anyone else I know."

"I hope so." As much as Yargazon terrified her, she hadn't meant to kill him.

Ozarson laughed softly. "The prettiest girl in Jazid fought with my fiercest general and carried me off. No one will believe me. They'll think I made it up."

She was glad he didn't really understand what had happened. His version of events was far more palatable. He hadn't seen all her bruises, for one thing. Her fight with Yargazon would leave some bad ones, including a black eye. Gouges ached where the skirt had bit into her skin when he dragged her across the carpet. And yet...she felt strangely exhilarated. She had fought a person who terrified her, someone far stronger and more powerful—and incredibly, she had *won*.

"You didn't really put us to sleep, did you?" Ozarson said. "We drank too much wine."

"You didn't drink any wine at all."

"Markus doesn't let me," he grumbled. "Major Gaizz does. So does General Yargazon. But never Markus."

She smiled at his grouchy tone. "Markus is a wise man."

"I've never known anyone who claimed to do real magic."

"Mages are rare."

"What's a mage?"

"A woman who does spells."

"Like the queens in Aronsdale?"

"Something like that."

He snorted. "Markus told me that wasn't true."

Allegra smiled slightly. "I think he's changed his mind."

He thought for a moment. "When he catches us, I'll say I told you to ride with me out in the desert. He'll believe me. I'm always saying I want an adventure."

Allegra knew Markus wouldn't believe it for a moment. But she said only, "Well, you shall have your adventure."

"I shouldn't run off. I have duties."

"You didn't run off." Guiltily she said, "I kidnapped you."

"As a hostage." He didn't make it a question.

"You know that's why I took you?"

"Isn't it?"

"Well, yes," she admitted. "I'm sorry."

"It's an honorable military tactic," he told her. "Jazid and Taka Mal have done it for centuries. A hostage exchange ensures no one attacks anyone else."

She was beginning to understand his response to what she had done. "Is that what you want? To resolve matters without a war?"

"Sometimes you must fight." He had the same withdrawn quality as when he talked about his father's death. "But sometimes—" He took a breath. "I wish we could find other ways than killing."

He had a great deal more to him than she had expected. "I wish that, too."

His voice turned wistful. "I dream about places with plants instead of sand. No one is angry or needs a sword. If I could decree it, I would." He sounded subdued. "But ordering people around—that isn't really what it means to be the atajazid. I have to do what is right for my people."

"It's true." She was struck by the boy's maturity. It also spoke well of Markus that the young king in his care understood the responsibilities of his position rather than just seeing it as a title that led people to kneel to him and cater to his wishes.

"We'll find you someplace beautiful," she added. She realized she wanted that for him more than she wanted a hostage. She knew she shouldn't let such feelings interfere with her plans. It was difficult, though; she liked him.

"My mother is in a place like that," he said.

His mother. Not the father he worshipped? "Ozarson," she said, then stopped, unsure how to ask about her.

He settled back in her arms. "You may call me Ozi." Then he said, "You're sort of my mother now, aren't you? Because you married my regent."

"If you would like." Using this boy for political gain was going to be a lot harder than she had thought.

He watched the shifting shadows of the predawn desert, all dim reds and browns. "I would like."

She spoke gently. "May I ask what happened to her?"

"My mother?"

"Yes."

He just shook his head and kept looking ahead. They rode in silence. Shadow didn't seem tired, but she thought they should stop soon, to tend the horse and break their morning fast.

Up ahead, a line of green edged the sands. If it was the river rather than a mirage, they had made good time. Had Markus come after them right away, he might have caught them by now. She had needed a spell to wake Ozarson, though. He had received more of her sleep song than the others, but probably not enough to make a large difference. Maybe everyone else was still out. Eventually they would awake, but without her intervention it might be a while yet.

"She was at the palace with me," Ozarson suddenly said.

"Your mother?" Allegra asked.

"Yes. When we learned about…about Father's death."

"How did you find out?"

"A company of the emperor's men came to the Onyx Palace. They said Cobalt had claimed the Onyx Throne." His voice cracked. "They had Father's body with them."

"Ah, Ozi, I'm so sorry."

He fell silent after that. She didn't push; this boy had too many nightmares in his life, he barely knew her and she had taken him away from Markus. She had expected him to seek control of Shadow or demand she return to the camp, but he seemed content to ride, nestled in her arms. Part of it seemed to come from his idea that this was an "adventure." But she remembered last night, when he had implied he didn't expect to live long enough to grow up. His fatalism broke her heart, and she felt it from him now, too, as if it didn't matter where he went, for he would be dead soon.

"Ozi," she said, hugging him. "I'll take care of you."

He rested his head against her shoulder. "You're only one girl. How can you stand against Markus's army?"

It was a good question. "Would you like to visit Aronsdale? We could go to the king."

"Why?"

"To ask for help."

"He'll send me to Cobalt, and Cobalt will kill me."

"I won't let him."

"How can you stop him? Do you know him?"

"No," she admitted. She was nobody in Aronsdale, as well. She had caught the attention of the castle mage, but that hardly meant she had the king's ear. She didn't really know how she could help Ozarson. He needed a stable, secure home and a normal life, neither of which were likely to happen.

Markus wanted to protect Ozarson by conquering anyone who threatened the boy. It was an endless cycle. Cobalt's father had attacked Aronsdale and lost; Cobalt avenged his father and ended up conquering many countries, including Jazid; now Markus sought to avenge his father. When he was done, who would be left, filled with misery and hate, to rise against Jazid? Markus and Ozarson would die then, possibly her, as well. Or she would become someone else's slave. She recalled the saying Rose T'Ambera had told her: *Men die and women suffer.* It would never end.

"We'll go to Aronsdale," Allegra said.

"Are there really edgerows there?"

"I don't actually know what an edgerow is," she admitted. "It's an old word. But we've beautiful meadows with flowers."

"I would like to go, Princess Allegra."

Saint Azure, was that really her title? "You mustn't call me a princess. People might guess who we are."

"What does Allegra mean?"

"It's from the musical term *allegro.* It means to play or sing sprightly. With energy."

272

"That's a good name for you."

"I like it." Up ahead, the green line was growing into a row of trees. She prodded Shadow and they galloped toward the oasis.

Caravans, families and riders crowded the banks of the Ata-Daz, or King's Courseway. It was only a moderate river, despite its grand name, but in the barrens of Taka Mal, it offered a ribbon of life. Sand covered Ozarson now, hiding the high quality of his clothes, so he and Allegra looked like a hundred other ragged boys wandering the river. No one paid attention to them, though some men spared a glance for Shadow. She could see why; he was a magnificent horse.

Ozarson gazed around as if he couldn't take it all in. When they dismounted to fill the water sacs, he stood on the bank and watched a gaggle of boys in ragged pants and no shirts splashing in the river.

"That looks like fun," he said.

"Go ahead and join them," Allegra said. "We could use a bath." She would have to find somewhere private, but she didn't see any reason why he couldn't go with the others. It would help their disguise; who would believe the Shadow-Dragon King of Jazid was carousing in the river with a cluster of other ragamuffins?

"I don't know how," Ozarson said.

She gave a snort. "Don't give me that, young man. Everyone knows how to take a bath. Even nine-year-old boys."

"I mean, I don't know how to play in the water."

Allegra blinked. "How can you not know how?"

"The camp has no children or river," he said. "Just springs. No one at the palace ever allowed me to go in a river. My mother bathed me in the royal suite."

"Oh." She let Shadow lap at the water. They were standing near a large boulder with moisture dampening its mottled surface. A man sat a short distance away, on top of the boulder, whittling a piece of wood. He glanced idly at them.

"Nice horse," he said, raising his voice so they could hear.

"He's a good one." Allegra hoped she didn't sound like a girl. "It's our father's."

"Hmm." He went back to whittling.

She nudged Ozarson toward the river. "Go on. Wash up."

He glanced at her, a blush on his cheeks. He took off his shoes and shirt and set them carefully in the grass. Then he waded into the water.

"Ho!" one of the boys shouted. "He's still *dry*." He hit the water and sent a huge swath over Ozarson. The atajazid stared at him, his mouth open, his hair and torso dripping.

"You'll catch bottle-bees," the boy said, laughing.

"He's on our team," another fellow said. He grabbed Ozarson's arm and pulled him away from the first boy.

An argument ensued over which team would get Ozarson, who was the largest of the boys. Allegra's heart lurched. He didn't know how to *play*. He held back, but the others dragged him into their game without realizing he had no idea what to do. She doubted anyone had ever splashed him in his life. If a palace servant had done so by mistake, he would have been reprimanded. Ozarson had only been seven when the army took him away. Had he spent the past two years with no playmates, only an army major who tutored him in academics and military strategy? No wonder he seemed bewildered.

Childhood had a healing power, though. Although he didn't loosen up as much as the other boys, he was soon splashing and laughing with them. Allegra tended to Shadow and checked his hooves for pebbles. Then she let him nibble grass. She sat near enough to the man on the boulder so people passing might think he was her father, but far enough away that he didn't pay her any attention.

Eventually the man finished his statue, a small bird, and put it in a sack. Then he called, "Ho! Devi! Time to go."

One of the boys stopped playing and turned with a thunderous look of protest. The argument that followed made Allegra smile. She had heard it often from her brothers when they wanted to keep playing in the lake and their father said it was time to go. For the first time since the T'Ambera had abducted her, she dared hope to see her family again. This freedom was tenuous, though. If Markus and his men hadn't already given pursuit, they soon would.

As Devi bid the others goodbye, his father glanced at Allegra. "Would your father consider selling that horse?" He indicated Shadow, who was peacefully cropping grass.

"I don't think so," she said. "He's mighty attached to it."

"Not surprised." The man hesitated. "He the one who gave you that black eye?"

Allegra bit her lip and just shook her head.

"Shouldn't go around hitting children," he muttered.

Devi came over, dripping wet, and glared at his father. "You could come back for me later."

The man smiled laconically. "Come on. You'll survive."

The boy waved at Ozi, who was wading out of the water. Then Devi took off, walking sulkily while his father handed him fresh clothes. Within moments, though, his interest was caught by the stalls that lined the bank, where merchants sold all sorts of goods, from food to bridles to mining equipment. People thronged the area, children ran and laughed, musicians sang for coins and acrobats tumbled in open stretches of grass. The place hummed with energy.

"This is fun," Ozarson said. He was dripping wet, and he held his shoes and shirt dangling in one hand. "Let's explore!"

Allegra indicated a secluded space between two outcroppings. "After you change. The travel bag has some dry clothes."

He fetched the dry clothes, then stooped behind the boulder so she could see only his head and changed into trousers and a worn shirt she had found in the hut at the horse pen.

When Ozarson finished, he and Allegra walked together, with Allegra leading Shadow. The boy stared around at everyone and everything.

"I've never been outside without guards," he confided.

"Does it bother you?" she asked.

"It feels good." He smiled just like Markus, with that gorgeous flash of white teeth.

Longing flooded Allegra, but she fought it. She didn't

want to miss Markus. He was the most maddening, arrogant man. Yet he could also be so compelling. Nor could she forget his beautiful body in the starlight. If she enjoyed making love to him, did that mean she wanted to be his wife? She felt as if her heart had betrayed her, trying to make her into someone she wasn't. It was all tangled up in her knowledge of his plans. Jazid and Taka Mal were going to war, and she was the only one who knew outside of his army.

"Do you want to fight Taka Mal?" she asked Ozarson.

He glanced at her. "Markus says we must."

"Markus may be wrong."

"He isn't often."

"He's not actually in the military, though, is he?" She had the impression he was a civilian.

"He served for ten years," Ozarson said. "Father made him a colonel even though he was young. But Markus decided to work on the palace staff. He used to say, 'Ozi, I'm a statesman, not a soldier.'" Pride touched his voice. "He's a great swordsman, though. You should see. No one can beat him. He led a company of men when Father went to war against Cobalt." In a subdued voice, he said, "They brought his body back with my father's."

Saints above. Most adults she knew would have reeled with the shocks this boy had faced at age seven. "But he wasn't dead."

"He was in a coma. They said he would never wake up. But he did before Cobalt's people knew. That's how we…" He stopped, then looked away.

"Ozi?" she asked.

"Look." He pointed at a stall. "They have so many shoes."

She could only imagine what it had been like for him to think he had lost his father and surrogate father on the same day. It was no wonder he didn't want to talk about it.

She peered at the stall. Sandals, shoes and boots hung from the overhead slats and were stacked on shelves. A heavy-set man stood calling out his wares. Watching him, Allegra had an idea.

"Let's go see," she said.

Ozarson glanced at her feet. "Major Taliz's boots fit you."

"Not shoes. Polish. Brown, I think. We'll need a lot." She patted Shadow's neck. "Everyone notices him. When Markus gets here, he'll ask people if they've seen us. Most won't notice two raggedy boys. But a huge black? That will stay in their minds. So we'll change his color. They'll remember a big brown horse."

"I don't think polish would work," Ozarson said, laughing. "It's probably not good for him, either."

"We should do something. I don't want to sell him. He's stronger than any other horse we could find. And he belongs to Markus." When she was free, she would try to have someone return the horse he so clearly valued.

Ozarson considered Shadow. "Mud could work."

"To make him look less valuable. Yes, that's a good idea."

They found a secluded place on the river and let Shadow roll in the mud, which he obviously enjoyed. As they continued on, the mud dried and flaked, turning his coat a mottled brown. It looked terrible, which was good, but Shadow grew annoyed. He swished flies with angry swipes of his tail and whinnied, baring his teeth.

Ozarson scratched the horse's neck. "Don't be mad. We'll clean you tonight. Besides, *we* think you look beautiful." He gave Shadow part of an apple. "See? We love you."

Shadow ate the apple and seemed mollified.

"We need more food," Allegra said. "I'd like to find a lookout, too, to see if we can spot anyone following us."

Ozarson waved his hand at the trees. "Have you ever seen so many? We can climb one! I've never done that."

She smiled at his enthusiasm. Every boy should climb a tree. "All right. After we buy food."

"My guards always take care of—" He stopped, looking confused. "Do you know how to buy food?"

She didn't know whether to laugh or cry at his questions. He was one of the smartest children she had ever met, yet in some ways, he knew less about life than a toddler.

"We go to a stall that has what we want," she said. "We haggle over price, the merchant gives us the food and we give him coins."

"Do we have coins?"

She regarded him guiltily. "I stole a bag from Major Gaizz."

"If Major Gaizz had the coins, they're mine. So you didn't steal them."

She smiled. "Let's spend your coins, then."

In no time, they had supplies and a spyglass. They found some sturdy trees and left Shadow at the bottom of one while they climbed into the branches. Ozarson took to it right away, and she could barely keep up with him. When they reached a good, solid branch, they sat on either side of the trunk with their legs dangling. They had a clear view of the land to the south. In the distance, the Fractured Mountains rose up, harsh and broken against the sky. It was so strange the way everyone went about their business here, oblivious to the three thousand warriors hidden in those mountains.

She scanned the desert with the spyglass. Red and yellow sands jumped into prominence, and jutting spars of rock.

"Do you see anyone?" Ozarson asked.

"Nothing." She lowered the glass. "I'd have thought they would be after us by now."

"Here." He held out his hand. "I'll look."

She handed him the glass, startled by his manner. He didn't ask, as most children would. He expected people to do as he bid. He wasn't arrogant, at least not yet, but neither did he know any other way. His differences were subtle enough that so far no one had noticed. She just hoped it stayed that way.

"I don't see anyone, either." He lowered the glass. "Yet. But you know Markus won't let us go to Aronsdale."

"He can't stop us if he isn't here."

Ozarson stared across the desert, then up the river, his face pensive. "It would be fun to travel like everyone else. To be a boy no one knows. No one special."

Allegra spoke quietly. "All your advisors want to put you on this throne and that. But you've never said what *you* want."

He thought for a long moment. "I am the Atajazid D'Az Ozarson. It is my right to rule from the Onyx Throne."

"But is that what you want?"

He regarded her steadily. "Yes."

Looking at him, for a moment she glimpsed his future, the day when this boy became one of the most formidable sovereigns ever known. The image vanished from her mind almost as soon as it came. Maybe she had imagined it; precognition was among the rarest mage traits. Even without it, though, she sensed the greatness in this child. Whether or not he achieved that potential depended on so many fragile plans.

"Do you want the throne of Taka Mal?" she asked.

"I don't know." He let out a breath. "General Yargazon says we must kill the queen and her baby. I don't want that."

"Maybe we can find another way for you to retake the Onyx Throne." She had no idea how a boy and a young woman could manage such a thing, but she didn't know what else to say.

"I don't see how going to Aronsdale will help," he said.

"They're the only country not controlled by Cobalt," she said, thinking. "He rules the Misted Cliffs, Shazire, Blueshire and Jazid, and his wife is the heir in Harsdown. Even Taka Mal has his troops and cavalry. Only Aronsdale is free of his influence."

"Not completely," Ozarson said. "His wife is kin to your king in Aronsdale."

"She's his niece." Allegra suspected Ozarson knew more

about the intrigues of the royal houses than most anyone. "Do you think that would make Aronsdale more likely to support Emperor Cobalt?"

"I don't know," he said. "Maybe not. General Yargazon told me that your king threatened to help Taka Mal *fight* Cobalt if the emperor invaded Taka Mal. It's because the queen of Taka Mal married a man related to the royal family of Aronsdale."

She wondered how they kept it all straight. "I can never sort out all those royal lineages."

"I had to draw family trees," Ozarson confided. "The queen's consort is Drummer Headwind. Drummer's sister is the mother of Cobalt's wife. The father of Cobalt's wife is your king's cousin. So your king considers Drummer his kin." His face darkened. "Queen Vizarana in Taka Mal told my father she would marry *him* if he allied with her against Cobalt. Then she married Drummer. She betrayed my father."

"But your father was already married."

He averted his eyes. "I know."

So even Ozarson's mother, the queen, hadn't been safe from his father's caprices. "Even in Jazid, it isn't legal for a man to have two wives."

"He was the atajazid. He could do what he wanted." The boy fidgeted with the hem of his shirt. "He already had a second wife. Queen Vizarana would have been the third."

"Saint Azure," she muttered. "How many did the man need?"

He looked up at her. "He told the queen of Taka Mal that

he wouldn't support her army against Cobalt unless she became his wife."

"I thought she offered to marry him."

"Well, no," he admitted. "She just asked him to ally with her. He said she had to marry him if she wanted his help."

"That puts a different slant on it, Ozi." It was beginning to make sense. With Cobalt threatening Taka Mal, it had given Ozarson's father a way to take the queen's throne—marry him in return for an alliance. By Jazid law, he would undoubtedly rule Taka Mal if he married the queen. But it couldn't be that simple in Taka Mal. Vizarana had married an Aronsdale man and continued to rule. Of course, he came from a country where the man expected to move into his wife's home and help with her livelihood. Allegra had hoped her husband would work in the dairy with her. Saints, what a thought, Markus milking cows.

She couldn't imagine a marriage between Queen Vizarana and Atajazid D'Az Ozar. No wonder Vizarana had turned to Aronsdale.

"Ozi, I don't know the answers," she said. "But I very much would like to go home. To Aronsdale."

He drew himself into a regal posture. "Then we shall go." His grin sparkled. "On the muddiest horse in Taka Mal."

With a laugh, she said, "Come on, you."

They climbed down the tree and up onto Shadow. Mud dusted all over their clothes, and they looked like itinerant wanderers.

So they set off for Aronsdale.

CHAPTER 14
THE SAINT VERDANT

They rode all day along the river, even *in* the river, to hide their trail. Every now and then, they encouraged the horse to roll in the mud, until they were all covered with caked dirt. They blended with all the other dusty travelers following the river, which offered the only viable route through a vast desert.

That evening, as the sun slanted across the land, they cleaned Shadow near a secluded waterfall. While the horse grazed, they climbed above the falls and sat eating their dinner as the sun sunk to the horizon. Allegra scanned the desert with her spyglass—

And sighted soldiers galloping across the sands.

"Damn!" She offered Ozarson the glass. "It's them."

The boy looked where she indicated. "Oh. Yes." He sounded disappointed. "They'll probably ride through the night until they reach the river."

"We're at least a day's ride west of where they'll hit it."

"They have more horses, supplies and scouts, though."

He considered her. "Maybe they'll assume you're taking me to Quaaz."

"It would be a reasonable choice. Yargazon might think I'm going to tell Queen Vizarana about the invasion."

"He must be embarrassed you knocked him out."

She suspected embarrassed hardly began to describe it. The General probably wanted to flay her. "We should leave."

Ozarson spoke firmly. "I won't let them hurt you. They must do as I say."

Allegra knew he couldn't stop Markus and Yargazon, but his intentions touched her. She said only, "Thank you."

They set off again, and kept going long after the sun left the sky in a wash of crimson fire.

Yargazon slammed her against the freezing wall. "You drove him to go, looking for you, when he should have stayed with the army. You endangered our plans and put him in danger."

She fought his hold. "Let me go!"

He swore at her and raised his arm....

"No!" Allegra woke with a gasp, shaking so hard, she almost slid off Shadow. And she *was* on the horse, leaning over his neck.

"You'll be fine," Ozarson murmured soothingly. "It's just a bad dream. I get them all the time."

As her mind cleared, she realized she was in front of him, and he was holding her as they rode. She barely recalled when he had told her they should switch places, acting more like an atajazid in charge than a hostage.

"Are you better?" Ozarson asked.

"Yes. You're right, it was just a bad dream." She feared it could become reality, but she didn't want to tell him.

"We should stop," he said. "Shadow wants to sleep, too."

"All right." She wished nothing more than to stretch out flat and sleep.

Ozarson reined in the horse, and they slid down. As he lifted off the travel bags, Allegra lay on the ground and closed her eyes.

Ozarson knelt next to her. "Don't sleep there."

"Shadow needs to rest," she mumbled.

"A little while. But if we don't stop long, we can reach the place where this river flows into the Saint Verdant by dawn."

She was drifting off. "It can wait an hour."

"Allegra, listen." He shook her shoulder. "I studied these places with Major Gaizz. The Saint Verdant is huge, the biggest river in the settled lands. Ships go up and down it, and that includes a scow schooner that's really *fast*. It can carry a horse. A barge carries horses, too, but it's so slow, you could ride to Aronsdale, quickly. The major's reports were over a year old, but if the schedule is the same now, the scow only leaves once every few days. It's scheduled for this morning, at dawn."

She opened her eyes. "As in, we could catch it, but Markus would have to wait days for the next one?"

Ozarson nodded, his face lit by starlight and a gibbous moon. "That's right. Unless he left the horses behind."

"They might do that. Buy more in Aronsdale."

He folded his arms against the cold. "If Markus goes to Aronsdale and they catch him, they might not let him go."

However confused she might feel about Markus, Allegra didn't want to see him hurt. And she realized now that she couldn't use Ozi the way she had intended. "I'll leave you at the dock at the Saint Verdant. You can go back with Markus. I'll return Shadow once I'm safe in Aronsdale."

He shook his head. "Markus won't stop looking for you. He'll make sure I'm safe and then he'll go after you even in Aronsdale."

She stood up, folding her arms against the cold. "Why? Because I took his horse?" She scowled. "After all, it's worth more than me."

"Don't say that."

Her anger simmered. "It's your law, not mine."

He gave a childlike snort. "They don't really believe that. All they *think* about is women. Women and war. They all want a woman, and almost none of them have one, so they're angry and they want to fight. So they say that thing about the horse."

She blinked at him. Sometimes children had far more wisdom than their guardians. "Even so."

"Legally you're his wife," Ozarson added.

"I hardly know him."

"But I do. He's never wanted to marry anyone before, even when my father pressured him to take a bride. He'll come after you." His voice was just audible above the flow of the nearby river. "And, Allegra, I *want* to go to Aronsdale. To see the king without him knowing who I am. To see what he's like. Will he help my people? How can I know? I could never go as the atajazid. Only this way, by pretending I'm no one."

"It's dangerous. Not just to you, but to Markus, too."

He spoke quietly. "If he invades Taka Mal, he could die more easily than if he comes looking for me."

He didn't say what they both knew, that Ozarson could also die that easily. "All right," she said. "We'll just sleep a little, then go on."

"You sleep now. I'll take care of Shadow."

She nodded and hoped their plan wasn't in vain, that tomorrow they wouldn't arrive at the ship to find Markus waiting.

Allegra had never seen docks as big as those where the King's Courseway poured into the Saint Verdant River. It was as if the entire world converged on this spot. The water stretched out to a distant shore she could barely see. Ships and boats of all sizes sailed the rivers, and men stood in them, calling out, raising sails, leaning into the wind. Fishermen thronged the docks, and the oily smell of their catch tickled her nose. Dogs ran everywhere and yapped at the red-terns that squawked in the cloudless sky.

"It's amazing," Ozarson said. "I never knew so much water existed!"

"I've heard the ocean at the edge of the Misted Cliffs goes on forever," Allegra said. "All the way to the horizon."

"I'll never know." His fist clenched at his side. "I'll never go to the Misted Cliffs."

His vehemence didn't surprise her, given what he thought of that country's sovereign. She indicated one of the bigger docks. A ship was tied up there, a schooner she thought, but she didn't know ships well enough to be sure. Criers were calling out port destinations, and many people were queued up to board, including someone with a horse.

"Do you think that's the scow?" she asked.

"It looks like it, doesn't it?" Excitement flared in his eyes. "Let's see!"

As they neared the ship, a man in a sailor's cap shouted at them. "The horse is two silver hexacoins. If you can't afford it, don't bring him."

Allegra raised her hand in acknowledgment, reluctant to call out an answer in what might sound like a girl's voice. Ozarson was looking everywhere, drinking in the sights as if he were a dry sponge. As they joined the line of people boarding, Allegra said, "Have you ever met Markus's mother?"

"A few times," he said absently as he craned his head to look at nearby piers. "She lives on Lake Baraza with her husband."

Her husband? "I thought she was a concubine."

"That was before. Allegra, look at all the sea creatures." He pointed to the pier next to theirs as a man heaved in a net of squirming, silver fish. A cork floater in the water bumped the dock, and river-weed trailed from his net onto the planks.

She smiled at his astonishment. "They're fish. They live in rivers, too, not just the sea."

"I know that," he said with offended dignity. His eyes were

lit with pleasure, though. "They just look so strange. We never see water animals with the army."

"Ozi, who married Markus's mother?"

"What?" He pulled his attention away from the fisherman. "The soldier who guarded her." He spoke awkwardly. "My father hadn't visited her in so long, I think he had forgotten about her. So he let her get married."

No wonder Markus understood why she wanted a guarantee he wouldn't do the same. He could have gone the other way and ended up like his father. Perhaps he and Ozarson were more fortunate than they realized in having their father ignore them, for neither seemed to have taken on his worst traits.

"What's his mother like?" she asked.

"She's pretty." Ozarson was inspecting the wood under their feet. He knelt down and peered through gaps between the planks. The river below sloshed against mussel-encrusted pylons. "*Look* at all that water."

Smiling, she took his arm and drew him up so they could move forward with the line. "It's a lot. But you have to watch where you're going, or someone will trip over you."

Mischief glinted in his eyes. "Markus's mother always scolded him like that. Even in front of his men."

She gave a startled laugh. "Really?"

"Once when I was five, he and his men came back from an army training exercise. They had been out for days. When he hugged his mother, she kissed his cheek. Then she wrinkled up her nose and said he smelled like a goat. In front of everyone."

Allegra smirked. "I'll bet he loved that."

"He made a joke. Everyone laughed." His eyes danced. "But when it was just him, her and me, he was so mad! He told her never to talk that way in front of his men. She said if he would take a bath, she wouldn't have to. I thought it was funny, but he didn't. He was furious."

Hah! Allegra wished she could have seen it. "Did he bathe?"

"For dinner. He changed his clothes, too."

Allegra smiled. Markus must have taken it to heart, given the care he took with personal hygiene even when he was on the run with his army. "That's a good story."

"It was funny to see his mother talk to him just like mine did with…" His smile faded and his voice trailed away.

"Ah, honey," she murmured. "I'm sorry to remind you."

"Honey?" He seemed bewildered.

"It's a term of affection."

"I've never heard that."

"You don't have honey?"

"On bread, if we can get it. I don't know from where."

"Bees make it."

"Bees!" He regarded her skeptically. "You made that up."

"It's true." What a strange life he had. He could tell her every detail of the military and political machinations among the royal families of the settled lands, but he didn't know where honey came from.

As they moved forward, she took several coins out of their bags, discreetly, so no one would know she had money.

As two scruffy boys, they were hardly likely targets for thieves, but anyone who saw Shadow might wonder.

Then they were at the front of the line. A man in a striped blue and white shirt and frayed trousers stood there, a cap at a crooked angle on his head. He was chewing, and Allegra smelled sour tobacco.

"How far you two going?" he asked.

"To Aronsdale." Allegra's pulse quickened. What if Markus had people on the docks seeking Aronsdale passengers? What if the ship didn't go that far or he said they were too young to go alone or he noticed she was a girl?

"A silver for each," he said. "Two for the horse. We provide water, but you pay extra if you need more feed. You can pay with hexas from Taka Mal, Jazid or Aronsdale. Animals stay on the lower deck. And listen here, boy. Take proper care of that horse or we'll put you all off at the next stop."

"We'll look after him," she promised, giving him the coins.

"Why two for the horse and only one for me?" Ozarson asked.

Allegra almost groaned. In his world view, a horse cost more than a woman, but *not* more than the atajazid. She needed to have a talk with him, and soon, or he would give himself away.

The man chuckled. "Because he's a big horse. You're just a turnip shoot."

Ozarson frowned. "I'm—"

"Here." Allegra grabbed Ozarson's arm and led him and Shadow onto the ship.

"What did he mean, a turnip shoot?" Ozarson grumbled. "I'm not a plant."

She lowered her voice. "You're not the atajazid, either, remember?" She glowered. "And if you're worth more than two silvers, so am I."

"Oh." Ozarson mulled that over as they walked Shadow down a ramp to the lower deck. The other horse was already in the cargo area, plus a goat, cow, various chickens and a goose.

Ozarson scrunched up his nose. "It smells in here."

Allegra laughed good-naturedly. "So it does."

Shadow whinnied as if to protest the indignity of a royal horse being quartered in such a manner. He had a lot in common with Ozarson, she decided. But they would survive. Although rough, the area was clean and spacious, with plenty of water.

"Here." She lifted the packs off Shadow and handed them to Ozarson. "After we get him settled, we can go on the upper deck."

Excitement filled his voice. "I want to watch the water! I can't believe there's so much. You could jump in and be covered."

"Can you swim?"

He shook his head. "I used to paddle around the bathing pool, when I was little. But Nanna held me so my head didn't go under."

"Nanna?"

He averted his eyes, suddenly intent on rubbing down Shadow. "She was my nurse."

Was. Past tense. She knew so little of what had happened to him, only that he had been with his mother when Cobalt's men brought his father's body and a dying Markus to the Onyx Palace. The men from the Misted Cliffs had taken control of the palace, including the royal family. So how had Ozarson ended up in hiding with a fugitive army led by a very healthy Markus and the general of his father's vanquished forces?

She spoke carefully, easing up to her questions. "Did Nanna care for you?"

"Until I was seven." He scratched the horse's nose. "We're going up top, Shadow. We'll come back down later." He made a face. "If we can stand the smell."

The deck jolted under them, and Allegra grabbed a nearby beam.

"We're moving!" Ozarson whirled around. "Let's go watch!"

The boy was off before she could answer. He took the rickety stairs two at a time and disappeared. Following him, she came up into a brisk wind just as the craft swooped away from the dock. Grabbing her cap, she worked the pins in her hair so they held the hat secure on her head. Cap or no, people might begin to suspect she was a woman, but they were closer to Aronsdale now, in an area of blended cultures, which would make her traveling on her own less unusual.

Before today, the only "ships" she had seen were boats that darted across the lake near her home. This was such a sight! Sailors were up in the rigging, and sails unfurled like billowing clouds. The schooner surged away from the banks—and away from any horseman who might gallop in to catch it at the last minute.

Allegra hung on to the stair railing and tilted her head into the wind, filled with elation. This ship could reach Aronsdale in no time. The Saint Verdant turned south at the border and cut back into Taka Mal, which meant the nomads must have crossed it when they took her from Aronsdale to Jazid. She had been so drugged, she didn't even remember. If she and Ozarson disembarked at the point where the river turned south, they could probably ride to Crofts Vale in less than two days.

Ozarson was at a rail of the deck, the wind tossing his curls as he leaned over to peer at the river. She went to him, surprised she could keep her balance on the swaying ship. Other travelers gathered along the rail, many waving to people on the receding dock.

The boy straightened as she came up next to him. "I love it!" He stretched his arms out as if to encompass the entire river. "Have you ever seen anything like this? It's magic!"

She smiled at his exuberance. "We might make Aronsdale in two days, if this wind stays strong."

"This is a good adventure." He indicated the rippling wake of the boat. "I could make an equation to describe those waves."

The idea intrigued Allegra. "How?"

"Some periodic function. Maybe sines and cosines."

"You know *trigonometry?*"

"Not very well," he said as if admitting a shortcoming,

when he was describing a level of mathematics most adult scholars in their lands didn't know. "But I'm trying to learn."

"You like math."

"I love it." He leaned on the rail. "Three times thirty-seven equals one hundred and eleven. That's the prime factorization. You know one hundred and eleven can't be prime because its digits add up to three. So it's divisible by three."

She laughed, delighted. "I'll teach that to my students."

Ozarson scowled, looking for all the world like Markus. "You shouldn't make things up."

"I'm not. And stop scowling at me, turnip sprout. Women can do math just as well as men."

"That's not true!" He squinted at her. "Is it?"

"It most certainly is."

"Not in Jazid."

She regarded him innocently. "Are you saying people in Jazid aren't as smart as in other places?"

"I am not!" He glared at her. "All right, Allegra. If you tell me the answer to this, I'll believe you. I have a dart board. It's perfectly round. The distance from the center to the edge is five times as long as my little finger." He held up the pertinent digit and wiggled it portentously at her.

She could already guess the type of problem. Something with the area or circumference of a circle. "All right."

"A smaller circle is inside the bigger one," he said. "It has the same center, but the distance to its edge is only three of my little finger. What's the probability that if I throw a dart, it will hit the smaller circle?"

"That's easy. Nine over twenty-five. Thirty-six percent."

He gaped at her. "Even Major Gaizz didn't do it that fast!"

"I told you," she said, relieved he had given her a problem she could do. "I help out at a school. All you have to do is take the ratio of the smaller area to the larger."

"Major Gaizz said it was easy when I explained," he allowed. "But he didn't know how to do it right away."

"How old were you when you made up the problem?"

"A couple of years ago."

At age *seven*? Even at fourteen or fifteen, the age when most children quit school, she knew of very few who could have done that problem. "You must learn fast."

"After Markus and I went into hiding, I was scared," Ozarson said. "Doing number games helped me calm down." His mood brightened. "I helped General Yargazon last year."

She couldn't imagine the ice-hearted general letting a child help him. Then again, he genuinely seemed to like the boy. Maybe it was just women Yargazon hated.

"What did you do?" she asked.

His voice warmed as he talked about what was obviously his favorite subject. "The math was easy. He was working out this war-games scenario. In one part, he needed to divide up the men so he had the same number in each group, but he had to plan for three different outcomes. He couldn't figure out the smallest number of soldiers he needed to have was eight per group in the first scenario, twelve in the second and fourteen in the third. He told Markus it would take over thirteen hundred! That's wrong. He just needed the least common multiple of eight, twelve and fourteen. One-hundred and sixty-eight."

"Did you tell him?"

"Of course." His mouth quirked up. "He thanked me and went on with his work. He thought I had no idea what I was talking about. Then Markus told him to see if it worked. When it did, the General laughed. He said I would make a great commander."

She would have liked to be a fly in that tent when it happened. "You should become a mathematician. You would be great at it."

His voice quieted. "I can't." He turned to stare out at the river. "I have duties."

I can't. Such simple words for so much pain. He couldn't pursue this great gift of his because he had to invade countries, wage war and conquer people, all to ensure his country survived.

Ozarson gazed over the water with his chin lifted in a regal posture she doubted he even realized. The wind blew his hair back from the same profile etched on Jazid coins. Watching him, a chill went up her spine. Greatness lived in this boy. Someday he would be a king like no other, his name remembered for ages. Whether it would be for great deeds or terrible, she didn't know, but he would become a legend.

If he lived.

CHAPTER 15
THE GILDED LAND

The day passed in a swirl of wind and colors. Allegra loved the river. She ate enough for the first time in days, and her bruises began to heal. Each time the schooner stopped on the river, she scanned the shore for Jazidian soldiers. She saw none. That night, she and Ozarson camped next to Shadow. At first, she watched over the boy. Incredibly, when she collapsed into sleep, he watched over her, the king of Jazid acting as a guard to a commoner in the smelly under-deck of a Taka Mal scow schooner.

The next day was just as exhilarating. As night fell, many passengers gathered on the upper deck. Everyone passed around wine bags, Aronsdale cheeses and citrus fruit from Taka Mal. They sang ballads and folk songs. It delighted Allegra to lift her voice purely for the joy of singing, with no worry about spells. Ozarson sat on a big coil of rope, listening, his eyes glowing in the light from covered lamps suspended on ropes. When someone launched into a ballad about a Jazid folk tale, he joined in with a boy's treble voice, untrained but clear and full.

That night, she and Ozarson slept under the stars, curled in a pile of rope. When a sailor called them a pair of turnip sprouts, the atajazid laughed. In the morning, they bought oranges from the citrus peddler. Their hexacoins were running low, though; if they didn't reach Crofts Vale soon, they would run out of money.

On the third morning, the Saint Verdant turned south-ward. The port-crier strolled through the ship, calling out destinations at the next stop—including the Pyramid Foot-hills of Aronsdale.

Allegra and Ozarson stood with Shadow on the dock. The horse snorted and shook his head. Ahead of them, beyond the pier, a few shacks lined a dirt road; beyond that, the Pyramid Foothills swelled into the sky. Compared to the soaring, broken majesty of the Fractured Mountains, these hills resembled beanbags strewn across the land. Grass rippled around the shacks, and scattered wildflowers added color to the edges of the road.

"Is this Aronsdale?" Ozarson asked.

"I guess so," Allegra said. It didn't look like much.

He glanced around. "We're the only ones who got off the ferry. No one else wants to go here."

"Not today." She started down the dock, leading Shadow. The aroma of baking crab wafted around them. "We'll ride south to Crofts Vale. We might reach it by tomorrow night."

He regarded her curiously. "Is your family there?"

"No." A surge of homesickness hit her. "They're farther west, near the border of southern Aronsdale with Shazire."

"Shazire." His gaze darkened. "Cobalt's lands."

"Actually his mother governs there."

"His mother?" He seemed mystified by that information. "A woman?"

Allegra smiled. "They usually are."

He walked for a while, thinking. Then he said, "His empire is Shazire, Blueshire, Jazid and the Misted Cliffs. But he calls it the Dawn Star Empire. Why?"

"I've no idea. For his wife, maybe? She's a Dawnfield."

"People say she's a sorceress," Ozarson confided.

"She's just a mage. Stronger than me, though."

"We're in the land of mages!" Ozarson ran down the dock. At the end, he spun around and spread his arms. "She'll put all of Aronsdale to sleep!"

Allegra burst out laughing. "I hope not."

"Let's go see Crofts Vale," he said, his eyes dancing.

Within moments, they were on Shadow, galloping down the road.

They reached Crofts Vale in the late afternoon of their second day in Aronsdale. Sunlight slanted across the hills, which were lush with grass. Skybells bloomed, and larks flitted through glades of trees draped with mossy vines. The fragrance of night-blooming starlights filled the air as the white flowers opened even though the sun had yet to sink behind the hills. A waterfall tumbled over a ledge and into a pool where Shadow stopped to drink. Above it all, Castle Suncroft stood on a hill, overlooking the village and countryside.

Allegra gazed at the castle. A croft for the sun. Such a modest name for so lovely a place. Towers with purple turrets rose at its four corners, and crenellated walls protected the interior. The setting sun gilded the castle and filled the valley with antiqued light, as if a gold haze shimmered within Crofts Vale.

Ozarson was sitting in front of Allegra, in her arms. He had been silent since they came into view of the valley, but now he said, "It's just as lovely as you said it would be."

"It is." This was actually her first time seeing it, too. She could understand why so many songs praised the beauty of this valley.

"Are we going to the castle?" he asked.

"To the village. The Song Weavers Guild." She couldn't just show up and ask for the king. The guild would send a message to Della No-Cozen, the castle's mage mistress, to let her know Allegra had arrived.

Allegra wasn't certain what to expect at the guild. She was many days late. They hadn't known exactly when to expect her, though, and she had been taking her time on the journey here, enjoying herself before the T'Ambera wreaked havoc with her life.

Boys and girls dashed in games of chase and jump-a-jump across the meadows, and adults relaxed in the grass, watching the children, picnicking, enjoying the evening. The women wore flowing tunics and leggings in green, blue, rose and yellow. The men had on dark trousers and shirts in bright colors.

Three girls tumbled into the grass only a few paces away from where Shadow was walking. They scrambled to their feet and ran after a boy who was laughing and teasing them with calls. When he saw them racing toward him, he shouted with alarm and took off, sprinting for a cluster of other boys farther down the slope.

Ozarson watched in silence. It was so unlike his usual response to new places, it worried Allegra.

"Ozi?" she asked. "Are you all right?"

"Yes." His voice had an odd sound. *Crying?*

"Honey, what's wrong?" she asked.

"Why do you call me that?" He *was* crying. "I'm not a sweet spread for a sugar roll."

"I thought you would like it here," she said.

"I do."

"But why does it make you cry?"

He sniffed and wiped his sleeve across his nose. "It's all so pretty. The children play and play. Everyone looks happy."

Allegra leaned her forehead against the back of his head, her heart aching. Aronsdale was no paradise. People here struggled for enough to eat, a family to love, a livelihood that would see them through their days. They had nothing of the wealth Jazid miners took for granted. But compared to what Ozarson knew, it probably looked idyllic.

"Do you want to play with the other children?" she asked.

"I don't know them," he said. "It's not like at the river, where no one knew anyone."

"No, I guess not." The other children would also realize he didn't come from here. Although most people in eastern Aronsdale had dark hair and eyes, possibly because far more Jazidian women ran away to Aronsdale than Markus thought, Aronsdale softened those who lived within its dales and meadows. Ozarson was pure Jazidian, with his obsidian hair, tilted eyes and proud features. Just as most people could tell a Jazidian thoroughbred from an Aronsdale horse, so she doubted anyone would mistake him for an Aronsdale boy.

They rode on, beneath the hill with its golden castle.

The Song Weavers Guild was in a large house of bronze-wood that turned coppery-red in the sunset. The stairs up to its wide porch were smoothed from years of feet going up and down them. Inside they entered a big room filled with serenity. Stained-glass windows glowed with aged sunlight and cast pools of gem colors on the floor. Bronze-wood tables stood around the room, surrounded by chairs with gold cushions. Shapes were everywhere, vines flowering with circles, squares, polygons and more. Shape carvings adorned the poles supporting the ceiling, borders on the walls, furniture, even worn patterns on the parquetry floor. For the first time in days, power stirred within Allegra.

Ozarson gaped at the room. "Is this where you live?"

"Maybe." Allegra no longer knew what would happen. She had cast more complex spells in the past few days than she had thought possible. The mage mistress had wanted to find a green or blue mage for Prince Aron. It seemed presumptuous to think they might have invited her to meet him, but she was beginning to wonder if Della No-Cozen had suspected her power more than Allegra had herself.

Allegra mentally shook herself. She had no business thinking about Aron. She was married. She could challenge the contracts since Markus had forced her into the union, but she wasn't even sure if she wanted to end her marriage. Then again, it probably didn't matter. Markus surely hated her now, after she took Ozarson.

She longed to go home, lean her head against her mother's shoulder and seek comfort in her family's love. But she had responsibilities. She had to warn someone about the Jazid army. She felt helpless to stop the war, but if she said nothing and thousands of people died, she could never live with herself.

A plump, older woman was coming toward them. Her brown hair curled out from under a white cap, and she had a white apron over her blue tunic. She stopped in front of Allegra and spoke coolly. "May I help you boys?"

With a start, Allegra realized how they looked: two grungy fellows gawking in the entry of a guild house for young women. She couldn't fathom why people mistook her for a boy just because she wore old clothes and flattened her chest, but it worked.

"I'm sorry." She pulled off her cap, letting her hair tumble around her shoulders. "My name is Allegra Linseed. I'm expected."

"Allegra!" The woman's entire manner changed. "Child, we've been worried sick."

"I had a...side trip." She suddenly felt tired. She didn't know what to say to anyone.

"Goodness, let's get you settled." The woman wiped her flour-dusted hands on her apron. "I'm Marnie, the cook. I'll show you where you can wash up and change. Then we can go meet the guild mistress." She frowned at Ozarson. "Your letters didn't say you were bringing a brother."

"He's my ward," Allegra said.

"Well, he can't stay in here," Marnie said sternly. She thought for a moment. "I guess he could sleep in the stables."

"The stables!" Allegra had no intention of leaving the king of Jazid to sleep in a stable. "Can't he stay with me?"

Marnie crossed her arms. "You can't have a boy with you."

"I can sleep in the stables." Ozarson looked delighted with the prospect. "I'll look after Shadow."

"Shadow!" Marnie exclaimed. "You've another boy here?"

Allegra smiled at her aghast expression. "He's our horse."

"Ah." Marnie relaxed. "Well, it's settled then." She even beamed at Ozarson. "You're a handsome fellow, eh? Better watch out or the girls will chase you."

Ozarson's face turned red.

"We should look after the horse," Allegra said, rescuing him. "I'll be back as soon as we're done."

"I'll tell the guild mistress you're here." Marnie's strict demeanor eased. "The boy can come into the dining room to eat. But he's to stay out of the rest of the house."

Allegra hoped Ozarson wasn't upset. For a child who was used to adults kneeling to him, the past few days must have been quite an experience. He hardly seemed to notice, though. He was already out the door.

Allegra spoke in a low voice to Marnie. "He's from Jazid. He lost his parents during the war."

The cook's expression softened. "Well, he can stay as long as he needs. In the stable, though. Just don't tell anyone."

"Thank you," Allegra murmured.

The stable turned out to be a barn with a couple of stalls. Fresh hay lay everywhere, filling the air with its aroma. She found Ozarson rubbing down Shadow. A boy with yellow curls was lounging against the half door of the other stall, watching him.

"That's surely the biggest horse I've seen," the boy said.

"He's part Jazidian Black," Ozarson told him.

"You from Jazid?" the other boy asked.

"That's right." Ozarson kept his attention on his work.

Shadow whinnied as Allegra came toward them. Ozarson whirled around, then relaxed when he saw her. "Look at all the hay." He motioned around the stable. "It's everywhere."

"What, your horse doesn't have *hay?*" the other boy demanded. With a grin, he scooped up a handful and threw it at Ozarson.

Ozarson dodged the flying hay, then stood with his mouth open.

Laughing, the other boy threw more hay. "You look like you forgot to think."

"Hai!" Ozarson glared, then grabbed a load of straw and heaved it at the towheaded boy.

Within moments, straw was flying everywhere. Allegra tried to duck into Shadow's stall, where he watched the proceedings with a dubious air. Then someone showered her with hay. With a whoop, she grabbed an armful and hurled it in the direction of whoever had attacked her.

"Allegra?" Marnie said from the door of the stable.

Laughing, covered with straw, she turned around. Except it wasn't Marnie. An older women with ruddy cheeks stood there, her face framed by gray curls. She was taller than most women, and her gaze held a calm authority. She wore a white and violet tunic with gold layers, the colors of the royal House of Dawnfield.

Mortified, Allegra stared at her. "Mage Mistress No-Cozen. I—I didn't expect you so soon."

"Marnie saw us walking in the village and called us over."

Allegra felt like an idiot, covered in hay, dressed in a stable hand's scruffy clothes, her hair tangled, her face smudged, standing with two rapscallion boys who gaped at the mage mistress.

"Us?" Allegra asked weakly, wondering if she was about to embarrass herself in front of someone else.

Della stepped aside—and a youth walked into the stable. Prince Aron.

CHAPTER 16
SUNCROFT

Allegra thought she would die of embarrassment. She went down on one knee with her head bowed. She had seen portraits of the prince, but even without that, she would have known he was a Dawnfield. He wore a violet and white tunic with the royal seal on the left breast, swords crossed on a field of stars.

Silence filled the stable. Aron said nothing, which seemed odd. She glanced to her left. The yellow-haired boy was on one knee with his head down, his hair falling across his face. Peeking the other way, she saw Ozarson—

Standing up.

Damn! He was watching Aron curiously, waiting to see what he would do. The prince looked back at him, puzzled. They were a study in contrasts. Ozarson was, for all appearances, a scamp in worn clothes. Aron looked exactly the way Allegra had imagined a prince, with a handsome face and light brown hair, the classic Aronsdale curls falling down his neck and over his ears. He couldn't be more than nineteen or twenty. Her age.

"Ozi," she said softly. "You must kneel. This is Aron, the king's heir."

He gave her a quizzical look, and she wondered if he had ever knelt to anyone in his life. She took his hand and tugged. With an awkward motion, he dropped to one knee and lowered his gaze.

The hay crunched and then someone knelt in front of Allegra. She looked up into Aron's face. He smiled and offered his hands to her. She didn't know what to do, so she took them.

He drew her to her feet. "You are Allegra? The mage?"

"That's right." She wanted to hide.

He let go of her hands and pulled straw out of her hair. Then he grinned, his boyish smile sparkling in a way guaranteed to break hearts all over Aronsdale. "That looked like fun."

Allegra flushed, acutely aware of Ozarson. He also stood up, though Aron hadn't given anyone else leave to do so. The prince seemed to have forgotten. He stared at Allegra, and she wondered if she had straw stuck in some strange way in her hair or clothes.

Then concern washed over Aron's face. "Who hit you?"

She put her hand on her cheek. The black eye had healed some, but the bruise was still visible. "I got into a fight," she improvised. "Just a little scuffle."

"A fight!" He laughed, and a brown curl fell into his eyes. Pushing it aside, he said, "I'll have to remember not to anger you. I'm afraid my combat skills are rusty."

Saint Verdant. Did he have to be charming as well as gorgeous? She knew why he was looking at her, asking her name. She hadn't been presumptuous. He was supposed to marry the strongest eligible mage. They had invited her here to help her develop, and Allegra knew now she had the ability they sought. If Prince Aron had found another mage to marry, he would already be betrothed. Well, he *wasn't* betrothed. She wanted to run, to hide from him, because he was fresh and sunny, perfect in every way, but she couldn't encourage him, for she already had a husband and saints help her addled brain, when she looked at Aron, she thought of Markus.

"I'm honored to meet you, Your Highness," Allegra said. "But I—I must clean up after my travels."

"You look lovely," he said. "Like a forest sprite."

How would she get out of this? "I must go now." Augh, that sounded rude, and to a member of the Dawnfield royal House no less.

"Perhaps you could dine with us tonight at Castle Suncroft?" he asked.

"Allegra?" Ozarson said. He sounded stiff. Cold.

"I, uh—I don't know—" She stumbled on the words.

Della No-Cozen came forward and extended her hand to Allegra, somehow gracefully extricating her from Aron's grip. "I'm sorry to put a damper on matters. But before Allegra goes anywhere, I need to discuss her placement at the guild." She gave Aron a stern look. "We must let our guest relax. She's had a long trip."

Aron gave Allegra a rueful smile. "If I've pushed, please accept my apologies. Perhaps another night would be better?"

"Thank you," Allegra said. "You're most gracious."

She felt Della watching her and suspected the older woman saw more than Aron did. Ozarson's presence was like a smoldering coal at her side. But she couldn't react, not here, not in any way that might give away his identity and endanger him.

Allegra's guild room was furnished with bronzewood pieces similar to those downstairs. Shape carvings scrolled in delicate curves along the door frame and windowsills, and sunlight poured through the arched panes. Mage power swirled in Allegra.

"Well, here we are," Della said.

"It's lovely." Allegra set her bags down on a stool. Then she laid her palm on the round table and murmured an ancient lilt:

Heal my heart, falling eve
Veiled in scraps of mist
Soothe and I will believe
In dreams I thought I'd missed

A green haze formed in her thoughts. She felt Della's mood, the mage mistress's worry for Allegra, her puzzlement over Ozarson—and her hope. It pleased her to see Prince Aron respond so well to the young mage she had invited to the guild.

Allegra spoke quietly to Della. "Please come in."

Della closed the door and joined her at the table. She

touched its varnished surface, then looked up at Allegra. "When I tested you three years ago, you had no green spells."

Allegra met her gaze. "A lot has changed."

The older woman glanced at her dusty bags, which had a tasseled cord in the Jazid style. "Did you really have a 'scuffle'?" She turned back to Allegra. "Why are you wearing those clothes? And that boy. He's from Jazid, isn't he?"

Allegra sat at the table and rested her elbows on it. Then she put her head in her hands. "Ah, Della. I can't go to the palace to dine with Prince Aron, not tomorrow or ever."

The mage mistress sat next to her. "Can you tell me why?"

Allegra looked up. "I was coming here to study. I rode the last part of the journey alone. The days were beautiful, and I was so happy." Her voice cracked. "So happily, stupidly naive."

Della's voice quieted. "What happened?"

"Do you know of the T'Ambera?"

Della let out a breath. "Ah, Saints, no, Allegra."

"They sold me as a pleasure girl," she said dully. "Or a wife, I guess. Eventually."

"Are you saying you're *married*?"

"Yes." She drew in a breath. "So you see, I cannot dine with that lovely boy who would have melted my heart twelve days ago."

"Allegra, wait." Della laid a hand on her arm. "If you were taken to Jazid, sold as a slave and married against your will, none of that's legal."

"It doesn't matter. Another man has had me. The succession rules wouldn't allow my betrothal to Aron."

"Don't be certain," Della said. "Dawnfield heirs have married widows, especially in the days when men died so much more often in war." She pushed her hand through her gray hair. "Nothing like this has ever happened. I've no idea what applies here."

"I need to see King Jarid as soon as possible." She hesitated, unsure how much to say. Della was a king's advisor, but Allegra didn't even know what to tell Jarid. "It's about something else, though."

"What?"

"I can't say. I'm sorry."

Della considered her. "Who beat you?"

"It was just a tussle."

"Those bruises may be fading," Della said quietly, "but I can tell. It takes more than a 'tussle' to do that kind of damage."

Allegra remembered how Yargazon had dragged her across the carpet, his brutal determination. "I fought with a man who works for my husband. He caught me trying to run away." In a low, angry voice, she said, "I left him chained and gagged, with his head split open."

Della looked at a loss for a response. "And your husband?"

"He might be looking for me. I'm not sure."

"What about that boy?"

"He was orphaned in the war." She sat back, fatigue settling into her. "He was traveling with my husband's men. I've promised to take care of him."

"What does your husband do?"

"He's—with the army."

"A soldier?"

"Not exactly." Allegra wasn't sure how it worked. The army answered to Markus, but Yargazon commanded them. "He travels with them."

"The life of an army tender is no way for a boy to grow up." Della regarded her with puzzlement. "If you were with the army, couldn't you ask an officer from the Misted Cliffs for help?"

It took Allegra a moment to untangle what she meant. Of course. Emperor Cobalt had taken command of the Jazid army and added two thousand of his own men.

She said only, "There was no one I could ask."

Della thought for a moment. "To have the marriage declared illegal, we would petition Cobalt's government in Jazid."

Allegra could imagine the political turmoil that would ensue if the king of Aronsdale asked the Dawn Star emperor to void the marriage of Jazid's fugitive prince regent.

"It's not that simple," she said.

"Tell me," Della urged.

"How do you tell— When a man—" Allegra stumbled with the words, clumsy in talking about this with someone she didn't know well. "If you lie with him, and there's pleasure—" Her face burned. "Why do I feel terrible? Why do I want to run and shout in anger? I didn't, in that moment—"

"That he aroused you doesn't mean it wasn't rape," Della said.

"He stopped. When I said no."

"Then why are you angry?"

Allegra took a breath. She told Della what had happened, sparingly, with nothing to reveal Markus's identity, no names, no mention of Ozarson. In constrained sentences, she described the days from when the nomads caught her until she escaped. Sometime during it all, tears started to run down her face, a release she hadn't known she needed until it happened.

When Allegra finished, Della exhaled. "I can't claim to have answers to something this complicated," she said. "But you have every right to be angry. It's not surprising you responded to him. He rode with you for days, always touching you in sexual ways. The nomads drugged and starved you, even withheld water. It's no wonder you were dazed. Then you were completely dependent on this man for food, shelter, even sleep, none of which he provided properly."

"Sometimes I wanted to rage," Allegra said. "But other times—" She thought of Markus lying next to her, his body silvered by the starlight, of the strength, the intelligence, the leader she had seen in him, of the admiration she fought so hard not to feel. "He was beautiful. I wanted to touch him. See his smile. Hear him say how good I make him feel." She gave an embarrassed laugh. "Have him stare in shock when I insulted him."

Della's expression gentled. "Maybe under other circumstances, the two of you could have met without anger. But he put you in an intolerable situation. He can't force you to become what he needs."

Allegra brushed the tears out of her eyes. It was a relief to talk to Della. Her confusion remained, but some of her anger had eased. "I just can't see Prince Aron."

"I'll talk to him. The last thing you need right now is another man pressuring you." She paused. "I've known Aron all his life. I doubt he'll care that you had this marriage before him. All I ask is that you don't shut out the possibility." Della rubbed her eyes. "I'm old, Allegra. I served as a king's advisor to Jarid's grandfather and now to Jarid. The Suncroft healer is a blue mage, but she's older than me. Aron's mother is the only other mage here who can do green or greater spells. None of the guild apprentices can go beyond gold. We need someone young to carry on after—after we're gone."

Faced with that painful declaration, Allegra couldn't refuse her. "I understand." Yet saying that much felt wrong, as if she were offering something she no longer had to give. Even if she never saw Markus again, he had left an indelible mark on her life.

"Allegra?" a boy said.

She looked up with a start. Ozarson had opened the door and was standing in its archway.

"Goodness," Allegra said. "How did you know where to find me? You shouldn't be here." Both the guild mistress and Marnie had made it clear that only women were allowed in this part of the guild house.

"I heard the cook talking to some girls." He stood tensely, his hand gripped on the doorknob.

Della looked from Ozarson to Allegra. "I think it will be all right for him to spend just a few minutes here." She smiled at Ozarson. "Will you be all right in the stable tonight?"

"Yes." He said only one word, but it crackled with tension, also a hint of the regal authority he would someday wield. His excitement from earlier in the day had vanished.

Della stood up and laid her hand on Allegra's shoulder. "I'll see what I can do about an audience with Jarid."

"Thank you." Allegra rose, as well. "For everything."

Ozarson stepped aside as Della left. Then he came in and closed the door. "Will you go to the castle with that man?"

"I told Della I couldn't," Allegra assured him. "That I was married." When alarm flashed on his face, she said, "Della thinks my husband is a tender with Cobalt's army."

His posture remained stiff. "And me?"

"I said you were an orphan who lost his parents in the war. Is that all right?"

He seemed as if he were balancing on a cliff. He came over and stood by the table, resting his palm on it. His fingers flexed until he was gripping the wood and tendons stood out on the back of his hand.

"And you?" he asked. "Will you go with these people?"

"Go with them?"

"To the castle."

Suddenly she understood. This boy had lost so much, the people he loved, his family and title. His future. She laid her hand on his. "I would never strand you. What happened with Markus and me has complications, but I will never leave you alone. I swear that to you, as your regent's consort and as a mage."

He stared at their hands, and his shoulders slumped as if he finally had release. Looking up at her, he spoke in a lighter tone. "The cook told me we could go to the kitchen for a snack."

A smile softened Allegra's face. The settled lands could plunge into war, with battles and magic blazing across the desert, but Ozarson would want to eat first. "We'll get a snack, I promise." She waved him in the direction of the stable. "*After* we wash up."

"I can use the pail of water in the stable." He looked inordinately pleased with the idea.

Allegra spoke warily. "Why is that particular pail of water such a fine idea?"

He regarded her innocently. "Thom is there."

"Who is Thom?"

"The stable boy." A wicked grin spread across his face. "I'll bet he needs a bath, too."

Allegra could just imagine. She held back her laugh and gave him a stern look. "When you come back here, young man, I want you cleaned up. Not covered in mud and hay."

"I will!" He was off before she could say more.

Allegra disliked leaving Ozarson in the stables at night, but he clearly wanted to be on his own. He and Thom got on well, and the other boy's father had no objection to Thom staying with him. He promised to check on the boys later.

The idea of having a friend his own age, without adults monitoring his every move, seemed so new to Ozarson, it tore at Allegra. So she made herself go to her own room. She wondered how everyone would feel if they realized the coveted Shadow-Dragon king sought by the warlords of half a dozen countries was snuggled in the loft of an Aronsdale barn that some optimistic person had dubbed a stable.

Up in her room, Allegra practiced spells. The green one she had made earlier had drained her, and she only managed to light a candle before exhaustion settled over her. It would be a while before her gifts returned fully, but they were healing.

Worn-out, she tumbled into the first bed she had slept in for days and let slumber take her.

The stable was empty.

Neither stall contained Shadow, nor were there two young rascals anywhere in evidence. Morning light filtered past the doors and drew a ruddy glow from leather saddles hanging on the walls. The scent of hay filled the air, rich and pleasant. But no boys and no horse.

Allegra walked out into an area of hardpacked dirt where Thom had probably walked many a horse. The stable was set back from the guild house, and a meadow stretched from here to the main building. A cluster of girls was sitting in the grass with an older woman, and light-pictures of flowers hazed the air above them. Allegra smiled, remembering how she had drawn such pictures when she had been young, learning from an elderly yellow mage in the village of Spindle Vine how to mold light with her spells.

The girls were laughing and chattering, but they fell silent as she approached. She was glad she had changed into the tunic and leggings the guild mistress had offered her last night, so she no longer looked scruffy.

"My greetings, Mistress Allegra," the woman said, a motherly type with a cheerful smile and gray peppering her yellow hair. "Welcome to the guild."

Allegra thanked her. If they recognized her, chances were they also knew why Della had arranged for her to come. It was awkward, given the situation, but she couldn't say anything. So she just said, "I wondered if any of you had seen the boys who slept in the stable last night."

That evoked a round of giggles, which didn't bode well. Girls in Aronsdale were nothing like those in Jazid. If they felt inspired to bedevil the boys, they would have no qualms about indulging the impulse.

"Young ladies," the woman said sternly. "What did you do?"

"They were making a lot of noise," a girl with a mop of gold hair said. "Running around, tussling and shouting and laughing. So we—" She paused for effect.

The woman frowned at her. "You did what?"

Another girl with innocent blue eyes said, "Why, we gave them a bath."

Allegra groaned. She couldn't imagine what Ozarson would do if a gaggle of girls attacked him with buckets of water. It was so far outside his experience, he had probably been dumbfounded into just standing there, gaping.

"And where did the young men go after this tumult of

yours?" Allegra asked. The situation would have been funny if she hadn't been so worried.

"What does *tumult* mean?" one of the younger girls asked.

An older one snickered. "It means we chased them, and they ran back into the stable."

"They aren't there now," Allegra said.

"Oh, they came out on the big horse," the girl said. "The new stable boy with black hair was riding it, and Thom was sitting behind him, holding on. The new boy yelled 'Hai' at us like he was some great warlord or something, and off they went."

That sounded like Ozarson, fending off a wild pack of warrior moppets. Allegra tried valiantly to appear stern, since laughing would only encourage them. "Do you know where they went?"

The girls shook their heads, and the teacher looked apologetic. "I suspect the boys rode out to the hills. Thom often does that to exercise horses for our guests."

"Ah. Well, thank you for your help," Allegra said.

The walk out of town didn't take long. As Allegra strolled through the meadows below the castle, a cloud drifted over her, its shadow moving along the ground. She could see a large horse on a distant hill, nibbling grass. Two boys were sitting nearby, one with black hair and the other with yellow.

She paused, torn between checking on Ozarson and leaving him alone. Were he any other boy, he would be fine. Even if he had been a stable boy, no other horses were in the stable, and Shadow probably did want exercise. If she went over there, it would look odd. But he wasn't any other child, and she feared to leave him even in situations that for another boy would be perfectly normal.

He needs to know what it's like to be nine. She prayed silently to Saint Azure, the patron of children. *Please let him have this time. Let him know some tiny part of childhood before his life takes it away from him forever.*

The castle stood above her, golden and out of reach. Two people were coming down the hill, a tall man who looked like a bodyguard and a girl of about fourteen with dark, straight hair and a violet tunic that fluttered in the wind. Allegra waited, uncertain if they were headed to Crofts Vale.

As they reached Allegra, the girl inclined her head. "My greetings, Mistress Allegra. I'm Sky Dawnfield. My father wishes to see you."

Dawnfield? Saints above. She was Aron's sister. The royal family did Allegra great honor, sending one of their own. She bowed to Sky, hoping she was using the proper protocols. "I'm privileged to meet you, Your Highness."

Sky lifted her hand toward the castle. "Shall we go?"

Allegra glanced at the distant hill. Ozarson and Thom were running after each other and tumbling in the grass.

"Is that the boy who came with you?" Sky asked.

Allegra nodded. "I'm worried about leaving him alone."

Sky peered at the hill. "He looks fine to me."

"I'm sure he is," Allegra said, as much to convince herself as anyone else.

She started up the hill with Sky, nervous tension coiling within her.

THE NIGHT BIRD

★ ★ ★

The Receiving Hall was long and elegant. Its walls gleamed with mosaics in gold, ivory and crystal, and arched windows graced one long wall, drenching the room with sunlight.

Allegra waited with Sky and the guard as her father's retinue approached from the far end of the hall. The four guards with him wore Dawnfield colors, white, gold and violet. The king dressed more simply, in a white shirt, dark trousers and knee-boots. His face had classic lines, with his straight nose and high cheekbones.

Sky resembled her father, whereas Aron had the tousled brown hair and fresh-faced quality so often seen in the Tallwalk Mountains of his mother's home. Jarid was more reserved, less open, less sunny. Although he had the pale complexion common in western Aronsdale, his straight black hair, streaked with gray, evoked the Jazid influences in his Dawnfield lineage. As he drew closer, Allegra realized he had violet eyes, the same as her own, unknown except in southern Aronsdale. She was startled to see a heavy scar that ran down his neck from his ear.

She sank down on one knee and bent her head.

"Please rise." Jarid's voice was oddly hoarse, as if he rarely used it. He never gave speeches; his wife, or more recently his son, always did the honors. Allegra had never thought much about it, but hearing him, she wondered if he found speaking difficult.

The king smiled at his daughter. "Thank you, Sky. I'll see you at dinner."

Sky nodded and left them, her footsteps quiet on the gold and white tiles. Jarid lifted his hand, inviting Allegra to walk with him. They strolled down the hall with the five guards.

"Della says you wished to speak with me," he said.

She wondered what else the mage mistress had told him. "It's about the past few days."

He glanced at her. "I understand you were betrothed to a Jazid man. Against your will."

Although it had been kind of Della to pretty it up, Allegra didn't want to mislead him. "I was kidnapped and sold to him as a slave. We weren't married until later."

He drew her to a stop, his gaze flaring with anger. "We have a treaty with Jazid. The late Atajazid D'Az Ozar and I signed it, and the government installed by the Misted Cliffs swore to uphold it. Any Jazid nomad who enters Aronsdale and abducts our citizens is committing a crime punishable by time in prison."

She grimaced. "I don't think the nomads or my husband care."

"The marriage isn't valid," Jarid said firmly. "We can dissolve it."

She regarded him uncertainly. "How?"

"We will present the case before the court Cobalt established in Jazid. They would also bring in a Jazidian judge. Your husband will be called to testify, as will the nomads." When she started to shake her head, he said, "Yes, I know, they will swear you wandered into Jazid. We'll deal with that." He regarded her steadily. "I will tolerate no one kidnapping my subjects. Nor will I allow them to abuse one of my strongest mages, a woman personally called to the castle by my own House."

His vehemence startled Allegra. She had feared he wouldn't believe her, but he seemed to understand exactly, which made her suspect she wasn't the first woman kidnapped this way. But what he described could never work. If she went to a Jazidian court and accused Markus Onyx of abduction—a man who was supposed to be dead, and who had a price on his head if he turned up alive—it would inflame an already explosive political situation. And of course, the entire matter of her kidnapping Ozarson would arise.

"Your Majesty." She spoke cautiously. "I'm deeply grateful for your support. But the situation has—complications."

He raised an eyebrow. "Such as?"

"My husband was with the Jazid army."

"Della didn't say much. Only that he was a tender."

"Not exactly." She hesitated, unsure how to approach this. "He isn't with the army that Emperor Cobalt took command of when he conquered Jazid."

"Jazid has no other army."

"It does." She took a breath. "The one raised by the outlawed Jazid military."

His expression darkened. "Do you realize what you're saying?"

"I think so." Seeing his reaction, she wasn't so sure, though.

"We have heard rumors," Jarid said. "And last year, a company of men from Jazid rode to Quaaz, the capital of

Taka Mal. They claimed, when met by the queen's army, that they came to warn her of an assassination plan. The queen had reason to believe they planned her overthrow."

"Yes." Allegra's gaze never wavered. "My husband is with that army. They were the ones who tried to kill her."

"They didn't fight. There were only a few hundred of them. They left Taka Mal and vanished." The king considered her. "The Jazidian authorities swear that company has dispersed. Cobalt has said if he discovers otherwise, he will have them executed."

She stared at him. "A few *hundred* men?"

"It's not as many as it sounds. Before the war, the Jazid army had thousands."

A chill went up her spine. "It still does. Three thousand."

His posture stiffened. *"What?"*

"They plan to invade Taka Mal. In weeks."

"Allegra, you can't honestly expect me to believe that."

"It's true." The words sounded absurd even to her. She had the proof in Ozarson, but she couldn't betray his trust. Nor could she betray Markus; she had begun to care for him too much. Yet neither could she mislead her own king. Which left her in an impossible situation.

He studied her face. "This story—kidnapping, forced marriage, a secret army—maybe these are the tales of a girl who fears a different future."

Allegra didn't know whether to laugh or cry. He thought she would make all this up to avoid marrying his beautiful, golden son? She truly would be a lunatic in that case.

"No," she said. "I was happy with my future." Before Markus had changed it irrevocably. "I wanted nothing else."

"Why would Jazid attack Taka Mal?"

"To gain control of the Taka Mal army so they can overthrow Cobalt's forces in Jazid."

"It wouldn't be enough men," Jarid said. "Cobalt has three thousand in Taka Mal and Jazid, and he has thousands more in other countries. Plus he has a thousand Jazidian warriors who swore him allegiance. Taka Mal has only about two and a half thousand. Even if the outlaws did conquer Taka Mal, why would the surviving Taka Mal soldiers agree to fight *for* Jazid?"

"They might." As much as she hated to admit it, she could see why Markus considered Yargazon an inspired strategist. "They wouldn't be fighting *for* Jazid, they would be fighting *against* Cobalt. People in Taka Mal and Jazid don't like the rest of us, especially the Misted Cliffs. They don't like our cultures, our influences, or our soldiers in their countries. A war between Jazid and Taka Mal is like a feud within the family. No matter how angry they are with each other, they will draw together when faced with the threat from outside."

"Perhaps." He was guarding his answers. "Centuries ago, their cultures were almost identical. But Taka Mal has changed."

"Even so." The strategies behind the councils she had heard were becoming painfully clear. "All those Jazid soldiers who swore allegiance to Cobalt—do you really believe they would fight their countrymen if they knew General Yargazon had raised an army to free Jazid? I would be surprised if any of them *didn't* desert the official army to join Yargazon's outlaws. Then Jazid would have—what? Three thousand men in the fugitive army. Plus one thousand deserters. Maybe two thousand more from Taka Mal." In a numb voice she said, "That's six thousand. Against Cobalt's three thousand. He would have to bring in more from other countries, which takes time and spreads his forces elsewhere too thin."

Jarid spoke coldly. "You know a great deal about military strategy that few people would even think about, let alone imagine taking place."

"I heard them talking."

He made an incredulous noise. "You want me to believe that the military leaders of a foreign army allowed a pleasure slave who belonged to one of their tenders to overhear their councils?"

Her anger sparked. "If they can't see a woman as capable of understanding them, that isn't my problem. It's theirs."

He crossed his arms. "And I suppose they discussed all this with the Atajazid D'Az Ozar."

She froze. Did he know about Ozarson? Then she realized what he had said. D'Az Ozar. He meant Ozarson's father. He wanted to see if she really had any idea what she was saying.

"He's dead," she said flatly. "Cobalt Escar cut off his head."

"I meant his son. The man who succeeded him."

Sweat was gathering on her palms. She had to be very, very careful. "Did you say 'man'?"

"That's right."

Did he mean Markus? Or was he trying to trip her up? "I was under the impression the atajazid was a boy."

"Perhaps." Jarid waited.

"They want to put him on the Topaz Throne," she said. "Then return him to the Onyx Throne."

"And the boy told you this?"

"No. He's protected. From everyone." Except mages with sleep spells.

"I see." He began to walk again. "Come with me."

Allegra fell in beside him. She held back her impulse to ask where they were going. This was the king of her country. He had practically accused her of lying to avoid marrying his son or else of knowing far more than any innocent person should about the military plans of an outlawed army—which could amount to her committing treason.

CHAPTER 17
THE GORGE

Lord Brant Firestoke was much older than Jarid. In fact, Allegra had heard that Firestoke had been a close friend to Jarid's grandsire, the previous king. Just as Brant had served Jarid's grandfather as an advisor, so now he served Jarid. Shoulder-length hair silvered by the decades swept back from his face, accenting his widow's peak. He watched Allegra with deeply set gray eyes, and his austere presence left her feeling much too young.

They met in an octagonal room on an upper floor of the castle. As she told Brant about the Jazid army, he paced the room. Jarid was leaning back in a chair at the octagonal table a quarter of the way around from Allegra. It was odd the way he had sat down. He felt for his place as if he couldn't see it. He obviously wasn't blind; his motions seemed unconscious, as if he didn't realize what he was doing.

When Allegra finished, Brant leaned against the sill of a window. "I doubt a dairymaid from southern Aronsdale could have made this up."

"I didn't," Allegra said.

"Where did you hear the name Yargazon?" Brant asked. "Few people know it outside Jazid."

"He leads the army," she answered.

"Kazil Yargazon," Brant said.

She shook her head. "His name was Dusk."

Jarid swore under his breath. "Hell and damnation."

"Is Yargazon a problem?" Allegra asked.

The king spoke dryly. "Well, given that he's considered the most notorious warlord alive by the emperor and a great war hero by the Jazid people, and that Cobalt has put the greatest price on his head of any war criminal in history, I would say yes, knowing he's raised an army is a problem."

"Are you sure they have the atajazid?" Brant asked her. "Cobalt claims he has hidden the child outside of Jazid."

"I'm certain Cobalt doesn't have him." Allegra still hadn't figured out how Ozarson had escaped Cobalt's men.

"I wonder if this boy even lives," Jarid said. "No one has seen him. His half brothers are dead. Why would he be alive?"

Her pulse stuttered. "His brothers died? How do you know?"

"You sound surprised," Jarid said. "Do you know different?"

"I know almost nothing about the House of Onyx," she said, which was as close as she dared go to the truth. "But I would feel terribly sorry for a child in the situation you describe."

"Don't," Brant said. "He would have grown into a monster just like his father."

"He's a child," Allegra said. "Children want to be loved. If he is, why would he grow into a monster?"

Brant sighed. "That is so painfully naive."

"Is it?" Jarid asked. "Maybe if Cobalt's grandfather hadn't beaten or whipped him every day of his life until he was able to fight back, Cobalt wouldn't feel driven to conquer the universe to prove to a man who's now dead that he isn't worthless."

Allegra stared at him. She almost asked how he could know all that about the emperor, but then she remembered. Cobalt had married Jarid's cousin. She rubbed her eyes, drained. "Yargazon's men think the previous atajazid, the man Cobalt killed, is a great hero."

Jarid scowled. "That atajazid started the damn war."

"I thought the emperor started it," Allegra said.

"It's true," Brant said. "Cobalt attacked first."

"With provocation," Jarid said. "Gods, was Ozar mad? What sane man would enrage Cobalt the Dark into a war?"

"I'm not sure I understand," Allegra said.

"The queen of Taka Mal kidnapped Drummer Headwind," Brant said, scowling. "They do that in Taka Mal and Jazid. Bunch of barbarians. They think it's perfectly fine to kidnap people."

"But Drummer married the queen, didn't he?" Allegra looked from him to Jarid. "To make a treaty with you."

"Eventually," Jarid said. "But first the Jazid king kidnapped Cobalt's wife. He made it look as if Taka Mal did it, and everyone believed the falsified evidence because of what happened with Drummer. Then the atajazid tortured Cobalt's wife. While she was *pregnant* with the emperor's heir. The atajazid had a Taka Mal traitor take her blood-soaked clothes to Cobalt and claim the general of the Taka Mal army had tortured her to death."

Allegra was grateful Ozarson wasn't present to hear this about his father. "You're saying the previous king of Jazid killed the emperor's pregnant wife and set it up to look as if Taka Mal did it. So Cobalt attacked Taka Mal in revenge?"

"That's right," Jarid said. "Except she survived. So Cobalt knows the truth. Some people even believe *Ozar* told him during the battle, while they were negotiating, to goad him into breaking the Alatian Code of War. If Cobalt struck first, Ozar could kill him without violating the Code." Grimly he added, "If that's true, Ozar fatally underestimated Cobalt."

Brant spoke quietly. "Ozar had five sons—four adults and the boy. Three of his sons died in the Rocklands, including the boy's regent."

"Markus Onyx," Jarid said. "We don't know much about him."

"Ozar's fourth son survived the war," Brant said. "So Cobalt executed him. Cobalt agreed to let the boy live, but many people think he had the child killed in secret."

"That's horrible," Allegra said. She hadn't realized Ozarson and Markus had lost their brothers as well as their infamous sire.

"The Jazidians hate their conquerors," Jarid said. "Their king may have precipitated the war, but if that hadn't happened, Cobalt would have eventually gone after Jazid anyway. It's a phenomenally rich country."

"This could explain a lot," Brant muttered. When Allegra gave him a questioning look, he said, "Cobalt has a big army. Eight thousand if you count the Jazidian soldiers. But they're dispersed among four countries. If he were to march an army on a few days' notice—say through Aronsdale—he could only marshal about two thousand."

Allegra wondered what made him think of that now. "His forces in Jazid and Taka Mal are spread too thin," she said. "And his men want to go home."

Brant didn't look surprised. "How do you know that?"

"From Yargazon's men."

Jarid snorted. "Apparently Cobalt isn't hiding their discontent as well as he thought."

"And you claim this outlaw Jazidian army will invade Taka Mal in three weeks?" Brant asked her.

"Or sooner," Allegra said. "They probably think I went to warn Queen Vizarana."

"Why?" Jarid asked. "You're the wife of a tender. Why would they even notice you had left, let alone think you would betray their plans to the queen?"

"They have strange ideas." She knew it sounded lame, but she had no better answer that wouldn't put Ozarson—or Markus—at risk.

"If this army exists and has the boy," Jarid said, "he could be an incredible rallying figure for his people. The balance of power in Jazid is barely stable as it is. His appearance could explode the political situation."

"Then hope Cobalt did execute him," Brant said grimly. "Saints only know what the child would be like with Yargazon as his regent."

"That's horrible, to wish death on a little boy," Allegra said. She almost added, *Why would the General be his regent?* But she caught herself in time. They thought Ozarson's brothers were dead—including Markus—which made Yargazon the logical choice as regent.

Jarid spoke as gently as his hoarse voice allowed. "None of us wish a child's death. But the freedom and well-being of several populations may pivot on his actions, even just his existence."

"You're so convinced he'll become a monster," she said, angry at them both. "Maybe he isn't the evil one. Maybe it's all the warlords who make him this 'pivot.'"

"I've no doubt it is," Brant said. "But that changes nothing."

"We do need to get out a warning." Jarid rubbed his chin. "I have the redwing carrier birds Queen Vizarana gave me last year. We can send them to her with a message."

"And to Cobalt," Brant said.

Jarid crossed his arms and regarded him implacably. "My responsibility is to my kin. Drummer."

"Drummer is also the empress's uncle," Brant said. "If we don't warn Cobalt, he'll be furious."

"That's Cobalt's problem." Jarid scowled at him. "We had nothing to do with his taking the Onyx Throne. Why should we help him keep it? I've signed no treaties to support these attempts of his to subjugate every damn thing that moves."

A door creaked. Glancing up, Brant smiled at someone behind Allegra. She wanted to turn, but she didn't wish to appear rude to the king.

Oddly enough, Jarid didn't seem to have heard. He pushed back his chair and stood up. "I'll send word to Drummer while we decide what to do about Cobalt."

"What you decide about Cobalt may be moot," a woman said.

Jarid spun around. Turning, Allegra saw a woman standing in the arched doorway. Tall and curvy, with rosy cheeks, she had a mane of chestnut hair exactly like Aron's, except hers fell in waves down her back. She glowed with health.

"My greetings," Jarid said, his voice warming. He turned to indicate Allegra. "May I present our new guild mage, Allegra Linseed." To Allegra he said, "My wife. Iris."

Allegra started to kneel, but the queen lifted her hand to stop her. She spoke in a rich voice. "I'm pleased to see you."

"I'm honored, Your Majesty," Allegra said.

Iris inclined her head. Then she turned to Jarid. "You had better come. They're here."

Here? Allegra thought. *Who?*

The Star Walk ran atop the great wall around the castle. Geometric crenellations sculpted its length: circles, diamonds, hexagons and, most of all, stars. From up here, a person could see for many leagues, gazing over the glades and rolling hills of Crofts Vale. Right now, soldiers in Aronsdale uniforms lined the walkway, including lookouts with spyglasses.

Everyone was staring to the south.

Far in the distance, an army poured into view from behind a cluster of hills. It must have been flooding out all morning, wave after wave of soldiers, tenders and horses. Allegra had never seen so many people together. They covered the land.

"Gods almighty," Brant said. "Even with the warning that they were coming, I didn't expect that many."

"Who is it?" Allegra asked.

"Cobalt," Jarid said. "We've known they were on the march for several days, escorted by my cousin, Muller."

Allegra didn't know the name Muller, but he had only one cousin. "Do you mean the King of Harsdown?"

Jarid nodded, his attention on the army. He took a spyglass one of his men offered and studied the army. "Muller has permission to ride through Aronsdale. Cobalt doesn't." Sourly he added, "Not that Cobalt asked. He just came. And he's not saying much." Lowering the glass, he regarded Allegra. "What do you know about this?"

She felt as if ice were in her veins. "Nothing."

Jarid glanced out again, then stopped and peered at the hill directly below the castle. "Who is that?"

Allegra followed his gaze—and her breath caught. Shadow was racing up the hill, ridden by Ozarson, with Thom seated behind him, hanging on to the atajazid's belt.

"That's a warhorse," Brant said. "Maybe it's a messenger."

Jarid trained his glass on Shadow. "No, just a couple of boys." He smiled. "Probably they're coming to warn us that a great army is invading Aronsdale."

Foreboding surged within Allegra. Ozarson knew she had planned to seek an audience with Jarid today, to warn him about the Jazid army. If he had seen Cobalt's army, saints only knew what he thought—or would say. She whirled and ran down the walkway, ducking past the soldiers on duty.

"Allegra!" Jarid's shout rang behind her.

Even knowing she risked offending the throne by ignoring his call, she kept going. She reached the tower at the end of the walkway and raced down the staircase that spiraled inside it. She heard people running, and someone called her name, but she kept going, desperate to reach Ozarson before anyone else.

The steps let her out into a wide hall. She ran along it until she reached the top of a staircase that swept down to the entrance foyer of the castle. In the great archway that opened from outside into the foyer, Ozarson was struggling with a guardsman. Beyond them, out in the sunlight, Thom stood with Shadow, holding the horse's reins and looking confused.

"I have to get by!" Ozarson cried. "Let me go!"

"It's all right," Allegra called as she started down the stairs. "He's with me."

The guardsman glanced up, his forehead furrowed, but he let Ozarson go. The boy dashed toward the stairs, started up them—and froze, his eyes widening as he looked over her head.

Allegra spun around. Jarid, Iris and Brant Firestoke stood

on the stairs above her, with several soldiers behind them. They had stopped, and were watching Ozarson with puzzlement.

"He's afraid of the army," Allegra told them. "His parents were killed in the war." She was talking too fast, but she couldn't stop. She started down to Ozarson, holding out her hand. "It's all right," she said. "No one will hurt you."

Ozarson raced up the stairs, reaching her when she was halfway down. He threw his arms around her, and she sank onto the step, holding him. She kept murmuring, "It'll be all right, Ozi. It'll be all right."

"It won't!" He raised his head, his gaze frantic. "It's the emperor's army."

"They don't care about stable boys." She looked at him hard, silently urging him to see past his fear and hear what she was saying. "You go back to the stable with Thom. You'll be fine."

Fear burned in his eyes. "He knows me. What I look like."

"Ozi," she said, warning.

"What does it matter?" A tear rolled down his face. "I'm going to die anyway."

"Gods, don't say that." Her voice shook, and she was aware of the people above them listening.

"I know that army." His voice trembled. "A company of those soldiers brought my father's body home after—after he died. A man led them. General Agate Cragland."

A sharp breath came from above them. Allegra may have never heard the name Cragland, but it obviously meant as much to someone here as to Ozarson.

"You don't have to remember," she told the boy.

He let her go and straightened up, almost as tall as Allegra with the two of them sitting on the stairs. His eyes blazed despite his fear. "They came to the palace with hundreds of men. They said Cobalt claimed the Onyx Throne, and I was to be executed."

She felt ill. "They told a seven-year-old boy they were going to kill him? What kind of monsters would do that?"

"They told my mother. They didn't know I was hiding and listening." His voice shook. "That night I snuck into the place where they had laid my father's body."

"Ozi, no." With horrible certainty, she knew what was coming. She couldn't stop it, couldn't protect the boy from what had already happened.

"His body had been laid on the floor." Tears ran down his face. "I pulled the cloth off his head and—and I tried to kiss his cheek." His voice cracked. "His head rolled away from me, across the floor."

Allegra wanted to hold him close, as if that futile gesture could banish the memory. But he kept going. "I tried to scream. It wouldn't come out. I—I put his head b-back on his body. Then I ran to my room. I put cloths around my neck, and a belt to protect it. I hid in my bed—crying—my Nanna—she came—my mother came—we all cried."

"I'm so sorry," she whispered. So sorry the world was filled with monsters whose greed and ambition mattered more than a child.

"General Cragland said they had to wait until Cobalt

arrived. All the leaders from the war were at a meeting. In Taka Mal. No one knew what they would decide. They couldn't—couldn't kill me until they knew." His face had gone deathly pale. "Cobalt arrived three days later. With his army. They came on and on, burying the world like a sandstorm, burying the palace, thousands, like a plague, like locusts that strip the land."

"Ozi." Allegra didn't know what to do, what to say.

He choked on the words. "Cobalt came into the hall where I waited with my mother. He was so big, his shoulders were so *big*. In armor and mail. The sword on his back was longer than me." Ozarson was shaking in her arms. "My mother cried. She had never knelt before any man but my father—but she threw herself on the ground before Cobalt and begged him to spare my life."

Tears ran down Allegra's face. No one else around them moved. The silence could have deafened. "What did Cobalt say?"

"He told her that he would let me live." Ozarson took a shuddering breath. "But they would take me away, far away, and she would never see me again." He lifted his chin. "I stood in front of him, and I said he was a fool to let me live, because someday I would cut his head from his body and avenge my father."

"Ozi," she whispered. "How did you get away? How did your mother and your nanna die?"

His voice was low, and sounded so very, very young. "General Yargazon came—he and his men smuggled me out. Cobalt's men thought Markus was dead. He almost *was* dead. Yargazon's men carried him. There was a river, a gorge. It was night—" He was crying, his words fractured. "Cobalt's men found out about our escape. They separated my mother, Nanna and me from the others. Cobalt had his sword up— he was going to k-kill me. Right there. I saw the blade coming down. But he d-didn't—didn't do it. He told his men to take me away instead. General Yargazon, everyone—they were down in the gorge, in a boat that could go over the rapids. My mother—she—she—" His voice caught on a sob.

"It's all right," Allegra murmured. "It's all right."

"No. It's not! She and Nanna—they grabbed me away from Cobalt's men and wrapped themselves around me." Then he whispered, "And they jumped."

"Saints, no," someone said.

"Into a gorge?" Allegra asked.

"Their bodies protected me. Just my leg broke." The words tore out of him. "Nanna d-died when we hit. My mother— She was alive—barely. She could hardly talk. She told me to avenge my father. Then General Yargazon reached us. He promised her, he swore on his soul and his life, that he would put me on the throne and avenge her husband. She was— She told me she was going to a golden place, that someday I would be there with her and Father and Nanna. And she—sh-she died." His voice broke as if he were shattering. "When you and I rode into Crofts Vale, with everything gold and green and all the children playing, I thought we had found that place. But it isn't. There is no place. Cobalt has come for me."

Allegra pulled him close and sat there rocking him while he clung to her, crying. She heard a rustle and looked up to see Jarid coming down the steps.

"Stay away!" she said. "All of you! *Stay away from him.*"

Jarid froze. Behind them, a clank of metal came from the foyer. Allegra turned with a jerk and saw an Aronsdale soldier entering the palace. Judged from his windblown hair, he had probably been out riding. Holding his helmet in his hand, he looked around, obviously trying to figure out what was going on with so many people in the entry.

"Sire." Seeing Jarid on the stairs, he dropped to one knee.

"Rise, please," Jarid said. "You have a report?"

Allegra wasn't certain why Jarid didn't go down, but she thought it might be for Ozarson. The boy could panic if anyone came closer to him, especially a king he had no reason to trust. He genuinely thought Cobalt's army had come to kill him. The worst of it was, he could be right. But they would have to take him from her first, which meant they would have to kill her, too.

"My patrol saw the army and headed back to tell you," the messenger told Jarid. "We took a group of travelers into custody."

Ozarson lifted his head from Allegra's arms and wiped his sleeve across his eyes. He watched the man with wide eyes, and Allegra felt him clutching the back of her tunic.

"Five men on horseback," the messenger said. "They refuse to identify themselves."

A man's voice interrupted him, rumbling as he stepped

around the soldier. In a deep, drawn-out accent, he said, "I will speak only to Jarid Dawnfield."

He stood in the light from outside, a barbarian warlord transplanted from a place of wildness, a warrior in chain mail and bronzed armor with a huge sword on his back and a black-plumed helmet under his muscled arm. His black hair was blown around his strong-featured face, and black stubble covered his chin. He faced them all, defiant and bold, his dark gaze smoldering.

Markus.

CHAPTER 18
THE HOUSE OF ONYX

"Markus!" Ozarson tore away from Allegra and ran down the steps to his brother. He threw himself into Markus's arms. The prince regent hugged him close, and as he lowered his head over his brother's, Allegra saw the immensity of his relief.

For several moments, they held each other. Allegra rose to her feet on the stairs. If Markus had only five men, she had little doubt King Jarid could hold him prisoner until they decided what to do. Aronsdale effectively had in their custody what remained of Jazid's royal House. Including her, unfortunately. Watching them, the last descendants of an ancient dynasty holding each other, she thought of all the violence others had committed to keep those two royals alive. Both Markus and Ozarson had suffered far too much in the name of conquest, honor, greed and vengeance.

After an eternity, Markus raised his head and looked at her. If a stare could have incinerated, she would have burned to ashes.

"Get down here," he said.

She stayed on the stairs. "No."

A rustle came from above her, and she looked up as Jarid came to stand with her. He spoke in a low voice. "The boy said, 'Markus.' The prince regent? Still alive?"

Allegra knew she couldn't hide their identities after what Jarid had heard. "He survived his injuries from the war." She spoke quietly. "He's been Ozi's guardian for most of the boy's life, even before their father died."

Brant Firestoke joined them on the stairs. "I would suggest we invite them inside. I sincerely doubt it's wise to leave the two of them standing in plain view that way."

Jarid grimaced. "Especially given who is pouring his un-invited army into my backyard." He went down the stair-case and across the foyer.

Markus watched him with suspicion, his arms protectively around Ozarson. The boy lifted his head. Although he stepped away from Markus with a self-conscious gesture, he stayed close to his brother, and the regent kept one arm around his shoulders.

Jarid stopped in front of Markus. Both men were the same height, though Markus was more heavily built. Both had black hair. Markus looked more atavistic, but Jarid had a roughness unusual in Aronsdale men, accented by the scar on his neck.

"Welcome to my home, Your Highness," Jarid said.

"Are you Jarid?" Markus asked.

"I am," the king said.

Markus met his gaze. "*Are* we welcome, Your Majesty?"

"You are my guests." Jarid indicated the foyer. "Perhaps you would come inside."

"Will Allegra stay?" Ozarson asked. Tears streaked his face.

"If she agrees," Jarid said, "then yes, certainly."

"I won't go without her," Ozarson told Markus.

"Why?" his brother asked, incredulous. "After what she did?"

Ozarson looked up at him. "I did it. Not her."

Markus started to answer, his disbelief obvious. Then he glanced at Jarid, who was listening intently, and closed his mouth. Jarid raised his hand, inviting them inside, and Markus walked warily, his arm resting on Ozarson's shoulders.

"Who are the men with you?" Jarid asked him.

Markus answered stiffly. "My bodyguards."

Jarid glanced at the Aronsdale messenger. "Have his men quartered with the army. Keep two guards on each one."

"As guests, of course," Markus said, sarcasm edging his words.

Jarid didn't answer.

Markus came up the stairs with Ozarson, and Allegra waited. When they reached her, Markus stopped, his gaze hard. "How could you do it?"

"Do *what?*" she asked in a low voice. "Yes, I took him as a hostage." She was so upset, she could barely speak. "All this fighting, fighting, *killing* one another. Hasn't he suffered enough? Haven't you? When will you have given enough of yourselves? When your country and your titles have destroyed both of you?"

Markus stared at her. She wondered if it had ever occurred to him that he had been just as manipulated, used and hurt by his life as had Ozarson. He didn't look at the world that way; he was doing his best to fulfill his duty as regent and to deal with the legacy of a father he had more conflicted feelings about than she suspected he could ever express. He was trying, under almost impossible circumstances, to be a good leader. Being away from the constant pressure of his presence, talking to Della, seeing him through Ozarson—it all helped her see this man who had become her husband. In his constrained world, what he had done with her was the only way he knew how to alleviate his crushing emotional isolation. It didn't change the anger she felt nor did it mean she could live the life he wanted for her, but at least she was beginning to understand.

It was a moment before Markus found his voice. Then he said, "We will discuss it later."

Ozarson was watching. Waiting. So was everyone else. Allegra took a breath, then nodded and went up the stairs with them.

Sky and cloud mosaics tiled the ceiling in the suite of rooms. The ivory walls had scenes of forests and lakes painted in their upper half. Markus and Ozarson sat on a couch with brocaded cushions and looked decidedly uncomfortable with the furniture and surroundings. Iris sat with Allegra on another couch across from them, and Brant Firestoke sat in an armchair facing inward to the couches. Jarid paced the room, then sat on the sill of an arched window with shapes carved into its frame.

"We've sent messengers to Cobalt's army," Jarid said. "When they return, we'll have a better idea what's going on."

Markus remained impassive. Ozarson didn't speak, either, but Allegra could read him better. He wanted to know what had happened with his army.

"We need to know more of Cobalt's intentions," Brant said. He regarded Markus. "For example, if he's going to Taka Mal."

"I've no idea what the emperor is doing," Markus said.

"What about General Yargazon?" Jarid asked. "You wouldn't happen to have some idea what he is doing?"

"No," Markus said.

"No?" Brant raised his eyebrows. "You wouldn't know if he just happened to, say, march an army into Taka Mal?"

"How could he?" Markus demanded. "They all betrayed their oaths to my father and joined Cobalt's forces."

"I wasn't talking about that army," Brant said.

Markus met his gaze. "I know of no other."

"Not even three thousand men hidden in the barrens of Jazid?"

Markus shrugged. "Three thousand men would be difficult to hide, I'd imagine."

Jarid leaned forward. "But useful in protecting the atajazid and his regent."

"I wouldn't know," Markus said. "We've been hiding alone."

"Just you, the boy and those four men?" Iris asked.

Markus looked at her with a start. His forehead furrowed.

He glanced at Jarid, then Brant. When both men continued to wait for his answer, he spoke tersely. "That's right."

"That isn't much protection," Brant said.

"With fewer people, it's easier to hide," Markus said.

"What if Cobalt comes here?" Iris asked.

Markus just looked at her.

"I'd like to know from *Cobalt* why the hell he's here," Jarid growled. "It's harder to get information from that man than taking water from a rock."

"He's going to Taka Mal," Brant said, his gaze on Markus.

"What are you going to do with us?" Markus asked.

"You're our guests," Iris said.

The prince regent frowned at her. "I spoke to your husband."

Jarid came to the couch where Iris was seated and braced his hands on the back, watching Markus. "As she said, you are our guests." He straightened up. "Your Highness, did any of your other siblings survive the war?"

Markus met his gaze with hostile silence.

"Your sisters?" Brant asked.

The prince regent stiffened. "The women of my family are no concern of yours."

"His sisters are probably married," Iris said. "They would be considered part of their husband's family rather than Onyx."

Jarid considered Markus. "Then you and His Majesty—" He inclined his head to Ozarson. "You are what remains of the Onyx royal family."

Markus continued his stony silence, but Ozarson glanced at Allegra. Allegra felt certain Jarid's question had a deeper meaning than just identifying Markus and Ozarson. She had no idea what, but Brant seemed to have no doubt.

"Jarid, damn it," Brant said. "If you give them asylum, Cobalt will be furious."

"Probably," Jarid said.

"Asylum?" Markus shot Brant an incredulous look. "Don't mock us."

"You have to give it to Allegra, too," Ozarson said.

"This is her country," Markus said quickly. "Why would she need asylum here?"

Allegra wondered at his reaction. So far he had kept her connection with him a secret. His marriage to an Aronsdale woman worked to his advantage, but it would put her in danger if other people discovered it, especially Cobalt. If she hadn't known better, she would have thought he was protecting her at his own expense, despite what she had done with Ozarson. Then again, given how confusing she found him, she probably didn't know better.

"Allegra is an Aronsdale citizen," Iris told the boy, her voice gentler than when she spoke to Markus. "Her marriage to the tender is almost certainly not legal."

"Tender?" Ozarson asked. "What tender?"

Markus spoke gruffly. "It means someone who travels with an army but isn't a soldier."

"I *know* what it means," the boy said.

"Oh, saints to hell and back," Brant said.

Jarid glanced at him with surprise. "What?"

Brant pointed at Markus. "She's married to *him*."

Jarid swung around to Allegra. "Is that true?"

She couldn't desert Ozarson or Markus with a denial. "Yes," she said quietly. "It's true."

"But what about Aron?" Brant protested.

"Aron?" Markus's face darkened. "You mean, *Prince* Aron?"

Iris spoke coldly. "That's right."

Allegra could barely breathe. *Saints almighty.* It was true. They had been considering her as a wife for their son.

"Allegra is mine now," Markus said. "My wife, my consort, my property. Would you let the Midnight Emperor execute a woman of your own country?"

"I'm not your property," Allegra said. Her thoughts whirled furiously, not only because of what she had lost due to Markus, but also because she *wanted* this maddening man.

He glared at her. "After what I paid for you, you most certainly are."

"This is Aronsdale," she said. "You can't own women here. Believe it or not, people consider us human."

Markus leaned forward. "You were in Jazid when I bought you. Our laws don't cease to exist because you left the country. I own you, Allegra, no matter where you live."

"Enough!" Iris said. "She was taken from Aronsdale in violation of a treaty your own father signed, Prince Markus."

"She was in Jazid when I bought her," he said. "That makes it legal. You can't dissolve our laws because it suits your purpose. *That,* Your Majesty, was also in the treaty."

"That may be," Jarid said coldly. "But no one here will let you force Allegra to stay with you."

"Which comes to the question he himself asked," Brant said. "Are we going to tell Cobalt she's the Princess Regent?"

"You may have to," Allegra said. "Because if he tries to execute Ozarson, he'll have to go through me first."

Markus gave her a startled look. "What?"

"Allegra, don't say that," Ozarson said.

Her voice gentled. "I gave my oath to protect you, Ozi."

"You can't protect him against Cobalt the Dark!" Markus looked as if he wanted to shake her. "I forbid you to kill yourself trying to do something impossible. Stay here. Be safe."

She spoke softly. "Some things are more important."

Jarid stared at her. Then he went back to pacing. Watching him, she felt as if they were holding Ozarson above a raging fire by a thread that could snap anytime. She got up and went over to the king, stopping him.

"*Look* at him." She indicated Ozarson. "You tell me this is the monster you all fear."

Jarid sighed. "It isn't that easy."

"Why not? You said yourself you had nothing to do with all this conquering Cobalt seems determined to inflict."

Jarid looked past her to Markus. "Why did you come here, knowing you would probably be taken prisoner?"

"To get my wife and my brother," Markus said quietly. "I hoped I could do it in secret."

"You had to know you could be discovered and lose your freedom," Jarid said. "Even your life."

"Yes. I knew." Markus spoke with the difficulty of a man

unused to speaking his emotions. "They are worth it to me. Both of them."

It didn't surprise Allegra that he was willing to risk his life for Ozarson. But for her? How could he want her that much when she made him so angry?

Brant was watching the king with a look of foreboding. "Jarid, don't be a fool."

Jarid considered his advisor, then Allegra, then Markus and Ozarson. To Brant, he said, "Better foolish than brutal." He turned to Markus. "I grant you asylum in my country. But you and your family will stay at Suncroft. And yes, as my prisoners."

Markus stared at him in disbelief. "Why would you risk Cobalt's wrath to protect us?"

Jarid' voice had a ravaged quality. "Maybe for another boy who lost his parents when he was six."

A chill went through Allegra. Did Jarid mean himself? Everyone in Aronsdale knew the story. Jarid had succeeded his grandfather because his parents died in an accident. He had spent his youth cared for by one of the highwaymen who had caused the accident, a thief who hadn't wanted to kill a little boy and had no idea of Jarid's identity. It wasn't until Jarid was twenty that his family had discovered he was alive and brought him home. Allegra knew nothing beyond those facts, but she thought there must be a great deal more when she saw the king's haunted expression.

Ozarson spoke. "I thank you for allowing us asylum, Your

Majesty. And I offer my condolences for your losses, however long ago they may have been."

Jarid inclined his head. "Well spoken."

Ozarson nodded with composure, but Allegra could see the exhaustion he was trying to hide. Markus looked worn-out, too.

Allegra glanced at Jarid. "Perhaps we could let His Majesty rest. He's had a long journey."

"I'm not tired," Ozarson said. "I'm hungry."

Markus chuckled and tousled his hair. "You consume more than my entire army."

Ozarson laughed, but an abrupt silence fell over everyone else. Markus glanced up, and Allegra saw comprehension dawn on his face as he realized what he had said.

"Your army," Jarid said slowly. "The army you know nothing about that even now is attacking Taka Mal."

Markus met his gaze and said nothing.

Brant swore. "Saints, man, if we're going to defy an emperor to give you asylum, you damn well better tell us everything."

"I have nothing to tell you," Markus said. "If you think claiming to offer us help will trick me into revealing information, I'm afraid you will be disappointed."

"Allegra told us she traveled with an army," Jarid said.

"She's a woman," Markus said, as if that explained something.

"And I'm a man," Jarid answered. "What the hell does that have to do with anything?"

"Women are unreliable." Markus glared at Allegra. "They say things they shouldn't."

She met his accusing stare. "You mean, things you don't want said."

"Women should obey their husbands," Markus told her.

"Women," she said, "should follow their consciences. If that means defying their husbands to save thousands of lives, they should do what they think is right. Not what their overbearing, I-am-the-center-of-the-world husbands demand."

"Good gods," Brant muttered.

"Center of the world?" Markus said, exasperated. "When did *that* one get in there?"

Jarid cleared his throat. "Perhaps we should see about having a meal brought up for His Majesty."

"I would like that," Ozarson said. He seemed bewildered by the exchange between Allegra and Markus.

Markus took a breath as if calming himself. Then he said, "Thank you."

They all stood, awkward with the tension. As the others started to leave, Allegra glanced at Markus.

"Stay," he said in a low voice.

Iris turned to her. "Allegra? Is everything all right?"

"Yes, I'm fine," Allegra said. "I'll stay here." She didn't understand how she could argue with such vehemence with a man and yet want to see him so much at the same time.

Jarid stopped by the archway. "Are you certain?"

"I'm sure."

She could tell they didn't want to leave her with Markus. But they did go, respecting her decision.

As the door closed, Markus looked around the room. "I can't stay here."

"Why not?" Allegra asked. "It's beautiful."

"It's for a *woman*."

She glanced around at the elegant furnishings. "Why do you say that?"

"Too flowery." He waved his hand at the couches. "And it's unnatural to live like this. All these chairs and things."

"It's all right," Ozarson said.

Markus laid his hand on his shoulder. "I need to talk to Allegra. I want you to stay here while we go in the other room."

Ozarson regarded him with undisguised worry. "Don't be angry at her. I told her to take me."

"Even so. I need to talk to her. Will you be all right?"

Although the boy didn't look pleased, he nodded and indicated an inner archway of the suite that opened into a room with full bookshelves lining the walls. "I can explore the library."

Markus smiled. "Good." He turned to Allegra and indicated another door. She nodded, for once in agreement with him. She didn't know how much of an argument they were about to have, but if Markus was as angry as she thought, it was better Ozarson didn't hear.

The door opened into a small chamber, which led them into a larger bedroom with a canopied bed made up with blue velvet covers.

"Who would sleep in that?" Markus said, perplexed. "It's awful."

Allegra couldn't imagine why he would say such a thing. She thought it was gorgeous. From the colors, gray and dark blue, she suspected it was intended for a man. Compared to his carpets and pillows in Jazid, though, maybe it seemed lifeless.

Markus closed the doors and turned to her with a hard gaze. "Ozi was crying when I got here. What did you do to him?"

"Nothing. He saw Cobalt's forces. He was terrified. He came looking for me."

"Looking for you?" His forehead furrowed. "You mean, he wasn't already here, in custody?"

"No, he was free," she said. "No one knew who he was. He had gone riding with another boy. They were *playing on the hills.*"

"Playing on the hills." He walked toward her. "The atajazid, playing on the hills."

She backed up a step. "That's right."

"Suppose he got hurt?" He kept coming toward her, his fists clenched at his sides. "Suppose he fell and broke his damn *leg.*"

She backed into the side of the bed. "He was fine."

"Fine?" He grabbed her arms and lifted her off the ground, then threw her across the bed. *"Fine?"* He got on the bed, and when she tried to roll away, he shoved her down. "Fine? You kidnapped him, dragged him across three countries and you say he was *fine?*"

"Markus, don't do this." Pushing up on her elbows, she slid away from him. "Talk to me. Don't hit."

"Like your *talk* with Yargazon?" He pushed her into the covers, pinning her to the bed with his body—and raised his fist. "Like the general you left bound and bleeding for an entire godforsaken day? You know what he said after he woke up? That I would be better off if you were *dead*. Why does that thought make *me* want to die?" He slammed his fist on the bed, so close that she felt the brush of air on her cheek. "Talk to you? When you put me in agony for days, not knowing where to find you or my brother?" He struck the bed even harder. Pillows jumped around them and the covers bunched under his fist. "How can I talk to you when I'm an overbearing, arrogant tyrant?" With every word, he hit the mattress.

The intensity of his reaction stunned her. She was scared in a way she hadn't been with Yargazon, because she had let Markus get past her guard and pin her down. He had never lost control this way before—except he *wasn't* losing control. He was hitting the mattress instead of her, over and over and over.

Suddenly he stopped and sat up so he was kneeling over her, straddling her body with his calves on either side of her hips. He grabbed her tunic and yanked it over her head. "Why do you wear this? It's ugly."

"Stop it." She fought with him, but he dragged the garment off her arms. When she rolled on her side, trying to get away, he pushed her onto her back and threw the tunic on the floor.

Dismayed, Allegra folded her arms over her breasts. "Markus, no, not like this."

He pulled apart her arms and pinned her wrists to the bed, on either side of her head. "You tear up my life, you have from the moment I met you, you take the only family I have left—I thought you would both be *dead* when I found you. Then what would I have to live for?" His voice wasn't loud, but it only made his fury more potent. "We had to send the army to Taka Mal before we were ready because Yargazon knew you were going to warn someone we were coming. I couldn't weaken it by taking a force into Aronsdale while the rest of my men went to war. Yargazon didn't want me here at all. We almost came to blows over it. I had to follow you with only a few men, give up my freedom, maybe even my life. You had no right!"

Her anger surged. "You had no right to take *my* freedom, *my* life, everything that mattered to me. I had to do what I thought was right!"

"You're my wife," he said. "Don't look at me with those huge eyes, Allegra. Don't destroy the foundations of my life and then expect me to treat you like a queen." He lay on top of her and kissed her. When she jerked her head away, he let go of her wrist and grabbed her chin. Then he held her, kissing her, forcing her jaw open so he could put his tongue in her mouth.

Allegra tore her head away from him. "Stop it!" She rolled him off her body and tried to scramble across the bed. Catching her around the waist, he pulled her against him, her back to his front. His armor pressed into her skin.

His voice caught. "You make me weak." He held on to her, his face against her hair, his arm around her waist. "I can't even make myself take from my wife what is right for a man to expect."

"It wouldn't be right." Her voice cracked. "It would be cruel."

He didn't answer. Instead he pulled her leggings and underclothes to her knees. When she grabbed for them, he caught her hand and used his boot to drag the garments off and swing them to the floor. "Why do you wear these ugly clothes? They cover up your beautiful body."

Her pulse had ratcheted up so high, she felt as if she were running a race. "Markus, let me go. Please."

"I *can't*."

She went still, uncertain what he meant. He lay on his side with one arm around her waist while he caressed her breasts with his other hand. As his breath quickened, his body went rigid. With a groan, he buried his head in her hair and whispered, "You're destroying me." Then the tension in his body suddenly released, and he sagged against her.

Allegra knew little about men and sensuality, but even she could tell what had just happened. She shifted in his grip, onto her back, and this time he didn't push her down. She sat up slowly, wary as she watched him. He lay sprawled across the bed, a warrior in full armor, mail and boots, the velvet covers bunched up and pulled apart around them.

"Sing me to sleep," Markus said in a low voice. "You put me to sleep for almost a full day, and I've barely slept since then."

He had tears in his eyes. *Tears.* The indomitable prince regent of Jazid was crying. She touched the moisture at the corner of his eye. Then she took a breath and looked around. The room was full of shapes. They bordered the windows, tiled the walls, scrolled the bedposts. She laid her hand against the headboard over circles in the carvings of shape-blossom vines.

Allegra sang in a minor key about the rising moon and a lion in the night. He didn't fight the spell, but even after so long with almost no sleep, his body didn't want to let go. Finally the spell caught, and slumber overtook him in a rush, like the cloak of night dropping across the desert.

❧ CHAPTER 19
A RIVER OF BATTLE

When Allegra was sure Markus wouldn't wake, she lifted his arm away from her legs and slid off the bed. Her clothes lay scattered on the floor. She crumpled to her knees and picked up her tunic. She didn't try to dress, though. Oil from his chain mail and dirt from his armor were streaked all over her body.

Her arm was trembling so much, she dropped her clothes. She stared at them, then rose to her feet. Surely a royal suite would have a bathing room. She went to a door on the other side of the room and opened it into a chamber with a small bathing pool. The water steamed, and the scent of box-blossoms drifted in the air.

Allegra went to the pool and let herself down into the bath. She didn't know how they brought in warm water, but she was immensely grateful. She wanted nothing more than to wash away the traces on her body of Markus's fury. She had expected him to yell or strike out; it had never occurred to her that he would spend his anger sexually. The more she knew him, the less she understood men. Or maybe it was just Jazid men.

It was a while before her pulse calmed enough that she could think clearly. In Aronsdale, what Markus had done would be considered an act of violence against his wife. In Jazid, not only was it acceptable, but he would have been expected to beat her and to feel justified, even encouraged, in forcing her. For a Jazidian man he had shown incredible restraint; for an Aronsdale man, he had shown a frightening lack of control.

Allegra rubbed her eyes. She was an Aronsdale woman. Markus was wrong for her in so many ways, she couldn't count them, yet he compelled her thoughts. She didn't see how this union of theirs could work. But he was trying, in the best way he knew how. And whatever she thought of him as a husband, she didn't doubt he was a good father to Ozarson.

She had tried to stop a war, but it had come out all muddled. In the process of her escape, Ozarson had come to mean more to her than her freedom. She couldn't turn her back on him. Which meant somehow she and Markus had to work out matters between the two of them. If they couldn't find a middle ground, she didn't know how they would manage, but for Ozarson—and yes, for herself—she would try.

After Allegra finished bathing, she toweled herself dry. She found some fresh clothes in the bedroom, a soft gray and blue tunic with leggings. Then she went into the main room. Ozarson was curled up on the couch, sleeping, and Della was in one of the armchairs, reading a book.

The mage mistress looked up. "My greetings, Your Highness."

Allegra winced. "Don't call me that, please. We have enough highnesses and majesties here already."

Della gave a wry laugh. "We do seem to have accumulated quite a few."

Allegra sat on the couch by Ozarson. "Has he been out long?"

"A while." Della indicated a book in his hand. "He picked that out of the library after he ate." She chuckled. "I'm not surprised it put him to sleep. He probably didn't understand any of it."

As Allegra gently took the book, the boy sighed and settled deeper into the cushions. She peered at the title: *Geometry for the Natural Sciences.* It was a treatise for scholars who studied the earth and stars.

"Actually he probably does understand some of this," she said. "He's unusually bright."

"That's amazing." Della closed her own book. "How is his brother?"

"Asleep." She hesitated. "Do you know how many people heard what Ozi told me on the stairs?"

"Jarid, Iris and Brant," Della said. "Iris told me. The men in the foyer and the other boy were too far away. They saw Ozarson crying and talking to you, but that was it."

Allegra smoothed Ozarson's bangs off his forehead. "So much has happened to him. I can't turn away, not even if it means letting the emperor know I'm married to a man he's sworn to kill."

"Are you sure?" Della said. "Don't expect the prince regent to change just because you both love the child."

"I know. We can only do our best."

"Allegra—about the auction." Della paused awkwardly.

She looked up at Della. "Go ahead."

"Was Markus Onyx the man who bought you?" When Allegra nodded, Della asked, "Who was the other man? Onyx isn't likely to be involved in an auction with just anyone."

Allegra folded her arms, feeling cold. "Dusk Yargazon."

Della stared at her. "Saints almighty. You really landed right in the middle of it all."

Allegra started to answer, then stopped when Ozarson stirred. It wasn't something she wanted to talk about in front of him.

His lashes slowly lifted. "Allegra?"

"I'm here," she said.

He sat up, rubbing his eyes. "Where's Markus?"

"He's sleeping in the other room."

Ozarson regarded her as if she were a vase that might break. "I didn't hear any yelling."

She smiled. "He didn't. We…worked it out."

"You don't have any new bruises."

"No." Then she said, "Did you expect it?" What he answered would tell her a great deal about Markus. Ozarson hadn't been the least surprised that Yargazon had beaten her.

"No," Ozarson said. "But I've never seen him so angry."

"Well, I'm fine. And so is he." Neither statement was true, but it would do. She glanced at Della. "Do you think someone could bring up some clothes for Markus? The trousers and shirts in the wardrobe aren't going to fit him."

"I'll check," Della said.

A door creaked in the outer entrance. Then a man in violet and white livery entered the room and bowed to them. "His Majesty, Jarid Dawnfield."

Allegra sat up straighter, and Ozarson shot her an alarmed look. "It's all right," she said, and hoped it was true.

Jarid entered with Brant and several guards. Allegra started to rise, uncertain how to greet the king, but he waved his hand for her to stay put. Ozarson sat tensely at her side.

"I need to speak with the two of you and the prince regent," Jarid told them. His face was unreadable. "As soon as possible."

"I'll go get Markus," Allegra said, uneasy.

In the bedroom, she found Markus was still asleep in his chain mail and armor. He looked as if he had been transplanted from a less civilized age into these cultured environs.

Allegra sat next to him. "Wake up," she coaxed.

No response.

She shook his shoulder. "Markus?"

He gave a snort and then snored.

Allegra laid her hand on the circles engraved in the headboard and sang the lilt she had used to wake Ozarson. After several verses, Markus rolled onto his back. He rubbed his eyes, then blinked at the canopy overhead. "How long have I been asleep?"

"About an hour." She smoothed back a lock of hair that had fallen into his eyes. It was exactly like the one she had brushed out of Ozarson's eyes. "Jarid is in the other room. He wants to speak to us."

Markus sat up, rubbing his neck. Then he wrinkled his nose. "I need a bath before I meet with a king." He swung his legs over the edge of the bed. "That rest felt good, though. I never sleep that well."

Allegra doubted he was usually that furious before he went to sleep, either. She said only, "You seemed tired."

He glowered at her. "I'm still angry with you."

In truth, he no longer looked at all angry. But she just said, "I know."

"I need to say something else."

She tensed for another onslaught. "Yes?"

He took a breath. "It took courage for you to escape that way. I hate that you left, and that you took Ozarson." He lifted his hand, then dropped it. "But it took courage." Then he added, "And, Allegra—it hasn't missed my notice that in support of my brother, you offered to stand as my wife in front of Emperor Cobalt, though it means you also risk execution."

She spoke quietly. "Ozi told me what happened. Everything. How he lost his mother."

"It's good he can talk to you. He's never spoken about it to anyone else that I know of." Markus shook his head. "It's a blur in my memory. Cobalt's men thought I was brain dead. Well, no one in that much damn pain could be dead. Though when Yargazon had me carried down to the gorge, I thought I *would* die. But I didn't." He exhaled. "Ozi's mother. And Nanna—"

"You knew his nurse?"

"She was mine, too, when I was his age."

"I'm sorry," she murmured. "For all your losses."

His gaze turned fierce. "She and the queen gave their lives so he could go free. I won't let their sacrifice be in vain."

"And when will it ever stop?" Allegra asked. "Would you have Ozi grow up into another Cobalt?"

"That's what Cobalt fears."

"Yet twice, when Cobalt could have killed him, he let Ozi live."

Markus stared at her, his head tilted to one side. It was a moment before he said, "I wonder why."

A knock came at the door. Allegra went over and found a man in Dawnfield livery holding a stack of men's clothes. He bowed to her. "For the prince regent."

She accepted the pile. "Thank you."

When she returned to the bedroom, Markus was standing by the bed, unfastening his chain mail. As he let it drop to the floor, she showed him the clothes. "I hope these are all right."

"As long as they fit." He pulled off his tunic and left it in a heap by his mail. Allegra wondered if he always treated his armor that way, or if someone usually picked it up for him. She set the fresh clothes on a table by the door.

He came over and cupped his palm around her cheek. "Just touching you calms me down. I don't know why."

Flustered, she drew away. "You must be very calm, then."

He gave her a startled smile. "Was that a joke?"

"I do make them sometimes."

"Not with me."

She could tell he was about to embrace her. "I should go back to the other room. King Jarid is waiting." She made a quick exit, before he started kissing and confusing her again.

Jarid and Della were relaxed in armchairs, deep in conversation. Ozarson sat at a round table by the long window, showing Brant Firestoke a school problem. Outside, clouds scudded across the sky.

"See, it's a square root plus a constant, all inside another square root," Ozarson said. "You set it equal to this term. Then square both sides. Sometimes it works, but you have to solve a quadratic and only one root is good. Sometimes it doesn't work. It depends on the numbers."

"That's clever," Brant said.

Allegra blinked at the sight of the fugitive Jazid king doing number games with a king's advisor from Aronsdale. Hearing a nine-year-old talk about quadratics was almost as strange. Few of her students ever reached that level before they left school to marry or work their farms. Lord Firestoke must have studied it, though. She wondered what it was like for Ozarson, when even so few adults could follow where he went with his intellect.

Jarid glanced at her. "Is he awake?"

Allegra nodded self-consciously. "He'll be out as soon as he cleans up." She remained standing, unsure how to act. She gathered she wasn't expected to kneel every time Jarid came into the room, but she had little idea how court protocols worked. Della had hinted in her letters that Allegra could learn at the guild, but Allegra hadn't believed they were considering her as a bride for Aron, so she hadn't thought much about it.

"Please sit." Jarid indicated the couch.

"Thank you." She sat across from him and Della.

"Your bruises are almost healed," Jarid said.

She touched her face. "They're much better."

He spoke awkwardly. "What happened to you— If I offend in my questions, please accept my apology. You're the only person from outside of Jazid who has been with this outlaw army, at least who has returned to talk about it. You've had contact with Dusk Yargazon. *No one* else outside their army can say that."

Allegra felt ill. She didn't think Ozi or Brant could overhear their discussion, but she spoke in a low voice anyway. "Yargazon wanted to kill me. No, not kill me. Just hurt me until I wished I were dead."

They stared at her, and Della's face paled.

"I'm sorry," Jarid said.

She couldn't answer. He was right. She knew the size of the army, where it had hidden, which commanders did what. She had lain in Markus's tent while he discussed strategy with his advisors. She had listened at dinner while they talked over the war. But she was Markus's consort. For her to tell Jarid any of that would be treason against the House of Onyx. Yet she had come here to warn her king about the army. She hadn't known she would feel this fealty to Ozarson, and she couldn't sort out her confused response to

Markus. She had agreed to stand by him, yet if she withheld knowledge about his forces, she was turning her back on her own people. No matter what she did, she betrayed someone.

She was grateful Ozarson was here, though, rather than with his army. Yargazon couldn't have left him behind; the Jazid army was his protection, the reason he survived. He would have stayed with the thousand or so tenders while the army fought, but if Taka Mal defeated Jazid, the tenders couldn't protect him. If she were willing to admit it, she also cared that Markus was here instead of marching with his forces. He probably hated it. But seeing him safe and alive mattered to her.

"Allegra?" Jarid asked.

She took a breath. "What did you want to know?"

"Do they plan to kill the queen and her family?"

She had expected him to ask about tactics, supplies, troops. Then she remembered; his kin had married into the royal family of Taka Mal. At least she had no qualms about answering that question. "Markus wants them as hostages. Yargazon wants them dead. They've targeted the queen, her child, her consort and Baz Quaazera, her cousin." Then she said, "Even Yargazon wants her consort alive, to use as a hostage against Cobalt."

Jarid exhaled, then glanced at Della, whose face had gone as white as linen sheets. She shook her head. "The treaty leaves no room for interpretation."

Jarid spoke grimly. "I know."

"I don't understand," Allegra said.

"He means his treaty with Taka Mal," a deep voice rumbled.

Allegra turned with a start. Markus was walking toward them, toweling his hair, dressed in dark trousers and a dark red shirt. He had shaved, and despite the toweling, it looked like he had brushed his shaggy hair. Lowering his arms, he considered the Aronsdale king. "Will you march with or against the emperor when you go to Taka Mal?"

Jarid met his gaze. "I haven't said I'm going to Taka Mal."

"If you don't support Taka Mal against the Jazid invasion, you're violating your treaty with them," Markus said. "And if you fight against Jazid, you're fighting for Cobalt."

"I've made no decisions," Jarid answered coolly.

"Do you have news of Cobalt's army?" Allegra asked Jarid.

The king nodded, and he suddenly looked tired. He glanced at where Ozarson sat with Brant. "Perhaps you should bring the atajazid over here."

Unease washed over Allegra, and she saw her tension mirrored in Markus's face. Without a word, he went to the table. As soon as Brant looked up, his smile faded. Fear surged across Ozarson's face, and Allegra wondered if he had really forgotten it or just kept it at bay by playing with numbers, which were always either right or wrong, with no moral ambiguities.

Ozarson came to sit on the couch between Markus and Allegra. Brant sat across from them in an armchair. Although Ozarson looked composed, his fear seemed like a tangible presence to Allegra.

"The envoy I sent to Cobalt's army has returned," Jarid said. "The situation is even more complicated than we thought."

Markus tensed. "Why?"

"It isn't just his army cutting across Aronsdale," Jarid said. "My cousin has brought over a thousand men."

A thousand? "But how?" Allegra asked. She understood how Cobalt could marshal his men; he had kept forces in Shazire, the country just south of Aronsdale, since he took over that country. But Harsdown was farther west, with the Boxer-Mage Mountains dividing it from Aronsdale. Unless Muller had his army near the southern border of Harsdown, it would take many days to bring it south and join Cobalt.

"My cousin, Muller, has had his men ready for a year," Jarid said. "Since the assassination attempt against Queen Vizarana. They've been doing maneuvers in southern Harsdown near the Shazire border in case they had to march unexpectedly." His gaze turned cold as he regarded Markus. "This army you claim doesn't exist invaded Taka Mal five days ago. They've already taken a portion of the country. They're expected to reach Quaaz soon."

Allegra felt as if she were falling into a whirlpool. No wonder Jarid hadn't asked about their plans. He already knew.

"I have no idea what this supposed army is doing," Markus said. "I've been looking for my brother and my wife."

Jarid clenched his fist in frustration. "Damn it, Onyx."

Markus said nothing. Ozarson sat between him and Allegra, his posture stiff, his face worried.

"What are you going to do?" Allegra asked.

"That depends," Jarid said. "The empress and her son are with Cobalt's army. He doesn't intend to take them to Taka

Mal." He spoke tiredly. "He had, in fact, planned to leave them here."

Ozarson's face paled. "But we're here."

"Let Ozarson go," Markus said, his voice urgent. "I'm the one Cobalt wants. I command the army."

"So you admit it exists after all," Brant said.

Markus never took his gaze off Jarid. "Let the boy go."

"You know I can't do that," Jarid said.

Ozarson looked up at Markus. "I wouldn't leave you anyway."

Allegra suddenly realized what Jarid *hadn't* said. "Does Cobalt know Markus and Ozi are here?"

"I haven't yet told him." The king exhaled. "And there, I'm afraid, lies another of our complications."

"*Don't* tell him," Markus said.

"I have to," Jarid said.

"You gave asylum." Allegra's pulse surged. "You gave your word."

"I intend to keep it." Jarid raked his hand through his long hair. "But you see, we have a new problem." He looked around at them all. "My envoy didn't return alone."

"No!" Ozarson cried. "He can't be *here.*"

"I'm sorry," Jarid said. "But I'm afraid he can. Cobalt has arrived. He's in the castle."

CHAPTER 20
MIDNIGHT EMPEROR

"Markus!" Ozarson jumped up from the couch.

"It's all right." Markus pulled him back down and held the boy against his side with his arm around his shoulders. Ozarson reached for Allegra's hand and gripped her fingers.

Jarid looked miserable. "I would have wished any other way to deal with this. But Cobalt has come with his wife and baby. My envoy didn't know you were here. If I don't tell him—" He took a breath. "Cobalt is usually a rational man. But when it comes to his family—" He shook his head.

"Your wife and children are here, too," Allegra said. "It's obvious you don't consider us a danger."

"I hope that makes a difference," Jarid said.

Allegra couldn't believe Jarid had sat so calmly, waiting for Markus to bathe, while the most notorious conqueror in known history waited elsewhere in the castle. She wondered if *anything* rattled Jarid.

"Cobalt and his wife are with Iris," Jarid said. "She's

getting them settled into a guest suite. He and I will meet when they're done." Quietly he added, "You three will come with me."

The blood drained from Ozarson's face. "I can't."

Markus leaned his head over the boy's. "I won't let him hurt you." They looked so alike, their hair falling haphazardly over their collars, somehow making them seem even more vulnerable.

"I meant it when I said you had asylum here," Jarid told them. "No one may harm you without going through me. That includes the emperor."

Markus looked up at him. "Why would you do that for us?"

"I gave my word." Jarid spoke uneasily. "Having Mel and the baby here complicates things."

"Mel?" Allegra asked.

"The empress," Della said. "She's the daughter of King Muller in Harsdown." She considered Allegra. "Mel's parents came from the same region of Aronsdale as you. And Mel is about your age. The two of you have a lot in common. You might like each other."

Allegra couldn't imagine summoning the courage even to speak to the empress that many people considered the reincarnation of a warrior goddess.

Jarid was watching her face. "Mel was betrothed to Aron for most of her life. We've known her for years. If Cobalt hadn't given her an ultimatum—marry him or he would take Harsdown by force—she and Aron would be raising their own family."

"Yes, well, at this rate we'll never get Aron married," Della muttered. "First Mel, then Allegra."

Allegra thought surely some imbalance existed in the universe when conquerors like Markus and Cobalt kept ripping away brides from someone like Aron, who as far as she could tell would make a wonderful husband to some fortunate woman.

Markus's face had gone cold. His voice was like ice. "I see."

"See what?" Jarid asked warily.

"If I die," Markus ground out, "Allegra can remarry."

"You think I'm taking you to Cobalt to get you *executed?*"

Markus's anger flared. "Men have killed for queens far less worthy than Allegra."

She could have fallen over at his words. If he felt that way about her, he certainly had an odd way of showing it.

"This is Aronsdale," Jarid said coldly. "Men don't go around killing each other to steal other men's wives."

Markus just shook his head. Allegra wondered what kind of life Jazidian families led, if a married man constantly feared someone would murder him for his wife. Rose's husband wouldn't even let her leave their home when Markus and Yargazon were in the camp.

"Allegra is my regent's consort," Ozarson told Jarid, lifting his chin. "Your son may not have her."

Jarid's expression gentled and it looked as if he was going to smile. But he answered Ozarson with respect. "I assure you, Your Majesty, we won't take Allegra away from you."

She noticed he didn't say, *Or your brother.* Could Jarid be hoping Cobalt would order Markus's execution?

The outer door of the suite opened. Footsteps sounded in the entrance foyer, and Queen Iris appeared with several guards.

Jarid stood, his posture tense. "Are they settled?"

"For now." Iris twisted the sleeve of her tunic. "Mel stayed with the baby. Cobalt is down in the Shape-Hall. I don't think you should keep him waiting."

Jarid turned to one of the guards, a man with more gold on his shoulders than the others. "Captain, send an octet of my soldiers to the Hall. I'll meet you there."

"Right away, Sire." The captain saluted and left, his boots loud on the parquet floor.

Markus stood up, his hands by his sides as if he were preparing to defend himself. "Guards to protect us? Or drag us away?"

"Whatever you may suspect of my motives," Jarid said, "I intend no betrayal. The guards are for your protection."

They headed to the Shape-Hall then, the best-known room in the castle. Even far off in her dairy, Allegra had heard of it, for the room also had another name. The Hall of Kings. It was where Jarid, the only king in all the settled lands to wear a crown, had gone to his coronation. Royal marriages and christenings took place there. Most of all, it was where visiting sovereigns met with the king of Aronsdale.

Today, they went to meet an emperor.

The Shape-Hall could hold hundreds of people. Mosaics of polygons and circles in gold, white and sapphire tiles gleamed on the walls. The floor tiles were gold and white diamonds. Sunlight poured through floor-to-ceiling windows bordered by shape-vine engravings. An ivory colonnade bordered the room, supporting a balcony. Far down the hall, a group of men waited by a window that overlooked the castle gardens.

One man towered over the others.

Ozarson tightened his grip on Allegra's hand, and Markus visibly tensed on the boy's other side. Four guards had come with them, and another octet was waiting at the entrance to the hall. Jarid, Iris and Brant walked at the front of their group, blocking Markus and Ozarson from view while they proceeded down the hall.

As they neared the others, Allegra had an eerie sense, as if time slowed. It came from the tall man. He was the largest person she had ever seen, close to seven feet, with a musculature to match. His hair fell to his shoulders, thick and black. He wore heavy black trousers and a black breastplate with chain mail. His face was like stone. Combined with his monstrous size, his appearance made him seem inhuman. More than his height dominated the hall; the sense of power he exuded overwhelmed everything and everyone.

This was Cobalt, the Midnight Emperor.

They came to a stop a short distance from his group. Even Markus didn't pause as they all knelt to the emperor. Jarid and Iris were the only ones who remained standing, and they both bowed deeply. Allegra felt Ozarson shaking at her side, and wondered how, at the age of seven, he could have stood up to this man and declared he would kill him.

Cobalt spoke in a bass voice. "Rise."

As they stood up, Allegra noticed Jarid's guards had closed around her, Markus and Ozarson. Jarid went forward to Cobalt, but Iris and Brant waited at the front of their group.

"Why so many guards?" Cobalt asked Jarid. He didn't sound suspicious or annoyed, just curious. His voice rumbled, deeper than any Allegra had ever heard.

"Your Majesty," Jarid began. It sounded odd to Allegra to hear the king of her country speak with such deference. Yes, he called Ozarson by a similar title, but this had a different quality. Fear underlaid the words.

"What's wrong?" Cobalt asked.

"I have guests," Jarid said.

"Is this a problem?" Cobalt asked. "Who are they?"

Jarid took a breath. Then he beckoned to Markus. Ozarson was gripping Allegra's hand so hard, her fingers ached. But she didn't try to loosen his grip.

Markus, Allegra and Ozarson walked forward, past the guards. She felt as if each step went through molasses. What was it about Cobalt that slowed her down? It wasn't any mage effect she knew, but it didn't feel natural. He turned to look, almost in slow motion, his black eyes boring into them.

Then Cobalt said, "What the hell?" He was watching Ozarson.

They all stopped, and the atajazid froze, his terrified gaze on the emperor.

"Come here, boy." Cobalt motioned him forward. "Let me get a better look at you."

Ozarson didn't move. Then Markus put his arm around his shoulders and guided him forward. Allegra walked on Ozarson's other side, holding his hand. They stopped in front of the emperor.

"Saints, boy," Cobalt said. He wasn't even looking at Markus or Allegra. "I saw you go over that cliff. How are you alive?"

Ozarson just kept looking up at him.

Cobalt waited. When the boy didn't answer, the emperor said, "We searched the bottom of the cliff. We didn't find any bodies."

"General Yargazon and his men took them," Markus said coldly. "Ozarson's mother and nurse were given a proper cremation."

Cobalt glanced at him. "Who are you?"

The prince regarded him steadily. "Markus Alexander Onyx."

Cobalt's face hardened with an anger that turned him into something other than a man. Allegra stepped back and Ozarson shrank against her side.

"The prince regent is dead," Cobalt said.

Markus raised his chin. "I live."

"For maybe one more hour." Cobalt swung around to Jarid. "How the blazes did you capture them?"

"I didn't." Jarid spoke quietly. "They came to me. I've given them asylum. They're under my protection."

The emperor stared as if the Aronsdale king had gone mad. Then he lifted his arm and pointed to Markus. "No asylum exists for that man. Everyone who tortured Mel will die." Some of the ice left his voice. "The boy was only seven. He's blameless, at least as much as anyone of Onyx blood can be. But not the regent. He will die as his father died."

"No!" Ozarson's voice cracked. "You can't."

Jarid stood his ground. "I gave them my word, Cobalt. You can't violate the asylum of Suncroft. You don't hold sway here."

"I will not have the outlawed regent of Jazid in the same *country* with my wife and son," Cobalt said, "let alone the same building."

"Then we must decide whom to move where," Jarid said. "Because we aren't executing anyone."

One of Cobalt's men stepped forward, a gray-haired officer in the blue and white uniform of the Misted Cliffs. He spoke in a gravelly voice. "The boy and his regent would make valuable hostages when we reach Taka Mal."

Cobalt considered the man. Then he turned to Markus, and the banked fury in his eyes belied his quiet tone. "Did you help them take her?"

"Take who?" Markus asked.

"My wife."

Markus's face paled, the first time Allegra had ever seen it happen. "No, I did not. I didn't know what he planned. Had I any idea, I would have tried to stop him."

"You lie so easily." Cobalt turned to Jarid. "Release them into my custody."

"I will not," Jarid said.

"I can take them by force. My army is only a few hours from your door."

Jarid blanched, but he didn't back down. "You would have to attack my army, then, in violation of your treaty with my cousin. Your wife's father. Will you start a war with Aronsdale, too?"

Cobalt's huge fist clenched at his side. "Why do you protect a monster?"

"You're accusing him of war crimes with no proof."

Allegra expected Cobalt to brush aside Jarid's objections.

Instead he walked away from them, past his men. The gray-haired officer joined him, and they stood looking out the floor-to-ceiling window. The man said something in a low voice, and Cobalt nodded, his face strained. Allegra caught a name: Agate. Saints. This must be General Agate Cragland, the man who had brought home the body of Ozarson's father.

Cobalt returned to Markus and considered the prince regent. Then he said, "My grandfather raised me."

Although Markus met his gaze, he seemed lost for a response.

"Stonebreaker Chamberlight," Cobalt said. "You are familiar with that name?"

"To some extent," Markus answered. "He knew my father."

"Yes, he did." Cobalt continued in the same measured tone. "He, your father and Dusk Yargazon swore a blood oath."

"I'm aware of that," Markus said.

"They were three of a kind," Cobalt said. "Three monsters. Why should I believe you are different?"

"My father wasn't a monster," Ozarson told him, defiant. "He was a great man."

Cobalt turned his dark gaze on the boy. "And you want to be just like him, no doubt."

"If I could be *half* of what he was, I would be honored."

"Your loyalty to your sire is admirable, boy. Perhaps I should tell you about your father's great deeds."

"Don't," Allegra said softly. "Please."

Cobalt glanced at her. "Come closer, where I can see you."

Allegra swallowed and let go of Ozarson. She went to Cobalt, and he studied her, his face puzzled. "You look like an Aronsdale mage girl."

"She is," Jarid said. "She's from the same part of the country as your wife's mother."

Cobalt scratched his chin. "Are you the nursemaid for this boy while he's here at the castle?"

She was having trouble breathing. "No. I'm one of his guardians."

"That makes absolutely no sense," Cobalt said.

"She's my wife," Markus told him.

Cobalt snorted. "No woman from southern Aronsdale would willingly marry a Jazid man."

A silence greeted his words. Cobalt looked around, studying each person. Then he turned slowly back to Allegra. "In fact," he said, "I wonder how a girl from Aronsdale even met the fugitive and presumed dead prince regent of Jazid."

Allegra was beginning to feel ill. Any answer she gave would only make matters worse. Her husband could die.

Cobalt spoke to Markus. "Men in Jazid buy wives, don't they?"

Sweat sheened Markus's forehead. "That's right."

"And you bought this girl?"

"Yes."

"From who?"

"A nomad."

"A nomad." Cobalt's eyes were burning. "A nomad who perhaps kidnapped her from Aronsdale?"

Markus didn't answer.

Cobalt swung around to Jarid. "If you protect this man, you are protecting the atrocities he commits, allows and condones." He lifted his arm and pointed at Ozarson. "That boy may be young enough to reeducate. But I will *not* have his regent anywhere near my wife or son."

Markus's voice snapped with anger. "I never condoned, allowed or participated in any way with your wife's abduction." In a calmer voice, he said, "Or in what your grandfather did to you. My father was his oath brother. Not me."

Cobalt lowered his arm, and silence filled the hall.

Then Cobalt said, "Your father once stood by and watched my grandfather beat me unconscious. I was *eight* years old. Younger than your atajazid. Your father just stayed there, drinking his wine as if I were some *dog* that had to be—" He took a deep, shuddering breath. Then he turned away from Markus and spoke to Jarid. "You have a dungeon here?"

Jarid nodded uneasily. "I do."

"Good. Put Onyx in it until we're ready for his execution."

"Cobalt—"

"Do it," the emperor said. "Or I'll have my men take him by force. If I have to start a war with Aronsdale, so be it."

"He didn't do anything!" Ozarson lunged toward Cobalt.

"No!" Markus grabbed him and pulled him back. In a low voice, he said, "Stay with Allegra."

"Your Majesty." Allegra's voice was shaking. "My husband is not a perfect man. But he is not a monster. He would never beat a child or torture a woman."

"You would defend a man who bought you like a slave?" Cobalt asked, incredulous.

"No," she said. "I'm defending the only real father Ozarson has ever known. And he's a good father. For the boy's sake, I beg of you, let his regent live. Don't condemn Markus and Ozarson for the sins of their sire."

Cobalt frowned at her. "Is that why you brought him here for sanctuary? Because you think he's a good father?"

"I only brought Ozarson here," Allegra said. "Markus came looking for us."

Cobalt peered at her. "How did you get here without him?"

"I stole his horse."

His eyebrows went up. "And how did you manage that?"

"I put Markus, Ozarson and his men to sleep."

"His men? As in, perhaps, Dusk Yargazon?"

"General Yargazon figured out I could do spells." Under the impact of his scrutiny, her words tumbled out in bursts. "When I sang. He put wax in his ears. He threw me down and we fought. I hit him with the candelabra. We fought more and I pushed him. His head hit a chest, and it knocked him out. Then I took Ozarson, stole Markus's horse and rode away."

To her unmitigated surprise, Cobalt smiled. "Do you by any chance know my wife?"

Allegra blinked. "No, Sire."

He glanced at Jarid. "I fear what could happen should they meet. They might overthrow everyone and take over all the kingdoms."

Jarid gave a startled smile. "Perhaps."

Allegra couldn't believe it. Cobalt the Dark, the Midnight Emperor, had made a joke. At least, she thought it was a joke. She wasn't certain. He looked intimidating even when he wasn't angry.

Cobalt turned to Markus. "And you came looking for the boy? Even though you knew you could die by doing it."

"Yes," Markus said. "And for her."

For an excruciating moment, Cobalt studied Markus. Then he swung around to Jarid. "Very well. I will allow you to keep him here." When Jarid started to respond, Cobalt raised his hand. "But only if you chain him in the dungeon for as long as my wife and son are in this castle. My men will remain as guards." He turned to Allegra and Ozarson. "You two will ride with my army to Taka Mal, to serve as hostages."

Markus's reaction was subtle, but Allegra recognized the slight lowering of his shoulders. As small a gesture as it was, she felt its immensity. Relief. He wouldn't die today after all.

"Allegra wouldn't be any use as a hostage," Markus said. "Not for leverage with my people."

"I'm not bringing her as leverage with your people," Cobalt said. "She's a hostage for your behavior. Just as you, imprisoned here, will be a hostage for your atajazid's behavior."

Allegra understood then what Cobalt intended. Markus's life depended on what she and Ozarson did as Cobalt's prisoners. Any attempt they made to escape could be the prince regent's death sentence.

The pitted steps led below the castle. Suncroft was named for light and warmth, but neither showed in this place of dank smells. A rat scuttled across the stairs, and Allegra jumped to the side. When a drop of water hit her cheek, she looked up to see a broken stone arch covered with lichen.

The stairs were too narrow for more than one person. Jarid went first, with a torch that cast oversize shadows on the walls. Two soldiers from the Misted Cliffs followed him. Markus came next, his hands bound behind his back, going slowly as he strove to keep his balance. Cobalt followed, holding another torch. Allegra went next, then two more of Cobalt's guards. The odor of burning torches saturated the air, and smoke curled around them.

Iris and Brant had taken Ozarson to his suite, despite the boy's protests. Allegra didn't want him to see Markus this way, and she thought Markus didn't, either. In fact, she suspected he would have liked her to go with Ozarson, as well. Cobalt, however, had given her no choice.

At the bottom, they walked along a rough-hewn tunnel. The wall on the left consisted of large stone blocks. The one on the right had three doors at evenly spaced intervals, each solid oak with a small, barred window at a tall man's eye-level. Strips of metal reinforced the doors, crusted with rust and lichen. Allegra wondered if anyone ever came down here.

Jarid fumbled with a hexagonal ring of keys as if he didn't know which he needed. He finally found one that unlocked the second cell. As the guards swung open the ponderous door, Markus watched, his face ashen. Allegra wanted to go to him, but Cobalt was standing between them. She remembered wishing Markus would suffer the emperor's anger, and the thought soured in her mouth. She couldn't have imagined then how much she would regret seeing that wish granted.

The guards took Markus's arms and walked him into the cell. Jarid followed, holding up his torch. Cobalt stayed in the doorway, so Allegra stepped past him with caution, acutely aware of his presence dominating the cell. His head almost touched the ceiling. When she tried to go to Markus, though, Cobalt caught her arm. He didn't let go until she stepped back to the wall by the door.

Straw had once covered the floor, but only a few blackened bits remained. The ceiling, walls and floor were built from stone blocks. Chains with manacles hung on the wall to the left. And that was it. An empty room that stank of rotting straw.

The guards brought Markus to the left wall. As they turned

him around and unbound his hands, he stared at Allegra. His face showed no emotion; he would never reveal his fear. But she felt it, perhaps because her spells sensitized her to his moods. It wasn't only his fear of Cobalt, who could still have him killed. For Markus—a man who needed constantly to be outside, walking or riding, someone who could never stay still—being chained in a cell would be a nightmare.

Jarid gave a key to one of his soldiers, and the man went to where the guards held Markus. As they manacled his wrists, Allegra sagged against the wall, feeling ill. When they chained his ankles, he had to sit on the floor, sideways to the wall with his right shoulder pressed against the stone. The shackles forced him to stretch out his legs because they weren't directly below those for his arms. It left him with his arms pulled tight over his head and his legs pulled tight along the wall.

Jarid glanced at Cobalt. "Is that really necessary? He couldn't escape here even if he wasn't in the chains."

"How do you know?" Cobalt asked. "We had him in Jazid, ready for burial, and then, suddenly, he's gone. Two years later, here he is, hale and hearty, sending an army to conquer Taka Mal. The chains stay."

Markus stared up at him, his face lit by flickering torchlight.

Allegra couldn't take any more; she stepped away from the wall before Cobalt could catch her and went over to Markus. Kneeling next to him, she spoke softly. "You'll be all right."

"Does the revenge feel fine?" he asked in a low voice.

"I would never wish this on you."

His face contorted. "My shoulder—can you push it?"

Puzzled, she laid her hand on his left shoulder. "Like this?"

"No." His face creased with pain. "The ridge, closer to my neck. You'll feel it."

Probing his muscles, she found a huge knot. "There?"

"Yes. Push. Hard—" He sounded as if he were gritting his teeth.

Allegra massaged the area, and suddenly the knot gave like the release of a bolt. Markus grunted, and his arm relaxed while relief washed over his face.

"What happened?" she asked.

"It's an injury from the war," he said. "I can't lift my arm above my head anymore. It spasms like that."

She stared at the chains pulling his arms. "Markus—"

"I'll be all right." Gruffly he added, "Take care of Ozi."

"I will."

Heavy footsteps sounded behind them, and then Cobalt was standing next to her. She looked up and felt as if the air went out of the room.

He indicated the doorway. "Wait with my guards."

Allegra stood up. "Please, can't you take off the manacles?"

"No." He regarded her with a hooded gaze. "Go with my men. I want to talk to you upstairs."

Markus stiffened. "Leave her alone, Escar."

Cobalt fixed Allegra with a hard stare and jerked his head at the door. Swallowing, she backed away, toward the entrance. Jarid started toward her, but Cobalt shook his head, and the Aronsdale king stopped. They all felt it, that

Cobalt's decision to let Markus live could change any moment, if anyone pushed him.

Cobalt turned back to Markus and looked down at the captive Jazid prince. "How many men have you put in chains, Onyx? How many soldiers have you had whipped?" His voice hardened. "How many innocent, vulnerable girls have you shackled for your pleasure?"

"You have no right to judge me," Markus said.

"Probably not," Cobalt said. "But the Onyx Throne is mine. Neither you nor your brother will ever sit on it."

"What are you going to do with Ozarson?" It was the first time Markus's fear had shown in his voice.

Cobalt pushed his hand through his hair. To Allegra's surprise, he said, "I don't know. Maybe take him to the Misted Cliffs and have him brought up there, by people I trust."

"No!" Markus yanked on the chains as if he could free himself by sheer force of will.

Cobalt looked at him for a long moment, and something subtle happened to his face. *Pain?* When he spoke again, he had a gruffer tone. "The boy is fortunate to have people who love him."

With that, the Midnight Emperor strode from the cell.

Allegra tried to go back in to Markus, but a guard held her back. As soon as Jarid left, two guards heaved on the door. It slammed shut with a crash that vibrated through the walls, leaving Markus alone in the dark.

CHAPTER 21
A MAGE OF CONSCIENCE

Allegra sat at the table in the Octagon Room while Cobalt paced. Jarid leaned on the windowsill, his arms crossed. Despite Cobalt's demands, the king had refused to leave Allegra alone with the emperor, and she was immensely grateful.

Cobalt finally sat down, several chairs away from her. He stretched his legs out under the table, and they seemed to go on forever. She had never seen a man with such long legs. His height, strength and sheer physical size shrunk the room.

"This marriage of yours," Cobalt said. "Do you want it ended?"

Allegra stared down at the table, thinking. What did she want? No easy answers existed. If she was no longer Markus's wife, they would ask her about Aron. He seemed a fine man. The two of them were similar in age, ancestry, culture, possibly even mage ability, if Dawnfield men did actually inherit the gifts bred into their line. It should be an ideal match. But when she tried to think of Aron, she saw Markus.

Her match with the prince regent was anything but ideal—and yet he stirred her heart in a way no man ever had before.

Allegra lifted her head. "No, I don't." She turned to Jarid, feeling like a traitor. "I truly am sorry." She wanted to say so much more, but she couldn't speak of such personal matters in front of Cobalt.

"Why are you telling him you're sorry?" Cobalt asked.

"She's a mage," Jarid said.

Still sprawled in the chair, Cobalt considered him. "And?"

"She's the strongest we've found in her generation of women." Jarid's voice cooled. "Except for Mel."

The emperor took a moment to absorb that. Then he raised his eyebrows at Allegra. "You would give up the chance to become an Aronsdale queen so you could remain the wife of an outlaw whose culture diametrically opposes anything you would want or choose?"

Allegra stiffened. "I decide what I want and choose."

"Not with a Jazidian prince," Cobalt said.

He had a point. "I can't give you answers I don't have. But Markus and I—" They what? Allegra hardly knew how to describe the way the two of them struggled with each other. She didn't see how she and Markus could find a life together. She couldn't stay with him in Jazid, especially with Yargazon in their lives. Nor could she imagine Markus living with her in Aronsdale. So where could they live? It was impossible. But she couldn't give up, not yet, for despite all their incompatibilities, Markus reached her as no one else had done. But she couldn't tell all that to Cobalt the Dark. So she said only, "We're trying."

"I suppose that's all any of us can do," Cobalt mused. He spoke thoughtfully. "We have the princess regent of Jazid here in Aronsdale, the Atajazid D'Az upstairs and the prince regent in the dungeon. A strange set of affairs."

"What will you do with us?" Allegra asked.

"A good question." He tapped his fingers on the table. "By the time we reach Quaaz, your husband's army will probably have been there several days. They may have taken the capital. If that happens, I'll have to fight a war." He glanced at Jarid, then back at Allegra. "Unfortunately Aronsdale and Harsdown may feel compelled to join with Taka Mal against me."

"I haven't said that," Jarid said sharply.

Cobalt's stare was impassive. "I haven't heard otherwise, either."

"Everything seems tangled," Allegra said, going for one of the greater understatements she had ever made.

"The loyalties are confused," Cobalt said. "Aronsdale has a treaty with Taka Mal. They will fight to defend the Topaz Throne. Which would appear to mean, they will fight Jazid. I hold Jazid. So are they fighting against me? But no, this outlaw army isn't mine. The fugitive army wants Taka Mal to increase its strength and defeat my forces. Also because Jazid just damn well wants Taka Mal."

"Jazid is dying," she said. "It's the richest country in the settled lands, and they're *dying*." She knew challenging the

397

emperor was dangerous. But Markus had strong reasons for raising his army, reasons connected inextricably with Cobalt. She steeled herself against her fear and regarded him steadily. "Are you helping them?"

Cobalt scowled at her. "It is impossible to help people who fight you at every turn." He motioned at Jarid. "Neither Aronsdale nor Harsdown is pleased with my holding Jazid. So maybe they want this outlaw army to conquer Taka Mal and engage my forces. But of course, they cannot stand by while Jazid attacks Taka Mal. So they want to help Taka Mal but fight me. Otherwise, they fear that when the dust settles, I will end up with the Topaz Throne."

Allegra didn't know what to say. It sounded like a mess.

The emperor was watching her closely. "What do you think, Allegra? Should I also hold the Topaz Throne?"

She felt as if a band were constricting her chest, cutting off her air. Of course she didn't think he should hold it. If things kept going this way, soon he would rule every country in the settled lands. She could hardly tell him that, though. So instead, she asked, "Could you keep it? To hold so many countries, you need a military you can trust. You can augment your army with those of other countries, but their loyalty won't be as strong, especially in Jazid and Taka Mal. The more places you take, the harder it becomes to keep them all." She took a breath, trying to calm her surging pulse. "Jazid raised an army large enough to threaten Taka Mal. They may take that country. Your forces are spread too thin. If you take Taka Mal, it will just get worse."

"So." He tapped his fingers on the table, and she feared she had gone too far. But he said only, "What do you think of this boy, Ozarson?"

"He's a remarkable young man."

"Brave."

She spoke quietly. "Yes. Very much so."

"And Dusk Yargazon?" Cobalt's voice hardened.

Allegra didn't want to answer. She had already said too much. But even through her apprehension, she understood the respect Cobalt was giving her, asking for her opinion and listening carefully, especially after the way Markus's people had treated her. She doubted Cobalt would ever sit talking strategy with his advisors while she "slept" in the room.

So she steadied herself and gave another understatement. "Yargazon makes me uncomfortable. He's cruel, he's brutal and he's a sadist. But he's also a brilliant commander. Markus needs him." Her gaze never wavered. "That doesn't mean Markus condones the rest of what he does."

"He can't have it both ways," Cobalt said. "Either he supports Yargazon or he doesn't." He studied her. "Ask yourself this. Who rules? That boy? I hardly think so. Your husband? He's what, thirty-six? Yargazon is nearly sixty. He has more years of experience with power than Markus has been alive. Yes, Markus needs him." He leaned forward. "The more you rely on what you need, the more you become that which you rely on."

She stared at him. "They're nothing alike!"

"And if you said that to your husband in front of

Yargazon? Would he agree? Or would he seek the General's approval, even if it meant hurting you in some way, emotionally, even physically?"

A chill went through Allegra. "I don't know."

"Cobalt, what do you want her to say?" Jarid demanded. "I don't see what grilling her this way accomplishes."

Cobalt pulled his long legs under him and rose to his feet. He went to one of the octagonal windows and stood gazing at the hills of Crofts Vale.

Allegra glanced at Jarid, baffled, and he lifted his hands with puzzlement.

Cobalt turned. "Allegra, I want you to answer my question again, and I want you to think carefully before you do. We can dissolve your marriage to the prince regent of Jazid, if you wish. Do you choose to remain his wife? Before you say yes, be sure that it *is* what you want and what you choose."

Was she sure? "I can't know what will happen, especially given how unstable everything is now. But I'm as certain as I can be."

He smiled slightly. "Does that mean yes?"

She nodded, hoping she wasn't making a terrible mistake. "Yes. I want to remain his wife."

He turned back to the window. Leaning his arm against the sill over his head, he watched the village in the hills beyond Suncroft. "Very well. Then I will let him live."

Allegra jumped out of her chair. "What?"

Cobalt turned back to her. "I said I will let him live."

She felt as if her heart slammed inside her. "And if I had said no, I didn't want to stay married to him?"

"I would have executed him."

She couldn't believe this. "How could you ask me to make a decision like that without telling me what hinged on my answer?"

He came to the table and stood on the other side, facing her. "I wanted your answer free and willing."

"Why?"

"I've already told you. The more a king relies on what he needs, the more he becomes that which he relies on." Quietly he said, "Markus Onyx needs you. He has managed, gods only know how, to earn your willingness to, as you said, 'try' with him. I have no doubt, Allegra, that a man such as Yargazon or Ozar Onyx would never have convinced you to say those words."

"No," she said, stunned. "They wouldn't have."

"Then it is done." With that, he nodded to Jarid and strode out of the room. The door swung open with a whoosh under his pull and closed with a loud bang after he left.

Allegra stared after him. Then she turned to Jarid.

The king walked over to her. "He can be overwhelming."

"What if I had said no?"

"Would you have grieved for Markus?"

"Yes!" She felt as if she had been running a race. "Even if I hadn't wanted to stay his consort, Cobalt had no right to make me responsible for his death."

Jarid laid his hand on her shoulder. "Cobalt always

intended to execute Markus. The prince regent was the first one whose death he demanded at the summit when we all met after the last war. It was the only way he would let the boy live. If you hadn't agreed to stay with Markus, Cobalt would have gone ahead with those plans. He didn't make you responsible for Markus's death. He made you responsible for his life." He grimaced. "If I were you, I would worry far more about that outcome."

"I just hate thinking of him chained down there." Allegra could still see Markus's bleak look as the guards slammed the cell door. "I wish Cobalt would let me see him, even if only to give him some light."

Jarid lowered his hand. "I never expected to use those cells. I'd planned on converting them to storerooms."

"Is it true, what Cobalt said, that you and the Harsdown king would rather fight against him than for him?"

"If I wouldn't answer that for him," Jarid said dryly, "I certainly won't tell the wife of the man whose army we would fight." He paced away from her, then turned around. "After you warned us about Markus's army, we sent redwings to the Topaz Palace with a message, and I dispatched a company of men to Taka Mal. The most important thing is to get Vizarana, Drummer and their baby out of there before the Jazid army gets them."

As much as it relieved Allegra that the royal family would have a chance to escape, she also knew that in the view of her husband's people, she had committed treason by warning Jarid, especially now that she had agreed to remain Markus's consort. Yargazon would demand she be sentenced, probably executed. It would have been far easier to say nothing—but she would have had to live for the rest of her life with the deaths that resulted. And she couldn't forget Ozi's pensive words: *Sometimes you must fight. But sometimes—I wish we could find other ways.*

"Is your army going to Taka Mal?" Allegra asked.

Jarid tiredly rubbed the back of his neck. "My generals have been preparing to march since we sighted Cobalt's army. We'll take about half my forces, between one and two thousand. Most of Cobalt's and my cousin's forces will camp here tonight, and we'll move out in the morning." He stood by a chair and felt for the table with one hand, again with that odd quality, as if he were blind. But he was looking straight at her. "As to what happens when we reach Taka Mal—" He shrugged. "That depends on what we find when we arrive."

Allegra had no doubt he knew far more about what he wanted to do than he intended to tell her. "Will you fight? Yourself, I mean." She was no military expert, but she was almost certain kings weren't supposed to go out on the battlefield.

He seemed surprised by the question. "In a sense."

"You're a mage, aren't you? I've heard stories." Impossible stories. "Tales about indigo spells and war mages."

His expression shuttered. "You shouldn't listen. People like to weave epic tales about royal houses. Reality is far different."

"Could you—" She took a breath, needing an answer she

had struggled with these past few days. "If you could use your gifts to do harm rather than to heal, would you?"

She immediately wished she hadn't asked. He *receded* from her somehow, drawing within himself. His gaze lost focus. He kept looking at her, but he no longer seemed to see. He reached for the chair, but he hit the back and knocked it over. Even then he tried to find the chair, as if he hadn't heard it fall and couldn't see it on the floor. Then he crouched down and felt around until his hand banged its leg. He picked it up and set it upright, then stood with his hand clenched on its back.

"Your Majesty?" Allegra asked, bewildered. "Can I help?"

Jarid reached toward her, and she stepped closer. When his hand hit her shoulder, he let out a breath.

"Sire?" she asked. "What's wrong?"

No answer. He pulled out the chair and sat down. When he put his hand to his neck, at first she thought he was loosening his collar. Then he pulled out a pendant.

A sphere.

It was a perfectly round ball of iridescent metal. He folded his hand around it and bent his head. Power swirled—and a green spell glowed around him. Not all mages created colors, but Jarid filled the room in emerald light. Allegra stared at him, stunned. She had never known anyone who could so easily create such a luminous spell. She felt it spreading throughout the castle.

He's searching for someone. She sat down, afraid to disturb him. The spell continued to expand. Such power! It was surely absorbing the moods of people throughout the castle, flooding him with emotions. She couldn't imagine how he endured it, unless he knew how to block out everyone but the person he sought.

Allegra wasn't certain how long they sat; moments or an hour. Then the door opened. Queen Iris stood in the archway, bathed in emerald light. As she came forward, Allegra left the table and moved back, out of the way.

Iris sat next to her husband. "Jarid?" She rested her hand on his where it lay on the table. "Can you hear me?"

He turned toward her and touched her face. He traced the line of her chin and cheek, then felt her hair. With an exhale, he dropped the metal sphere against his chest. As the spell faded, he folded his arms on the table and put his forehead on his arms.

Iris laid her hand on his back. "Can you speak?"

No answer.

The queen looked up at Allegra. "What happened?"

"I a-asked—" Allegra took a breath to stop her stammering. "I don't know. We were talking. He went into a trance. I think."

"What were you talking about?" Iris said.

"The armies and Taka Mal." She had been nervous about her own conflicts with spells and violence, and the intensity of his reaction frightened her. "I asked if he could use his mage gifts to do harm rather than to heal."

Iris's face paled. "Ai, no wonder." She leaned over Jarid, her hands on his shoulders. "Come back, love."

He lifted his head and felt for her face, then kissed her. His eyes were unfocused.

Standing, Iris drew him to his feet. "Come, sleep. Perhaps it will be gone when you awake."

He gave no sign he heard. He started to walk, feeling his way along the table, and she helped guide him, her hand on his arm.

"I'm sorry," Allegra said, dismayed. "What did I do?"

Iris looked back at her. "Nothing, child. It's not your fault. Here, come with us."

Allegra joined them. Once they were in the corridor outside, with no chairs or tables, Jarid seemed better. But he kept his hand over Iris's on his arm, and his gaze remained unfocused. Allegra felt certain he could neither see nor hear. He couldn't even talk. *Why?*

She could hardly believe what he had done, calling forth such a tremendous power from the highest possible shape. If a green spell of that magnitude came so easily to him, what else could he do? Could the impossible be true, that he was an indigo mage? This might be the price he paid for that immense power, the loss of his senses.

Iris took them through back halls, choosing narrow corridors with fewer mosaics. They ended at a side door. Allegra opened it for them, but it wasn't until they were inside that she realized they were in the royal chambers. The understated elegance made the rooms no less breathtaking. Gold and white gleamed, from the gilded walls to the drapes to the chandeliers. Exquisite patterns of interlocking rings bordered the archways, and hexagonal tiles patterned the floor. The goldwood tables were octagons or circles. Roses and violet royal-buds bloomed in white vases set within wall recesses. It stunned Allegra that they allowed her into their private rooms.

Iris guided Jarid to a worn armchair. He visibly relaxed as he let himself down into it, and Allegra wondered if it was his favorite chair.

"Do you want anything?" Iris asked him.

He touched her face, his fingers skimming her cheek as if to reassure himself she was there. Then he waved his hand, sending her away.

Iris turned to Allegra. "This is a private matter. We would like it to remain that way."

Allegra stepped toward the door. "I'll go."

"No, I didn't mean that." Iris rubbed her eyes, then dropped her arm. "I would like company. If you don't mind."

"It would be my honor to stay." Then Allegra added, "I'll say nothing about what happened."

"Thank you." Iris lifted her hand to a nearby couch. "I should stay close, in case he needs anything."

Allegra glanced at Jarid. He had leaned back and was staring at the ceiling with an unfocused quality. She thought it must be terrifying for him to lose his sight.

"I'm sorry," she said to Iris as they went to the couch. "I don't know what I did."

Iris sat down with her. "It's happened a few times before. He'll come out of it." Her face was drawn. "He will."

Allegra doubted Iris was anywhere near as certain as she tried to sound. "Is it something to do with his being a mage?"

"In a sense. Our inability—our *refusal*—to do harm is a foundation of what it means to be a mage. What we do to others, we do to ourselves."

Allegra smiled wryly. "I almost put myself to sleep when I used the spell on Markus and his men."

Iris nodded. "You can give sleep because you sleep. We feel only emotions we can experience ourselves. I can heal a wound that isn't mortal, for it could eventually heal itself." Even after so many years at Suncroft, she had a tinge of the dialect from the Tallwalk Mountains of her home. "But I canna heal a mortal wound."

"I never thought of it that way," Allegra said. "It makes sense."

"You have studied the different types of spells, yes?"

"Some." Allegra wondered how this connected to Jarid. "Red brings warmth and light, orange eases pain, yellow soothes emotions, green senses them, blue heals wounds, indigo heals emotions. Except—" She hesitated.

"Yes?" Iris asked.

"Do indigo mages actually exist? Legends say the House of Dawnfield once had such…" Allegra trailed off, not wanting to tell the queen she found such stories hard to believe.

"I'm not an indigo, if that's what you're asking." Iris's expression shuttered. "Nor is my husband."

Allegra wondered why she had withdrawn. "Blue, then?"

"No."

Allegra waited. "Your Majesty?"

Iris spoke as if she hurt. "If my husband considers using his abilities in battle, he loses his sight, hearing and speech. I fear that if he ever uses spells in war, it will destroy him." She glanced at Jarid. "His parents were killed by highwaymen when he was six. Jarid blamed himself. What can a child know? He turned his power against himself—and for fourteen years he was deaf, blind and mute. He lived in a hovel with one of the highwaymen able to do nothing but make spells." In a quiet, even voice, the queen of Aronsdale said, "He spent fourteen years purifying the spells of a violet sphere mage."

The blood drained from Allegra's face. Violet came *after* indigo. Such a mage was beyond her ability to comprehend. In a low voice, she said, "The power to save lives."

Iris met her gaze. "Or take them."

"He can kill with his spells," she said numbly.

"Aye." Iris watched her husband. "You asked him a question he has struggled with since we saw Cobalt's army. Perhaps this is his way of focusing inward to search for answers."

"I didn't mean—"

Iris laid her hand on her arm. "He must wrestle with this himself. It isn't up to you or me or anyone else."

A sudden thought hit Allegra. "Is Aron a mage?"

"Aye. We don't know his full power yet. Blue, maybe indigo."

"Gods." Allegra felt like an imposter. "Why am I even here? My spells are such silly, puny things."

Iris's expression softened. "Della tells me they are lovely and pure."

"And weak."

"Don't be so hard on yourself. The Dawnfield traits have been forged over millennia." Her gaze looked much older than her face. "My husband can use violet spells anytime. He has the greatest power of any mage alive. But the price he will pay, if he does—I doubt he will survive."

Softly Allegra said, "Perhaps his senses won't come back. He would have to stay here, then."

"He would hate himself for it." Iris let out a breath. "Each of the few times this has happened, I have feared that he wouldn't recover."

Allegra thought of Markus chained in the dark. Jarid lived in a cell of his own making that was as much a dungeon as the one that held her husband. Then she thought of Ozarson. All of this—armies on the move, mage powers gathering, the survival of royal Houses against Cobalt's inexorable power—it had all been put into motion by one boy who had lost so much.

❧ CHAPTER 22
THE LONG ROOM

Two guards escorted Allegra to her suite. Ozarson came running out of his bedroom as soon as she entered the main parlor.

"Is Markus all right?" the boy asked anxiously. "Did they hurt him?"

Della walked into the room. "You've been gone so long."

Allegra sat on a low table, bringing her eyes level with the boy's. "Markus will be fine." She struggled with the words, because he obviously hadn't been fine when she left. "They just put him in a big room under the castle."

"I know what a dungeon looks like," Ozarson said. "We had them at the Onyx Palace."

"He's going to be all right." Allegra prayed to Saint Azure that was true.

"Did they leave a torch for him?" When she just kept looking at him, he said, "Did they leave him water? Food? Can he get to the water? Can he *move?*"

"He's fine," Allegra whispered. How could she tell him the answer to all his questions was *no.*

"They can't chain him." Ozarson's voice cracked. "He can't stand to be confined. He needs to be out, moving all the time."

She tugged him down next to her. "Markus is strong. He's probably faced far worse than sitting in some dungeon."

"Do you know how long they will keep him there?"

"Until we get back from Taka Mal." She didn't add, *If we do.*

Dismay filled his face. "That could be a long time!"

Allegra put her hands on his shoulder. "Ozi, listen. He's safer in that dungeon than going into battle."

Ozarson looked away, biting his lip.

Della came over and sat in an armchair next to him. "Your brother is a strong, brave man. He will get through this."

"They won't let me see him," Ozarson said. "I asked the guards to take me, but they told me the emperor says I must stay here."

"I think he wants to separate you from Markus," Allegra said.

"You must go see Cobalt." Ozarson's voice cracked. "Talk to him. Please."

Allegra's heart ached. How many times had he pleaded for the lives of people he loved? He had lost his father, three brothers, his mother, his nurse. Now the biggest constant in his life, the man who had been more like a father to him than his sire, sat chained in a cell, imprisoned by the same warlord who had brought such destruction into this child's life.

Damn Cobalt Escar. Allegra took a breath. "I can't promise anything. But I will see what I can do."

Della looked at her sharply. "You can't naysay the emperor."

"I won't." Allegra felt queasy. It had been a long day, and

night was settling over the hills. She didn't know if she had the reserves to face Cobalt again. But she couldn't stand here with Ozarson looking at her this way and not at least try.

The boy inclined his head. "Thank you." His voice quavered.

She smiled wanly. "Don't thank me. It may come to nothing."

Then she left, to challenge an emperor.

Two guards stood posted outside the suite, both with blue and white surcoats bearing the Chamberlight sphere. She didn't understand how a man called The Dark could rule a House called Chamberlight.

The guards bowed, rather than kneeling to her as they had done before. Apparently people knelt when first introduced to a sovereign, but they didn't keep doing it during a single visit or if they lived with the person. After that, they bowed. It seemed that practice extended to consorts, as well.

"May we assist you, Your Highness?" one of the guards asked, a husky man about half a hand span taller than her.

Allegra steeled herself. "I would like to see the emperor."

The two guards exchanged glances and looked uncomfortable.

"If he says no," she added, "I'll leave immediately."

"He may not want his evening disturbed," one guard said.

She suspected they didn't want to be the ones to disturb it. "I'll tell him it was my idea to speak with him. Only mine."

"You needn't," he said gruffly. "I wouldn't ask you to be bringing his anger on yourself."

"I won't." Softly she said, "Please."

The guard looked at the other man. Allegra didn't know what communication passed between them, but the first man finally nodded to her. "All right, then." He stepped aside so Allegra could leave the suite. "We'll go."

A long table stretched the length of the darkened hall. Most of the room lay in shadow. Halfway down, a window extended from the floor to the ceiling and let starlight pour across the floor. Cobalt sat at the end of the table closest to the door. An oil lamp shaped like a falcon sat near him, shedding light across his work as he studied a map of the desert. A pair of wire-rimmed spectacles sat by the lamp.

The guards took Allegra through the door behind Cobalt, but when one of them started forward, Allegra caught his arm. She had to do this herself. He paused, then let her go on alone.

She walked through the shadows, her heart beating hard. Just as she was about to speak, Cobalt looked up with a start.

"Ah." He smiled. "I'm glad you came down."

Allegra stopped, bewildered. He had known she was coming? And he was *glad?* Just as surprising, this monster of darkness had a quite attractive smile.

"Is the boy settled all right?" Cobalt asked.

All right didn't remotely describe how Ozarson felt. But she said only, "Yes, he's fine."

"Good. I didn't want to disturb him." Cobalt dropped his head against the high back of his chair and rubbed his eyes.

Disturb him? Confused, Allegra stayed put, waiting to see what he would do. He pushed back his chair, then got up and walked down the hall. He stopped at the window and leaned his arm on it above his head while he stared out at the night.

"It's so hard to believe Markus Onyx survived," he said.

"It is?"

"I was certain he died." Cobalt swore under his breath. "I should have him killed, damn it."

She froze, terrified to say the wrong thing. "You gave your word."

"And I will keep it." Then he said, "When I look at that boy, I see myself almost thirty years ago. And in thirty more years? Will he be the one sweeping across these lands, seeking the death of our son? I was a fool to let him live. But I couldn't—" He shook his head. "I had the chance to kill him. That night, when we caught him above the gorge, I could have done it. I had my sword above his head, ready to bring down. Just one more second. But I *couldn't.* He stared at me with those terrified eyes, so brave and defiant. Gods, Mel, he was only seven." He turned to her. "I couldn't kill him."

Saint Azure. Without his glasses, and with her in the shadows, he thought she was his *wife.* She stammered, "Sire. I'm s-sorry. I believe you have mistaken me for someone else."

"What?" He beckoned to her. "Come closer. Let me see."

Allegra walked forward until she stood before him. Cobalt stared at her, shadows and silvered light on his face. Then he swore under his breath. "It seems I cannot help but earn my damn name."

"Escar?" Her voice trembled.

"No." He grimaced. "The Dark. The idiot who tells a man's wife he should kill her husband and the child she loves."

"Sire, please. Let me see my husband."

"I'm sorry. But no."

"What would it harm?" She willed him to change his mind. "I only want to offer a little comfort."

"He's in a dungeon," Cobalt said. "You don't comfort people in dungeons."

"He gets claustrophobia. It's hard for him to stay still, especially inside buildings instead of tents where he's closer to the land. He has a war injury. He can't lift his arm above his head." Her voice cracked. "Sire, at least let me give him water."

He shook his head. "No."

Remembering what Ozi had told her about the Onyx Palace, she said, "Ozar Onyx kept dungeons. You are not such a man as he." She hoped her words were true.

"You're right," Cobalt said quietly. "I'm not. But his son stays in the cell."

Of course, she thought. *You and Markus want the same thing: the Onyx Throne.* Her anger sparked. "Always you men must fight and conquer. Take. Kill. All for thrones named after damned rocks."

"Ah, well. I suppose." His voice gentled. "Allegra, I bear you no ill will. You were thrown into a terrible situation. But reality won't disappear because a beautiful girl with golden hair and a grace of spirit softens the heart of an evil man."

She wondered who he was talking about, Markus—or himself. "I don't claim Markus is a paragon. But he isn't evil. Can he be cruel? It's within him, yes. He lives according to the ways of a harsh, brutal land. As a boy, as a youth, the two men he had to pattern himself after were his father and Dusk Yargazon. Yes, that affected him. Yet despite all that, he has retained a goodness of heart."

"He's fortunate to have someone like you to see him that way." He rubbed the small of his back tiredly. "I have a great deal more work to do this night."

"Of course, Sire." Allegra bowed, struggling to contain her disappointment. "Please accept my apologies for disturbing you."

Then her guards took her back to her suite.

That night, she held Ozarson while he cried, for he believed he would never again see Markus. After he fell asleep, exhausted, she tucked him into bed and went to her room. She created a spell, singing of comfort as she reached out to the man under the castle. But she had too little strength to find him, and in the end she collapsed into a fitful sleep.

Allegra awoke sprawled across the bed, fully dressed. She stared at the canopy overhead until her mind caught up with her waking. So much had happened in so few days.

From the soft light coming through the window and the trill of birds, she thought it was dawn. She pulled herself from the bed, tired but unable to rest. She should check on Ozarson, who hadn't slept enough since they had left Jazid.

Allegra bathed and changed into a blue tunic and leggings. When she walked into the main parlor, she found a circle-maid setting out a gold tray bearing china dishes heaped with sweet rolls, honey, jams, hard-boiled eggs and slices of meat. The aroma of chocolate wafted on the air.

The maid bowed. "My greetings of the morning, ma'am."

"Thank you," Allegra said. It felt strange having people wait on her. At home, everyone pitched in with chores.

Ozarson wandered into the room, rubbing his eyes. In his borrowed sleep trousers and shirt, with his curls mussed up, he looked even younger than nine.

"My greet—" Allegra broke off as doors banged open at the front of the suite. Boots thudded in the entrance foyer.

Ozarson turned to her with a jerk. "What is it?"

Allegra moved to stand with him. "I don't know."

A knot of warriors strode into the room, all in armor and mail, their breastplates emblazoned with the Chamberlight sphere. The circle-maid slipped around them and ran out the door. A grizzled captain and another soldier at the front were gripping the arms of a prisoner with his hands manacled in front of his body and connected by one chain link—a man with curly black hair and dark circles under his eyes.

When the captain shoved Markus forward, the prince staggered and fell to his knees a few paces from Allegra and Ozarson. She started toward him—then froze as another man strode forward.

Cobalt.

The emperor wore full armor and heavy boots. He held

a black helmet shaped like the head of a jaguar under one arm. The sword strapped across his back was longer than any Allegra had ever seen, and its gigantic hilt stuck up over his shoulder. He filled the room with his power, like a conqueror who could shred the entire building simply by the force of his will.

He spoke to Allegra. "You have half an hour. Then we leave for Taka Mal." He threw a key to her, and she barely caught it. "That unlocks his manacles. You can clean him up, whatever you want. He'll come with us as a hostage. But if he's not ready to leave in thirty minutes, he stays here in the dungeon."

With that, he spun around and left the room, accompanied by his men, their boots resounding on the floor.

Stunned, Allegra dropped next to Markus. As he lifted his head, Ozarson fell to his knees and threw his arms around his brother. "You're here!"

Markus managed a smile. "It seems so." He tried to reach out to Ozarson, but he couldn't manage it with his hands manacled.

Allegra wrestled with his shackles until the key clicked in their locks. When they fell open, Markus grunted with relief. They clattered on the floor, black and ugly, freeing his lacerated wrists. He grabbed his left shoulder, his arm shaking, and clenched the spot where his muscles had gnarled yesterday.

"Here." She moved behind him and massaged his shoulder. It felt terrible, knotted and spasmed in many places.

"Ah, gods," he groaned. "Yes, do that." As the knots eased, he said, "I was afraid I'd lose the use of my arm."

"Why did Cobalt let you out?" Allegra asked.

"I have no idea."

"Allegra talked to him last night," Ozarson said.

She winced. "I didn't think I helped at all."

"Whatever you did," Markus said, "I'm eternally grateful."

"You have to get ready!" Ozarson said. "We can't let them put you back down there."

Markus tried to climb to his feet. His legs buckled, and with a grunt, he collapsed to the floor.

"Here." Allegra put one arm around his waist, and Ozarson did the same on his other side. Together, they helped him stand.

"The water in the bathing pool is warm," Allegra said. "You can soak there. It will relax your muscles."

"Yes." His gaze raked over her, and she was beginning to understand him, at least enough to know that what he needed had nothing to do with water.

Allegra spoke to Ozarson as they helped Markus limp to the bedroom. "Can you get our things ready?"

"I'll get everything I can," the boy said. "But we don't have travel packs."

"They'll give us what we need." She wasn't sure of that, but she had no intention of wasting time searching for anything.

At the bedroom entrance, Markus grasped the lintel of the archway. "I can walk now," he told Ozarson. "You go get ready."

The boy glanced uncertainly at Allegra.

"It's all right," she said.

"She *helped* you," Ozarson told Markus, his expression worried.

Markus smiled and tousled his hair. "I know that."

Mollified, Ozarson headed back to his room. Allegra helped Markus into the bedroom and closed the door.

"I hate this place," Markus muttered. "All doors and walls. It's suffocating."

"Come to the bathing room," she said. "It's more open."

The small pool was steaming with heated water. Water mosaics tiled the walls, and a high window let in early morning light. It had no furniture, which might remind him of home.

"Gods," he murmured, staring at the bath. "So much water."

Allegra blinked. She had always taken water for granted. Maybe in Jazid it was worth more even than the gems they mined.

"Do you want help?" she asked, suddenly shy.

He touched her cheek. "Are you all right?"

"Well, yes," she said, puzzled. She wasn't the one who had spent a day locked in a pitch-black, suffocating cell.

"Then, yes," he said. "Stay." He didn't ask what she had meant by *help*; he just grasped her tunic and pulled it up. As she helped him take it off, his palm scraped her breast. He rubbed his hand over her nipple and let out a breath as if an emotional spasm were easing within him much as his shoulder had loosened. When he dropped her tunic by the pool, she instinctively folded her arms over her breasts.

"Don't do that, night bird," he said softly. "You're beautiful."

Self-conscious, but aware of their limited time, she tugged down her leggings. He put his arm around her waist and lifted her against him, her front against his side, and slid her clothes off faster. She closed her eyes, trying to relax as she put her arms around his neck. Kneeling by the pool, he set her in the shallow end where the side sloped back so a bather could lie down. The water came to her shoulders and rippled against her skin. He undressed quickly, leaving his grimy clothes by the pool. As he slid into the water, he pulled Allegra into his arms so they were lying on their sides on the sloped surface, most of their bodies in the water. He didn't speak, he just held her with his head against her hair.

"It's all right," she murmured. "It's over."

"For now." His hands moved over her, touching. She slid her hand shyly across the muscled ridges of his abdomen.

"You should have stayed with me in Jazid," he said. "Then we wouldn't be Cobalt's prisoners."

"Ah, Markus," she said. "Why is it all right for you to hold me prisoner but not for him to hold us?"

"It's not the same. You took Ozarson." He caressed her breasts, waist, hips, thighs. "Cobalt may still execute me. I would never have done anything like that to you."

"He swore he wouldn't."

"Because you intervened on my behalf." He drew back to look at her. "Why? You despise me."

"I don't want you to be hurt!"

He spoke wryly. "I thought I was a pig."

"You're a man. A complicated, violent man. Markus, I *don't* despise you. Not at all." She hit her palm against his chest. "But you took my freedom. I can't fight every law in Jazid. It's always about *you,* what you want, where you go, touching me, lying with me, dressing me, using me for your pleasure without thinking how I feel."

"That's not true." He cupped his hand around her cheek. "*Always* I think of you. It's making me insane." He pulled her close and spoke against her ear. "I don't want this weakness, but I can't stop feeling it any more than I can stop needing to eat or drink. Looking at you, touching you, lying with you—it's pleasure, yes, but more than that. It's— I don't know. Like I'm dying for water in the Fractured Desert, and you're the Saint Verdant River. If you don't let me have you, I'll die of thirst."

Flustered, she said, "You're lying in a pool of water."

"Ach! You're impossible." Sliding his hand behind her head, he kissed her deeply. "I need you now," he growled. "Or you will have a lunatic in this pool of water."

Her voice softened. "Then have me now."

It was all he needed. He rolled her onto her back and shifted his weight so he was on top of her, his hips settling between her thighs. The power in his muscular body seemed barely contained. He caressed her, his hands strong and sure.

When he entered her, he pressed his lips and teeth against her neck. She let go to the sensations of his strong body against hers. The water was silken on her skin, and it surged while he made love to her. She was in the center of a storm borne of his anger, fear and pain, but it wasn't directed against her; she was the vessel that contained it. The force of his passion could have been overwhelming, but knowing he wanted her that much excited her, kept her holding him, her arms around his solid waist, her breasts against his chest with its thick, curling hair.

His rhythm increased, becoming more demanding, more urgent. The muscles in his body went rigid, and he groaned, pressing down on her, straining, his hips jerking. They slid down the sloped side until he was kissing her with their lips just at the water.

Markus exhaled with a gasp, stirring the water, and his body finally relaxed. As his weight settled, he eased her back up the side, enough so her nose didn't go underwater. Then he laid his head next to hers on the slope and was still. Allegra closed her eyes, her own body still unsettled. He lay next to her, breathing deeply.

Too deeply, in fact.

"Markus." She nudged his shoulders. "Don't go to sleep."

With a sigh, he lifted his head. A satiated look had replaced his intensity. He brushed his lips across hers, gently this time. "You sing to me even when your voice is silent, night bird."

"If I'm a bird, you must have such a name, too." When his look turned wary, she smiled. "But not the pig."

"My mother says I smell like a goat," he offered.

She laughed softly. "Not that, either. A lion."

He kissed her, his lips lingering as he slid his hand between her thighs. It aroused her even more, and she wasn't sure what she wanted him to do, only that she didn't want him to stop. She tilted her hips up and pushed against his palm.

He rubbed her in slow circles. "I wish we could stay here."

She agreed. But she said, "We can't...be late."

His finger slipped inside her, tantalizing. "Later, hmm?"

Oh, yes. Later, definitely. She nodded, knowing they had to hurry, but she felt restless and flushed, wanting him.

Markus slid into the water and ruffled his hands through his hair, making the curls float. He came up, sitting on the bottom of the shallow pool, and shook his head, splashing water everywhere. He rolled his shoulders, then jerked as the injured side spasmed.

Allegra slid behind him and massaged the scar tissue on his shoulder. "Does that help?"

"Ah, yes." He sounded blissful. "Very much."

"We should go." But she kept massaging, aware of his back against her front, his muscles sensuous under her palms.

With reluctance, he said, "Yes. We should." When she took her arms off his shoulders, he stood up, water cascading down his body, and stepped out of the pool.

It was the first time Allegra had seen him in daylight. He was as impressive as in the starlight, but she saw now what she had missed before, because she had been shy about touching him. Scars covered his body, especially his torso.

She started to ask, then stopped when she realized he would probably describe being hacked on a battlefield. She couldn't bear to hear about him being hurt that way, particularly given how close they were to another war.

They went to the bedroom and changed. Markus's armor had long since disappeared, but someone had left more clothes. He chose riding trousers and a blue shirt with blue embroidery on the cuffs. Although the threadwork barely showed, it seemed an odd choice for someone with such strong ideas about what he considered masculine. Then she remembered how his Jazid clothes had fastened, with complex loops sewn in the leather. Maybe the embroidery reminded him of his home.

Allegra searched the room until she found a stack of games. The playing pieces included two dice cubes, a wooden pyramid with four sides and a little hole at its point and a metal ring. She put the ring on her big toe. She tied a cord through the pyramid to make a necklace and she tucked the cubes into a pocket of her tunic. She had lost the dodecahedron from Ozarson's toys, but she had the octahedral block, which she pocketed with the cubes.

Markus watched her as he drew on his boots. "It isn't just round things, is it?"

"No," she admitted. "Any geometrical shape works."

He came over and touched the pendant hanging between her breasts. "Lucky necklace."

Allegra smiled and folded her hand around his. "Markus—"

He waited, then spoke curiously. "Yes?"

"I'm glad you're here."

He started slightly, as if stunned, then raised her hand and pressed his lips against her knuckles.

"How did you know I would be in Aronsdale?" she asked.

He lowered her arm, holding her hand. "I wasn't sure. But it seemed what you would do." He shook his head with a grimace. "Yargazon was convinced you went to Quaaz. We rode along the King's Courseway for a while, but we couldn't pick up your trail. So we decided he would take the army to Quaaz while I came here." Then he said, "Actually, I chose. He wanted me with the army. He was furious I decided otherwise. But he couldn't stop me."

It gratified Allegra to know he was willing to stand up to the powerful general. "Before the T'Ambera caught me I had been coming to Crofts Vale to study at a guild for mages."

"It is important to you, yes? Learning these spells?"

"Yes. Very."

"Can you study even if you don't stay here?"

It was a good question. "Possibly." She thought of Cobalt's men. "We should see if Ozi is ready."

Markus nodded, and they went out into the parlor. They found Ozarson eating breakfast.

The boy looked up with relief. "I saved you some food."

Markus sat down and started eating without another word. Allegra settled next to him and grabbed the last roll before he could inhale it.

"You're hungry," Ozarson said, watching his brother.

Markus took a hard-boiled egg. "It's been a while."

"They fed you, didn't they?" Allegra asked. He had been in the cell for a day.

"Nothing." He shook salt and pepper on his egg. "They gave me water this morning when they took me out."

Allegra and Ozarson waited while he ate his egg and attacked a slab of meat. Finally Ozarson said, "Markus?"

"Hmm?" The prince regent glanced at him. "Why do you look so worried? I'm fine."

"Father used the dungeons at the Onyx Palace," Ozarson said. "He told me once that sometimes he had people in them for seasons at a time. Even years."

"Yes. He did." Markus lowered his fork and spoke quietly. "And yes. Some of them died."

"That can't be true!"

"You never knew our father that well, Ozi."

The boy bit his lip and turned away.

The grate of wood came from the entrance, followed by a tramp of feet. Eight Chamberlight warriors entered the parlor. Cobalt hadn't come this time, but Allegra had no doubt he intended the message implicit in their behavior. Their military bearing, the way they entered with no warning, their large forms turned even more imposing by their armor and swords—it all heightened the sense of their power over the three people they had come to collect.

"It's time to go," the captain with the grizzled face said roughly. He was holding a blue-plumed helmet.

Markus stood, followed by Allegra and Ozarson. One of

the warriors stooped to get the manacles Markus had left on the floor, and the captain spoke to Allegra. "The key."

Feeling ill, she said, "It's in the lock."

The captain motioned the prince regent forward. Allegra could see Markus clenching his jaw as he complied. They turned him around and pulled his arms behind his back. He stared at her as they fastened the manacles and closed them with loud snaps.

Then Cobalt's men took the three of them away.

CHAPTER 23
DAWN'S MARCH

Soldiers were everywhere. Thousands. Three armies converged at Suncroft: Chamberlight, Harsdown, Aronsdale.
Allegra could only stare in astonishment.

The guards escorting Markus, Allegra and Ozarson
stopped a short distance outside the castle and stood waiting.
People covered the hills: men strode in groups, warriors
oiled weapons, horses trampled the grass and tenders packed
up cooking pots, extinguished campfires, loaded supplies
into carts. A stream of humanity flowed between Crofts Vale
and the encamped armies. Barracks for the Aronsdale soldiers
were on the other side of the castle, and a good portion of
the population in Crofts Vale were the families of the men
quartered there. A good portion of Jarid's men would stay
here, though, with several companies of Cobalt's men to
protect the Dawnstar empress and her son.

Most of the soldiers around Crofts Vale wore armor emblazoned with the crossed swords of Aronsdale, but many
Chamberlight men were mixed in with them. To the south,

the jaguar flags of the Harsdown army rippled. Pennants snapped everywhere. A woman from Crofts Vale untied a ribbon from her hair and gave it to a man in Aronsdale armor. He put his arm around her waist and kissed her, then tied the ribbon to his spear.

Markus stood with Allegra, scrutinizing the forces. She could almost feel him sizing up what he saw, the men, horses, weapons. His gaze burned. If all these men fought for Cobalt, the prince regent's forces would lose.

"Markus, Allegra, look," Ozarson said. "It's Shadow." His voice brightened. "And Thom!"

Following his gaze, Allegra saw Thom leading Shadow through the crowds. His father walked with him, a slender man with brown hair streaked by the sun.

"Who is that?" Markus asked. "Why does he have my horse?"

"Thom is the stable boy at the guild," Allegra said.

"Thom!" Ozarson called out, waving.

Their guards tensed, and one dropped his hand to the sword sheathed on his belt. Then the grizzled captain said, "It's just the boy with the horse." That apparently made sense to the others, for they relaxed.

Thom thrust Shadow's reins at his father, then took off running up the slope. His father followed with Shadow and studied the Chamberlight warriors. With so many soldiers about, Thom seemed oblivious to the tension of the eight surrounding Ozarson, but his father obviously noticed them.

Thom threaded his way past the guards, oblivious to their hard stares. "Where were you last night?" he asked Ozarson.

The atajazid motioned at Suncroft. "Here."

"Hai! At the castle?" He pretended to punch Ozarson in the arm, and Ozarson laughed. "They have better stables here, eh?"

One of the guards reached to pull Thom away, but the captain shook his head. Allegra wondered if it was as odd for them to see the atajazid—the king whose existence had spurred this great confluence of armies—acting like a normal boy.

"I didn't sleep in the stables last night," Ozarson said.

"No? I know you didn't sleep in a castle!" Thom peered past Allegra to Markus, who was watching him curiously. "Who are you?"

The prince regent blinked at him. "Markus."

"I remember!" Thom said. "You're the soldier who was here yesterday."

"He came from Jazid to find me," Ozarson told him.

"Thom," a man said. The boy's father was a short distance away, beyond the guards, holding Shadow's reins. The big horse whinnied and pranced as he tried to follow Thom.

"Let the horse go," Markus said. His deep voice carried with a snap of authority.

Thom's father shot a startled look at Markus. He dropped the reins and motioned toward Allegra. "There she is, boy. Go on."

As the guards around Allegra stepped aside, Shadow

walked forward—not to Allegra, but to Markus. The great horse nosed Markus's shoulder, then snuffled and tried again.

Markus laughed, averting his face from the insistent horse. "I'm glad to see you, too. But I don't have any treats." With his hands behind his back, he had to turn to keep his balance as the horse pushed him.

"Just scratch his neck," Thom said cheerfully. "He likes that...." His voice trailed off as his gaze fell to Markus's manacled hands. His eyes darted to the armed warriors around them, and for the first time he seemed to realize they weren't just soldiers milling about.

"Thom," his father said. "Come on back."

"Ozi should come with us." Thom turned a worried gaze on Ozarson. "We can watch the armies from the hill."

Allegra sensed Ozarson longing to say yes, to run off with his friend and watch from a safe distance. And in that aching moment, she saw something die inside the boy. It was as if another piece of his childhood fell away, broken off, irretrievable.

Ozarson spoke quietly. "I can't go with you, Thom."

"What's wrong?" Thom lowered his voice. "Are you in trouble?"

"Thom!" His father's voice was urgent. "Come back here." He shot a worried look to the east. "*Now*. Hurry up!"

Allegra followed his gaze—and inhaled. Cobalt was riding toward them with several officers. The emperor sat astride a huge black warhorse, a mammoth animal large enough to hold even someone his size. His men were leading two horses draped with Chamberlight colors, blue and white.

Thom started toward his father, then paused, looking back. "Ozi?" His gaze darted to the emperor.

Ozarson's voice caught. "Goodbye and be well."

Markus spoke in a low voice. "Allegra, take Shadow."

She caught Shadow's reins just as Cobalt's group reached them, and the emperor reined his horse to a stop. Markus stepped out to face him. He waited, a solitary man with his hands locked behind his back facing warriors astride giant horses.

The emperor motioned to his men. One rode forward, bringing one of the extra horses. Watching Markus, Cobalt indicated the horse. "You can ride that one. Allegra will take yours."

Allegra closed her eyes, so relieved he wouldn't put Markus back in the dungeon, she almost missed Markus's response.

"...manacled, I can't keep my balance," Markus said.

"You'll manage," Cobalt told him curtly. He jerked his head at the horse. "My men will help you up."

Ozarson came to stand with Markus. It was impossible to miss the fear in his eyes, but he carried himself with remarkable aplomb. He addressed Cobalt as if he were speaking man-to-man. "Your Majesty, I thank you for releasing my regent from the dungeon."

The emperor regarded him from high on his mount, and Allegra could have sworn he almost smiled. He inclined his head to Ozarson as if they were both of an age. He indicated the other horse, which another of his men had brought forward. "You may ride that one."

Allegra stiffened, and Markus tensed, as well. Yes, Ozarson was comfortable with horses, but riding a giant warhorse on his own was another story. Could a child even control a horse that size? She didn't miss the thrill that flashed on Ozarson's face, though. Cobalt had chosen to treat him as a man rather than a child. She just hoped Cobalt's treatment didn't extend to the sentences men meted out to their enemies.

"He's too young for that horse," Markus said.

Cobalt looked down at Markus. "Then he can ride with me."

"I can go on my own," Ozarson said quickly.

A soldier brought over a three-legged stool and let Ozarson use it to climb onto the horse. The animal stepped restlessly as Ozarson slid into the saddle, and the boy grabbed the reins with a jerk. One of Cobalt's officers rode forward, leaning over to help. By the time he reached the boy, though, Ozarson had his animal under control.

The guards helped Markus onto his mount. They looped and tied the reins, letting them lie where he could have grabbed them had his hands been free. Markus's gaze flicked to the ground far below. He had nothing to keep him in the saddle except stirrups and the pressure of his legs on a horse he had never ridden. His horse, though spirited, responded well to the directions he gave with his knees and legs. Allegra didn't doubt that with his experience, he could manage, but for an entire day? She wished Cobalt would let him ride

Shadow, an animal he knew. Then again, that was probably why the emperor separated them; Shadow would be more than willing to abet any escape Markus tried.

Thom watched Ozarson with his mouth open. His father stayed at his side, his hand clamped on his son's shoulder. Taking a breath, Allegra handed Shadow's reins to one of her guards and walked over to Thom. Two of the other guards came with her, including the hard-faced captain. She felt his impatience, but she kept going, determined to speak with Thom and his father.

Thom's father tensed as she approached and he drew his son closer to his side, though she thought it was more to keep him away from the guards than from her.

Allegra stopped in front of them. "I wanted to thank you." Her voice caught. "For giving him a day."

"A day?" Thom's father asked. "Who do you mean?"

She tilted her head toward Ozarson, who was riding behind Cobalt's men. "Ozi."

The father paled. "Who is he? He called that man his *regent*."

Allegra spoke quietly. "The boy is the Atajazid D'Az Ozarson of the House of Onyx. The man is the prince regent of Jazid, Markus Onyx."

"Saint Citrine!" Thom looked suitably impressed. "And I just thought he was the smartest stable boy I ever met."

Although she wasn't certain Thom understood the significance of Ozarson's title, the father was a different story. His face went ashen. "That boy slept in the *stable* with my son."

"And for one day," Allegra said softly, "he got to be just

a boy with his friend. It means more than you'll ever know. It will probably never happen again."

The guard captain spoke to her. "We must go." Despite his respect, his words brooked no refusal. If she delayed any longer, they would probably put her on Shadow whether she agreed or not.

"Goodbye," she murmured. Thom's father nodded, and she thought he understood.

When Allegra returned to Shadow, the guards helped her mount. Up that high, she had a better view of the ocean of soldiers. The armies went as far as she could see to the south, east and north, and Crofts Vale lay to the west. Far ahead, a Chamberlight officer was riding alongside Markus. She followed them, headed downhill.

Another man came galloping up to Cobalt and reined in to speak with the emperor. Cobalt listened, then stepped his animal around to face Castle Suncroft. Others glanced back, as well, and soon everyone, on the ground and on horseback, was stopping to look.

Puzzled, Allegra brought Shadow around. A woman had come out of the castle with six guards and was striding down the slope. A mane of yellow curls blew back from her body in the wind. As she drew nearer, Allegra saw she had the face of an angel. She dressed like a warrior, but the clothes looked far different on her. The leather trousers fit tightly to her long, long legs. They were too wide for her waist, so they rode low on her curved hips. She had on a black leather vest a man might wear, but without chain mail or other garments.

It left a strip of skin visible above the waist of her pants and did nothing to hide her womanly form. She carried a baby in one arm, a big, strapping toddler who alertly watched everything going on around him.

The woman passed Allegra without a glance for her or anyone else. She was looking ahead. Allegra brought Shadow around in time to see Cobalt jump down from his horse. When the woman reached him, he embraced her, one arm around her waist and the other on her arm where she held the boy. Then he kissed her, towering over even her tall form, his big hand splayed against her back while her yellow hair blew around them.

Saint Verdant, *that* was the Dawnstar empress? No wonder tales proliferated of how men walked into doors or stumbled over their feet when she went by. Allegra couldn't imagine why Della had ever compared her to the empress. Mel Dawnfield was so far out of her league, Allegra felt like an insubstantial nobody.

Cobalt drew back and spoke to his wife. She said something, and he *laughed*. In one moment, he went from being the dark, threatening conqueror to a handsome man. He lifted the child out of her arms and held him up high, grinning as the boy cooed. Cobalt the Dark, smiling at his heir. That child would someday inherit an empire—perhaps one that included Taka Mal.

Soon Mel headed back to the castle with the boy, surrounded by her guards, and Cobalt swung back up on his horse.

So they set out, headed for the deserts of Taka Mal.

★ ★ ★

Allegra's guards wouldn't let her ride with Markus or Ozarson, who were well ahead of her. Ozarson managed his horse well, and Allegra soon realized the animal was more docile than its size and military finery implied. For a while, Cobalt rode with Markus, no doubt questioning his prisoner about the Jazid army, though she doubted he had much luck. Eventually he went on ahead, leaving two Chamberlight guards with Markus.

The end of the Chamberlight army overlapped the front edges of the Aronsdale forces. Harsdown came last, led by Muller Dawnfield, the empress's father. Allegra saw mostly Chamberlight men. About an hour after they started out, though, a group of men with horses draped in Dawnfield colors came riding along the Chamberlight army. With a start, she recognized the man in their center. King Jarid.

He came up beside her. "Good morning, Allegra."

"Your Majesty!" She almost added, *You can see!* but stopped herself, aware of the people around them. "How are you this morning?"

"I'm well. Much better." He tilted his head toward the south. "Iris sends her greetings."

Looking back, she saw Iris riding with Aron. Even knowing mage queens had always gone to war, Allegra tensed. What if Iris was hurt? Then it hit her; if she had married Aron, she could have ended up riding to battle, as well.

Mage queens supported the army with spells to spy, heal and improve morale. By seeking their enemies with emotion spells, a mage could pick up hints of their plans and affect the morale of the opposing forces. Aronsdale soldiers fought in shape formations, mostly polygons, because the queen could then use spells to focus them into a stronger unit. Although Aronsdale was a small country and had never boasted a large army, their mages had always given them an edge. But a great deal of danger existed for the queen, not only because of her proximity to the battles, but also from the backlash of her spells, should any cause harm.

Historically Aronsdale kings were statesmen and warriors rather than mages. Jarid broke the rules with his incredible power. He was watching Allegra closely, and she had the unsettling sense he had formed a spell to detect her mood. Yet she saw no green light. Colors didn't show for every mage, but she had already seen his. If he could stop the colors, he had far more control than she had thought possible.

"Each of us has to decide how we will use our gifts," Jarid said. "You have to choose."

With a start, she realized he was answering her question from yesterday. Embarrassed, she said, "Some of us have so little from which to choose." She felt inadequate among these people, a minor mage with inconsequential talents caught in eddies of the great currents sweeping around those with true gifts.

"You shouldn't devalue yourself," he said. "Not every mage needs to move mountains."

She spoke wryly. "Perhaps I could manage a molehill."

"Allegra, listen." He reined in his prancing horse to keep

it beside her. "If ever you need support, talk to me. Hell, reach for me when you sing your spell. You needn't be isolated."

"Thank you, Sire," she said, surprised. Mages couldn't combine their talents as far as she knew. But she had no idea how to understand a gift as powerful as his.

Jarid inclined his head. He rode on then, cantering with his men. She smiled when she realized he was discreetly observing Cobalt's forces. The Midnight Emperor wasn't the only one fishing for information about the other armies.

The grizzled captain from the Misted Cliffs maneuvered his horse closer to Allegra. The cold stare of the man's gray eyes startled her.

"Is everything all right?" she asked.

He leaned over and took the reins of her horse.

Allegra grabbed for the reins. "What are you doing?"

"Sit still." He drew Shadow away from the other riders, off to the side, out of the flow of the army.

"What's wrong?" Allegra asked. Something had changed. Yes, he had been wary before; Cobalt's men had no reason to trust the consort of Jazid's prince regent. But this was different.

When he didn't answer, she looked around to see if anyone was leaving the main column. Markus and Ozarson were so far ahead, she could no longer see either of them. King Jarid had fallen back to his own army and was riding with his officers, deep in discussion. Iris and Aron were even farther back. She didn't know anyone else.

The captain led her toward a line of trees.

"What are you doing?" Allegra asked, alarmed.

He shot her a warning glance and touched the dagger at his belt. "Don't talk." He guided their horses under a screening canopy of branches. "Get off." He swung his leg over his own horse and jumped to the ground.

Allegra slowly let herself off Shadow. She started to fall, but the captain caught her, and set her on her feet. Then he let go as if she burned, and he quickly stepped back when she turned around to face him.

"Over there." He motioned at several trees within the grove that grew close together, their foliage like a screen of leaves.

"Why?" She was guessing he had acted on his own, rather than on any orders, which only worried her more. "What do you want?"

Anger flashed across his face—and fear? Why by any saint would this gnarled warrior be afraid of her?

He drew the dagger from its sheath and motioned at the trees. When Allegra turned toward them, the captain grabbed a handful of her tunic at the nape and shoved her forward. "Over there, witch!"

Witch. Saint Azure, she had forgotten how some people viewed mages. He must have overheard her talking with Jarid. She had no idea how people in the Misted Cliffs felt, but if this was any example, she didn't want to know more.

"What are you—" She broke off as he pushed her face-first against the trunk.

"Quiet," he said. "Don't talk. Don't *sing*."

She braced her palms against the tree, her heart beating

hard. Surely he wouldn't stab her. No matter what he thought of her abilities or her husband, he had no authority to harm her, and Cobalt wanted her as a hostage.

The captain put his hand under her hair. When she inhaled sharply, he said, "No sounds." He found the thong of her necklace and pulled out the pyramid she had hidden under her tunic.

Well, damn. He had figured out she might hide shapes. One aspect she was discovering about leaders such as Markus and Cobalt: their success came not only from their own intelligence, but also from their ability to pick officers with similar talent. Which was great for them, but had ended up being her bane.

Metal flashed in her side vision. His dagger. She tensed, ready to shout for help, but he only cut the thong so he could pull off the necklace. She stood with her cheek and body pressed against the tree while he checked her clothing and took the dice cubes and octahedron she had stashed in her pocket.

"You can turn around," he finally said.

Allegra faced him with a scowl. "Are you done?"

He stepped back from her. "Take off your boots and socks."

Double damn. He had thought of all her hiding places. She sat on the ground and tugged off her riding boots. The captain crouched down, his blade at the ready, and slid each boot away after she took it off. When she pulled off her socks, the ring glinted on her left toe. She reached for it—

"Don't move!" He pulled the circle of metal off her toe and slipped it into a travel pouch tied onto his belt. After

443

scanning her other foot, he released a breath and some of the tension eased in his shoulders. "All right." He motioned at her boots. "You can put those back on and get on your horse."

Disgruntled at losing her shapes, she laced up her boots and stood, keeping her hands out so he wouldn't think she was up to any mischief. She supposed his reaction made sense, given that he served an empress who had become a legend for her powers. Of course he took precautions against a mage of their enemies. It would have been funny if he hadn't been so intimidating; she couldn't imperil a flea, unless he counted a good night's sleep as danger.

The captain walked her back to her horse before sheathing his dagger. He helped her mount Shadow, then swung up onto his own horse. As they returned to the army, Allegra brooded. Without her mage shapes, she was even more defenseless than before.

❧ CHAPTER 24
A PRINCE'S RANSOM

In the sunset, the Pyramid Foothills resembled ruddy towers. The armies made camp across the border from Taka Mal where the Saint Verdant River turned south. The Rocklands of Taka Mal lay to the east. The main battle of the Sun-Dragon War had been fought there, but now the rocky plains lay empty and barren, blistering during the day and icy at night. Tomorrow the armies would travel northeast, cutting across a corner of the Rocklands and venturing deep into Taka Mal, headed for Quaaz.

Allegra expected Cobalt to insist she remain in the custody of his army, but Jarid convinced him to let her stay with Aronsdale because he had given her asylum. The tents used by the Aronsdale army were far less opulent than their desert counterparts. Jazid tents had furs, carpets, cushions strewn around and gem-encrusted chests; Aronsdale tents had pallets on the floor, riding bags or a duffel, and maybe a table and chairs. It made sense to Allegra; Jazidians lived in their tents, but the Aronsdale structures were only temporary shelters.

Aronsdale was also relatively poor, whereas Jazid was saturated with gems and precious metals.

Several warriors escorted her to a tent and remained outside, guarding the entrance. Sitting on the pallet, she pulled the thin blanket around her shoulders, chilly in the night. When a rustle came from the entrance, she tensed, wondering what else would happen. The grizzled captain pulled aside the flap and stood there, his face impassive. The blood drained from her face. But instead of threatening her, he stepped aside—and Markus walked into the tent.

Allegra exhaled, her shoulders easing down. After the captain dropped the flap, Markus stood rubbing his wrists as he scrutinized the tent, studying everything.

"Markus?" she asked. "Are you all right?"

His expression softened as he came over and dropped down next to her. "It was a long ride." He showed her his wrists, which were bruised from the manacles. "Not so comfortable."

Allegra took his hands and pressed her lips against his skin. "They shouldn't restrain you." She couldn't imagine going all day with only her legs to control a horse. "Did you see Ozarson?"

"They let me tell him good-night." He put his arm around her shoulders and drew her close. "He's all right, I think. Tired. It upset him that they wouldn't let him come with me."

Allegra could tell it hadn't only upset Ozarson. "Do you know where he is?"

"Not too far. A few tents over."

Relief trickled over her. She would have rather he stayed with them, but at least he was close.

Markus lay on the pallet behind her, on his back. "Sing to me, night bird," he said wearily. "Sing your magic."

She turned toward him, sitting on her hip, her weight on one hand. He had closed his eyes, but his body remained tense.

"I can sing, but I won't be able to make a spell," Allegra said. "That guard captain took my shapes."

His eyes snapped open. "Did he hurt you?"

"I'm fine. He didn't do anything except growl."

Markus threw his arm over his eyes. "This is a nightmare."

"Why do you say that?" The ride was unpleasant, certainly, but compared to the dungeon, it seemed like a gift.

"We'll reach Quaaz in a few days," Markus said. "My army will also be there. Even if they've taken the capital, Yargazon won't be ready for Cobalt." He rubbed the heels of his hands in his eyes. "I hadn't expected the emperor to raise this many troops so fast. Especially not from Harsdown."

"He may not have," Allegra said. "No one knows if Harsdown or Aronsdale will fight for him."

Markus looked at her. "Did Jarid tell you anything?"

"Not a thing." She smiled slightly. "I believe his exact words were, 'If I wouldn't answer that for Cobalt, I certainly won't tell the wife of the man whose army we're going to fight.'"

Markus rested his arm over his eyes again. "The dragon only knows what Yargazon will do when he learns Cobalt has both Ozi and me as hostages."

"Do you think he will trade?"

He spoke uneasily. "After the way we argued before we split up in Jazid, I've been wondering."

"He's doing this for Ozi. Surely he must have wanted you to explore every possible avenue to find him."

"Yes. He does. But he was angry that I defied him." Tiredly he said, "He'll negotiate for you and Ozi. I don't know if he will for me."

Allegra wondered how he could be so intelligent and miss the obvious. "He will. Believe me. He was angry because he doesn't want you hurt, Markus. He sees you as a son." With a grimace, she added, "I hope he *doesn't* negotiate for me."

He pulled his arm down so he could look at her. "He will."

She shifted uncomfortably. "He's that angry?"

Markus pushed up on his elbows. "He was in those chains for sixteen hours. He demands sixteen hours with you in recompense, to apply whatever punishment he deems appropriate."

The blood drained from her face. "Markus!"

"Don't look at me like that, kitten," he murmured. Sitting up, he shifted position so he could put his legs around her body. Then he pulled her into his arms. "I won't let him touch you." He spoke grimly. "But if he takes Quaaz before your king's warning reaches the royal family, he will execute the queen and her heir."

"How can he be so cold?" Allegra asked. "We're talking about the murder of a mother and her two-year-old child."

"Of course he should let them live," Markus said bitterly. "Every conflict fought since Cobalt went on this rampage of his has been the result of heirs left to live when someone should have killed them."

"It has to stop somewhere." She gave him a good, long look. "Cobalt let you live."

He bent his head over hers, cradling her in his arms. "I've no wish for Vizarana or her baby to die. But what do you expect in wartime? That we'll all get together for a tea party?"

What an image. She smiled wryly. "You and Cobalt, with tea and scones."

"That would be a sight." He let out a breath. "King Jarid swore, in his treaty with Taka Mal, to defend the Topaz Throne. If Yargazon takes the throne for Ozi, then what? Jarid has sworn asylum to *Ozi,* of all the bizarre developments. If Ozi becomes king of Taka Mal, what will Jarid do?"

"His treaty is to defend the royal family of Taka Mal," Allegra said. "That's not exactly the same as defending the throne."

"Well, no. But if Yargazon kills the queen of Taka Mal, will your king attack my army? If he does, Harsdown may follow. Then they would be supporting Cobalt. The Taka Mal army would probably stop fighting my army and *join* us, because they would rather have Ozi on their throne than Cobalt. And here is Jarid, sworn both to protect Ozi and fight for Taka Mal. What does he do?" His breath stirred her hair. "If Cobalt ends up with both the Onyx and Topaz thrones, he'll control every country in the settled lands except Aronsdale. Jarid *knows* that. He would be mad to fight for Cobalt. But if he fights against him, he will be fighting against the empress—who is his kin. His House will be going to war with itself. The dragon only knows what would happen."

"You're right," she said, subdued. "It's a mess."

He tangled his hand in her hair. "We have too many rulers and too few thrones. Some of us will die."

"The solution is easy." She laid her head against his shoulder. "Cobalt should give the Onyx Throne back to Ozi."

He gave a strained laugh. "So he should."

Allegra sighed. "It would be so much easier to hate Cobalt if he were a monster. But he's not."

Markus put his hand under her chin and tilted up her face so she was looking at him. "What power do you mages have? What do you do—you, the empress, this man Drummer, that fire opal girl? How do you quench the fires in those of us with violent hearts?"

"I can't do anything."

He kissed her. "You do more than you know."

She hesitated. "Fire opal girl? Who is that?"

"Ginger-Sun. She was the girl who escaped Yargazon after he put her on the rack. She's the consort of Baz Quaazera, the cousin of Queen Vizarana. He commands the queen's army." After a moment, he said, "Ginger-Sun is the reason Yargazon wanted an Aronsdale girl with fiery hair. Hers was like that."

"And she's a mage?"

"Apparently. She escaped Yargazon's camp by starting fires. The men think she used spells."

"It's possible." Small flames were simple to do. Allegra had lit a candle as her first spell. But escaping an armed camp would require a far more powerful blaze. "It wouldn't be easy."

A smile ghosted on his lips. "Maybe she used this mysterious kindle-powder Yargazon's spies say Taka Mal isn't inventing."

"How can they be *not* inventing it?"

"Well, I don't know. Supposedly they've tried, but it doesn't work." He eased her down on the pallet, on her back. Mischief flashed in his gaze. "Kindle my fires, night bird."

She put her arms around his neck. "You've already teased me with water." During their interlude in the pool this morning, she had felt as if he had played her to a crescendo and then left her alone before the music finished.

He kissed her while he slid his hand under her tunic and over her breasts. Her nipples hardened when he rolled them between his fingers, and her body responded with a surge of desire. But when she pulled his shirt out of his trousers, he caught her hand.

"Not here," he said. "Not in the middle of a war camp."

"I want to see you." Her breath was quickening. "*Feel* you."

He finally let her take off his shirt. When he sank between her legs, the rough cloth of his trousers scraped sensually against her inner thighs. The muscles of his chest shifted against her skin, the wiry hair brushing her erect nipples. As his passion built, she felt like a leaf caught in a whirlpool. He needed no miradella to make her want him; he was his most potent aphrodisiac. When he lost control, she let go, as well, and drowned in the sensations that shuddered through her body.

It almost let her forget the fires of war poised to consume their lives and leave only ashes.

★ ★ ★

The second day of their ride passed like the first. Allegra remained under the hostile gaze of the captain as they crossed the Rocklands. The sun beat down on terracelike formations stepping endlessly across the desert, and the broken land sweltered.

That night, they camped beneath rocky peaks where the Citadel of the Dragon-Sun sat high above the desert. On the third and fourth days, they forged through low mountains. In the evening of the fourth day, they reached the great basin that for more than a thousand years had served as home to the ancient city of Quaaz.

A harsh voice woke Allegra. She lifted her head in the dark, groggy and confused. Markus lay at her side, his front to her back, his arm around her waist. She thought he was sleeping, but then he said, "Did you hear someone?"

"I think so," she said.

He rose to his feet, looming over her, dressed in his pants and boots. As she pulled on her tunic, the flap of the tent swayed. Light filtered through the walls, and the smoky tang of a torch drifted to her. Markus had just taken a step forward when the grizzled captain fastened up the flap and entered the tent. Despite the late hour, he wore full armor and chain mail—and he had his sword drawn. The torchlight outside glinted on the blade.

"Come with us," the captain said. "Both of you."

Sweat gathered on Allegra's hands, though the air felt chilly. Her pulse raced as she stood up by the pallet.

"Go where?" Markus asked. He stood with his arms by his sides, ready to fight. Bare-handed, he faced an armored man with a sword, and more armed warriors stood outside, visible in the torchlight. Allegra came up to him, and he put back his hand, stopping her.

"You will come with us," the captain repeated. *"Now."*

"On whose orders?" Markus asked.

The captain's face clenched, and he jerked his hand in a signal. Nine men entered the tent. Markus pulled Allegra to his side, his arms protectively around her, and she held him around the waist, her fingers clenched on his belt. They stood half-dressed and unarmed in the midst of ten Chamberlight warriors in full battle dress with their swords drawn.

The captain stepped toward them.

"We'll go!" Markus said. He kept his arm around her shoulders as they stepped forward, and she held on to his waist, half-awake and bewildered. The soldiers swept them out of the tent. The rocky ground stabbed her bare feet, and icy starlight frosted the camp. The Chamberlight men led them past dark tents until they reached a large one where the light inside turned the walls silver.

"Wait here," the captain said. Allegra thought if a man's voice could have become a weapon, his would have stabbed Markus. He disappeared into the tent, but reappeared almost immediately and motioned to them. She stumbled as they entered the tent, and Markus tried to catch her as she fell. She landed on one knee with a cry. In the muted silence, even that small noise sounded loud.

"Get up," the captain said.

"Help her, for saints' sake," a man said.

As Markus helped Allegra to her feet, she strained to see who had spoken. It sounded like Jarid. Smoke drifted from the torches and curled around many people in the tent, stinging her eyes after the dry, chill air outside. The guards prodded her forward. Markus walked with his arm around her shoulders, and she had both of hers around his waist. With the two of them bleary-eyed and confused, she didn't see how anyone could think they posed a danger.

As her eyes adjusted, she saw Jarid sitting on a heavy chest. Her relief was short-lived, for Cobalt was behind him, pacing back and forth. Other men stood around the tent. Some were Chamberlight officers, but most were Aronsdale. Many of the Aronsdale officers looked strange, though. Something was wrong with their uniforms.

One man in particular caught her attention. He was standing by a tent pole, his arms crossed. Although she had never seen him before, she *knew* him. He had the yellow hair, blue eyes and graceful build common in southwestern Aronsdale. The same traits people called "angelic" in the women, they tended to call "too pretty" in men, but she doubted anyone would use those words for this warrior. He wore armor, a burnished breastplate and glinting mail. Gray streaked his hair, and his face had the character of a man who had endured much in his life and survived.

He wore no insignia to indicate his rank. Instead a jaguar emblazoned his breastplate. She didn't understand why someone in the Dawnfield colors wore a jaguar. It was, she realized, why some of the other officers looked strange. Their armor bore a jaguar instead of the crossed swords of Aronsdale.

Markus stopped in the middle of the tent with his arms around Allegra. "What do you want with us?" he said.

Cobalt pointed to a low chest. "Sit."

As Allegra sat on the chest with Markus, sweat beaded on her forehead. She pulled her tunic farther down over her thighs, painfully aware that she was the only woman in the tent.

Another Chamberlight man strode inside, and someone else pushed another person after him—a boy.

Ozarson.

The atajazid tripped on the rug exactly as Allegra had done and stumbled forward. He was wearing the soft black trousers and shirt he slept in, and his curls were tousled all over his head. He stared around with wide eyes.

The guard shoved Ozarson down onto the carpet next to the chest where Markus sat. Kneeling, the boy stared up at the towering guard, then turned a bewildered gaze to his brother. Markus put his arm around Ozarson's shoulders and sat holding him and Allegra, looking around at the gathered warlords. The grizzled captain and two other men stood behind them with their swords drawn.

A child cried somewhere deeper in the tent. It sounded like a baby or a toddler, perhaps one or two years old.

"What the hell?" Markus said.

The man with gold hair spoke curtly. "You would know. You've created your share of hells."

The child whimpered, and a woman murmured to it in the shadows behind the officers. Allegra tried to peer into the darkness back there, but she could only catch a glimmer of light. A gauze drape hung between this main area and whatever lay beyond.

Cobalt came over to them and stared at Ozarson. "So," the emperor said coldly. "Not only are you a Shadow-Dragon King, it seems you now also rule Taka Mal."

Ozarson looked up at him, his mouth opening.

Satisfaction flickered on Markus's face. "Then your armies were too late. Quaaz has fallen."

Saints almighty. *It had happened?* In all the epics, the rescuing army galloped onto the scene just in time to save the beleaguered heroes. They weren't supposed to arrive too late, after the enemy had already won.

Fast on the heels of that thought came another: Where was the royal family? The warrior with gold hair and the jaguar on his breastplate couldn't be Drummer Headwind. Drummer was younger than the queen, who was in her mid-thirties. This man looked fifty. He wore Dawnfield colors, but with the wrong emblem.

Then it hit Allegra: This was Muller Dawnfield, the king of Harsdown. Jarid's cousin. He wore the Harsdown jaguar, which had once symbolized Cobalt's throne. Cobalt's father had attacked Aronsdale and lost, and in doing so, he had lost his throne to the House of Dawnfield. Now Muller claimed the jaguar.

The gauze at the back rippled and a woman stalked forward with feral grace. She was the most furiously beautiful person Allegra had ever seen. Wild black curls tumbled around her face and shoulders, disarrayed as if she had been riding in the wind. Her upward-tilted eyes were huge and black, and fierce with anger. She wore the riding trousers of a Zanterian merchant, the suede dyed a rich crimson. Her red jerkin had a fringe with ruby balls, and gold rings hung from her ears. In the sheath on her belt, a dagger glinted with a topaz in its hilt. She came to stand in front of Markus, and he watched her with recognition.

Then she spit in his face.

Markus jumped up—and every man around them lifted his sword. Cobalt drew his with an uncanny speed, faster than anyone else, though he was the largest man by far, the heaviest, and Allegra would have thought the least agile. Before Markus was upright, Cobalt had the tip of his sword at the prince regent's throat.

"Sit," the emperor said.

Markus stared at the sword, the tip of which just touched his neck. Then he sat slowly, with care, as Cobalt lowered his sword.

The woman turned her blazing gaze on Ozarson. Her husky voice simmered with fury. "You will never sit on my throne."

The boy stared as if he were seeing a goddess. He didn't seem to know whether to be terrified or in awe. If Allegra hadn't known better, she would have thought he had just fallen in love.

Queen Vizarana took a deep breath. Then she spun around and stalked to the other side of the tent. After a moment, she turned and came back. Fury still seethed in her gaze, but she had it more in control.

She considered Allegra. "You're the mage?"

"Yes." Allegra barely controlled her stammer. She didn't know what she had expected from the queen of Taka Mal, but she hadn't been ready for this force of nature. The child who had cried in the back of the tent must be her heir.

Markus looked around the tent, his forehead furrowed. "Is your consort here?"

"No." Vizarana's voice turned harsh. "Most of him is in the camp of your army, Markus Onyx." She said his name as if it were a curse.

Allegra's palms felt clammy. "Most of him?"

Cobalt motioned to one of his officers. The man came forward with a scroll and an ivory box tiled in gold and onyx. Cobalt took both and handed them to Markus. "Look."

When Allegra saw Markus's expression, her unease grew. He knew or at least suspected what that box held—and he dreaded it. She wanted to look away as he opened the container, but she made herself watch. The interior was padded and lined with black silk.

A man's bloodied large toe lay on the silk.

Ozarson's face paled. "Markus?" He looked up at his brother as if willing him to say this was a mistake.

Face drawn, Markus closed the box and carefully set it on his knee. Then he untied the scroll. As he unrolled it, Cobalt spoke. "Read it aloud. Let the boy hear what his generals do in his name."

Markus read in a flat voice. "To His Imperial Majesty, Cobalt Escar. The screams of your kinsman are most satisfying. If Queen Vizarana reaches the Aronsdale king before we catch her, show her the toe. She will recognize it by the birthmark. Assure her that I intend to send all of her consort back to her. Whether or not he arrives piece by piece depends on you. Send me Allegra, and I will stop cutting Drummer apart. Send Ozarson and I will stop interrogating Drummer. Send Markus, Ozarson and Allegra, and I will return Drummer. Each day you delay, I will cut another piece off Vizarana's pretty consort and send it to you. Dusk Yargazon, General of the Army."

"Gods," Allegra said. "He can't mean it."

Markus looked ill. "We never planned this."

"He can't!" Ozarson spoke frantically to Cobalt. "Give me a parchment and pen. I'll write to him. Command him to stop."

Cobalt stared at the boy, his face impassive. "And he will say we coerced you." He shifted his dark gaze to Markus. "You claim this wasn't part of your 'plan.' You expect me to believe you never intended to take Drummer hostage?"

"A hostage, yes," Markus said. "But not like this."

"It makes no sense," Allegra said. "What can he hope to gain?"

"I should think it's obvious," Vizarana said coldly. "Your husband. You." She turned her fiery gaze on Ozarson. "This child who mistakenly believes he can usurp my throne."

"But it will antagonize Drummer's kin," Allegra said. "Even if you get Drummer back, this will only make Aronsdale and Harsdown more likely to join Cobalt. Which works against the Jazid army."

Cobalt glanced at Jarid and Muller. "It is a conundrum, yes? Avenge Drummer—and give me the Topaz Throne."

"You will not have it," Vizarana told him calmly.

Cobalt turned his formidable stare on her. "If I rescue your consort and take back Quaaz, I keep the throne."

Vizarana crossed her arms. "You've done neither." She scowled at him. "My army isn't defeated. After we bring down this force that came sweeping out of Jazid, maybe I should take *your* throne."

"That would prove interesting," Cobalt said dryly.

Allegra suspected "interesting" was far too mild a word for a challenge between Vizarana and Cobalt. She spoke with deference to the queen. "You escaped the Jazid army?"

Vizarana lowered her arms. "We received King Jarid's warning in time. We almost made it out before Yargazon's men stormed the city walls. When they breached the palace, Drummer misled them long enough for Ginger, my daughter, and me to get out."

"Ginger?" Markus asked. "You mean the fire girl?"

Cobalt jerked his chin toward the curtained area at the back of the tent. "She's with the queen's child. She won't come out here. She's a Dragon-Sun priestess."

Muller came to stand with Cobalt. "Would it be so wrong

to let Allegra go back? If Yargazon keeps his word, Drummer might survive longer."

"No!" Markus said. "You can't send her back without me."

Vizarana stared at him, incredulous. "You would let him torture my husband just so you can be with your wife?"

"If he gets Allegra," Markus said grimly, "she's the one he'll torture."

Ozarson's voice cracked. "I won't have this done in my name."

"It's you that Yargazon wants," Muller said to Ozarson.

"I'm not so sure." Cobalt narrowed his gaze at Markus. "This is as much about you. Yargazon wants to control you, doesn't he? But it's harder than he expected." He motioned toward Allegra and Ozarson. "Maybe you aren't so much your father's son after all. Otherwise, this remarkable woman would never have stood by you, nor would this boy love you as he does." He rubbed his chin, his expression thoughtful. "You went to Aronsdale without Yargazon's support. You act as your own man even when he forbids it, eh? He can't control you, and if he can't control you, he'll never control the throne."

Markus met his gaze. "I'm no one's puppet."

"I still don't understand," Allegra said. "Even if his threats convince you to trade all three of us back, it works against him because it pushes Aronsdale and Harsdown into allying with you."

Vizarana snorted. "If he acted like a civilized human

being, what motivation would Cobalt have to trade three people for one?"

"They aren't Cobalt's damn hostages," Jarid said. He was sitting on the chest, one leg bent, with his elbow resting on his knee. "They're in my custody." The scar on his neck darkened in the torchlight.

"Either way," Cobalt said, "we have three people he wants and he has one that we want."

"Oh," Ozarson suddenly said. "No, that's not why he sent his ultimatum this way."

Cobalt looked down at the boy. "You know otherwise?"

"Don't you see?" Ozarson said. "It's obvious."

"Ozi," Markus began. He sounded worn-out.

"Let him talk," Allegra said.

"Look around," Ozarson told them. "At everyone."

Cobalt glanced around, then turned back to the boy. "I see many grim-faced soldiers waiting for you to get to the point."

"You're here," Ozarson said. "The Dawnstar emperor." He indicated Vizarana shyly. "The queen of Taka Mal." He glanced at Jarid. "The king of Aronsdale." Then he nodded at Muller. "The king of Harsdown. And me. That's almost every ruler in the settled lands, fugitive or not. King Jarid's men went in to get Queen Vizarana and her family. I know how General Yargazon thinks. He doesn't care about codes of war. He probably had spies looking to follow—"

"Gods *almighty*." Cobalt swung around. "Everyone out of here!" He grabbed Markus's arm and hauled him to his feet, then literally threw him toward the grizzled captain. "Split up the three of them. The only reason Yargazon's men haven't moved yet is because these three are in the tent. They needed to find out where we had them, so they waited until we brought them here. Now they know."

A warrior pulled Allegra up, and another had Ozarson. They strode to the entrance in ground-devouring steps, pulling her and the atajazid, and she had to run to keep up. A baby cried somewhere, and a woman spoke softly, urgently.

Then they were outside, running through the dark. Stumbling, with rocks stabbing her bare feet, Allegra bit the inside of her cheek to keep from crying out. People were running past them in the darkness, men in armor.

Suddenly the man on Allegra's right spasmed as if someone had struck him. He stopped and stared at her with shock. Then he crumpled to the ground.

She dropped next to him. An arrow had hit his neck, one of the few places on his body with no armor or mail. She laid her hand on the wound, on either side of the shaft, trying to stop the bleeding. She needed a shape! She couldn't heal him, but she could help him survive until the doctors—

Then she realized it didn't matter. The man was dead.

"Saints, no," she whispered, taking her hands from his neck. Blood dripped from her fingers, but it no longer pumped out of his wound.

Ozarson spoke dully next to her. "This man is dead, too."

She sagged as people ran by them in the dark. Swords clanged somewhere. She and Ozarson stayed crouched by the fallen bodies of two warriors much larger than either of them, which in the darkness probably made it difficult to tell them apart from the dead.

"Ozi," she said. "Keep low." He was a shadow in the starlight, but she could see his frightened eyes. "Do you recognize the arrows that hit them?"

"Jazidian."

"How could Yargazon sneak your forces up here? They would have to get past sentries from four different armies."

"I don't think he did," Ozarson said. "It was probably just a few men, enough to attack one tent."

"That's suicide!"

His voice shook. "Even if every man that he sent died, they had only to kill the people in that tent. Or just *one* of them. Cobalt."

A chill went up Allegra's spine. It probably couldn't have worked, but it wasn't impossible. If it had succeeded, then in one attack, Dusk Yargazon would have killed every sovereign in the settled lands—except Ozarson. They would have been within reach of putting the boy on the throne of the Dawnstar emperor.

"Ozi, listen," she said. "Never, *never* tell General Yargazon you're the one who warned Emperor Cobalt. *Never.*"

His eyes widened. "I didn't— It didn't occur to me—"

"I know." She held her breath as more men ran past them.

"Allegra." Ozarson pressed something into her hand.

"What—" Then she realized what he had given her. The dodecahedron. "I thought I lost it."

"I found it in the travel bags."

"But why did you bring it?"

"No one would search a Jazid boy for a mage shape." Softly he added, "It's a Platonic solid. Twelve sides, all regular pentagons. Surely that must be powerful."

"Yes, very," she whispered, hiding it in her pocket. "Thank you." A twelve-sided form like this might burn her abilities to ashes, but if she could control it, she could make incredible spells. It stunned her that he had figured out so much about her spells. But then, Ozi was no normal boy.

"Ho!" someone shouted. "There's children here!"

A warrior dropped by Allegra and grabbed her arm. "Not a child. A woman!"

Another man crouched by Ozarson. "Your Majesty! Dragon's blessings, we've been worried."

As the man holding Allegra turned toward Ozarson, his grip on her arms loosened. She wrenched free and tried to lunge away, but he caught her easily around the waist and yanked her back.

"Give me a cord," he said to the other man. "It's her. The witch who took the atajazid."

"Don't hurt her!" Ozarson said.

"We won't," the other man said. He was between Allegra and Ozarson, so she couldn't see the boy anymore. She fought the man holding her, raking her fingernails down his arm, but gauntlets protected his hands and forearms, and he had armor everywhere else. Her silk tunic caught on his mail and ripped.

"Your Majesty, we'll get you to safety," the other man told Ozarson. "I'd lay my life down before I let anyone take you."

"Thank you," Ozarson said in a low voice.

The other man handed something to the one holding her, who then twisted her arms behind her back and bound her wrists together. "Help!" she shouted, then choked as he shoved a wad of leather into her mouth. He pulled back two straps attached to it and fastened them together behind her head. Then he leaned over her, pushing her forward with his arms wrapped around her torso so she couldn't struggle. The stench of his sweat nauseated her.

"What did you do?" Ozarson said.

"She's fine," the man assured him. "We need to get you out of here, and if she shouts, she'll bring Cobalt's men." Grimly he added, "If she sings, the dragon only knows what she'll do to us."

"She won't harm you," Ozarson said.

"We can reach the horses from here," the man holding Allegra said. They were crouched in the dark, and the sounds of battle had moved beyond them.

"Where is Prince Markus?" the other one asked.

"Cobalt took him," Ozarson said. "Can you find him?"

"I wish we could." The man spoke kindly to the boy. "But we'll be lucky if we can get the two of you out of here."

"You'll have to run with us, Your Majesty," the other man said. "Stay bent over as much as you can, and keep close."

"You have to guard Allegra, too," Ozarson said.

"We will," the man holding her said. "You have our word we'll get both of you back."

"All right," Ozarson said. "Let's go."

No! Allegra shouted, but it came out as a muffled grunt. Ozarson couldn't see well enough to realize what his men were doing to her. She didn't doubt, either, that he believed going with them was the right thing to do. Why the blazes wouldn't he? They were his army, who answered to her own husband. He didn't understand what would happen if they took her back without Markus to keep Yargazon away from her.

The man holding her stood, still bent over, with one arm clamped around her waist and his other hand gripped on her upper arm. The second warrior grasped her other arm and they took off running, dragging her between them. Rocks and stubby plants stabbed her feet. She fought their hold, to no avail. When she balked, they lifted her off the ground and ran holding her up so her feet dangled. It hurt her arms and shoulders so much that when they put her down again, she kept running.

They half slid and half ran down a rocky slope at the edge of the camp. Sentries should have been patrolling the hill, but either they had died or were fighting elsewhere. Allegra couldn't see or hear Ozarson. It was all happening too fast.

Then they were out of the camp and racing through the dark.

⚷ CHAPTER 25
SHADOWS OF NIGHT

"The horses should be over there." The man spoke in a low, urgent voice.

The warriors stopped, and Allegra sagged in their grip, out of breath, barely able to draw in enough air past the gag. Dark bluffs surrounded them.

"I see the horses," Ozarson said. He sounded far away. "Two of them."

"I'll take you on one," the man told him with respect. He turned toward the other soldier. "You can bring her."

"Allegra?" Ozarson said from somewhere. "Are you there?"

"She's here," the man said.

Her stifled protest was almost soundless. With her wrists tied behind her back, she couldn't use her arms, so she twisted her shoulders back and forth, trying to free herself. One of the men put his arms around her, his front to her back, holding her still while the other man disappeared into the darkness. A horse snorted, and someone spoke in a low voice. Allegra caught bits and pieces: "…leave saddle… riding blanket… Hold the reins, Your Majesty.…"

The man reappeared out of the shadows, walking a horse without a rider. "Here, Zeik." He handed the reins to the man with Allegra. "You can take her in."

No! Allegra redoubled her efforts to twist free.

The man holding her, Zeik apparently, handed her to the other man. She kicked at him, and her foot hit a boot, then his knee. He swore under his breath and pulled her hard against him so she couldn't kick.

Zeik swung onto the horse. He reached down, and the other man lifted Allegra up to him. She wrenched back and forth, fighting them. The gag muffled her shouts, but in the silence of the night, even her grunts were audible. She twisted hard and began to slide off the horse. Zeik hauled her back up, then dragged her leg across the animal so she sat astride in front of him. He clamped his arms around her torso to hold her in place.

"You got her?" the man on the ground asked.

"Fine." Zeik sounded out of breath. "We should split up. It will increase the chance that at least one of us gets through."

"Dragon willing, we'll both make it. Good luck."

"And you." Then Zeik set off through the night.

Allegra eventually wore herself out struggling and sagged in Zeik's hold with her head hanging down. As exhaustion caught up with her, nightmarish images flickered in her mind. Over and over, she remembered the man next to her collapsing in the dirt, an arrow in his neck as he died.

Her jaws ached. As soon as Zeik had a chance, he readjusted

the gag so the leather ball settled firmly in her mouth, filling it and pushing down her tongue. He did something with the straps, locking them behind her head. When he finished, she doubted she could have taken the thing off even if she had her hands free. They had figured out too well how to "disarm" what they considered a weapon—her ability to do spells.

The pound of hooves sounded nearby, several horses perhaps. Zeik guided his mount behind a large bluff that rose as a darker shadow in the night. He laid the blade of a dagger flat against her neck. "Hold still. No noise."

Allegra barely breathed. After the riders passed, Zeik set off crossways on a steep hill instead of riding down to flatter land. His horse had to step carefully on the precarious slope. At first she hoped the slower pace would make them easier to catch. She soon realized why he had done it, though; no other riders were up here.

After a while, Zeik said, "I know you're evil. A witch. If you could sing, you would curse my soul." He shifted her in his arms. "But hell, I can't help it, you just seem like a frightened girl to me, one who's so pretty, men can't think straight around her. Even powerful men." Then he muttered, "Especially them. They're used to getting what they want. But even when they *have* you, they don't."

She had no idea what he meant by the last statement, but he had it right about one thing: She was frightened. Terrified.

Some time later, he said, "The General is a good commander. Harsh, it's true. But a man must be harsh to conquer

470

the barrens of Jazid. He pulled our forces together out of nothing. He gave us hope when we had none. He brought the atajazid and Prince Markus to freedom. It's my honor to follow him." He sounded as if he were arguing with himself. "Nor is he weakened by sentiments that would undercut his strength."

Allegra didn't doubt he felt what he said. But she wondered whom he was trying to convince—her or himself.

They were riding around a jumble of rocks when he brushed back her hair and leaned down so his lips touched her cheek. "Still, if I had a woman like you, I would never hurt her."

Then don't take me to Yargazon, she tried to say. It came out as a faint, scared sound.

"Don't cry." He sounded miserable. Then he gave an angry whistle. "Damn it, stop weakening me!" After that, he said no more.

Eventually they reached flatter land. He made an odd noise, like the call of a blackwing hawk. As they continued on, another call drifted on the air. A rider appeared out of the darkness, almost upon them before Allegra realized he was there.

"Zeik," the newcomer said.

"It's me," Zeik said.

The other man, apparently a sentry, exhaled. "The dragon has blessed us twice this night."

"Twice?" Zeik asked. "Did the atajazid make it back?"

"He did indeed." The sentry's tone lightened as he rode

with them. "We've been quiet, no noises, but the men are rejoicing."

"At least some good came of this night."

"What happened with the raid?"

"Everyone else in the tent escaped," Zeik said sourly. "As soon as they started to disperse, we attacked."

"Only two of you have made it back." The sentry sounded subdued. "It looks like all the rest were killed."

"It's a sad business," Zeik said. "But they died for the atajazid, that he could go free."

Tears gathered in Allegra's eyes. Yargazon's plan had failed—almost. In the greater scheme of these history-making events, she was nothing, just one girl with a bit of mage power. Whether she ended up in Jazid or Aronsdale made little difference in the long view. It mattered only to her, who would suffer the brutal consequences of her capture, one small victory in a failed attempt to murder all the leaders of the settled lands.

They reached the Jazid camp and rode among shadowed tents. Sentries passed them, patrolling in the dark, and the one escorting them quietly sent another soldier out to keep his watch. He took Zeik deeper into the camp, past other guards. Ahead, a dim light grew larger. They were approaching a tent whose sides glowed from the inside. As Zeik reined in his horse, a stable boy ran to them.

Zeik dismounted, then reached up and pulled Allegra off the horse. The dodecahedron in her pocket jabbed her thigh as the tunic hiked over her leg. Zeik put her on her feet, and for a moment he kept holding her, even though she was neither falling nor fighting.

The sentry jumped down and handed his reins to the stable boy. As the youth led away the horses, Zeik took her arm. "Come. The General is waiting."

No! She balked, refusing to move. Zeik jerked her, and she stumbled a few steps. When she held back again, he and the guard took her by the arms and dragged her forward until she managed to pull her feet beneath her. They stopped in front of the tent, and the sentry went on inside, leaving Zeik and Allegra waiting.

Please. She tried to say it, but even she couldn't decipher the noise she made. She looked up at Zeik and willed him to relent, to show mercy, to take her away from here.

"Your eyes are as big as moons," he said, his voice strained. He cupped his hand around her cheek.

A tear ran out of her eye. *Please don't do this.*

"Ach," he muttered. "Don't look at me that way."

The sentry opened the tent. "You can bring her in." He lifted the flap and stepped aside.

Zeik's expression hardened, and he pushed Allegra through the entrance as if he were angry at her for his own compassion. The light wasn't bright inside, but after so long in the dark, she had to squint. The reek of scorched hemp saturated the air. Three men sat around a low table, studying maps and other parchments. A torch burned in a stand behind them, lighting their area but leaving the rest of the tent in shadow. She recognized all three: Generals Yargazon and Ardoz and Colonel Bladebreak. As Yargazon looked up, Zeik saluted, his fist turned up to the sky.

"Well done, Lieutenant," Yargazon said. "Excellent work." He indicated a pole that held up the roof to Zeik's left. "Put her there." Then he returned to his meeting.

Zeik took her to the pole and shoved her down on her knees. Crouching behind her, he worked on the thongs binding her wrists. When he freed them, she tried to bring her arms in front of her body, but he pulled her hands over her head. By the time she realized what he intended, he had stretched her arms tight and bound her wrists to a metal loop jutting out from the pole above her.

Don't, she tried to say. *It hurts.*

He avoided looking at her as he pulled her calves so she was sitting with her legs bent to the side. He tied her ankles to a metal loop jammed into the ground. She felt ill when she saw the blood that stained the rug—near her big toe.

"Stop looking like that," he said in a low voice. "Your spells won't work on me." He hesitated, then pulled her tunic down, over her thighs. The cloth was too torn to cover much, especially with her arms pulled over her head, but his gesture of kindness made another tear roll down her cheek.

Zeik's face contorted as if he were in pain. "I'm sorry," he muttered. When he reached up to her hands, for one incredible moment, she thought he would free her. But he was only checking the knots around her wrists. He pulled one, securing it perhaps. Then he stood up and turned toward Yargazon.

The General glanced up. "Thank you, Lieutenant." He inclined his head. "I'm pleased. You will be rewarded."

"Thank you, sir."

Regret showed on Yargazon's face. "We will hold a memorial for those who lost their lives tonight. Their sacrifice in rescuing the atajazid will be remembered. If you would like to speak for them—?"

"Sir, yes, I would," Zeik said. "Thank you."

"Very well, Lieutenant. You may go rest." The hint of a smile touched his expression. "It's well deserved, young man, and we've a few hours before we fight at dawn."

Zeik saluted and left the tent, accompanied by the sentry. Allegra felt as if her last hope of mercy had vanished. Not that she had really believed he would help her. But at least he had shown remorse. Watching the officers conferring with Yargazon, she wondered if they even cared what the General would do to her. She had thought Ardoz might, but neither he nor Bladebreak even acknowledged her presence. Perhaps they truly did think her evil.

Although she was too far away to hear all of their war council, she caught some. Their forces had occupied the palace in Quaaz, but the Taka Mal army continued to fight. Carrier birds had taken news of the invasion to Cobalt's forces in Jazid, and many Jazidian soldiers had deserted that army to join Yargazon's fugitives. Tonight Jazid and Taka Mal had called a temporary truce. They were waiting to see what would happen with Aronsdale and Harsdown, and for the arrival of the extra men from Jazid.

They also talked about the suicide raid. They had known it had little chance of success and that it violated accepted codes of war. They had been willing to try anyway, for if it had succeeded, the sun would have risen on a very different world. Ozi could have been close to becoming ruler of all the settled lands.

Yargazon finally set down the map he was holding and rubbed his eyes. "It's been a long night."

"So it has," Bladebreak said. "But when the men realize His Majesty has returned, it will improve morale."

"There is that." Yargazon rose to his feet with the others.

They spoke for a bit about inconsequential matters, and then Ardoz and Bladebreak bid him good-night. Ardoz glanced at Allegra as he and the colonel were leaving the tent, and a frown creased his face. He turned back to Yargazon. "Be careful with her, Dusk. Markus doesn't want her interrogated."

"Don't worry," Yargazon said. "She'll be fine."

Liar! Allegra thought. When Ardoz nodded and left the tent, she cried, *Come back!* but even she barely heard her muffled call.

Yargazon stretched his arms and rubbed the small of his back. He turned almost lazily toward Allegra. "So," he said. "The witch comes home."

Don't, she thought. She was having trouble breathing.

He came over and sat next to her with one leg stretched out and the other bent at the knee. Leaning his weight on one hand, he traced his finger up the inside of her elbow. With her wrists pulled over her head, her sleeves had fallen down to her shoulders, leaving her arms bare.

"You're quiet tonight. Good." He touched her neckline. "This rag, however, offends me."

Don't hurt me, she thought, knowing it was futile.

He dropped his hand to his belt and pulled a dagger out of its gold sheath. As she stared at the knife, blood drained from her face. With methodical, relentless motions, he slit the neckline of her tunic, then ripped the cloth down her front. He cut off the sleeves and pulled away the scraps until none remained. Then he sat, his gaze traveling over her body.

"I've wanted to do that since I first saw you," he said.

Her face flamed. She instinctively tried to pull her arms down to cover herself, but she could do nothing. He dropped the remaining rags of her tunic in a pile, and she saw the pocket that hid the dodecahedron. Unreachable.

Yargazon pointed his dagger at a structure half-hidden in shadow across the tent. "Do you see what's up there?"

She squinted into the dark, but she could make out no more than a framework with a row of shapes along its top, cups or bottles perhaps.

"They're hourglasses," he said. "One hour each. Do you know how many are there?"

She shook her head, and a curl fell into her eyes.

"Sixteen," he said. "One for each hour you left me chained." He picked up her curl and twirled it in his fingers, then deliberately let it fall back into her eyes. "You will pay for that." Folding his hand around her breast, he pinched her nipple. Then he leaned forward and kissed her cheek, his lips brushing the strap of her gag. "Sixteen hours for sixteen hours," he murmured.

No! Clenching her teeth, she wished she did have the power to curse him. *May you lose everything you've ever cared about. Everything you love. The war. Markus. Ozarson. Everything.*

Yargazon sheathed the dagger. Then he rose to his feet and walked to the row of hourglasses. He took one and turned around, holding it up so she could see. "The first hour," he said. He flipped it over and set it on a table where she could see it better. Sand began to pour from the upper into the lower half.

As the General walked back to her, Allegra flattened herself against the pole and wished she could shrink into it where he couldn't follow.

He stopped in front of her and looked down as he unbuckled his leather belt. "You may belong to *him*," he said, his voice low and angry, "but I'm the one who controls you." He pulled the sheathed dagger off his belt and dropped it on the ground. "I will own you, Allegra, despite what those marriage documents say, because after tonight, you will *know* I'm the one who has claimed your spirit."

Then he swung the belt.

The sand poured, and Allegra cried. She tried to distance herself from Yargazon and his swings, tried to think of Aronsdale, rolling green hills, her friends, Prince Aron, kindnesses she had known or of Markus's gentler side, instead of the violent warlord who wanted to conquer her in the same

478

way he sought to conquer the brutal land that had forged him in the crucible of its merciless sun.

At one point, after Yargazon's blows had become especially violent, he took a long breath and stepped back. Sitting on a crate, he leaned against a pole behind it, the belt hanging loose in his hand while the clenched set of his features eased. He closed his eyes, and his body relaxed for the first time that night.

Allegra breathed in ragged gasps, fighting for air, her face wet with tears. When she realized he had fallen asleep, relief surged through her. She didn't know what he would do to her for sixteen hours, but surely if he kept this up, she wouldn't survive.

Yargazon eventually lifted his head and rubbed his eyes. The intensity came back into his gaze as he watched her shuddering by the pole. Then he went to the shelf with the hourglasses. The first one had run out, so he took the second and lifted it so she could see. Then he flipped it over and set it on the table with the sand running. He returned to the pole—

And swung his belt.

Her existence narrowed to each moment, one after another. She withdrew deep within herself, seeking a place where nothing could reach her, none of the cruelty that stamped this world.

A call came from outside the tent. "Sir?"

Yargazon lowered his arm, the belt hanging from his hand. He wiped his other arm across his forehead, blotting the sweat from his exertions. Allegra shook with silent thanks for the reprieve.

The General strode to the entrance and swept aside the flap. "What is it?"

"A messenger arrived," a man outside said. "With a scroll from Emperor Cobalt."

"Bring it in," Yargazon said, moving aside.

The man who entered wore black armor and a heavy sword across his back. He handed Yargazon a scroll and stood waiting while the General read it.

"So." After rolling up the scroll, Yargazon tapped it against his fingers. "It looks like no one is sleeping tonight." He walked over to Allegra and looked down at her. "Cobalt is willing to trade Markus for you and Drummer. How absurd, to think I would send back the wife of the prince regent."

Die, she thought. *Have a terrible convulsion and die in agony.* She knew too little about Jazid to know whether Yargazon had overstepped himself, but she couldn't imagine he could do this to the prince regent's wife. He was betting on his irreplaceable value to control Markus's anger.

You can't control him, she thought. Yargazon had misjudged Markus this time. Maybe he couldn't understand the prince, for Markus acted differently with him than with other people. He didn't want to appear weak to the General. But Markus wasn't Ozar Onyx.

Yargazon turned to the other man. "Is the messenger from the emperor still here?"

"Yes, sir."

"Good. I will speak to him." Yargazon sheathed his dagger on his belt and fastened the belt around his waist, once again the General in perfect array. He crossed the tent to his shadowed wall of time and set the second hourglass on its side, stopping the flow of sand. Glancing at Allegra, he said, "We'll finish when I return."

With that, he strode from the tent.

Allegra sagged against the pole, so relieved that she wanted to laugh, then cry. Then she wanted to rage. She yanked on the cords binding her wrists—

And they slipped.

Allegra froze. She looked up at the knot, the one Zeik had tightened before he left. At least she thought he had tightened it. Yet now it was coming apart.

Her pulse jumped. She yanked on the bonds over and over, and with each pull, the knot slipped a little more. When it finally unraveled, her arms fell into her lap. Her muscles hurt from being held in one position for so long, but she ignored the ache as she attacked the restraints on her ankles. They were tighter than the ones on her wrists, but Zeik hadn't pulled them as secure as possible, either. *Thank you,* she thought to his image in her mind. *Thank you, forever.*

As soon as her feet were free, she grabbed the dodecahe-dron out of her tunic pocket. But the wretched gag silenced her. Metal clasps were embedded in the ball of leather, with straps that pulled around her head, under her hair and locked in the back. She couldn't pull the leather out of her mouth or the strap over her head, and without her voice, she had no spell.

Allegra ran to the nearest chest and opened the top. Scrolls filled it. She kept searching, fast and furious, knowing Yargazon could return any moment. She found a chest with his uniforms and put on one of his shirts, hiding the dodeca-hedron in its pocket. She went through more chests, throwing out contents, until she found a shaving blade. Clenching the hilt, she ran to the back of the tent and hacked a hole, then pushed through it, out into the night.

She ran past dark tents, trying to ignore the pain from the welts on her body and lacerations on her feet. She found a row of supply carts and crouched behind them, straining to breathe. Then she went to work on the gag. The lock mechanism wouldn't release. The strap consisted of metal strips, so it couldn't stretch over her head, and the knife wouldn't cut it. She used the tip of the blade to dig through the strap that held the ball in her mouth, gouging the place where a stud held the leather in place. She hacked at it, striving to shred the gag without hurting herself.

Finally! The stud fell out of the leather. With a gasp, she yanked the gag out of her mouth and threw it on the ground. She gulped in air, nearly choking with her need to breathe.

Calm down. She took a steadying breath, then pulled out the dodecahedron and clenched it as she marshaled her thoughts. What spell to use? She couldn't put everyone here to sleep. They probably had precautions in place now, too. It was easy to counter her spells; they had only to shut out her voice. The last time, she had needed to affect a few people, walk a short distance while putting people around her to sleep and sing in the desert. Even that had drained her. She still hadn't fully recovered. Now she didn't know who to put to sleep, and she had only one chance. If her spell didn't succeed, she would do no more than warn Yargazon about her escape.

Allegra rested her forehead against the big wheel of the cart. In an act of mercy Zeik probably considered weakness, he had given her a hope of escape. But she had no resources. She could barely walk. She needed water and sleep. She was deep in a camp with many sentries. Tomorrow they would resume fighting the Taka Mal army, which hulked somewhere out in the basin. She had nowhere to go, no place to turn, and if Yargazon caught her— No! She couldn't go back to that nightmare.

Ozarson was here somewhere. Could he protect her? Allegra hesitated. She had kidnapped him. He later came willingly, but this army was the closest he had to a home. He would be horrified if he knew what Yargazon was doing to her, but despite his title, she doubted he could stop the General. Too many complications existed in Ozi's life, as the atajazid and now, saints forbid, as the conquering sovereign in Taka Mal. He was vulnerable. Brave, yes, and intelligent. But he was only nine. If she sought him out, the General would retaliate against her, possibly even in subtle ways against Ozarson.

Drummer was here, too. Bile rose in her throat as she

recalled the blood in Yargazon's tent. She couldn't heal Drummer; she wasn't a blue mage. But she could ease his pain and help him escape. If he could walk. It was probably a stupid idea; she couldn't even escape herself. But she needed to do something.

Demoralized, Allegra closed her eyes. Then she took a breath and sang, her voice soft, a ballad about green hills and sunlight. She wove a gold spell to keep anyone nearby asleep so they wouldn't catch her, and a green so she could search for Ozarson and Drummer. King Jarid had called his wife using a green spell, so it had to be possible to find a person that way, though she had no idea how.

Her spells wavered. The dodecahedron had too many sides, and she couldn't grasp its power. She lost her grip and the spells faded. She hurt so very, very much, and Yargazon had barely started with her. He wouldn't let her die, but that only meant hour after hour of pain. Nor did she know how far he would go. The marriage contract had gone on at great length about how Markus could kill any man who slept with her. But Yargazon had an army at his disposal, and he had spent decades building his power base. If he wanted the prince regent's wife, she wasn't certain even Markus could stop him.

"Please," she whispered. "Help me." But no one was here to answer. She had only herself.

Focus! She concentrated on her spells and her power swirled, more than she had ever wielded. But she couldn't quite grasp it. Nothing was distinct. It was as if she stood on the shore of a lake and tried to hold the water. The spells ran through her fingers.

A sense of someone's pain trickled past her, but without a warrior's hard edge. This was a gentler mind. Vulnerable. Then she *knew*. Like recognized like. She had touched another Aronsdale mage.

Allegra climbed to her feet, hanging on to the cart. The surge of energy that had driven her escape from Yargazon's tent was gone, leaving exhaustion. She leaned over the cart while her head swam. Then she took a step toward that faint sense of recognition. Pain stabbed her feet, and she crumpled against the wheel. Gritting her teeth, she pushed away from the cart and hobbled behind a line of tents. Cold wind ruffled her black shirt, and silver braid on the shoulders and cuffs glinted in the starlight. The shirt came to midthigh, with the sleeves dangling past her hands. She heard the clank of a sentry on patrol and barely ducked down behind a barrel of water before he walked past. Then she went on, searching for Drummer.

He'll be in the next tent. She needed to lie down, but she forced her burning feet to keep stumbling. She couldn't give up.

Allegra knew when she reached Drummer. Only traces of the green spell still vibrated within her, but it was enough, for he burned like a flame. She knelt behind the tent where she sensed him and hacked at the cloth until she could squeeze through the hole. Inside, darkness surrounded her. She tried to stand, but pain jagged through her feet. So she crawled. The soft rugs under her hands and knees soothed her bruises and cuts.

Her hand hit a mound.

Allegra jerked back, sitting on her haunches. She heard someone breathing, slow and ragged. Stretching out her arm, she touched a cushion, then several others. She felt farther, and her hand brushed across a blanket. She froze when she realized her palm was resting on the back of a person lying in front of her.

Turning her concentration inward, she focused on a new spell, the simplest of all. When she opened her eyes, dim red light surrounded her. A man lay sprawled on his stomach, asleep, his face turned toward her. Yellow curls fell across his eyes. It had to be Drummer; he was probably the only man in Taka Mal or Jazid with hair that color. A blanket covered him to his waist—and whip marks crisscrossed his back and arms. Her tears gathered again, this time for him.

Allegra recognized him, though they had never met. The same hills and valleys she called home had nurtured his mage gifts. He looked just like the other youths where she lived, with the handsome features and boyish face. He had the slender, lithe build of an Aronsdale man rather than the height and musculature of Jazid's native sons. He could have been a farm boy from down the road. Except he was here, in agony, imprisoned while invaders used him as a pawn in their machinations to wrest the throne of his adopted land away from his wife and child.

When she saw the bloodied bandage on his left foot, which stuck out from the blanket, she almost threw up. She laid her hand on his forehead, and found him burning with fever. Dismayed, she closed her eyes, concentrating. She crooned softly, weaving an orange spell to ease the misery of his injuries.

It wasn't enough. Drummer needed a blue mage who could heal, either Jarid or Iris, possibly Aron. She felt as if a weight were crushing her. He couldn't walk, and she couldn't carry him. She would have to drag herself out of here, find a cart and an animal to pull it, bring it back, put him in it, cross the great Quaaz Basin and climb up the hills to the encamped Aronsdale army. She folded her arms across her stomach and rocked back and forth, knowing she couldn't fix this, that this man with such luminous mage power could soon die.

Light flared across the tent.

Allegra froze, then shielded her eyes with her hand. Her spell died, but it was too late. Two men entered the tent, holding a torch that threw huge shadows on the walls. General Ardoz and Colonel Bladebreak.

"I don't see the light anymore," Ardoz said.

Bladebreak indicated Allegra. "It was around her."

As they walked over, Allegra felt as if she were falling off a cliff with nothing but jagged rocks below. She tried to scramble to her feet, but her movements were slowed by pain and fatigue, and she barely made it up by the time Bladebreak reached her. He easily caught her around the waist. He held her with one arm, her front against his side while he handed the torch to Ardoz.

"No." Allegra's voice cracked.

"Come now, Allegra," Bladebreak murmured while Ardoz put the torch in a nearby stand. "It's all right. You'd better sit."

She resisted when he pushed her down, but her legs buckled. He set her so she was sitting sideways to him, between his legs, her side against his chest. He pushed her knees up to her chest, then put his own legs around her, one pressing her shins, the other her spine, then slid one arm around her waist and put the other around her shoulders. She had always liked it when Markus held her that way, but now she thought she would hate it forever.

Bladebreak pressed his lips to her temple. "Were you waiting for us, hmm?"

"Stop it." She tried to push him away, but he brushed aside her hands.

"Why is she here?" Ardoz asked. He knelt next to Drummer and laid his palm against the prince's forehead.

"Maybe Dusk wanted them together. She must have been with him. She's wearing his shirt." Bladebreak touched one of her wrists, then her ankles. "That's odd."

"What?" Ardoz unslung a drinking bag from his shoulder and uncapped a narrow spout at the top.

"She isn't restrained," Bladebreak said. "She could have just walked out of here."

"I can't walk," Allegra said. "My feet are injured." She had the desperate hope that if they thought Yargazon had left her here, they might not mention her to him.

Ardoz tilted the water bag to Drummer's lips, trying to get him to drink. "He's burning alive," the general muttered.

Bladebreak spoke against Allegra's ear. "You put us to sleep that night, didn't you? Before we even got started, you knocked us out." He ran his tongue around her lobe. "You shouldn't have done that."

"Don't." Allegra turned her head away.

"Why do you all grab her that way?" Ardoz asked. "Leave the poor girl alone."

Bladebreak lifted his head. "They do that to you, these witches. Make you want them." He indicated Drummer. "Admit it. You wanted to come in here to see him."

"I want him to live," Ardoz said curtly. "If he dies, we have no hostage to trade for Markus."

Bladebreak brushed Allegra's hair back from her face. "You should have listened to Jasmine," he told her. "She's never suffered. I protect her. But you fight, you disrupt, you resist. You taunt us with your defiance. What did you expect to happen? You have to pay the price for your behavior."

She wondered who protected Jasmine from him. "No matter what you do," she said in a low voice, "I'll never bend to your will."

"Think again, girl," he said. "I can do what I want now."

"No, you can't," Ardoz said. "She's Markus's consort." He took a cloth off a nearby pile and dampened it. Then he laid the compress on Drummer's forehead. "Why is it that the women who cause such turmoil, the ones who bring down dynasties and change history—why are they always the ones who make the men who want them the most miserable?"

Bladebreak grunted. "The dragon only knows."

"You can't have her, Ivan."

"I never said I wanted her," Bladebreak said crossly, though he was still embracing her. "But I'll tell you this—Markus is better off without her."

Ardoz looked up—and Allegra knew. He hid his reaction well, but her mind was sensitized from her mood spell. Markus may have promoted Ardoz and then let his memories of the general fade, but Ardoz had never forgotten.

"Markus needs her," Ardoz said. "And if he needs her, he will have her. So leave her the hell alone."

"Fine," Bladebreak muttered. He motioned at Drummer. "You can't have him, either."

"Don't be absurd." Ardoz dampened another cloth and cleaned a cut on Drummer's back. "I want him to live, that's all."

Bladebreak snorted. "Right."

"You don't want him to live?"

"You really think he might die?"

"His fever is worse," Ardoz said. "Dusk pushed him too hard during the interrogation."

"He's as weak as a girl," Bladebreak said. "A child probably knows more about the queen's army. They obviously don't tell him anything. He's just her pretty, captive consort."

"Either that," Ardoz said, "or he held out against even Dusk."

"A trained officer couldn't do that. This minstrel would have crumpled right away if he knew anything."

Ardoz indicated Allegra. "Would you have thought she could do what she's managed? Or that the fire opal priestess could have been so strong? These mages, they look soft and pretty, Ivan, but I think they have steel inside."

Bladebreak snorted, what sounded like disagreement. He kept her trapped between his legs, caressing her body whenever Ardoz wasn't looking. Allegra wanted to slap him, but she knew if she struck, he would hurt her, and she didn't think she could take any more. Ardoz continued to treat Drummer's wounds. From the last shreds of her spell, Allegra could tell his ministrations helped the prince.

Their contradictions drained her. Bladebreak, Yargazon, Zeik—they kept *touching* her, a caress or kiss, even their voices softening, as if they had a right to those intimacies, as if what they felt was affection—yet the threat of violence saturated their behavior. With Yargazon, the brutality was deliberate, but she didn't think the others even realized it. Bladebreak didn't think twice about stroking the consort of the prince regent while his own wife slept nearby. The imbalance in their culture, with so many men for every woman, sexualized everything. They acted as if they thought it gave their women an intolerable power over them. They couldn't see her as human, only as a threat.

What astounded her wasn't that Markus had absorbed those ideas, but that he tried to move past them. Maybe having known Ardoz helped him understand Allegra, because he had already once stepped outside the rigid constraints on love in his own culture.

Bladebreak idly slid his hand over Allegra's fist. Then he said, "Are you holding something?" He pried open her hand and took the dodecahedron. "What's this?"

"A good luck charm." Her pulse leaped. "Please don't take it."

"Why not? Maybe I should keep it."

"Ivan, give it back to her." Ardoz brushed the curls off his patient's forehead. "Drummer?" he asked. "Can you hear me?"

The prince stirred, but didn't open his eyes.

"If you wake up," Ardoz said, "I can give you some water."

Drummer's lashes lifted, then lowered.

Bladebreak held up the dodecahedron, examining the small block. "Why should I give anything back to her?"

Ardoz looked up at the shape—and Allegra knew with terrible certainty that he had either learned or deduced the truth about how she made spells. She felt dizzy with fear, for if he revealed her, she had no doubt Bladebreak would retaliate against the "witch."

"Ivan, stop tormenting her," Ardoz said. "Let her have the toy." With amusement, he said, "Unless you like playing with children's blocks."

"Very funny," Bladebreak said sourly. He pushed the block into Allegra's hand. She sagged with relief, afraid to look at Ardoz or do anything that might spur him to change his mind about revealing her.

Bladebreak motioned at Drummer. "Ask him about the army. Sometimes people talk when they're asleep."

Ardoz brushed the curls off Drummer's forehead. "Tell me, golden prince. What is kindle powder?"

"For saints' sake," Bladebreak said. "Ask something useful."

"You never know what will be useful." Ardoz spoke to Drummer in a soothing voice. "You can talk to me, princeling. I won't hurt you. Tell me about kindle powder."

Drummer shifted and murmured in his sleep.

"What was that?" Ardoz lowered his head. "Gum?"

"Gunpowder," Drummer mumbled. "Doesn't work…"

"Powder?" Bladebreak asked. "What, he needs women's cosmetics? He's not beautiful enough already?"

Allegra thought Drummer probably meant the gumpowder used in Aronsdale to make paste, but she kept quiet. Reminding them that he came from a country they despised wouldn't help him.

Ardoz massaged Drummer's neck under the spill of his curls. "What is gunpowder?"

"Called that…in old scrolls…tales of lost continent."

"He's telling us folktales," Bladebreak said. "How useful."

"Do you think your powder will ever work?" Ardoz asked Drummer.

"Someday…" Drummer sighed, and his breathing slowed as he sank deeper into sleep.

"Well, you see," Bladebreak said. "If he knew anything, Dusk would have had it out of him by now."

"I suppose." Ardoz moved down to Drummer's feet and began changing the bandages. When he uncovered the foot, Allegra cringed. In the shadows, she could just see the stump where his toe had been.

"This is bad," Ardoz said. "He needs a doctor."

"The army doesn't have a doctor," Bladebreak said.

"We can have one brought from the palace."

"Heh. That's right." Bladebreak gave a relieved laugh. "I keep forgetting we have their resources at our disposal." He rubbed his hand down Allegra's back. "We can't leave her without restraints, though. We'll take her to Dusk, see what he wants."

No. Allegra's sense of panic flared. She *couldn't* go back to Yargazon. She clenched the dodecahedron and the jagged edges of a spell skittered around her mind, slipping by, slipping by. She had the sleep song in her mind, but she needed to sing, to *hear* the words, and it would take time to build a spell once she began. But the moment she started, they would gag her.

Frantic, with a force driven by desperation, she sought the only person who had ever spoken to her of mages working together, perhaps the only person alive who could manage such a feat.

Jarid, help me! The plea burst out of her, and she *reached* with a strength that in normal times, she could never have done.

Nothing.

Please. She whispered the word in her mind. Then, frantic, she shouted the thought. *Please! Jarid, help me.*

Suddenly the song flooded her mind—and she understood. In his fourteen years of blindness, Jarid had achieved what no other mage had ever done—he could make spells simply by envisioning the shape rather than touching it. In his fourteen years of deafness, he had learned to hear in his mind as clearly as if he spoke aloud. He took her song and filled her with it. For one spectacular moment, her song and his power swelled together.

With a groan, Allegra released her spell. She thought she would explode into fragments, burn to ashes, blaze in a million fireworks. She could barely contain the immensity of the power he lent her. And in that instant of union, she thought, *Sleep.*

The world burst apart. Then the backlash of the spell hit Allegra and oblivion claimed her.

CHAPTER 26
THE SLEEPERS OF ALTAIR

Allegra lifted her head. The world was a blur. Gradually she realized she was lying against someone. Colonel Bladebreak. He had fallen to the side and lay sleeping, one of his legs under her and the other thrown across her body.

It took an effort to push him away and sit up. Drummer lay on his stomach, the blanket covering his hips and legs. Her stomach lurched at the blood that stained the bandage on his foot. But he was breathing more easily than before. Ardoz was sprawled on the carpet, fast asleep, his fingers tangled in the cloth he had used to clean his hand.

Allegra felt slowed and thick. She climbed to her feet, then swayed while nausea swept over her. How long had she slept? The tent was light as if the sun had risen. Weren't the armies supposed to be in battle? It had been close to dawn when Bladebreak and Ardoz found her. Surely by now someone had noticed them missing.

She limped to the entrance. Dimly, in the back of her mind, a thought surfaced. She should hide. But she couldn't hold on to the thought. The spell had scorched her mind, seared away her mage gifts and left her dull.

It was quiet outside. Nothing stirred. She saw no people or animals. From the position of the sun, dawn must have been at least an hour ago. She went down a row of tents and passed a sentry snoring on the ground. She kept going through a silent camp, past sleeping soldiers and still tents.

Eventually the tents thinned out, until she was limping across the desert. She had been walking in a haze, aware of only what lay in her path. Now she stared around. Behind her, crags and low hills sheltered the Jazid camp; in front of her, a barren plain stretched out. In the distance, the towers of glorious Quaaz gleamed like an enchanted city out of a mythological tale.

She kept going.

She reached companies of the Jazid army that had been forming up at the edge of the plain in the predawn hours. They were in armor, their swords ready—and they all lay on the ground, row after row of warriors. Asleep. Their horses stood by them. Asleep.

She kept going.

Her world narrowed to the pain in her feet and the relentless sun as it rose in the sky. Quaaz was located on the only large lake in Taka Mal, but she saw no sign here of the rivers that fed that vital body of water. The ground was packed hard by fighting that had already taken place. The armies had claimed their dead and injured, but she passed a crushed helmet here, a torn leather strap there, an empty water bag half buried under a rock.

She kept going.

And when she reached the Taka Mal army sprawled at the far edge of the basin, she limped among the sleeping men. All of them, rank upon rank upon rank. Sleeping.

She saw movement.

A man was walking among the Taka Mal warriors. Allegra stopped, uncertain what to do. She knew when he sighted her, for he called to another man and pointed toward her. She thought of running, but she had no idea where to go. She was on a plain. It had no place to hide. She couldn't run anyway. She could barely walk.

The two figures approached her.

It soaked into her mind that these men wore armor with the Harsdown jaguar on their breastplates. One stopped a short distance away and the other came closer, a burly fellow in his forties, with a wide face that gave him a stoic appearance. A shock of golden-brown hair fell down his neck. His expression was odd. It took a moment before she realized it seemed strange because of his concern. Nothing covetous. No submerged desire to inflict violence. No anger or hatred or lust or cruelty. Just concern.

"It's all right," he said gently. "I won't harm you."

Allegra backed up a step.

The man raised his hands as if to show her he had no weapons. He had a sword strapped across his back, however. Dully, she realized the warriors sleeping around them had curved swords. Curves and shapes…

"I'm Arkandy," the man said. "Sphere-Colonel Arkandy Ravensford, Harsdown Seventh Regiment."

She had no answer for that.

The other man joined Ravensford. With his dark hair and eyes, he could have been from anywhere: Misted Cliffs, Aronsdale, Shazire, Taka Mal, Jazid. He had the jaguar on his breastplate, though. He spoke to the colonel. "I called over the medical cart."

Medical cart. That stirred Allegra's memory. "Yes," she said. "For Drummer."

Both Ravensford and the other man stiffened. Ravensford said, "You know where we can find Drummer Headwind?"

"I can show you." She turned and stared across the basin at the distant bluffs where the Jazid army was camped. Had she truly walked all that way? Too far…never make it back…

Someone caught her as she fell.

"No." Allegra twisted away from his hands and crumpled to her knees. "Don't touch me."

Ravensford crouched down without touching her. He motioned to his right. "Can you climb in there?"

Numbly she looked up. A cart with a canvas roof and open sides waited a few paces away, with two oxen to pull it. Several Harsdown soldiers stood there, including one who wore a uniform instead of armor and mail. A patch on his shoulder showed the candle insignia that symbolized the medical corps.

Allegra tried to get up, but it hurt too much. Her vision blurred. Ravensford was watching her with a strange expression, as if he simultaneously wanted to comfort her and kill someone. He spoke kindly. "I won't touch you without your consent. No one will. I don't know who left those welts and bruises all over you, but believe me, no one here will do anything like that. We can help. If you can't get into the medical cart, I can carry you. But only if it's all right with you."

She trusted no one. But she didn't miss the contrast; Colonel Bladebreak's first response upon finding her was to embrace and fondle her, despite her protests and injuries. This colonel's first response was to express concern and ask her consent to help.

"Yes," she whispered. "Carry…"

Ravensford picked her up with one arm under her legs and the other around her back. He rose to his feet and carried her to the cart. As he laid her inside, under the shade of its roof, the doctor said, "She's the only conscious person we've found in the entire army."

"Maybe the Jazid army wasn't affected," Ravensford said. "I think this is Allegra Onyx. She and the atajazid were taken last night by Yargazon's men."

Allegra Onyx? That wasn't her name. She was Allegra Linseed. Or maybe Jazid men renamed their wives for themselves.

The doctor climbed into the cart and sat near Allegra while he opened a battered satchel. One of the soldiers climbed onto a plank seat at the front and prodded the oxen into motion. They didn't go very fast; Ravensford and the other soldier were able to walk alongside the cart.

When Allegra realized they were headed toward the foothills near Quaaz, she said, "Wait. No." She pulled into a sitting position, facing backward in the cart, and pointed toward the Jazid camp. "We have to get Drummer."

Ravensford held up his hand to the driver, and the other man brought the oxen to a halt. The colonel turned to Allegra. "Drummer is in the Jazid camp."

Her mouth felt dry. "We have to get him before they wake up."

The doctor made an incredulous noise. "They're asleep, too? Saints almighty, is *anyone* awake?"

"That's how I escaped." As Allegra's numbness was wearing off, she could feel her injuries. "No one was awake. I can show you where to find Drummer." Her voice caught. "If he doesn't see a doctor soon, he'll die." She feared it would be her fault, for she had put to sleep anyone who could have helped him.

Ravensford motioned to the driver, who brought the cart around. Soon they were headed across the sun-drenched basin toward the distant crags that sheltered the Jazid army. The doctor took bandages and bottles out of his satchel, but when he leaned toward Allegra, she shook her head. She couldn't bear to have anyone touch her. He started to protest, but whatever look she had on her face stopped him. He exhaled, then settled back and returned his potions to his satchel.

They continued on, but they were going slowly, much too slowly. "Are all the horses asleep?" Allegra asked. "We should bring Drummer out as fast as possible." She wanted to get Ozarson, too, but she doubted they could risk going after more than one person.

"Some of our horses are awake," Ravensford said. He thought for a moment. "A medical cart has immunity in many places during combat, but for us to go into the midst of the Jazid camp with you in the cart is too much of a risk. What if they wake up?" Then he added, "Or you could be lying, sent by one of your husband's generals to trick us."

"I'm not lying." She could see why he was worried, though. "But it's true, I don't know when they will wake up."

"How can thousands of people be asleep?" the doctor asked. "We can't wake anyone."

Thousands? Allegra finally began to comprehend what she was seeing. Had she and Jarid done this? She slumped back, her head falling against the pole that held up a corner of the canvas roof.

"Allegra?" Ravensford asked.

"Yes?" she asked.

"Then that is your name. You're the regent's consort."

"Is Markus all right?" It hurt to ask about him, given what had happened, for he was the one who allowed Yargazon free rein.

"He's fine," Ravensford said. "Just asleep."

"But…isn't he with Cobalt's army?"

The colonel regarded her steadily. "They're asleep. Cobalt's men, Jarid's, everyone. The Harsdown army was the farthest away, so whatever happened didn't affect all of us."

She lifted her head. "King Jarid is probably awake." If she had recovered early, he would, too.

"He wasn't when we left this morning."

"Neither was I. But I am now."

The colonel's forehead creased. "Why would that matter?"

She bit her lip, staring toward the distant hills. Then she said, "We did it."

"Did what?" the doctor asked kindly.

She looked at him. "I sang."

The doctor glanced at Ravensford, and the colonel shook his head, his expression puzzled.

"Many people sing," the doctor said.

"They were going to give me back to Yargazon." The words felt like broken glass to Allegra. "He had fourteen more hours he meant to work on me. And the others—they wanted—" Her voice cracked. "They were going to go out today and kill and kill and kill, because nothing ever stops them, nothing, and when they came back, Drummer and I would be the prizes, the spoils of war, and I couldn't take any more. So I—I—" She couldn't continue.

Ravensford stared at her. Then he thumped the driver's plank. The man guiding the oxen started, then brought the team to a stop.

"Tell me, Allegra," Ravensford said. "Tell me what you did."

"I used a shape I wasn't ready for. I sang a spell of sleep. Jarid added power. But it was too much. I broke."

The doctor stared at her. "Are you saying you did this with a *spell?*"

She met his incredulous gaze. "Yes."

"How could that be possible?" the doctor asked.

Ravensford spoke. "In extreme adversity, people can do incredible things. A man holds up the roof of a collapsing house to save his loved ones, a mother heaves away a huge boulder to rescue her child." Softly he said, "Perhaps a mage calls forth a power greater than she could normally handle."

Allegra could only say, "I don't know." She sagged against the pole, needing it to stay upright.

Watching her, Ravensford spoke to the doctor. "Take her back to the camp. She needs to see Jarid, if he's awake."

"No!" Allegra said. "We have to get Drummer."

"I'll go scout the Jazid camp," Ravensford said. "See what I can find out. Can you tell me how to reach Drummer?"

Allegra described his location as best she could. Her dazed walk through the Jazid camp was seared into her memory.

"Can he ride?" Ravensford asked.

"He's asleep." She thought of his torn body sprawled in the tent. "I don't think he could ride even if he were awake."

A muscle twitched in Ravensford's cheek. To the doctor, he said, "Send someone to help me, with the fastest horse you trust to carry an unconscious man. If the Jazid camp is asleep, we'll get Drummer. If they're awake, we'll come back."

"I should go with you," Allegra said.

"You must rest. Recover." In an oddly strained voice, the colonel said, "Regain your mage gifts."

Sadness tugged at Allegra. "I don't think I can."

"If you don't," he said, "who will awake the sleepers?"

With that, he set off for the Jazid camp.

Allegra passed out on the way to the Aronsdale camp. The next time she became aware, she was lying in a blurred gray and blue place. The day's heat blistered, but it receded when hands laid wet cloths across her fevered skin.

Jarid visited. He knelt by her pallet and spoke softly. She didn't understand, but his words were like cool water on her burning skin. He held his sphere, and his miraculous blue radiance filled her, a gentler, more nuanced spell than she had ever known. Her pain receded. The blue deepened into an impossible color, indigo, and the agony in her heart over Markus and Yargazon eased. Even an indigo couldn't take away emotional pain, but he helped her to heal. The world faded and sleep folded her into its softness.

The day had slipped into evening by the time Allegra awoke. She lay on her back gazing at the tent above her head. A blue tassel hung from the apex of its peaked roof. When she felt strong enough, she slowly sat up and looked around. A table across the tent had bandages, pots and fluted bottles, and a basin of water. Several other pallets lay on the floor, but it was a moment before she realized someone lay in one of them. A blue sheet covered him to the waist. He was on his stomach, his head turned away, but she recognized the yellow curls spilling down his neck.

She stood up carefully. Someone had changed her into a blue shift that came to her knees. Her welts had healed far more than should have been possible in less than a day, and the blisters and cuts on her feet didn't hurt nearly as much as before. She crossed the tent and knelt next to the man. Lash marks showed on his skin, but as with her welts, they had healed far faster than normal.

Allegra touched his shoulder. "Drummer?"

To her surprise, he turned onto his back. Now that she could see him in better light, she realized he had the classic Aronsdale blue eyes, said to be granted by Saint Azure himself. Long, gold eyelashes framed them, thick and curled. They were gorgeous. She hadn't realized just how handsome he was, even by the standards of her people. No wonder the queen of Taka Mal had wanted him.

"Who are you?" he asked. His voice rasped, and she flinched, knowing what had injured his vocal cords. Screams.

"My name is Allegra. I was Yargazon's prisoner, too."

"The green mage from last night?"

"You could tell? I thought you were unconscious."

"Mostly. But I knew you were there, offering comfort." Softly he said, "Thank you."

"I'm sorry I couldn't do more."

He gave a ragged laugh. "Jarid tells me you put thousands of people to sleep to get us out of that camp."

Including Drummer. "When did you wake?"

"About an hour ago."

"Are you all right?"

"Fine." He laid his arm behind his head, his elbow bent, and stared at the peaked roof where shadows were gathering. "My wounds will heal." He sounded listless.

She had a feeling it wasn't that simple. "And your voice?"

It was a moment before he answered. "I was a minstrel and an acrobat before Jade and I married. I suppose it's not the life for everyone, but I loved it. I used to sing to her. But now…I don't know. And with my foot like this—" He let out a breath. "At *least* I have the foot. If Jarid hadn't helped, the doctor says he would have had to amputate. Because of infection."

"I'm sorry," Allegra said. She understood well the grief of losing his songs. "Surely your voice will heal."

"Perhaps." His face gentled. "Hell, I'm free of Yargazon. And my wife and child are alive. That's what matters."

"I miss my family," Allegra said. "They don't even know what has happened to me." She hadn't yet had a chance to send them a letter. She couldn't imagine what they would think when they found out about her marriage. Drummer was one of the few people who would understand what she faced as the consort of a foreign sovereign. Now that he was safe and the immediate crisis was over, perhaps he would be willing to talk about it. If he could adapt to Taka Mal, hope might exist for her and Markus.

Allegra spoke awkwardly. "Would you mind if I asked about your marriage?"

He regarded her curiously. "What would you like to know?"

"Is it true the queen took you as her consort the same way my husband had me brought to Jazid?"

His grin flashed, and in that instant he turned into the epitome of the Aronsdale male, with his sunny appearance and sparkling eyes. She couldn't fathom why people in Jazid denigrated him. In Aronsdale, women had probably fallen all over themselves to catch his attention.

"I've no idea about your wedding," Drummer said good-naturedly. "But I doubt it was like mine. We had to sneak off in the middle of the night so no one could stop us."

"Then you went willingly?"

"Well, yes." He was watching her closely. "You didn't?"

"I was kidnapped in Aronsdale. They sold me."

Drummer grimaced. "Ah, yes. This barbaric penchant of theirs for stealing mates. They grabbed me at night." He gave her a crooked smile. "Maybe I should be insulted. Vizarana didn't pay anything for me. She just locked me up in a suite of the palace."

Allegra shuddered. "Don't be insulted. Believe me."

His smile faded. "I think maybe it wasn't the same for you."

"No," she said wanly. "It was a nightmare."

His voice quieted. "I was only a political prisoner."

"Did she take advantage of the situation?"

His devastating smile returned, but it was gentler this time. "I suppose. I never felt coerced. Her generals would undoubtedly say I took advantage of her." Mischief flashed in his eyes. "I kept trying to kiss her when I wasn't supposed to."

"She's a lucky woman."

"I'm glad someone thinks so." He grimaced. "So many of her people can't see beyond my having been her exotic Aronsdale prize. But I do love her."

Allegra didn't know how she felt about Markus. Thinking about him hurt too much. "Why do they hunt us? It's like we're prey."

A voice spoke behind them. "I would also like an answer to that question."

She looked around with a start. Jarid was walking over to them. Rather than armor, tonight he wore dark trousers and a blue shirt. He sat on the floor with them, with his elbow resting on his bent knee. He could have pulled over a stool, but he didn't seem inclined. Allegra would have never expected the king of her country to sit so casually on the ground.

"I didn't mean to eavesdrop," he said. "I heard you as I came in."

Drummer pushed up on his elbows, then winced and lay down. Allegra nodded to the king, unsure if she should bow when she was sitting in a medical tent. Jarid didn't look as if he cared. The strain on his face had aged him years in one night.

"Is everyone still asleep?" Drummer asked him.

"The armies are waking," Jarid said. "So far, no tragedies. The injuries are mostly dehydration and burns from the sun."

"The spell seemed so innocuous," Allegra said. Putting so many people to sleep for so long suddenly didn't look harmless. "Did you wake them?" she asked Jarid.

"I helped. They started coming to on their own about an hour ago." He tilted his head as he considered her. "I've never made a sleep spell before. How did you do it?"

"I'm not sure." It embarrassed her to explain her inadequate attempts to the greatest mage alive. "My husband suffers from insomnia. The first time, I was trying to help him. It's like offering comfort, but so much that the person falls asleep."

He gave a wry laugh. "It's certainly the most innovative way I've ever heard of stopping a battle."

Drummer pushed himself up, persisting this time until he was sitting on the pallet. He took a blue sleep shirt that was crumpled by his pillow and slipped it on, wincing as he pulled his arms through the sleeves. His legs were under the sheet with his bandaged left foot sticking out the end.

"You're moving better," Jarid said.

Drummer answered wryly. "Moving at all is an improvement."

Jarid glanced at Allegra. "How do you feel?"

"Tired. But better. Thank you for helping." She hesitated, then asked, "What happened with Yargazon?"

"Nothing that I know of," Jarid said. "We didn't risk trying to reach anyone else. A few people were already waking up."

"I would have gone after Yargazon anyway," Drummer said flatly. "And killed him."

Allegra understood his reaction, and he had endured far worse than she at Yargazon's hand. She didn't want the General dead; she wanted him to suffer. Endlessly. But not at Ozi's expense. "Is the atajazid all right?" she asked.

"I assume so," Jarid said. "He's still in the Jazid camp." He considered them both. "When the two of you are ready, we need to meet with the other army commanders."

"They're going to talk?" Allegra had been afraid to hope.

"A truce has been called. For now." Wryly he added, "You frightened a lot of people, Allegra. No one knows what you're going to do or who you're going to do it for."

"But I can't do any—"

He held up his hand. "Let them worry that you might. It's valuable for negotiations. And it will protect you." He tilted his head toward Drummer. "Both of you."

"Protect us?" Drummer asked uneasily. "Why?"

"I'm afraid it's true, what Allegra said," Jarid answered. "Aronsdale mages are no longer safe. It's my responsibility to see to your protection." Then he added, "Our protection."

Allegra couldn't imagine Jarid needing protection. A violet mage. Had he not refused to use his abilities in violence, he could have become a tyrant far crueler than Yargazon or Cobalt. He didn't need to put people to sleep—he could kill them.

"The days are gone when mages can go unnoticed," Jarid said. "We're no longer fables told to children at night. It started twenty years ago, during the war between Cobalt's father and myself. I brought down part of Castle Suncroft in the last battle. You can't hide that. Two years ago, Mel shattered the Rocklands with lightning. Then Baz Quaazera married the fire opal mage. Drummer, you try to hide what you do, but rumors are always swirling about you." He glanced at Allegra. "Your husband told me the specifics he and Yargazon gave the nomads for the woman they wanted. It was an exact description of a mage girl from southwestern Aronsdale. They may not have realized what they were seeking, but they knew your people existed and were valuable."

"Wait, slow down," Drummer said. "Her *husband* and Yargazon?" He stared at Allegra. "Who the blazes is your husband, that he associates with Jazid's most brutal war criminal?"

Allegra forced herself to meet his gaze. "Markus Onyx."

"Gods almighty." Drummer stared at her. "No wonder you're upset about the marriage."

Allegra flushed, unable to answer.

"He's asking to see you," Jarid told her.

"I can't," she said. "Not yet."

Jarid spoke quietly. "For what it's worth, Allegra, when he learned how we found you, he was ready to kill General Yargazon."

"He won't," she said. "Yargazon is the closest he has to a father now that his own is dead."

"Do you love him?" Jarid asked.

She wasn't certain why the king of Aronsdale cared, but after all he had done for her, she felt she should answer him. "I think so. But I can't live the way he does. If we were in Aronsdale, it would be different. I would have the support of the culture. But I can't imagine living in Jazid."

Drummer spoke. "Jarid, it's hard even for me, and I live in Taka Mal, which is less rigid than Jazid." Anger edged his voice. "Many people there don't see me as a man, because of the way I look. They think I'm not quite human, but some exotic colt their queen caught. They don't say it aloud, maybe they don't even admit it to themselves, but I've stopped making green spells when I'm with the royal court, because their reaction is so intense. And I'm not under the kind of pressure she would be in Jazid. It would be asking a lot of her."

Allegra stiffened as she looked at Jarid. "You *want* me to go with Markus?"

"Not unless you wish it. But it will come up in the summit." Jarid tilted his head toward Drummer. "His marriage established a treaty between Aronsdale and Taka Mal. You're in my custody, under my protection, a citizen of my country, and you married Jazid's prince regent. This morning you and I stopped a battle. Everyone will want to know if I'm considering a treaty with your husband."

"But if you have a truce," she said, "doesn't it mean neither you nor the Harsdown king has to decide whether or not to fight?"

"Only if the truce holds," Jarid said. "Unless we come to terms in this summit, the fighting will start again."

Drummer crossed his arms. "Taka Mal will never recognize the atajazid's claim to the Topaz Throne."

"And Cobalt won't relinquish the Onyx Throne," Jarid said tiredly. "I see no solutions, especially if General Yargazon is able to secure Quaaz."

Drummer's fist clenched in the blanket. "He's a war criminal. He should be executed."

"He's a war criminal because Cobalt declared him one," Jarid said. "Unfortunately, the only crime we can prove is that he cut off your toe. And even that isn't certain."

"You have my testimony," Drummer said. "Saints, man, you have my damn *toe.*"

"The evidence isn't the problem," Jarid said. "It's whether or not he broke laws."

Allegra couldn't believe it. "How can you say that after all he's done?"

"Because everything he's done is legal in Jazid." The king sounded as if he felt heavy. Weighed down. "His army has taken every Taka Mal town on their route to Quaaz. They've taken Quaaz. They claim to have taken the throne. If the atajazid can hold it, then Jazid rules here, which means the laws of Jazid hold."

"I was a political hostage," Drummer said tightly. "You don't maim and torture such prisoners."

"You're right, according to unwritten rules of war, we don't. But that's the key word—*unwritten*. He broke no actual laws." Jarid rubbed the heel of his hand over his eyes, then dropped his arm. "I've talked to Markus. He says the custom of returning a hostage in pieces hasn't been done for centuries, but he's certain it's still part of Jazid's legal code."

"That's appalling," Allegra said.

"Jazid doesn't rule here," Drummer said. "Yargazon may have forced my family to seek protection, but Baz Quaazera commands our army, and they haven't stopped fighting." Wryly he added, "Sleepy or not."

"Nothing about this situation is clear cut," Jarid said. "But some facts are painfully clear. Aronsdale is surrounded at every border, and our mages are becoming prey. Especially those like you and Drummer, from the southwestern regions."

"Why us?" Drummer asked. "Mages live in other places, too."

Jarid smiled slightly. "Don't either of you own a mirror?"

"Well, actually, no," Allegra said. Jasmine had thought it absurd she had no interest in looking in a mirror.

"Why would I want a mirror?" Drummer said. He was leaning on his hand, and Allegra could tell he was tiring. So was she.

"People covet you," Jarid said. "You're mages, you're sensual and you look helpless." He flicked his hand through his black hair as if showing it to them. "Almost everyone in the settled lands has darker coloring and more height than you. People associate those traits with strength, not only in Jazid, but everywhere. Gold hair, blue eyes, even violet—you find them only in southwestern Aronsdale. Your slender builds, gentleness, softness, the beauty of the women, and forgive me, Drummer, but the prettiness of the men—it makes you seem defenseless. People don't think of you as normal, and yes, maybe not fully human. It never caused problems during the generations of peace because no one noticed southern Aronsdale. You were insulated. But as our mages have become known, so has the desire of others to own you." His voice tightened. "I'll be damned if I let conquerors violate my country to take the most vulnerable of my people."

Allegra gaped at him, and Drummer turned red.

After a moment, Jarid spoke awkwardly. "Maybe I said too much."

"No. No, you didn't." Allegra found her voice. "I just can't see myself that way."

Drummer snorted. "I'm just a minstrel, Jarid."

The king spoke quietly. "And I'm just a blind, deaf, mute boy who grew up in a hut. But whatever we are, tomorrow we must be more for this summit of sovereigns."

THE NIGHT BIRD

★ ★ ★

Allegra stepped outside the medical tent into a cool night beneath a canopy of stars veiled by translucent clouds. Two guards flanked the entrance, though whether to protect or imprison her, she didn't know. Both were tall and broad, and wore armor with the crossed swords of Aronsdale on their breastplates. Their plumed helmets covered their upper faces, leaving only their chins visible. It unsettled her; she had never realized how much she relied on expressions to help her understand people. When she couldn't see their faces, they became more intimidating.

"Princess Allegra?" one of the men asked. "Can we help you?"

"I would like to see my husband." She had tried to sleep, unable to face him, but her tangle of emotions had only grown worse, until it drove her out here.

The guards exchanged glances, and the other man nodded. The one who had spoken said, "I'm Major Lachlan. I'll take you."

"Thank you," Allegra said softly. She didn't miss the difference between the kindness of these Aronsdale guards and the severity of Cobalt's grizzled captain from the Misted Cliffs.

She walked with Lachlan through the night, her feet protected by soft slippers. Lights showed here and there from torches or cooking fires, but the camp was mostly dark. Sounds drifted: the murmur of soldiers discussing a game of color-stones, the clank of a cook stowing a cauldron, the sizzle of water on a fire. Some people glanced her way, but most ignored her. As far as anyone knew, she was just another tender on an errand.

When they reached a blue tent with a peaked roof, Lachlan stopped. Two soldiers stood by its entrance, as imposing as the two outside the medical tent. Lachlan spoke with them in low tones, but she caught, "Onyx consort" and "visitation rights."

Lachlan turned to Allegra. "They'll take you in. If you wish to return to medical, one of them will take you back."

Allegra nodded her thanks. She didn't know the protocols for royal consorts yet, but her response seemed to satisfy him. A guard lifted the tent flap for her, and she went inside. The tent was similar to the one where she and Markus had slept before, with a table, two stools, a pallet and braziers in two corners. Markus was seated at the table with his dinner set out on pewter plates. He had a mug halfway to his lips, but when she entered, he slowly set it down.

She stopped in the center of the tent. "Markus—"

He stood carefully, as if she were a skylark doe that would bolt at the slightest provocation. Dark rings showed under his eyes, and his hair was a mess, as if he had raked it with his hands many times. He started to come around the table, then hesitated, watching her uncertainly. She also started toward him, but stopped almost immediately. Finally he let out a breath and walked over to her.

"I'm glad you came," he said.

Allegra laid her hand against his chest, the cloth of his shirt soft under her palm. She wished she could feel his heartbeat.

Markus put his hand over hers. "Gods, Allegra, if I could take into myself the pain of what he did to you, if I could free you from that anguish, I would do it a hundred times over."

"I didn't—" Her voice broke as she reached for him. He drew her into his arms, and they stood embracing, his touch so very, very careful with her injuries. She closed her eyes while her body shook with the silent tears she had pent up all day.

He kept whispering "I'm sorry" over and over.

When her tears spent themselves, she pushed back, her palms on his chest. "Markus, I'll never be able to be around him. If you go back—" She couldn't say any more.

"I'll protect you, I swear."

"You can't always! And I shouldn't have to live needing that protection." Her hands clenched, and the rich material of his shirt crumpled in her fists. "You can't abhor the cruelty in Dusk Yargazon and yet let him vanquish countries in your name."

He caught her hands. "The world isn't drawn in such easy shades of light and dark."

A tear slid down her cheek. "As long as he remains your right hand, I cannot live with you as your wife." She wanted to hold him, touch his strong body, inhale his scent. Instead she released his shirt and dropped her arms by her sides. "Each day you allow him to continue as the power behind your reign, you become more of him and less of what is best within you." In a ragged voice, she said, "You could be a great leader, Markus. I won't be the excuse a demon like Yargazon uses, in his craving for power, to destroy a good man."

"You want me to deny what I am." He lifted her hand to his cheek. "I'm a prince of the desert, not of your lush, rolling Aronsdale. Make no mistake, Allegra—Yargazon *will* pay for what he did to you. But I need him. Look at what he accomplished, starting from nothing, with the emperor set against him." Softly he said, "I would conquer a world for you, night bird, but I cannot stop being what defines me."

"You're more than you know." Her voice caught. "But you'll never find out as long as he darkens your life."

His gaze never wavered. "The darkness is already in me."

"It shadows you, maybe even adds to your strength. But it doesn't define you." She willed him to hear, really *hear* her. "If you continue with him anywhere, I can't go with you."

"Allegra, don't say that."

"Yargazon told me things last night." Her voice cracked. "He'll never rest until he takes me from you. Until he owns all of me, my body, my spirit, my will, my soul. He wants me broken and on my knees. I *will not* live in fear of the man you turn to as your greatest strength."

His gaze darkened. "He'll never have you."

"Why does he hate me so much?"

"He doesn't. You threaten him. The dragon knows, he would never admit it, but I think he's afraid of you." He took both of her hands. "You challenge him. You refuse to submit. That's why he wants to break you. But I swear, he'll never hurt you again."

"How can you swear that? It's impossible." She felt as if her chance for a life with Markus was slipping through her fingers like the sand in Yargazon's hourglasses. "No matter how much you refuse to see it, he's hurting *you*. Destroying you." She made herself say what she had come to tell him. "Tomorrow, at the summit, I will stand with you. But when all is decided and done, I won't live where your general holds sway."

"You're my wife. You must go with me."

She let go of his hands. "You can't take me against my will, not with the Aronsdale army here."

His face turned cold in a way she had never seen before. "Do you think to marry the son of your king?"

"Markus, don't."

He was staring as if she were a will-o'-the-wisp that would disappear any moment. Although he spoke with anger, she heard the pain under his words. "As long as I live, no other man will call you his wife. I'll never release you from the contracts."

Allegra felt as if she were breaking in two. Talking to him hurt too much. Softly she said, "Then I'll live my life alone."

She turned and left then, before her heart could shatter.

CHAPTER 27
THE LOST CONTINENT

In the sharp clarity of a desert morning, in legendary Quaaz, the warlords gathered. They came from five lands: Aronsdale, with its rolling hills and lush meadows; Harsdown, a place of cool autumns and apple orchards; Taka Mal, where ancient legends saturated the land; Jazid, with its starkly beautiful mountains spearing the sky; and the Misted Cliffs, whose emperor had reached out the long arm of his power from the snowy cliffs of his home to the burning deserts.

By mutual agreement, they met in the Topaz Palace, in the Hall of the Dragon-Sun, nominally hosted by the royal House of Taka Mal, though the Quaazeras were in exile from their own city. Every leader from the assembled armies attended, with no exception, to ensure none tried to kill the others. The Hall gleamed like a sunrise. Gold-veined pillars bordered the room. Arched windows spanned the walls, and sunlight poured across a floor tiled in red and gold. Outside, the fabled gardens exploded with color. Blossoms spilled out of flower beds and trailed over trellises and stone arches.

Fountains sculpted like dragons breathed arches of priceless water instead of fire.

King Jarid entered the hall with his retinue, austere in dark trousers and a white shirt. His hair grazed his shoulders, thick and streaked with gray, but it didn't hide the scar on his neck. Prince Aron walked at his side, the same height as Jarid, broader in the shoulders, brown hair curling over his ears. Hale and strong, bursting with youth, his face unmarred by life's pain, he was the ultimate Dawnfield heir. Watching him with a mage's sense, though, Allegra wondered if he would rather be practicing spells than sitting in a war council.

Allegra entered with Markus and four guards. They took their places at the far end of the great oval table and stood next to their chairs, with Jarid between Allegra and Aron. The Dawnfield prince glanced at her and flushed, then looked away as if it hurt to see her. Maybe she was naive to think they would have matched each other so well. But they would never know. Impossible as it seemed, she loved her husband. She could neither stop what she felt for Markus nor become a woman of Jazid. She saw no more hope for the two of them than she did for a peace settlement.

Markus stood next to her, his gaze burning with a wildness nothing could tame. He wore dark clothes instead of armor, but nothing could disguise the warlord within him. Next to the men of Aronsdale, his fierce presence simmered.

King Muller led the Harsdown retinue. Dawnfield violet and gold edged his white surcoat, though it bore the jaguar emblem on the chest. Muller wore Dawnfield colors because he had no claim to the colors of the House of Escar, which had ruled Harsdown before him. Ebony and blue symbolized the House of Escar. Cobalt-blue: It was what gave the emperor his name.

Colonel Arkandy Ravensford, the man who had found Allegra among the sleeping army yesterday, came with Muller. A gray-haired man walked on Muller's other side, someone so well-known, even Allegra recognized him. Sphere-General Samuel Fieldson, formerly of Aronsdale, now commander of the Harsdown forces.

When the queen of Taka Mal entered, the force of her presence blazed. To say Vizarana Jade Quaazera was arresting was akin to saying the lava in an erupting volcano was warm. She wore a gold silk tunic and trousers, with a dagger at her belt. Weapons were forbidden at the summit, but no one challenged her. She raked her gaze over every man in the room as if sizing them up and discarding the results. Allegra wondered if it had occurred to all those kings in Taka Mal and Jazid who were so intent on choosing wives to give them strong, fierce, powerful sons that they might end up with strong, fierce, powerful daughters instead.

Drummer entered with Vizarana, his appearance far different than when Allegra had last seen him. He wore gold trousers and a light shirt with topazes on the cuffs. His yellow hair gleamed. Although he walked with crutches, he moved with a natural agility that made Allegra suspect it wouldn't be long before he recovered. Compared to all the brooding lords here, he was sunlight. If he felt self-conscious entering this place of towering warriors, he gave no sign.

Two Taka Mal generals flanked the queen and Drummer. The older man with silvered hair dazzled in his red and gold uniform, with a sash across his chest that bore five disks enameled in sunrise colors. The other general looked so much like Vizarana, he could have been her brother. But she had no siblings, which meant he was almost certainly Baz Quaazera, her cousin, the commander of her armed forces. Given the pride that blazed in his eyes, Allegra doubted he would ever rest until he took back the Topaz Throne for the queen—or died in the effort.

The Jazid warlords came next.

The Taka Mal retinue had just stopped by their chairs when the color suddenly drained from Drummer's face. Following his gaze, Allegra felt as if ice formed within her. Yargazon was entering with Ardoz and Bladebreak. She wanted to bolt from the room, and it took a great effort of will to remain.

Yargazon regarded her coldly—and with satisfaction. Her clothes covered the welts he had left on her body, but he knew she felt that measure of his revenge.

The General glanced at Drummer, and the prince stared back, his hands clenched on his crutches. In that instant, Allegra wondered how Markus could live with himself, giving Yargazon free rein. Fast on the heels of that thought came another: How had Markus turned into a decent human being given the father figures in his life? Maybe good existed in Yargazon and Ozar, but Allegra knew Ozar Onyx only by his deeds, and she would never see anything but Yargazon's brutality.

Markus, too, was staring at the General. To anyone else, his face may have looked impassive, but Allegra saw the tightening of his lips, the twitch of his eyelid. It had to be excruciating, knowing he could be condemned to death for what Yargazon had done. She had little doubt Vizarana would demand Markus's execution, and Cobalt still wanted him dead.

It wasn't until she heard Markus's indrawn breath that she looked at the other men with the General. No, not the men—

The boy.

Like his father before him, Ozarson dressed in black. His dark hair gleamed. Allegra didn't know if the other leaders here had expected him to attend, given his young age, but she felt certain Yargazon had tried to forbid it. With Markus as a hostage, no one could override the General's authority except Ozarson. The boy must have insisted, which meant he had stood up to Yargazon.

The atajazid regarded the gathered leaders, and they stared back at him. Allegra saw wariness in their expressions, hostility, and curiosity, too, about a child no one had seen for two years, while speculation about him ran rife. When Ozarson saw Markus and Allegra, his shoulders lowered the slightest bit, as if he had tensed for a blow and now realized it wouldn't come. She wondered if the others here sensed the power in this boy, the signs of the formidable man he could someday become. It already showed in the lift of his strong chin, the confidence of his posture as he took his place at the table and the intelligence in his eyes.

Then Cobalt entered—and the room seemed to shrink.

Almost seven feet tall, with a massive physique, he towered over even the Jazidians. He wore his black hair in a warrior's queue, and he had on dark clothes with no adornment except a jaguar in dark blue on his belt. General Cragland came with him and other officers Allegra didn't know. It didn't matter who they were. Cobalt's presence dominated the room.

They were all gathered then, standing by high-backed chairs, Aronsdale at the far end of the table, Harsdown to their right, Taka Mal on their left, with Jazid and the emperor toward the other end. Bodyguards for every leader stood around the walls, towering, imposing. Daunted, Allegra realized that except for Vizarana, who had a lifetime of dealing with these people, she was the only woman.

Cobalt spoke in his impossibly deep voice. "Let us begin."

Everyone took their seats, clothes rustling. The emperor settled back, one elbow resting on the arm of his chair, and said, "We are met today to decide who will hold the Topaz Throne."

"The Topaz Throne is already held," Vizarana said. "By me."

"How odd, then," Yargazon mused, "that my soldiers occupy your palace while you, your child and your cousin's consort are with the Aronsdale army." He glanced at Drummer as if just remembering his existence. "Oh, and him, too."

Drummer's fist clenched on the table. Vizarana's hand dropped to her dagger as her gaze stabbed at the General. Yet neither she nor Drummer lost their calm.

Baz Quaazera leaned forward. "Your soldiers may be in the Topaz Palace, Yargazon, but they're losing on the battlefield. It's a lot easier to occupy a building than a country."

General Ardoz gave him a sour look. "The last I saw, General Quaazera, your fearsome troops were asleep."

"A trait seemingly shared by yours," Muller Dawnfield said. "When my men rode into your camp yesterday, your infamous Jazidian warriors were out like babies."

Everyone at the table glanced uneasily at Allegra. The queen considered her, then let her gaze travel over the others until it came to rest on Cobalt.

"You have a price on General Yargazon's head," Vizarana told him. She jerked her head at Markus. "And on his. Well, you have them both. Carry out their sentences. Execute them."

"Prince Markus is in my custody," Jarid said sharply. "If you plan to kill him, you'll have to go through me first."

General Cragland spoke from his chair on the emperor's right. "Everyone here is under the protection of the Alatian Codes of War. No one can be imprisoned, attacked or killed at this summit." He regarded Markus, then Yargazon. "Not even those under a death sentence."

Although he didn't say, *Even those who deserve it,* the words seemed to hang in the air. Markus sat listening, his face as cold as the first time Allegra had seen him.

Baz Quaazera spoke to Yargazon. "Look at the numbers. You have, what? Four thousand men, counting the Jazid deserters." He let the word "deserters" curdle on his tongue. "I have two thousand, and Aronsdale and Harsdown together brought over three thousand. The emperor has another two, in addition to the thousand already here. That's eight thousand."

Yargazon didn't look in the least daunted. "Three thousand Dawnfield," he mused. "To fight for whom? And what do we have? Four thousand Jazid, two thousand Taka Mal. Six thousand total. Three thousand Dawnfield and three thousand from the emperor also makes six thousand. An interesting balance, there."

No one answered. Allegra didn't envy the queen her decision. Her forces alone couldn't defeat Yargazon. If Cobalt's men joined hers, along with Aronsdale and Harsdown, they had a good chance of defeating Yargazon, but Cobalt would then move his men into the palace. Unless Aronsdale and Harsdown were willing to challenge him, he would take the Topaz Throne. But if the queen formally relinquished the throne to Ozarson and joined forces *with* Jazid, it would swell their ranks enough to defy Cobalt.

It was excruciating. Allegra feared that if they couldn't reach a decision here, the Dawnfields would stand by and let Jazid keep the throne. Yargazon would win. She hated that he had set it up so well; she wanted him to fail so much, it burned inside her. But he had a good chance of achieving everything he and Markus had set out to do.

Two unplayed cards remained on the table. The first was Markus. Whatever her husband might think, Allegra knew Yargazon wanted him back. Cobalt could claim the Onyx Throne and enforce that claim with his army from now until the end of time, but to the Jazid people, Markus was their true ruler until Ozarson came of age. Jazid needed him as a rallying figure, a leader, a symbol that the royal house continued. Nor was it only political; as much as Yargazon was capable of loving a son, he felt that way about Markus. But he would have to negotiate the prince regent's release, which put Jarid Dawnfield in a powerful position.

The second card was the mages who had come with the armies. Allegra knew she could do nothing more to affect the war. Nor did Drummer have that level of power. Jarid did, but he wouldn't use it in violence. Iris was a healer, and Aron was still learning. But she wondered if anyone besides the mages themselves realized those limitations. Yesterday everyone had seen what looked like proof of a new mage force. She wasn't certain how they could use that card, but it had to be worth something.

Baz Quaazera spoke. He had a powerful voice; even his quiet tones reached every corner of the room. "The question of these war crimes must be decided before we go any further."

"We are shielded here under the Alatian Code," Yargazon said.

"Only until the summit finishes," Vizarana said. Her voice could have chilled ice. "You would do well to remember that."

Ardoz leaned forward. "Are you suggesting something illegal has transpired, Your Majesty?"

No, Allegra thought. She didn't think she could bear it if they discussed what had happened to Drummer or to her. She doubted Yargazon cared that he transgressed against the moral codes of those he tortured; in his view, she and Drummer weren't human.

General Cragland spoke. "The legalities depend on what

legal code you apply. And that depends on what country rules Taka Mal."

Allegra let out a breath, and she felt Markus shift next to her. An unsettled stir went around the table. It all came back to the standoff: they had to determine who supported whom.

Then Ozarson spoke. "No, it doesn't."

Surprise at the interruption flashed on Yargazon's face and his mouth tightened. But he spoke smoothly. "His Majesty has taken the throne of Taka Mal, so the question of who rules is moot." He glanced at the boy. "Perhaps you would allow your humble servants to discuss—"

"No." Ozarson stood his ground, but Allegra could tell that under his composure, he was scared. He spoke to Drummer. "Your Highness, I greatly regret you came to ill use while a guest of my House. I hope we may in some way offer compensation for the misuse of our pol-political protocols." He stumbled over the last words as if he wasn't sure what fit the situation.

Everyone stared at the boy. A muscle twitched in Yargazon's cheek. He sat forward, one fist clenched on the table.

"You speak well, Your Majesty," Drummer said. Wryly he added, "Perhaps in compensation, you might direct your armies to withdraw from Taka Mal."

Ozarson actually smiled. Before he could respond, Yargazon cut him off. "His Majesty has had a difficult time these past few days." He glanced at Ozarson. "We can discuss this later."

The boy started to speak, and Yargazon's face hardened. Biting his lip, Ozarson fell silent.

Jarid spoke. "Whether or not compensation can be offered to one hostage won't change the situation for others."

Allegra could almost feel Markus tensing next to her. They all knew which "other" hostage Jarid meant. The prince regent.

Yargazon spoke to Jarid. "Perhaps we should discuss—"

"No." Markus's voice rumbled. "The question of compensation must be settled. As Ozarson's regent, that task comes to me."

Allegra could almost hear the words he didn't add to Yargazon: *Not to you.*

"You don't appear in a position to settle anything," General Cragland told Markus. Cobalt sat next to the general, seemingly at ease, his booted foot crossed over his knee, his elbow resting on the arm of the chair. Allegra didn't believe he was anywhere near as relaxed as he appeared. She doubted he missed a single detail here. She prayed to Saint Azure her husband took care with his words. Even if she never saw him again, she wanted him to live.

Markus glanced at Jarid, and the king inclined his head in a subtle agreement that the prince regent should continue. Markus addressed the others at the table. "The Rite of D'Azare dates from a thousand years ago. It's been centuries since anyone invoked it, but in Jazid it's legal."

"What the hell is a right of Dalkazarre?" Baz growled.

"D'Azare," Markus said, with the glottal scrape in his throat native only to Jazid. "Sending your hostage back in pieces. One of my ancestors, the Atajazid D'Azare, began the practice."

Drummer stiffened, and Vizarana's gaze narrowed at Markus. "You've a charming family history," the queen said sourly.

Markus continued in a neutral voice. "If negotiations led to an arrangement deemed satisfactory to the army, and the hostage was still alive, he was returned to his people. Whatever remained of him. If he had died, his body was sent back to his kin."

Allegra felt ill. Could she truly be married to someone who descended from such a line? He had nothing to do with the brutality of his ancestors, but his total lack of emotion as he described their actions chilled her.

"Do you have a purpose in relating this grisly story?" Muller asked. "I don't see how this helps your position."

"Compensations existed for those injured in the rite," Markus said, "if it was later determined the codes of war were violated."

Ozarson jumped to his feet. "Markus, no!"

"What the hell?" Baz said.

Ozarson started around the table toward Markus—a blatant violation of the boundaries that the delegations had all established—and every bodyguard in the room went on alert.

Yargazon grabbed him. "Ozi, no," he said in a low voice. "Stay here." He nudged Ozarson back into his chair.

"I don't understand," King Muller said, looking from Ozarson to Markus. "What sort of compensation are you suggesting?"

"He isn't," Yargazon said shortly.

"Markus, that wasn't what I meant," Ozarson said.

"I know," Markus answered. "But your instincts are right." His voice had the warmth that always came when he spoke with the boy. It didn't surprise Allegra, but she saw shock register on the faces of the others present. None of them had reason to have seen his gentler side.

"I forbid it," Yargazon said.

Markus slammed his palm down on the table so fast, several people jumped. "You forbid nothing! Or shall I exact compensation for what you did to my *wife?*"

"It is I who am owed compensation," Yargazon ground out. "Fourteen more hours."

Shrivel up and rot, Allegra thought at him.

"Prince Markus," Vizarana said. "Just what compensation do you offer my husband?"

Markus cleared his throat and took a breath. "I believe the appropriate procedure would be that King Jarid offers it to you."

Jarid cocked an eyebrow at him. "Perhaps you might enlighten me as to what I'm offering Her Majesty."

"Balance," Cobalt said suddenly. "That's it, isn't it? Yargazon had a hostage. But so does Jarid. Yargazon mutilated his hostage." He motioned toward Jarid as he spoke to Markus. "The compensation is that Jarid do the same to you, yes?"

Markus's gaze never wavered. "That's right."

"Now wait a minute!" Drummer said.

Vizarana's eyes blazed. "Fine. I accept the terms. Cut off the prince regent's toe and send it to me in a box."

"I concur," Baz rumbled.

"Saints, no," Allegra said. Had her words in the tent last night forced Markus to this?

"Hold on!" Jarid said. "I haven't agreed to anything."

"Compensation has been offered," Vizarana said. "And accepted."

"No!" Ozarson said. "Take mine!" He jumped up, his face flushed, and turned to Vizarana. "Your M-Majesty, the responsibility for the army is mine. So should be the—the compensation."

"Ozi, no," Markus said, rising to his feet. "No one is going to cut off part of your foot." He looked as upset as when he had raged at Allegra for kidnapping the boy.

"The crime was done in my name," Ozarson said.

"Your Majesty." Yargazon laid his hand on the boy's arm. "Please. Sit. The terms can't include you." He didn't look any happier than Markus about this development, but Allegra noticed he didn't offer himself in their place.

"For saints' sake," Jarid said. "I would never do that to a child."

Ozarson took a breath and settled on the edge of his chair, his hands clenched on the table. Markus sat down, as well, in almost the exact same position.

Jarid frowned at Vizarana. "You truly want me to do this?" He tilted his head toward Markus. "As he offers?"

Drummer started to speak, then stopped when Baz shook his head.

The queen met Jarid's gaze. "Yes."

Cobalt was frowning, but Allegra didn't see why. The situation would have little impact on what happened with his part in the war, and he had no love for Markus. To put it mildly.

Then again, maybe it did have significance. Cobalt didn't want the queen to ally with Jazid. If this gruesome "compensation" appeased her anger, she might consider the unpalatable option of joining with the army that had invaded her country.

"Surely there are other terms you would accept," Jarid said.

Vizarana motioned toward Allegra. "Her."

Allegra blinked. "What?"

"No!" Markus said. "She had nothing to do with what happened to your husband."

"I don't want her damn toe," Vizarana said. "Just her time."

Allegra couldn't fathom this turn of events. "But why?"

"I want to talk to you," Vizarana said. "In private."

"No," Markus told her.

"It's out of the question," Yargazon said.

"It seems General Yargazon and I are actually in agreement on something," Cobalt said. "I also say no."

Allegra was growing annoyed. "It isn't for any of you to say yes or no. If my speaking with Her Majesty will keep my husband in one piece, I'll do it."

"Then it's settled." Vizarana leaned forward in preparation for standing. "We can meet now."

"Nothing is settled." Markus scowled at her. "You will tell me what you want with my wife."

Vizarana turned her fierce gaze on him. "I don't answer to your demands, Onyx, any more than I answered to your father."

"No, you just betrayed your alliances," Yargazon said. "Maybe you intend to suggest the prince regent's wife do the same?"

Allegra felt as if she were a leaf tossed in the currents of their intrigues. "I'm agreeing to a discussion. No more."

Markus spoke in a low voice meant only for her. "Don't."

"I should see what she wants," she said softly.

Jarid was the only one near enough to hear them, but everyone seemed uncomfortable. Yargazon's anger practically flamed in the air. Allegra didn't know what to think. She saw no solution to this mess except war and death.

Vizarana escorted Allegra down a pathway with trees arched overhead. Guards from Aronsdale and Taka Mal followed at enough distance to allow them some privacy. They entered a garden where vines heavy with fire-lilies looped over trellises. Cat sculptures peeked out from among trees, and a small waterfall burbled beneath an arch of stone. It was extraordinarily lush for the desert.

"This is lovely," Allegra said, self-conscious with the queen. "Except for the Saint Verdant, I haven't seen so much water since coming to Jazid."

"We're fortunate here," Vizarana said. "The water comes from the lake."

"Ah." Allegra felt strange, making small talk while four armies hulked around the city.

The queen sat on a stone bench by the waterfall and waited while Allegra settled on the other end. Then she said, "This spell, putting so many people to sleep—you can't do it regularly, can you?"

Although Jarid hadn't actually asked her to lie, Allegra knew he didn't want anyone to know. She said only, "I've made sleep spells often." That was true. Sort of.

The queen raised her eyebrows. "For thousands of people?"

She exhaled, unable to lie. "No."

"Drummer thinks you did it in desperation, to save him and yourself, and that it destroyed your ability to do spells."

Allegra didn't want to dwell on what she had lost. She could no more imagine living without her spells than being blind. "Maybe someday it will come back."

Vizarana spoke quietly. "My husband would have died. You gave him back to me, at great cost to yourself. You forever have my gratitude."

Allegra nodded, unsure how to respond. Vizarana didn't seem to expect an answer, though. She considered Allegra. "Tell me what you think of this boy, Ozarson."

"He's a remarkable young man." Allegra smiled. "It would probably embarrass him to hear me say this, but he's very sweet. Brave. Incredibly smart."

"That's an odd description for an Aronsdale woman to give of a Jazid man." Wryly the queen said, "Even one who's only nine."

"I doubt Ozi will ever be like his father," Allegra said. "But what happens in the next eight or so years will make a dramatic difference. If Markus raises him without Yargazon's influence, I think Ozi could become an inspired leader. If Yargazon raises him, especially without Markus—" She shook her head. "So much depends on Markus. But no matter how much he abhors Yargazon's personal behavior, I don't see him repudiating the General."

Vizarana grimaced. "I don't suppose you could put Yargazon to sleep permanently." When Allegra gave her a startled look, the queen sighed. "Maybe not."

"He is—" Allegra couldn't think of anything tactful to add, so she said nothing more.

Vizarana rose to her feet and paced to the waterfall. "Prince Markus is a hostage of your king." She turned to Allegra. "Maybe he should become a hostage in Taka Mal instead."

Allegra couldn't imagine Jarid turning Markus over to the queen, especially given that Vizarana wanted Markus dead. She said only, "I don't follow you."

"Jarid could release Markus into custody of my House," Vizarana said. "You would be free to live here with your husband, if you wished, without the threat of Dusk Yargazon. Ozarson would relinquish the Topaz Throne but live here, as a hostage rather than a sovereign."

Allegra couldn't believe she so blithely suggested the impossible. For all that the hosting of such political "guests" had a long history in the settled lands, she saw no motivation for anyone to agree to such an arrangement in this case.

"It seems unlikely," she said.

"A few days ago, I would have agreed," Vizarana said. "I'm no longer sure." She rested her hand on a sculpture of the Dragon-Sun with its wings spread wide. "I would *never* have expected Ozar's sons to offer that ancient compensation, or for the boy to insist on taking his regent's place." She turned to Allegra. "I spoke at length with Jarid last night, and he has said similar about how they surprise him."

"That may be," Allegra said. "But I can't imagine they would relinquish the throne or have Markus come here."

"Don't be certain." Vizarana studied her. "I need you to answer a question. You must think with great care before you do."

"Yes?"

"This boy. Ozarson. If he were to grow up here, with you and Markus as his guardians, without Yargazon—would he become a man of good character? A decent man."

Allegra didn't hesitate. "Yes." But she had to add, "If Yargazon can hold Ozarson's claim to the Topaz Throne, he would never leave Ozi alone here with Markus and me."

"My throne," Vizarana said flatly, "is not up for claiming." She tilted her head toward the hills where their armies camped. "We have by no means lost this war."

"It will be ugly no matter what happens," Allegra said quietly. "If Jazid loses, there is still the emperor."

"Maybe." Vizarana watched her intently. "What if Prince Markus had reason to relinquish this claim on the Topaz Throne?"

Allegra couldn't imagine any reason. "He won't."

"For the sake of argument, suppose he did. Yargazon would have to take his army back to Jazid. Cobalt must leave Taka Mal then. He can't declare war on me without provocation. The Dawnfield armies would join us against him. *That* instance is specifically in my treaty with Aronsdale."

"Why would Yargazon take his army home?"

"If the prince regent orders it, he must comply."

"Even if Markus relinquished Quaaz—which I can't see happening—his army has taken other villages in Taka Mal."

"Terms would have to be worked out," Vizarana acknowledged.

Allegra shook her head. "My husband won't send Yargazon home."

"And if I gave him a good enough reason?"

"What reason?"

Vizarana gazed at the spires and bulb towers of her palace. Softly she said, "Dragon-Sun guide me."

Allegra waited, wondering what drove the submerged conflict she sensed in the queen.

Vizarana turned to her. And then she said, "If my daughter and Ozarson are betrothed now and marry when they come of age, it will meld the Houses of Quaazera and Onyx. Ozarson would never sit on the Topaz Throne, just as Cobalt will never sit on the Harsdown Throne. But a child born to my daughter and Ozarson would rule Taka Mal." She regarded Allegra steadily. "If Prince Markus will accept this arrangement and agree to let Ozarson live here, we can avert a war no one but Yargazon and your husband wants. The Topaz Throne will stay in my line *and* go to Onyx." In a low, fierce voice, she said, "And someday my House may raise an army that *no one* on this Lost Continent can withstand."

A chill went up Allegra's back. She suddenly remembered Ozarson standing at the rail of the ferry, his hair blowing back from his face. In that moment, she had seen not a boy, but a king beyond all others.

She mentally shook herself. That "premonition" had probably been born of fatigue more than anything else. She understood Vizarana's logic—and her anguish. The queen wished happiness for her child. If Ozarson were his father's son, Vizarana would no more want her daughter married to him than she had wanted to become Ozar's queen.

Yargazon would never agree. But Markus? A tendril of hope crept into her thoughts, then shriveled. The General's hold on Markus was too great. Or maybe it was true, what Markus had told her last night, that she wanted him to be someone other than who he was or desired to be.

So many questions needed answers. She hardly knew where to begin. "What did you mean by the Lost Continent?" she asked.

"Surely you've heard the tales," Vizarana said. "Supposedly an ancient mage cursed these lands. Each century we would become more hidden from the world, until one day we would be forever cut off. Some people think it's already happened."

Allegra had never thought much of the legend. She remembered Drummer's mumbled words to Ardoz about a lost continent. "It seems an odd thought."

"Our priestess finds many odd tales buried in the archives." The queen's voice quieted. "However, we must speak of the reality we face today."

"I don't know if the betrothal could work." Allegra steeled her resolve. "But if you wish me to bring this idea to the prince regent, I'll talk to him."

Vizarana inclined her head. "Please do."

CHAPTER 28
THE DEATH OF INNOCENCE

The only light in the Aronsdale tent came from coals in a brazier shaped like a horse. It dimly lit Markus's face as he sat cross-legged on the pallet with Allegra.

"It would never work," he said.

She willed him to consider the compromise. "Ozarson could live here in Quaaz, rather than in hiding."

He held up his hand with his thumb and forefinger almost touching. "We're this close to taking Taka Mal. I don't think the Dawnfield armies will help Cobalt."

"Yes, you might conquer this country," Allegra said. "But at what price? More death and destruction that drives yet someone else's thirst for vengeance?"

"That's the price of war."

"You don't have to fight!" She wanted to shake him. "Jarid will never release you to Yargazon. You're a hostage for the General's behavior. Dusk Yargazon will raise Ozarson. Is that what you want?" Sitting in front of him, grasping his hands, she said, "I don't know if Jarid will give you to Taka

Mal, either, but surely he'll consider it. He doesn't want to choose sides in this impossible war. And think of this, Markus. No one wants to risk Jarid and me doing more spells. They're afraid. It could encourage them to consider this compromise."

"I would still be a hostage," he said.

"You would have both Ozi and me. And your House will someday rule in Taka Mal." She didn't know if having her meant enough to him to give up Taka Mal, but Ozarson was another story. "If you let this war go on, you'll have neither."

His voice hardened. "I won't stay a hostage, Allegra, no matter what your king—or his son, Aron—do."

"Is that what you want? To break my country, too?" It was the only way he could force Jarid to release him.

"We didn't come to fight Aronsdale," he said. "If we must, we will, but that isn't my wish." He closed his hand around her forearm. "I won't be anyone's hostage, Allegra."

"You would rather fight?" She thought of the threatening blend of sexuality and aggression she had felt from Yargazon and Bladebreak. "Do you enjoy war so much?"

"Do you think I would have resigned my commission if I did? I was a good officer. I earned my rank through more than heredity. But I prefer governance. Except that isn't what fate handed me." Bitterness tinged his voice. "What would I like? For Cobalt to return the throne and pull his troops out of Jazid. While we're dreaming, let's add a population of ten million with a social and governing structure to support that many. A medical system that provides decent

care. Guilds, real cities, a system of roads, wells and irrigation, and hell, if we're really dreaming, how about it
goddamn *rains* more than twice a year." He lifted his hand,
then dropped it. "That isn't going to happen. And Cobalt
isn't going to leave unless we force him out."

Allegra wondered what would have happened if Cobalt
had never taken Jazid after Ozar's death. Markus would have
made a good leader. Cobalt was too removed from the
country. His people there were primarily military, and they
considered the Misted Cliffs their home. Although Cobalt
didn't seem to wish ill for the country, she didn't think he
cared about developing it, not in the way Markus dreamed.
Cobalt wanted the immense riches Jazid had to offer; beyond
that, it seemed fine with him if they went on as always.
Markus looked to what his country could become, visions
that he, and Ozarson after him, had the ability to make real.

"Work with the Quaazeras instead of trying to crush them,"
she urged him. "Your two Houses together may someday
defeat Cobalt." If the emperor brought all his forces to bear,
he would have over eight thousand men, but he would have
to pull them out of other countries he held. It was a risk. A
big one. "If Jazid and Taka Mal strain his forces to breaking,
he might let Jazid go rather than imperil his sway elsewhere."

"We can defeat him now," Markus said.

"Even if you win here, you still lose."

He frowned at her. "What does that mean?"

"Suppose you get what you want," she said. "Taka Mal
joins you and helps free your country. Then what? Do you

think they will just accept Jazid sovereignty? You have to hold what you win, Markus, and you need only look at Cobalt's reign to see how difficult that is. He's not the most involved sovereign, but he's not hurting Jazid, either, and even then, your people resent him. How will the people here feel about Ozarson taking the throne by force? Vizarana offers you a genuine alliance. It isn't what you want, and I truly am sorry. Believe it or not, I agree Ozi should sit on the Onyx Throne. But ultimately, what the queen offers is better than what you will win even if everything goes as you hope."

"Every campaign has its ill side." He shook his head. "Dusk will never agree to her idea."

"*You're* the prince regent, damn it!" She jerked her hands away from him. "Be a man of vision."

His voice hardened. "I see. So it's 'vision' only when it agrees with what you want."

"Ah, Markus, maybe I just don't have the ability to show you why I think it's better." She shook her head and started to rise.

He caught her hand and tugged her back down. "You aren't staying here?"

"I can't."

"I don't want you to go."

"Markus—"

"Stay, Allegra." He pulled her into his arms.

Allegra pushed against his shoulders. "Let me up." She heard the quaver in her voice and hated her rush of fear. But after what had happened with Yargazon, she wasn't ready for physical intimacy. Markus wasn't hurting her, not after Jarid's spells had helped her wounds heal. But she ached inside in a way even an indigo spell couldn't soothe, and when Markus's touch turned from simple embraces to more, it was too much.

"Don't do this." Markus sounded bewildered. "First you hate me, then you love me, then you hate me. I can't bear it." He drew back her head and kissed her. "Just love me."

"Markus, stop." She pulled away, panic lurking at the edges of her mind. He didn't understand about Yargazon, but that just made it harder to talk about it with him. And he was holding her with his legs on either side of her body. Two days ago it wouldn't have bothered her. She had *liked* it. But now it reminded her of how Bladebreak had held her. She hated that he and Yargazon could so deeply injure the fragile affection she and Markus had been building, but she couldn't stop her reaction.

"This is what I am," Markus said. "Either accept me or leave me. Don't torment me this way."

"I can't stay with you. Not like this."

"Why?" The words tore out of him. "Always you say this. You can't stay with me. You can't bear my decisions. You despise me. Well, more the fool am I, because no matter how much you push me away, I can't let go. You say I held you against your will. But you've put me in a prison I can't escape. And now you want me to become a hostage for years, possibly for the rest of my *life*."

"Markus, no, I don't despise you. It's just——" She wrestled with the words. "This is like last night."

He stared at her in disbelief. "You're comparing me to *Dusk?*"

"No! I don't know. Markus, let me go. Please."

"No." He bent his head and kissed her again.

Images of Yargazon ripping her tunic, touching her body, kissing her, burst into her mind. She saw his hunger, saw him raising the belt. She jerked back from Markus and hit her fists on his shoulders, though in her mind she was striking Yargazon. "Don't hurt me!"

He grasped her hands and held them in front of his body. "Everything I am hurts you." He spoke as if his heart were breaking. "I never claimed to be a good man. But gods, I've tried. I've never beaten you, never forced you in bed, never denied your humanity. But you want me to bend so much, I'm *breaking.*" He took a breath. "You have to tell me something. Say it, and I'll let you go from this tent, from my life, from everything. I want to hear it before you leave me."

Her pulse lurched at his tone. "Tell you?"

His voice was barely audible. "Say, 'I love you, Markus.'"

She stared at him. Did he feel the only way he could hear those words from her was to force them? She hated that she was starting to cry, and she wasn't even sure why, if it was for him, for them or because of last night. "What has your life done to you, that you can't separate love from violence?"

"You won't even say it now, will you?"

"Please. Let me go." A betraying tear ran down her face.

"Hell's dragon, don't cry." Markus groaned and released her. Allegra scrambled to her feet, and he rose more slowly.

When she backed to the entrance of the tent, he didn't stop her. She paused with her hand on the flap. He stood watching her, his hair tousled, his clothes rumpled, with the intensity that had always both compelled and frightened her.

"You didn't need to threaten me to hear those words," she said softly, hurting so much. "You needed only to say them yourself."

Then she left.

In the relentless light of dawn, they all reconvened in the Hall of the Dragon-Sun, the lords of the settled lands, the queen of an ancient dynasty and a boy far too old for his age. Allegra thought it truly was a Lost Continent, lost to violence and anger. They would talk and challenge and posture, and when it was done, they would go back to their armies and start fighting again, until one side wiped out the other.

When Vizarana met her gaze, Allegra could only shake her head. She felt everyone watching them. Speculating. She had told only Markus about her discussion with the queen. Drummer knew; she saw it in his tensed posture. With that slight shake of her head, he let out a breath, though whether in relief or disappointment, she didn't know. She doubted he and Vizarana wanted their daughter betrothed to Ozarson. But the alternatives were worse.

When everyone had taken positions by their chairs, Cobalt said, "Let us begin."

Before anyone could sit, Muller Dawnfield spoke in a tired

voice. "To what point? Let's be done with this. I have made my decision. I will not join this battle of vengeance."

Allegra drew in a sharp breath, and Jarid jerked as if Muller had unexpectedly struck him in the knees. She didn't know how Markus felt; she couldn't look at him. Everyone stayed on their feet as if the announcement had frozen them in place.

The only person who appeared pleased was Yargazon. He turned to Jarid with satisfaction. "Is that your decision also?"

The Aronsdale king glanced at his cousin, and Muller regarded him with what looked like apology. Both men seemed worn-out, and Aron wasn't much better off.

Jarid turned to Vizarana. "Your Majesty." He spoke with impeccable formality. "I will honor the terms of our treaty. My forces will join yours."

Her exhale was almost invisible, just the barest lowering of her shoulders, but that slight gesture spoke volumes about her relief. She inclined her head. "We thank you for your support."

Yargazon didn't react, but Allegra knew he could do the numbers as well as she. Counting the Jazidians who had deserted Cobalt's army, he had almost four thousand men. If Jarid and the queen combined forces, they had about three thousand. Cobalt had another three. The numbers didn't tell the whole story; Allegra had no doubt Yargazon's men were well trained. They also knew desert fighting better than either Cobalt's or Jarid's men, whereas the Jazidians who had deserted Cobalt's army had been training with soldiers from the Misted Cliffs, learning their methods. No one had enough of a margin to ensure victory.

Cobalt spoke in his rumbling voice. "Do you wish to continue these talks, General Yargazon?"

"Wait," Jarid said. "There is more."

Cobalt frowned at him. "More of what?"

Jarid was standing in front of his chair with his hands on the table as if reassuring himself it was there. Although he was looking at Cobalt and could obviously see the emperor, Allegra suspected he was close to losing that ability.

"I will also fight against your forces, Your Majesty," Jarid said, "should you seek the Topaz Throne."

Muller spoke in a steady voice. "And so would I."

Allegra felt ill. The battle between Jazid and Taka Mal would be ugly no matter what. If after that, the House of Dawnfield turned against itself, even Muller fighting against his daughter's husband, it would be a tragedy.

Cobalt spoke tightly. "You would fight Jazid's army *and* mine?"

"If necessary," Jarid said.

"Well, hell," Yargazon drawled. "Maybe we could bring in Shazire, too. Then we could have a four-way battle."

Allegra wanted to punch him. Jarid's men would have to fight side by side with Cobalt's soldiers, knowing they might soon be called on to attack those very same men. No wonder Muller refused to send his forces into battle for Taka Mal. But Jarid had little choice if he meant to honor the treaty. Allegra wanted to rage at the universe. The General's chances of winning improved with his enemies divided and demoralized. The universe had no justice, that a monster like Yargazon triumphed.

Baz Quaazera pushed his hand through his hair. He moved as if he were weighted down. "We are decided then. The negotiations here have failed."

Ozarson stood with one hand on the table, his fingers pressed against the wood. Allegra would have so much preferred to see confusion on his young face than understanding. But he knew. Oh, yes, he knew. They were going to war for him. Hundreds had died, and thousands more would before this ended. He would live with the knowledge that for his reign, the settled lands underwent one of the worst bloodbaths in history.

Markus made a low noise, barely audible even to Allegra. He sounded as if he were being strangled. Then he raised his voice and said, "No."

King Muller stiffened, Yargazon tensed and Cobalt turned his harsh gaze on the prince regent.

"No?" Jarid asked him. "No what?"

Allegra looked up at her husband. She expected to see the hardened warlord. Instead he had a hollow gaze and pain etched on his face. He didn't look as if he had slept at all last night.

Markus spoke to Vizarana. "Your Majesty. Yesterday you presented an offer to my wife. I would ask you now present it to the atajazid, for his consideration." He turned to Ozarson. "The decision of whether or not to accept the alliance must be yours, since it's your life that will be most affected."

The relief that poured over Allegra was so intense, it felt visceral. She breathed slowly, trying to calm her surging pulse.

"What offer?" Yargazon asked.

Cobalt narrowed his gaze at Vizarana. Like everyone else, she and Drummer were still standing. Her reaction was subtle; she simply took her husband's hand, which was lying on the table. Drummer closed his fingers around hers. They leaned the slightest bit toward each other, and he bent his head over hers, his light curls a contrast to her dark ones. He said something, and she nodded. He looked as if he were tearing apart. Allegra recognized the look. Her father had worn it the day she left home.

Vizarana faced Ozarson. "Your Majesty," she began. "My husband and I offer you the betrothal of our daughter, Zarina Quaazera, to become your lawful wife when the two of you are of age. Your heir will inherit the Topaz Throne." She took a breath. "In return, your army will withdraw from Taka Mal, and you will remain here with your regent as hostages to prevent the army's return."

Ozarson's mouth fell open. In the same instant, Yargazon said, "What the hell? Absolutely not!"

Protests rumbled all around the table, though Jarid's, "Saints almighty," came out over the rest. Allegra couldn't follow who was saying what, with so many voices.

"Quiet!" Cobalt hit the table with his fist.

Everyone fell silent.

Cobalt spoke sharply to Vizarana. "You're suggesting a treaty by marriage between Taka Mal and Jazid?"

"It does work," she said. "As you would know."

"It's out of the question," Yargazon told her.

General Ardoz spoke. "I fail to understand how you could think we would let the atajazid live here as a hostage."

Markus scowled at him. "To stop the war, obviously."

Yargazon regarded him intently, his brow furrowed. Puzzled. His gaze flicked to Allegra, and his already tensed posture stiffened even more. The antipathy in his gaze felt like a blow.

To Markus, the General said, "It is a war you have a good chance of winning."

"At what price?" Markus pushed his hand through his hair. "With the betrothal, we achieve our goals without the bloodshed. And with no more mage spells."

A shifting of weight came from around the table while people glanced toward Allegra and Jarid, then looked away quickly, as if they didn't want to be caught staring.

"Achieve *what?*" Yargazon pointed at Cobalt. "He would still have the Onyx Throne. Ozi would still be a fugitive, except he couldn't even live in his own country. It reeks, Markus. It reeks to the goddamned sky."

"We've already taken part of Taka Mal," Colonel Blade-break said. His voice hardened as he spoke to Vizarana. "You're deluded if you think we would relinquish it."

"Wait." Ozarson sounded so boyish compared to the rumbling men. He spoke to Jarid. "My regent and his wife are your prisoners. What would happen to them if I went to Taka Mal?"

"Ozi, you can't be considering this," Yargazon said.

"I would have to discuss it with Queen Vizarana," Jarid told the boy.

"If King Jarid allows it," Vizarana said, "we will arrange for them to live with you."

"As hostages?" Ozarson asked.

Vizarana met his gaze. "Yes."

"No," Yargazon said. "It's unacceptable." He spoke to Ozarson in a low voice. "Your Majesty, we are so close."

"I know," Ozarson said softly. "I just—" He took a deep breath and shook his head.

Cobalt pointed at Markus. "If you release this man into Taka Mal custody, my promise to let him live is void. I gave that oath with the assumption he would be held in Aronsdale. Not Taka Mal."

"Will you kill everyone I love, then?" Ozarson asked. His face paled, but he didn't back down. "You took everything. My country. My throne. My father. My brothers. My nurse. My *mother*." His voice cracked. "I have only one person left. Are you going to kill him, too? When you're finished taking everyone and everything I've ever loved, will you be happy?"

Cobalt stared at him. The silence at the table was complete.

The emperor spoke in an unexpectedly gentle voice. "I've found no joy in your losses."

Ozarson took a breath and turned to Vizarana. "If I can live with my regent and his wife, I will accept the b-betrothal, be your hostage and tell the army not to fight."

"Saints almighty," someone said.

Yargazon put his hand on Ozarson's shoulder. "Ozi, you can't. We will talk of this later."

"No." The boy turned toward Yargazon as if for protection and wiped his palm over his eyes. But he raised his gaze to Cobalt. "Are you going to fight here if my army doesn't?"

"No," Cobalt said quietly. "If you withdraw your forces, I will withdraw mine."

Vizarana closed her eyes and her hand tightened on Drummer's fingers. Such understated signs of her feelings, but Allegra had no doubt her relief was profound.

"And my regent?" Ozarson's gaze was stark as he regarded Cobalt. "Will you kill him if he tries to come to Taka Mal to be with me?"

For a long moment, the emperor stared at him. Then Cobalt took a deep breath. "If Prince Markus remains a hostage in Taka Mal with no access to his armed forces, I will not seek his death."

Ozarson nodded, his eyes glossy from unshed tears. He spoke uncertainly to Markus. "We have occupied part of Taka Mal. I don't know how to figure out what will happen with that."

Markus managed a smile. "We'll help you."

Allegra wanted so much to reach out to Ozarson. She stayed put, knowing it would embarrass him here in front of all these leaders. His heredity had taken his childhood—but for today at least, it wouldn't crush him with the weight of ten thousand deaths.

CHAPTER 29
HEART OF TOPAZ

Allegra leaned her forearms on the balcony wall and gazed at the palace gardens awash in the afternoon sunlight. A long stretch of grass sloped down to the lake of Quaaz. Trees draped with vines drooped over the water, and sun-snaps grew in profusion, mixed with skybells. Even this high up, she could smell the heady scent of rosy box-blossoms. Goldwing larks trilled, and butterflies floated in the air. The scene took her breath. Give the desert a little water, and it bloomed gloriously.

Eventually she went back inside the suite where Queen Vizarana's soldiers had brought her after the summit this morning. The empty suite. Other guards had taken Markus to meet with Vizarana, Ozarson, Cobalt, Yargazon, Baz, Jarid, Muller, and who knew how many other officers to discuss what would happen to the villages Markus's army had already conquered. Taka Mal would have to make concessions to Jazid if they wanted this compromise to work—which ironically meant they would also be making those concessions to Cobalt, who remained the ruler of that country.

Guards outside the suite prevented Allegra from leaving, but they otherwise left her alone. Too agitated to sit, she wandered through the rooms. The walls were like sunrises, painted red near the floor, shading up through gold and yellow, then into blue near the ceiling. Red-glass lamps shaped like dragons hung from the rafters, and parchment-thin screens painted with delicate birds graced the airy rooms.

She was in one of the parlors pouring a glass of orange juice when the outer door of the suite creaked. She walked into the main parlor just as Markus and Ozarson came through the entrance.

"Allegra!" Ozarson's face lit in welcome.

Markus spoke in a subdued voice. "Good afternoon."

"We've come to invite you to the ceremony," Ozarson said.

Curious to know what had happened, she said, "What ceremony?"

The boy's face turned red. "My marriage."

Markus smiled. "Betrothal."

Ozarson looked as if he wanted to run outside and hide. "Yes. That."

"It's not all that bad," Allegra told him, charmed by his embarrassment. "Someday you might even be glad."

He regarded her skeptically, but said nothing.

Behind them, a Taka Mal guard entered the suite. When Markus turned around, the man bowed to him. "You have a visitor, Sire."

"Who?" Markus asked, his posture tensing.

"A General Ardoz, from your army."

"Oh. Yes." Markus cleared his throat. "Bring him in."

As the guard left, Ozarson blinked at Markus. "We just talked to him."

"I know." Markus's face shuttered as he glanced from the boy to Allegra. "Why don't the two of you go change for the ceremony?"

"But, Markus," Ozarson said. "I wanted to ask him—"

"Ozi, you can talk to the general some other time," Allegra said. She didn't know when, given that Ozarson would be here and Ardoz would be somewhere else, but she could tell Markus wanted privacy. "We need to get ready. You don't want to be late to your own betrothal, do you?"

"Oh. No, I guess not." The boy didn't look certain about that, but he went with her.

After Allegra left Ozarson in his room, she went to the master bedroom. The maid had left her some clothes, and she changed into a tunic and trousers of brocaded blue silk. Gazing at the bed, she wondered if Markus would ever grow used to sleeping off the ground. She hoped so, for she wanted him to be as content as possible. At least the decor here was a lot like that in Jazid.

She paced around the room and used up more time brushing her hair, but eventually she walked back to the main parlor. When she heard Ardoz's voice, she stopped, unsure what to do. She was in an alcove next to the parlor, and a burnished gold mirror on the opposite wall showed Ardoz and Markus standing in the other room. They looked so similar, both strong and broad shouldered, though Ardoz was a bit taller than Markus, with gray in his shock of dark hair and more aquiline features.

"I know," Ardoz was saying, his voice low. "But I waited anyway."

"Basil, I'm sorry." Markus lifted his arm as if to touch him, then dropped it again.

"Don't be sorry," Ardoz said. "I always knew it wasn't your preference." He gave Markus a rueful look. "It was just so hard to think straight, ever since the first time I saw you, so strong and proud." He just barely touched one of Markus's curls. "And who has hair like this? I could have brushed it for hours."

Markus laughed self-consciously. "I did like that."

"I know." Ardoz lowered his arm. "But not enough."

Markus spoke quietly. "I don't want you to think— It wasn't only because I was lonely. Gods know, Basil, sometimes I thought the loneliness would kill me. But I would have never—not with anyone else." He stopped, his discomfort obvious. But he didn't step back. "Be well. May you always have the best."

Ardoz grinned at him. "I already have."

Incredibly Markus blushed. "For gods' sake."

Ardoz's face gentled. "Goodbye, Mark."

Markus touched Ardoz's face, the slightest brush across his cheek. "Goodbye."

The general left then. Allegra thought she would have been shocked, but she felt only regret at stumbling onto their farewells. She withdrew down the hall, leaving Markus his privacy.

★ ★ ★

Allegra walked with Ozarson and Markus into the entrance foyer of their suite. Ozarson looked serious in his formal black clothes, and Markus seemed more subdued than usual. She didn't ask about Ardoz. If he ever wanted to talk about it, she would listen, but if not, she would respect his silence.

Ozarson opened the outer door and looked up at the guards. The four soldiers bowed to him, then moved aside and accompanied them down the gleaming topaz corridor. The wall sconces held frosted glass lamps with ruby accents, their flames flickering.

Walking through the palace felt odd to Allegra, for despite its opulence, it was a prison. For Markus, these golden rooms would be as confining as a cage. He might never again ride with his people, sleep under the stars or see the mountains and deserts of the home he loved. She wondered if she could ever fully appreciate the magnitude of what he had given up to make this alliance work.

"Thank you," she said.

Markus smiled at her. "For what?"

"Everything." She watched Ozarson walking ahead of them. "I know you didn't want this."

"Ah, well." He spoke awkwardly. "It could have been worse."

"What did you all decide about Taka Mal?"

"The queen ceded a portion of the land we took," Markus said. "The Saint Verdant River now defines Taka Mal's southern border with Jazid. That area isn't heavily populated by Taka Mal standards, only about two hundred thousand people. The people can leave, if they want, and relocate in Taka Mal territory. But if we can convince a substantial number of them to stay, it will greatly increase Jazid's population."

"What about your army?" She couldn't imagine Cobalt letting four thousand men go free.

His eyes glinted. "It's a hell of a fighting force."

"I know," she said dryly. "I doubt Cobalt or Queen Vizarana appreciates that, though."

"That's why they're letting the men settle the land Taka Mal ceded to us, so they'll stop fighting. About two thousand want to stay. It's what they had planned to do if we took the country. I'll be expected to help integrate the Jazid citizens with the Taka Mal population." He cracked his knuckles restlessly. "I doubt I'll be able to travel. But the queen has asked me to act as an advisor for the blending of the two cultures in my capacity as Ozarson's regent." Wryly he said, "No life of ease. I have to work for my keep."

She suspected he far more preferred that to doing nothing. "And the rest of the army?"

His satisfaction vanished. "Cobalt gets them. In return, he won't execute them."

"*Two thousand* Jazid men?"

"Yes." His gaze darkened. Even a tenday ago, she couldn't have deciphered the expression, but she knew now exactly what it meant. He was furious.

"You can't be serious," she said.

"It's the Jazid army," he answered curtly. "He rules Jazid."

"Doesn't he have to put the deserters on trial?"

"Technically, since they're still in his army, they aren't deserters." The lines around his mouth creased with his displeasure. "But damn it, Dusk didn't train them for Cobalt."

"What about Yargazon?" Just saying his name made her queasy.

Markus didn't answer. Instead he watched Ozarson up ahead of them. The boy was looking around with undisguised appreciation at the gilded walls and their mosaics. "Ozi has never lived anywhere like this. The Onyx Palace is starker, and he spent the last two years with the army."

She didn't let him evade the question. "And Yargazon?"

"You won't like it."

"Cobalt is letting him *live?*"

"Yes." He spoke evenly. "It was my condition for giving up those two thousand soldiers."

Allegra wanted to hit him. But she held it in. Markus had given up more than she had ever expected in that moment he had asked Ozarson to consider the queen's offer. She hadn't believed he would ever repudiate Yargazon, yet incredibly, he had done it. He had given up his kingdom and his army because Allegra had asked him to do it. She was still reeling with that knowledge.

"What will they do with Yargazon?" she asked.

"He's going to retire." Markus even said it with a straight face. "Under guard, of course, to make sure he complies with the terms of this new treaty. He'll return to his home in Jazid."

Allegra snorted. "And I'm sure Cobalt believes him." It didn't surprise her that the emperor demanded an entire army in return for Yargazon's life, given that the General would undoubtedly start trying to outwit his "retirement" as soon as he was back in Jazid. "So he wins again."

Markus shook his head. "In Dusk's view, he's lost everything that ever mattered to him. He wanted to *fight*. He thought we could defeat Cobalt. He may be right. But the cost was too high." After a moment, he said, "It's more than the war, Allegra. Ozi and I were the closest he had to a family." He touched her hair. "And he wanted you. It obsessed him. I don't know why, for he genuinely believes you sought to ruin his relationship with Ozi and me and our plans for Taka Mal. The way he sees it, you 'won' by corrupting me and destroying Ozi's future. You have everything Dusk wants."

It was an outlook so different from her own, she didn't know what to do with it. "Do you see me that way?"

"Gods, no!" He gave her a wry smile. "You make me think. Which is good. I may not *like* it, but that's my problem, not yours."

She exhaled, relieved. "Yargazon wasn't actually the one I meant, though. It's *Cobalt*. He always comes out ahead, stronger, more powerful. Now he has more land and a bigger army."

Markus lifted his chin. "For now."

For now. With this alliance between Taka Mal and Jazid, saints only knew what would happen. Ultimately Taka Mal and Jazid would become one, in spirit if not in who actually claimed the throne—and when that happened, she wondered if even the emperor could stand against their fierce soul.

"Did King Jarid agree to let you live here?" she asked.

"As a prisoner, yes." He winced. "Better than his dungeon."

"How does it work? Do we—do we have to live in cells?"

"Dragon's breath, Allegra. Of course not." He motioned to Ozarson. "He and I will stay in the suite we have now. We'll always have guards, and we can't leave the palace without an armed escort. But it's more like we're guests than hostages."

"You and Ozarson? Not me?"

"You are free to leave. If you want." Awkwardly he added, "Or to stay. If you want."

To leave. Or to stay. "Markus—would you have considered the queen's proposal if I hadn't asked you to do it?"

"No, I don't think so." He took a breath. "You see the world in ways I find difficult. But if you will stay with me, I'll try to understand."

Allegra thought of everything he had given up for her, and she didn't really need to debate her answer.

"I'll stay," she said.

His face relaxed. He took her hand as they walked together.

Vizarana and Drummer were waiting in an alcove of the nursery. Baz Quaazera was with them, and a striking woman who was surely his wife, the Dragon-Sun priestess. A cascade of red-gold hair tumbled down her back. Although she had the upward-tilted eyes common in Taka Mal, they were green instead of dark. She wore a long yellow skirt and a bodice that left her lower abdomen bare. She regarded Allegra with a serene gaze and inclined her head as one mage would to another.

"Zarina is sleeping," Drummer told them. "She usually does at this time of the day."

Ozarson shifted his feet. "Maybe we shouldn't wake her up."

"It's all right." Vizarana's face gentled when she spoke to him. "Come in, please."

They walked into the nursery, an airy room with blue walls and a white ceiling. Toys were strewn in one corner, balls and stuffed animals. A child lay curled under a blue quilt in a small bed with raised sides to keep her from falling out. They stopped just within the archway, except for Vizarana and Drummer, who went to the bed. The queen bent over and picked up the child, cradling her in her arms. The girl was about two years old, with dark hair and a sweet face. She snuggled against her mother and murmured, "Pappy."

Drummer laughed softly. "I'm here, little one." He tapped his finger on her hand, and she gripped it with her eyes closed.

When Drummer beckoned to Ozarson, the boy started with alarm, looking young and uncertain. Then he drew himself up straighter and went over to them. He peered at the girl. "She's pretty."

"Her personal names are Zarina Bell," Vizarana said.

"Bell?" Ozarson asked.

"It's my mother's name," Drummer said. "Many people where I come from have names based in music."

"Oh." Ozarson squinted at Zarina. "Is she asleep?"

"A little." Then Vizarana murmured, "Wake up, sweetings."

"Mummsi," the girl said drowsily. Her huge eyes opened and she regarded Ozarson. "Boy-boy?" she asked.

"His name is Ozarson," Drummer said. "Your husband, someday."

Ozarson turned even redder than before. "Don't be sad," he told the girl earnestly. "I'll try not to be a bad husband."

"Busbus," Zarina murmured. She yawned and closed her eyes.

"Well." The queen caught her lower lip with her teeth, and Allegra saw a sheen of tears in her eyes. When Vizarana glanced at Markus, he went to stand with them. The priestess came with him, her long hair rustling with her elegant walk.

"We will have the more elaborate ceremonies later," Vizarana told Markus. "Since we've already agreed on the basic terms, my people and yours should have a preliminary draft of the contract for you this evening, and we can settle on details. However, this will formalize the betrothal."

Markus nodded his acceptance. "That will work."

She took a breath, then shifted into a ceremonial cadence. "Does anyone here have cause to dispute this joining of the royal Houses of Onyx and Quaazera?"

Allegra held her breath, afraid someone would speak and destroy this precarious solution to a brutal war.

After a moment, the priestess spoke in a melodic voice. "Your Majesty, Ozarson Onyx, Atajazid D'az, Shadow-Dragon Prince of Jazid, do you accept this betrothal?"

Ozarson looked up with wide eyes. "Yes? I mean, yes, I do."

She inclined her head to the boy, then said, "Your Majesty, Vizarana Jade Quaazera, Atatakamal D'oz, Dragon-Sun Princess of Taka Mal, do you accept this betrothal in the name of your daughter, Zarina Bell Quaazera?"

"Yes," Vizarana said. A tear gathered in her eye.

"Then it is done." The priestess smiled at Ozarson. "You're betrothed."

Watching him, a chill went through Allegra. An image formed in her mind—Ozarson towering and dark, a powerful man taking his place on a huge black throne. A stunning woman stood at his side, her head lifted, her eyes wild and fierce with Quaazera pride. She wore the red trousers and jerkin of a Taka Mal warrior-merchant, with a sword at her side. A belt of metal cylinders crisscrossed her torso. Ozarson gripped something Allegra had never seen, an elongated metal object with a cylindrical snout and a massive grip. She didn't know what it meant, but she suddenly felt cold.

The image faded, replaced by a nervous boy standing with his future bride. Allegra shook her head, wondering what was wrong with her. She needed more sleep.

Be well, she thought to Ozarson and Zarina. *No matter how difficult the path you trod, may you always have love.*

Markus leaned with his back against the palace wall where the balcony rail met the side of the building. Allegra stood a pace away, her elbows on the rail, looking over the gardens and beyond to the lake. She held the dodecahedron in one hand.

"It will be strange living here," Markus said. "I've never been in a place with so much water. It feels exorbitant."

She smiled at him. "It seems dry to me. Especially the air."

He held out his hand as if to ask a question. She took it, and his shoulders relaxed. He drew her into his arms, and she stood in his embrace, her cheek resting on his red silk shirt, her palm against his chest. They both looked out at Quaaz, he gazing over her head. Afternoon sunlight slanted across the city.

"You told me something last night," Markus said.

Allegra knew what he meant; she had said she would leave him. But that had been before his decision to end the war. His incredible decision.

"Things are different now," she said. She had thought he understood when she said she would stay with him, but perhaps he still wasn't certain.

"Are they?" He sounded oddly strained.

She watched a hawk drift over the city. "Yargazon is gone."

"I don't mean that." He spoke with difficulty. "You said I had only to tell you something and you would respond in kind."

Her breath caught. Suddenly nervous, she said, "That hasn't changed."

"It's hard for me." He spoke quietly. "My father never told my mother he loved her. Because he didn't. I don't know if he ever truly loved any woman. Maybe Ozi's mother, but I doubt he told her, either. All I ever knew, all my life, was that with women, a man employed force, commands and control. You didn't love a woman, you used her, for pleasure, for status and for children."

"You aren't your father. Or Dusk Yargazon."

"No. It seems I'm not." He brushed his hand down her hair in a caress. "Because I do truly love you, Allegra. And if you will let me, I will try learning to do this marriage business better."

She closed her eyes, far more glad to hear the words than she had been able to admit even to herself. "I would like to spend my life with the man I love. With you."

He said only, "Good," but his voice caught on the word.

"Do you remember when you wrote our marriage contract?" she asked. "You put something in I didn't understand."

"What was that?"

"You swore to honor the vows of our union." She hesitated. "In Aronsdale I would know what it means. But I don't in Jazid." Or Taka Mal, for that matter.

"It means the same everywhere, night bird," he murmured. "I believe the language in Aronsdale is, 'I will cleave to you and only to you for as long as we both shall live.'"

It meant more to her than she knew how to say. He had given her that vow despite all the reasons a Jazidian man in his position had to withhold it, and he had even taken the time and effort to find out the wording her own people used.

She lifted her hand and held it palm up to the sky. The dodecahedron gleamed. Power stirred within her, a gift she had feared she would never know again, one as ancient as her people in Aronsdale. She sang a simple song that had come down to her people over the centuries:

His kiss so sweet, his heart so bold
Embracing me with love's true hold
Sweet passion, where the starlight pours
Whispers of love, forever more

A sphere of golden light formed on her palm like a promise, that even a harsh land could miraculously come alive with the balm of water. The spell encompassed them, and Markus held her in his arms.

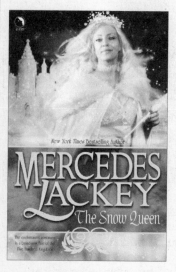